The Infinity Code
Book 1
The Rise of the Antichrist, the Apocalypse, and Armageddon

Kalb Kinu

Cadmus Publishing
www.cadmuspublishing.com

Do not judge me by the designation on the front of this book. You have no idea who I am or who I was. I admit for a while I was lost; I've done great evils and I became a sinner. I've embraced every demon this world had to offer until I reached bottom and then was saved by GOD. Do not judge this book by its cover alone, its contents are designed to open your minds. Do not judge its contents based on what you've always been taught because many of the beliefs you hold are false. The first error you've made is believing that the Apocalypse coming was going to be a bad thing. The dictionary says it's a cataclysmic event in which evil forces are destroyed but when it was given it was simply meant as to reveal the hidden truth which is what the Infinity Code is all about. My first truths are these; I am here to bring mankind the first steps of its Apocalypse. I am the bringer of Revelations and bearer of the PROOF this world has always wanted. I am God's champion. I am here to destroy evil.

Dedications

To my youngest son, who always had my heart keeping it safe from turning to stone.

To my middle son, who's spirit is so infectious he helps me to smile in the face of hate.

To my oldest son, who's unparalleled love and devotion shine like a beacon, guiding me as I walk alone.

I Am nobody
I come from nothing
This poem will bare
A truth I bring
These words together
Become a foresight
If you but harness
Your God's warm light
A liftetime of wrongs
I try to make right
For I Am nobody
Yet still I fight

Prologue

I think I was always supposed to be hated. Or maybe, to be judged. I didn't know who I was or who I was supposed to be. You didn't know who I was or who I was supposed to be. So much was lost in translation and the truth lay somewhere between fact and fiction. This is what I will give you now. A story you're not going to believe. A story that I tried my hardest to make look like any other story. A story that must appear familiar for it to work the way it is intended. Like a regular story. My story. The story of my life that no one ever knew… not even me.

I am many things but above all, I am sorry. Sorry for what I've become. Sorry for the things I've done. And sorry for what you are about to read. I am no author but I must try so please forgive my mistakes as I am sure you will find some. Most, simple errors, others on purpose. They may not seem logical but I have my reasons and those closest to me will see more than a story. They will know what this is really all about. Sure, I added a little sugar to the medicine, some milk for the babies and meat for men. This is only in the hopes that it goes down easier because it must be taken by everyone. So as you read, peel back the layers to find the gems I've scattered throughout. Some buried deep, some cleverly disguised, others on top but one… one is on display. My diamond for the world. So I urge you, do your own research, challenge my words and everything you find before forming your own opinions.

There have been no others in existence who can do what I do, exactly the way I do it. I've done my own research and looked but I always came up empty. I tried to explain it to the people that I loved. People I trusted the most but I always stopped short. I remember one time I sat chatting with our oldest child. I tried to say it. I tried to explain things my mind could do. The places I could go but when I received incredulous looks from my family ,

I stopped short. I always stopped. How do you tell your brothers with their ironclad beliefs that we are alone in the universe? That you've mingled with other beings? How do you tell your religious mother with her immovable faith the truth about hell? The thing is, you don't. You keep it to yourself, bottled up inside so people don't call you crazy. So people don't SEE that you're crazy. Until one day, fate slaps you in the face. What you are about to read may seem like a sci-fi or fantasy but it's the first piece of my story. And if you decide not to believe, well then I hope at least you enjoyed the story. But those of you who dare to wonder, dare to believe and then dig for themselves will find a harvest. After it's all picked clean, at the bottom you will see the real treasure, that it's the truth.

Table of Contents

CHAPTER 1

The infinity code is where all the unknown truths of existence lay hidden. It is its dissection, to find all of its purposes, meanings and possibilities. These can be found in tiny hints and fragments randomly scattered throughout all realities. It's not known here on Earth because most of you are still under the illusion that this is the center of it all. That you are alone in your universe, or even worse, that yours is the only universe. I'm here to pull back the curtain, to reveal the secrets, to make everything unknown known. The first truth I'll tell you is that the spirit world is real and by the end of this book not only will I convince you of this, but truly I can prove it.

Reality popped into existence without a sound, like turning on a light, there just suddenly 'was'. My eyes darted back and forth frantically as I took in my surroundings, hands clenching nervously as I tried to grasp what had just happened to me. What was still happening to me. I was in a small circular clearing in a very dense forest of pine. The light gray bark on the trunks rose up into a dark green canopy of needles so thick I could only see a few feet through their branches. An unfamiliar sun hung overhead in the clear blue sky. Soft yellow tendrils swirled around the orb, it's light dull and flat compared to the blazing radiance of the sun that warmed our Earth. I didn't even have to squint while looking at it.

I shifted my weight from foot to foot and felt a soft crumbling underfoot and looked down to see I was standing on a blanket of moss. Dead, grey and white with small patches of green life speckled throughout. I stared down and started wiggling my toes, catching small pieces of the broken plants and wedging them between my toes, only then realizing I was naked. What is happening to me? Where am I? Did I die? My breath came quicker at the thought of being dead and having arrived at a new place... a new world? A new universe? Wherever it was, it was not Earth. I gulped in a lungful of air and let it out slowly, trying to calm myself and come to grips with this experience. I closed my eyes to help settle my nerves and only after doing this could I feel the link. I could feel a connecting pressure at the base of my brain before sensing it shoot straight into the air. Beyond just the air, it reached across galaxies, universes, and dimensions. Wherever I was, I wasn't dead. At the end of this link I could still feel my body, dull and distant but also familiar. It pulled at me, sucking at my consciousness like a vacuum over dust. My eyes opened and the feeling instantly receded. I placed a hand on my chest and one on my stomach to help try and stop hyperventilating. I knew none of this was possible but at the same time it was also my current reality. I spun in a slow circle taking in by surroundings. Directly behind me, in what appeared to be a child's writing, was a wooden sign with bright red letters spelling "HERE". The arrow on the sign pointed down a narrow, weedy path with the branches cut away. This way to hell, I imagined its secret meaning but then why would it be made so poorly? Maybe demons and the like were just really dumb. Most likely, this wasn't hell, I hear that place is supposed to be hotter but always wondered, how would anyone know unless they've escaped it?I considered my options and realized it was either stand here arguing with myself, take the cleared path, or wander aimlessly through the pine needle filled woods like an imbecile. I stepped forward slowly, the soft ground muting any sounds and I gained a small amount of confidence from that. I pulled the sign from the ground, holding it like a bat in case of danger then proceeded forward. I moved hesitantly at first then faster as I realized that there was nothing around. No bugs, no animals, no people, just me. I briefly considered the possibility I was in a barren world but then remembered the sign I held clutched in my hands.

Someone had clearly made this sign, had written on this sign, not only does that signify life, it signifies intelligent life. Life that has a language and can communicate.

I crouched low and tried to search down the path as far as I could to see where it bent slowly to the right. Images of little grey men with big bulging eyes flitted through my head as well as green toad- like beings with dozens of eyes and tentacles instead of arms. Whatever they turned out to be, I knew I wanted to see them before they ever saw me. I scanned to my left into the closely cropped pines with their pointy branches and tiny green dagger needles then looked down to my naked body. If something did come, hiding was out of the question. I resumed my pace but at a crouch. If I made myself smaller maybe they wouldn't notice the giant pink fleshy thing on the only path in a sea of green. I didn't care, it made me feel better. After several minutes and a few turns I could see the path end into a clearing. I dropped lower and strained my senses. A gentle breeze brought the smell of tree bark and fungus to my nose but I detected nothing else. I started forward again but this time at full attention, ready to risk the dive into the woods and all its regrets at the first sign of alien life.

I neared the clearing and was finally able to see through the greenery. A large brown structure sat off to the side that looked like a house. I stood next to the last tree, hand on one of its sawed off branches and poked my head out to have a better look. It was a house. It had a red roof made of clay tiles and brown rough wooden siding of what I'd guess to be pine since it was the only tree I've seen in this place. There was a window facing me and I couldn't see where the door was from this angle. I sat for several minutes scanning for life or even any recent activity. The building sat on a small property only about a half an acre wide. On one side there was an old well right out of the story books. Slimy dark bricks formed its circular body with two wooden boards going up to support its tiny roof of rotting shingles. Between the boards sat a metal crank with rope and a bucket hanging from it. On the other side of the yard was a small two track road, each track made of a soft light brown sand seperated by more of the moss that seemed to be everywhere and on everything. In the center of the yard closest to the building was a scarecrow with a bullseye on its chest. No, a practice dummy. Its hempen wove shirt was covered with small holes and there were even a few on its faceless head. Perfect. At least I know that whoever lives here is not only armed, but must have some skill because they practice. I stood up slowly. Hopefully they're afraid of naked pink beings they've never seen before. With the amount of time I had sat thinking and no signs of life I decided to be brave and venture closer to have a peek in the window. I scurried over, still at a crouch, arms and wooden sign held out to the side for balance, hoping to remain noiseless. I gently touched the wall just beneath the window and drew in a sharp breath, held it, then ever so slowly raised my head up and peered in.

I dropped back down quickly, my mind racing with what I had seen. It was a small bedroom with a door on the opposite side. To the room's left was a simple dresser made in all right angles with a single knob in the middle of each of its three long drawers. On the right side of the room was a black chest with golden trim that resembled a treasure chest and directly beneath the window was a bed. An occupied bed with a young boy sleeping in it. He was human. Or looked exactly like a human anyway, I thought. This can't be real. None of this makes sense. I must be dreaming. I decided to inspect my surroundings once again, searching for some sort of oddity, something out of place or im- possible that could only happen in dreams. After a few moments I found nothing but it didn't change my belief. If this is a dream, then maybe I could control it. I focused and tried to imagine the trees were different. Those trees aren't green, they're red. Then I tried to believe it. The world rippled into clarity like opening a murky window. The air was more crisp, the sky's blue deepened and the sun radiated its yellow warmth onto my skin. The moss beneath me felt like a silk blanket over a pillow of cotton and even the greens of the needles changed in shades, from that of swamp water to the darker greens of an alligator.

Slowly it faded away and I sat puzzled. Clearly I had done something so this could be a dream but normally dreams changed randomly and without explanation. It didn't make sense. I tried to imagine a bird into existence but nothing happened. What I did next I should drop a little back story into first. At the time I was still young, months left before I was even old enough to get into a bar and like what was common with most kids of a younger age, I wanted to be cool, good looking, rich, famous, powerful, all of the above. But my biggest secret fantasy was I wanted to be powerful. Not president of the world powerful, superhero powerful. I'd often find myself daydreaming about it. Unfathomable powers, save the girl, kill the bad guys, you get it. I was always the good guy and would always be saving some damsel in distress with my unique abilities.

So this is what I decided to try next. I held my arms out to the side with my hands upright, fingers spread and relaxed. I tried focusing my thoughts, concentrating hard, attempting to force power from my outstretched hands. The feeling of butterflies tickled from my armpits to my wrists and my arms went numb but other than that, nothing.

I stood up and tried to shake feeling back into them as I contemplated. I knew I was close, my arms going numb was proof of that but maybe I was just doing it wrong.

I flexed my muscles and pointed a finger at a nearby tree and tried again. The world started to go vivid as I stared at the tree, all my focus and attention bent on making something happen. Anything happen. Seconds came and went then minutes. I let my arm fall as I tried to figure out what I could do differently. Maybe I was trying too hard.

Maybe I was handling this like using a sledge hammer to repair a set of spectacles, it's just not going to work if I was being too forceful.

I cocked my head sideways and let my eyes lose focus. I let the soft breeze glide around me and my skin absorb the gentle warmth of the sun. I could feel its warmth. I could sense its warmth radiating down in slow tiny drops like the mist of an early morning sprinkle. I noticed it being absorbed into the moss, the trees, into their endless needles and into me. I wanted more. I breathed it in but not just with my lungs, with my entire body. It beckoned to my call and I was slowly filled with a power like nothing I'd ever felt. It was waking up after being dead. Or maybe like stepping into a hot tub after being in a snowstorm. I felt stronger, faster. I felt alive. I stood, enjoying it for some time, just watching it dance in the sunlight as it filled me and everything I could see. I was elated, completely engulfed in my euphoric trance.

"Hello." a small voice spoke from behind me and I spun around quickly to find the boy standing there with a shy grin spread across his face. "Are you here to save me?"

He stood at the edge of his house holding a bundle of clothes with a sword laying across them. His light blue eyes and round face went well with his ash brown hair that danced lazily in all directions like it had never seen a brush in its life. A tattered brown robe similar to the one on the target dummy was tied at his waist with a white rope in a single knot holding it shut. He looked every bit like the cliché monk out of some secret hidden temple only found at the tops of mountains. Except he was young, on the verge of his teen years and monks usually didn't have hair but I could be wrong. The smile he still wore was clearly forced and his eyes were down like he didn't want to stare directly at me.

"How...umm..." I didn't know where to start. He was a human. He could speak. This was a dream. "Hello." I finally replied, setting aside the dozens of questions I had that needed answering.

He rubbed one foot with the other, head still down. "I'm Deffy."

I stared at him curiously. "Nice to meet you Deffy, I'm [Earthen Name Omitted]"

His eyes shot up and locked onto mine for a brief second then returned to the ground. "You're not supposed to use real names here. It could be dangerous. You should make a new one." He paused, "But I won't tell no one until you do."

I didn't understand how a real name could be dangerous but decided that I'd put some thought into a different one anyway to be safe. I've never really liked my real name anyway.

"Immi helped me make a sign for someone to save me so if you're here for that then we should probably go soon." He handed me the bundle without looking.

I grabbed them, noticing some sort of kilt, a tunic and a belt for the sword and started putting them on, deciding to inquire further into his statements. "Well what am I saving you from?" I asked, finishing and sheathing the sword with hidden fascination. He paused, considering my question for a second, "Um, just Tad and Scar, but if we don't wait you don't even have to fight them though. Immi said it's fifty fifty you'd lose.`` Then he started to walk towards the two track without bothering to see if I had heard or even if I was about to follow. I stepped quickly to catch up as I thought about what he had said. Tad and Scar? Scar sounded like some made up name for an evil villain but what was Tad? Was that even a name? Also why would this young monk need saving from them unless he was some sort of prison- er and what was the comment about fifty fifty I'd lose? This was a strange dream indeed and doubt started to creep into me. There was something different about this place. I've heard of people having vivid dreams they were sure were real. I've even had some myself but this was beyond that. This had noise, touch, smells and I'm pretty sure dreams don't have smells.

I reached him in a few long strides and slowed my pace to match his. "First things first, why do you need saving from Tad and Scar?" I asked, each of us walking in his own dirt track.

"Well because they don't let me have fun and I can't never leave and I can't never have friends, I just have to make stuff."

They sounded like some strict guardians but nothing worth saving from. "That sounds mean but do you really need to leave?" I stared at him to see if he had any reaction but he didn't. "I'm sure they care for you. I can talk to them-" He stopped and glared at me for a brief second like I was a mute yodeler. "Tad and Scar are both Favored Few." Then he continued walking like it explained everything. I had no clue what the Favored Few were or how it was supposed to clear up my misunderstandings. "Hey umm, Deffy? What are the Favored Few and... I don't think you should be running away without letting someone know first."

Where were this boy's parents? If either of them was his parent wouldn't he have said mom or dad. Oh man, what if Tad was his mothers name?

He didn't slow as he responded. "I thought about it a lot. I think I figured out a way for Immi's plan to work best. If we time it out and jump in the trees before they come into sight but we're far enough from the house to where they can't see us come out then we can escape and nobody has to fight or die." That gave me pause. Losing didn't just imply a fight, he thought it would be to the death. Who is this Immi girl and why is she feeding such terrible stories into a young boy's head?

"Ok, ok. Slow down. You need to explain some things. What are the Favored Few and why would I have to fight them?" To the death apparently. "Are they your-" I was cut off by his reply

"Favored Few are fighters who do bad things for their masters so they can be rich I think. And they don't care for me. They don't care for no one and if you don't fight them then they'll kill you." He gave a short pause. "And me."

Well that's exactly what to the death was and at least this was a good reason for him to be running away. I couldn't imagine living like that, no one to love you or play with. Clearly I could assume these two were not in any way shape or form acting with his best interests in mind if he thought they would kill him... for any reason. "And after I save you, then what? You have another home? A family? Maybe some parents somewhere?" He kept his eyes forward and his pace brisk as we strolled. The thick pine forest to either side still showed no signs of other trees of even different life other than the moss that spread over everything like an old blanket.

After the silence drug on for a bit he finally responded, one quick word and nothing further. "Nope." like he was reluctant or not sure of his own answer.

I felt bad immediately at mentioning it so decided I'd play along to help raise his spirits. "Then I guess I'll just do my best to save you. What's the worst that could happen? I can't die anyway, this is just a stupid dream." I muttered the last part to myself then put on a confident smile.

He stopped in his tracks without looking up as he shook his head. "Now it's fifty fifty." he sighed. "Now you have to fight them." He turned to look at the woods on both sides of him and with a shrug as if it didn't matter, strolled into the thick forest.

I regarded him for a moment while he made his way in a dozen paces or so and then crouched down under one of the low hanging branches where he was barely visible.

"Hey." I called out, "Why are you in the woods? Are they close?"

He shrugged again then sat, picking at the moss between his legs. I followed him in, moving branches out of the way as I passed and letting them sling shot behind after. I chose the tree next to him and plopped down, the soft vegetation lightly crunching beneath my weight as I tried to get comfortable.

"You don't know why you are in the woods or you don't know if they're close?"

He lifted up a section of moss and pushed his finger through the dirt. "Both," he stated flatly.

This was a hard conversation to have. The boy wasn't just young, there was something different about him. An innocence rarely seen in kids of that age. A shy gentleness like he was blissfully unaware of everything except his eyes said different. His eyes could take you in in a single glance, judge your worth, read your soul, see all your darkest secrets and know you inside and out.

I chuckled softly at the awkwardness of it all. "If you don't know why you're in the woods, then why don't we walk back to the road?" I asked as I stared, trying to get a read on him.

"Immi said that if you said you couldn't die because you thought it was a dream still then nothing was going to stop you from trying your new sword and abilities and I should sit in the woods while you do." He pulled a small twig from the dirt, inspected it between his fingers then discarded it away and continued prodding the soil. "But she didn't say why so I'm just gonna sit here until the fightings done."

My brows narrowed as I considered his words. It sounded like this Immi knew I'd be here, knew what would happen like she could predict the future. "And what did she say I'm supposed to do until this fight?"

He plopped the moss back to its original position with a sigh, shrugged again, then peeled up another small section.

So apparently she had predictions for him but none for me. I didn't let it bother me. I never really believed in predicting the future or prophecy. They always seemed so flimsy to me. If someone came up to me and said they could predict the future or had a prophecy, I'd listen at first then just do the opposite of whatever they told me. For example, if I was told tomorrow I would fall while going for a walk, I'd stay in bed and never let my feet touch the ground. Or today you'll see the love of your life, I'd blindfold myself. I don't know why. I just don't like the idea of something else dictating my choices.

My thoughts cut off as a new sensation started to overwhelm me. I could feel something... pulling at me. Pulling at everything, similar to what I had done before. It was distant, really distant but whoever it was was so incredibly strong I could feel them using the energy from the plants and trees around me even though they were miles away.

"I can feel the essence being pulled in that direction." a deep gruff voice spoke from behind where the road was and I turned to look.

"How can you feel it? Is it that sword you had the kid make ya?"

The first man nodded and I realized he must be feeling the same thing that I did. I regarded them both closer, the one who had just asked the question had dark hair slicked back on his head where it fell about shoulder length. A hooked nose sat between two dark eyes and a jaw so pointy it could be used as a door wedge. A thin leather tunic covered his gangly arms and chest and he wore a kilt similar to mine. In fact, it was the exact same. I was wearing this man's kilt, I realized.

"Yeah. I bet the boy has something to do with this." the first man answered in a low tone. "I'm tired of babysitting him out here in the middle of nowhere. I'd just like to give the little bastard a beating for getting our pay docked then leave him out here to rot."

He continued to stare in that direction and I noticed he too was wearing a kilt similar to ours but his shirt was jet black and had no sleeves. His bald head rested on a wrinkly wide face that looked like he used it to break down walls. He was thicker and shorter than his companion and as I observed further, I noticed a line across his arm from shoulder to elbow. Thick angry skin appeared to be stretched out and clearly the wound hadn't been cared for properly when he took it.

This one had to be Scar and if I had to pick, I'd guess he would be the better fighter. Thick heads like those tended not to feel pain and the mark on his arm proved he'd been through some at some point in his life but-

My thoughts were cut off again as a tremor shook through me. Small at first then growing more and more. Whoever or whatever was doing that was shaking the foundations of this place like it was nothing and at a distance too far to even gauge properly. I only had myself as a comparison but I couldn't even guess at how many times more powerful this being was then me.

Then it vanished. Completely gone without a trace.

"I never knew it could cause that." Scar spoke slowly, like he wasn't sure how to proceed.

Tad nodded, "Let's get back to the house and see if that worthless brat knows what's going on."

They started walking, continuing to stare in the direction the source had winked out at. Clearly they didn't like the kid and wanting to give him a beating was proof enough for me of their intentions. This was a dream after all. My dream and I had powers here that only existed in dreams so I was confident in myself. I'd step out and confront these two but I needed to say something first. Something witty or something to strike fear then attack. Or maybe, something funny. Sometimes humor could throw a person out of sorts when they're not expecting it.

I started to crawl on hands and knees in an attempt to stay under the branches and make less noise, this way my sudden appearance behind them would add some mystery to it all.

"Immi says don't try to be funny." the boy suggested without looking. "Because it won't be."

I paused for a second, I had decided on humor but how could she have known? Well if she didn't want me to be funny then that's exactly what I was going to do. Unless she knew that too... Nope, no second guesses. If she told me not to be, then I would do the exact opposite.

I crept onto the road about twenty paces behind the two men, stood straight and spoke loudly.

"What kind of man steals another man's skirt?" Both men spun. "What?"

"Sorry. I just noticed we all had the same fashion sense. That or we're all clearly shopping in the wrong stores." Neither of the men responded or moved in anyway, just sat staring. "Nothing?" I asked, holding both of my hands out. "Come on guys, that was gold."

Scar continued to inspect me while the other looked back and forth between us nervously. He's not sure what to do and is looking to Scar for direction. That would make him the superior, I guessed.

"What is this? Some sort of childs prank?" His voice was deep and raspy like his voice box was in his chest. "I don't do well with people who think they're funny." His eyes stayed locked on mine and I shrugged his comment away.

"No surprise there. People who want to give children beatings," I emphasized the word to let them know I had heard their talk. "usually aren't the humerus type." I tried to act relaxed but I was coiled like a viper ready to strike out at the slightest hint of movement.

"What did you do with the kid?" Scar asked, his feet slowly parting as he spoke.

"And how are your eyes glowing? Ain't no such thing as a male Sovereign so how'd you do that?" Tad asked, rocking nervously.

How are my eyes glowing? What kind of stupid question was that?

"He can speak like us so he must be like us. The kid had something to do with this I'd bet."

Now I was thoroughly confused. I'm wearing this man's outfit and all the two cared about were my eyes and ability to talk. If this was a dream, it was definitely an odd one.

"Listen, my eyes aren't glowing and I always talk this way."

A flicker of movement caught my eye and Scars as well as the boy moved to hide further behind the trees.

"Ahhh," Scar realized, standing a little more confidently. "What we have here Tad is a good old fashion thief." he proclaimed in triumph. "He's in league with the boy. He had him make some- thing to change his eyes but the brat wasn't smart enough to change the color. He stole the clothes, stole our yielder and is now trying to scare us off so we don't chase him." A smile spread across his face as he started to believe his own conclusions and the two began to appear at ease.

He turned back to where Deffy sat in the woods. "Tad fetch him out. I'll take care of this one. I think it's time I had a bit of fun with me new sword." A devilish grin spread on his face and he lowered his head, drawing his weapon.

Now I've watched a lot of movies and even been in a few fights myself, mostly with my brothers so it goes without saying... I couldn't fight my way through a cobweb. But what I did have was wits. When a person lowers his head like a bull, he intends to charge and if he's making it that obvious then to him I was less than a threat.

I had to use this to my advantage. I did not want to be like that and underestimate him back. I decided to play it safe. The first thing I needed to do was protect Deffy, the second, even the odds.

From the corner of my eye I could see Tad slowly turning to walk towards the hidden child. He wasn't even paying attention in the slightest, sword not drawn, eyes away.

I cleared my mind to feel the energy around me, confident my new found ability was still there.

I hope this works. I pulled as slowly and as gently as I could, drawing in just enough to use without being noticed and hoping the world didn't intensify like it did before.

Scar shot forward like a dart, sword pointed straight out, aimed at my gut. I stepped to the side, planting my right foot and at the last second tried something new. I pushed the energy out through my leg and the result was as hoped.

I blasted through the air, my next step not touching down until well over ten feet away. I planted and sprung forward again pulling my fist back and trying to focus some energy into my punch.

Tad turned just in time to take the blow directly in the face instead of the side of the head like I had aimed but the end result was the same. He did a full somersault in the air before he finally touched the ground where he crumbled and rolled until he hit a tree with a solid thump and a groan.

With only a second to make sure he wasn't getting up I spun back towards my aggressor. He stood dumbfounded, staring at his companion.

"Oops." I joked with an exaggerated grin. "I've got lousy aim."

He continued to look between me and the fallen man, his confidence slowly being replaced by doubt.

I pulled in some more energy and this time clarity radiated into the world as I faced him squarely.

He took a defensive step back. "Who... what are you?" I shrugged. "Your guess is as good as mine."

Let's take a pause. I'm ahead of myself. I know it's the middle of our first scene but I need to put down some backstory to answer Scars questions for you. What I was, was just like you, although different in many ways. So how did a person from Earth end up in a different place away from your world? Well that's what I'll touch base on next. The how and why of what happened. The part that made me shed my Earthen body and do something no one else has ever accomplished.

CHAPTER 2

Whether you prefer to call it the spirit world or Heaven, proof of it being real has always been impossible for you. In my research I've found mention of this other dimension in literally every religion I've read on and this fact cannot be ignored. But how does one reach such a place while firmly imprisoned in a physical reality like yours? There is an ability I have that others have similar to mine. An ability that involves the use of a 'link'.

I was in a field of long grass that swayed back and forth to the demands of the breeze. Tall dark trees full of triangle shaped leaves skirted its edge and fireflies floated up in all directions then winked out like embers from a fire. A giant pale moon hung half full in a deep purple sky that held only a few scattered stars. I had just arrived but what I was doing here or why I came was lost to memory.

I held my hand out to my companion as I whispered, "Let's go this way." then gestured toward the middle of the mystical meadow.

She smiled fondly, the color of her eyes obscured by the shadow of the night. Her long curly blonde hair swayed easily as she nodded her agreement. I walked at a slow crouch in an attempt to stay hidden from whoever or whatever we were sneaking away from. I led her a short distance until we reached about dead center of the small clearing then turned to face her.

"This should be good." I whispered again. "There's no way anyone will think to look for us out here."

She smiled at me playfully. The kind of smile that was se-duc- tive and mischievous at the same time. Luscious red lips parted, showing her perfectly white teeth and I smiled back. She was beautiful. Beyond beautiful. Her slender shoulders and small waist only accentuated the curves of her chest and thighs.

I looked to where she still held my hand. Obviously she was interested. I put forth my other one and she clasped it with hers. We stared into each other's eyes for a minute, the tension building. Her smile faded as I pulled her closer, neck bending to one side as her eyes shut and our lips touched.

A low growl rumbled itself into existence from somewhere close behind and she pulled back in terror.

"What was that?" Then she peered around nervously. "I'm not sure." I admitted, annoyed by the distraction.

"Will you look?" she pleaded, staring at me in anticipation.

How could I say no to that face? "Fine. It's probably just someone messing with us. Or maybe thunder in the distance." I was making excuses to help keep her calm.

I stood up to see over the tops of the neck height grass that encompassed us and not even a dozen feet away, I saw the shoulders and back of a bear slowly circling.

I lowered myself again easily to come back face to face with her. She must have been able to read my expression and realization and fear spread across her features.

"What-"

I put my hand over her mouth as fast as I dared and shook my head no, putting a finger over my lips.

We needed pure silence. This thing was so close it could have heard my heart thumping out of my chest.

I turned back to watch the wall of green reeds in the direction I had seen it and I could feel her pressing herself close to me. I knew she expected me to protect her but what could I do against a bear of that size?

I thought back to everything I've ever learned about the wild. You raise both hands above your head and make loud noises. Or was that a moose? If being attacked by a bear try to hit it in the nose? Or was it the eyes? Or was that a shark?

I turned back to her as I made up my mind to take a chance on the one swing I'd get, if any, and let her run to safety.

Another growl came then, this one closer. This one lower as if in anticipation of something. We were found and I knew it.

"Run." I whispered. "Run and try to find help." I squared myself up to the direction it had come from and shrugged her hands off of me. I would need to be able to react and fast if I was to have any chance.

"But... what if..." She cut off with a gasp as I pushed her away and stood.

"Just go!" I shouted.

The grass parted and a massive face emerged. Its head was low, eyes reflecting the moonlight and massive teeth glistened as its lips curled back.

She ran.

I heard the soft shuffle of pant leg on pant leg get fainter as she

sprinted away.

I clenched my fists and raised them both above my head. "GO AWAY BEAR!" I yelled, my voice cracking. This wasn't a bear, it was a demon. Its lifeless eyes appeared to glow as I stared into them. Then the bear decided to stand. Its head slowly going higher and higher and soon it towered above me, threw back its head, and roared.

My wits fled in all directions like cockroaches under a light. All that was left behind was pure terror. Mind numbing, body freezing terror. I sat motionless, too afraid to do anything.

The bear's head tilted down towards me then and emitted a low chuckle.

Did it just laugh? I must be going crazy?

Its huge paw swung forward and grabbed just below its neck and pulled down to its groin with a metallic zipping sound. The costume fell away and someone stepped out of it, laughing hysterically.

"You should have seen your face." he snorted, wiping a tear from his eye. "This is priceless."

"Hughbert?" I asked in confusion, everything that transpired still fogging up my thought process.

He came closer and stood before me. "Man," he bragged, face still full of mirth, "That was worth it."

I decided the best choice was the eyes and I swung.

I awoke later not remembering the rest of the dream but that's what it was. A plain old dream just like everyone has. Nothing fancy, nothing unusual.

Later that same day I saw the friend that showed up in my dream and it popped into my head so I decided to tell him about it.

"What a terrible dream. Don't blame me for how stupid they are. You're the one that thinks it up."

The comment didn't mean much to me at the time but ultimately it was probably one of the first life changing things that was ever said to me. I dwelled on it only a little bit, wondering how people could control their dreams. At the time, I never could, not very well if at all anyway and it bothered me. That little bit of annoyance, that tiny kernel of reproach I had at not being able to control something that other people could would blossom into the single most important discovery of my life.

The next night I fell asleep on a couch at my parents house. I was still young enough to stay with them sometimes but old enough to do what I wanted. Shortly after, I began to dream.

A normal dream where we don't really control anything we just observe and react to whatever our subconscious is playing out for our enjoyment.

In this particular one, we were at a social gathering at a local pow-wow grounds. There were people and cars scattered around, laughter and yelling in the background and I sat standing with my older sister and her best friend.

"Give me a cig." she demanded and put her hand out while we surveyed the area, scoping to see who was all there and who wasn't.

I took out my pack and handed one over then popped one in my mouth and lit it.

No sooner had this happened did she speak out. "Crap. Mom's coming." then dropped her cigarette to the ground, stomping it out quickly.

We were both of age to smoke but chose not to do so in front of our mother out of respect. She stepped up to the side of us, a large smile on her face.

"What are you guys doing here?" like she was surprised to see us at a party for people our own age.

I sat motionless, lighter in one hand, cigarette in the other, hoping she didn't notice. Drums started to beat out loudly and a surprised look spread across her face.

"I love listening to the drums." she exclaimed, looking around as if searching for something. She noticed the lighter in my hand, snatched it away and with one flick of her thumb she had it lit and above her head, swaying back and forth to the sound.

All of the sudden she was standing closer to a bush that appeared as if from nowhere and she was oblivious to the dried branches and leaves that surrounded her. The flames licked at them and it all went up like it had been doused in gasoline with a whooshing sound.

"Ma!" I warned but she didn't notice.

Whoosh. Whoosh. Whoosh.

More and more of the woods around her started to go up and people ran in fear, screaming as she still sat there swaying under the flaming bush.

Realization that this was all a dream washed over me and my friends' words sat at the forefront of my mind. If I could think this stuff up then I could control it too. Had to control it. I focused, at first only concentrating on putting out all the flames at once but it didn't work. I felt in control but it wasn't enough, I had to try harder.

What I did next is hard to explain and may be even harder to grasp but it was the key to my success. I pulled at my own consciousness, tugging it forward in a way to be more a part of the dream. To become more conscious without waking myself up. To stay in the dream but fully awake. What happened was I ripped my consciousness away from my brain. I felt myself fall beneath my own body, hang there suspended for a second, then shoot off across dimensions.

Stars, solar systems, entire galaxies whipped by so fast it gave the image of flying through a tunnel just like the ones everyone associates with death and space travel. They were extremely accurate. Too accurate, clearly people have done this before and lived to tell about it. The next thing I knew, I was in a field. The small field where the story began. The field with the wooden sign written by a boy in need of saving.

CHAPTER 3

There are esoteric religions all over the globe that claim to visit the spirit realm. The technique on how it's accomplished takes years to master and they save it for only their devote and elect. In my searching, I've found one thing that I've experienced in my travels that is similar to their accounts. The thing that allows me to hop across dimensions. The link.

"I guess it doesn't matter either way." Scar stated flatly. "Stealing from our master is punishable by death. I've killed all types before, you'd just be the first knick to add to the new blade."

He shot forward without warning, his sword held out about level with my side and I moved quickly to block. He planted his foot, spun, and suddenly the sword was coming from the other direction.

The power that coursed through me made me more alert, stronger, faster, almost to the point where it seemed to slow down time. Even with all that, I still barely managed to block. I realized then, dream or no dream, I had no clue how to use a sword.

In one fluid motion his sword rebounded off my clumsy block. He used this motion to swing it low at my leg in what I assume was an attempt at ham stringing me. I swung down to intercept but the blade lodged itself in the dirt near my foot with a gravely crunch that actually prevented me from taking off my own toes.

The move was so awkward he took a step back to reassess me. I tugged my sword back up and could feel my confidence fading. This is a dream so I can't die. I'm supposed to be the hero.

The thought did little to reassure me as I regripped the sword firmly in my hands and held it out diagonally like they do in the movies.

He threw his head back and laughed. "The easiest way to spot someone who knows how to fight with a sword is their grip and their stance. You see, you've got to grip the sword like it's your prized chicken's neck and you're carrying it through a fox den my pappy used to say. If you hold it too loose it'll jump out of your hands and into a fox's belly before you can ever grab it back. Grip it to hard and you'll pop it's head off." He smiled again. "You're popping it's head off. That's why your blocks are rattling down your arms and into your teeth." He stood, flicking the dust from his shoulder. "And you're standing like you just shat a brick of gold and are now defending your prize." His left hand went down to his boot and he pulled out a concealed dagger. "You shat gold son?" he questioned with a chuckle. "As I see it, you're fast enough to stop one attack at a time but not two." He rolled his shoulders then spat to the side, lowering his head.

He was right of course. I could barely stop his sword swings, what was I supposed to do about his other hand now having a dagger. All my experience with weapon fighting amounted to me trying to decapitate a brother with a plastic sword from the dollar store… and he usually wasn't even looking when I attacked. As inexperienced as I was, I don't think that made me completely useless. This was my dream after all. I pulled at the power I could still feel surging all around me like a torrent of wind but with a physical presence that gave a sort of thickness to the air. Like standing in an extremely dense fog while it swirled around you. Even with the endless amounts that thrashed about me, I could only draw in a tiny trickle.

I tried to focus in an attempt to draw more. I strained for it, tried to expand myself beyond what I held, desperately pulling at it, willing it to enter me.

The small amount I harnessed spread through me evenly and I could feel every fiber of my muscles as they responded to it. My mind slowly focused and time seemed to slow, my reflexes heightening beyond anything I've ever been capable of.

He came at me in a burst of motion, sword aimed dead center at my chest. I swang up, deflecting the blow and his dagger shot out towards my side. I had no way to block so I spun, sending it just wide. He pulled it back, dragging it across my ribs and leaving a gouge in the leather tunic but not piercing flesh.

He smirked wickedly at his accomplishment and leaped forward again. Sword thrust, block, lunge with dagger, side step, watch for dagger on retraction. Missed. Sword thrust, block again, dagger, sidestep again and back to prevent. Sword thrust, block, preemptive side step.

His second sword swing caught me completely off guard. I threw up a panic stricken block with my sword that prevented him from taking off my arm at the shoulder but not enough to stop it from biting deeply into the muscle, sending pain flaring throughout my arm.

I gasped as it overwhelmed me. Pain like this didn't happen in dreams or if it did, it was supposed to wake you up. I suddenly became very conscious of my Earthly body as it called for me to flee this place and back to its safety, away from the pain and exhaustion.

I ignored it and noticed a new sensation blossom when his fist slammed into my side, sending another shockwave through me that caused me to stagger backwards.

My true body screamed as I struggled to keep my grip on this reality and my balance while my feet did their best to respond. I took a few more steps backwards and could feel warmth slowly spreading from where he had hit me in my side and making its way towards my hips. The warmth intensified into a searing heat like I'd just caught fire.

I put my hand to it, touching a soaked tunic covered in blood. My blood. I looked up at him in bewilderment while he held the dagger out in front of him.

"You realizing now it wasn't gold?" he observed with a throaty laugh.

I couldn't understand this. Any of it. This was supposed to be a dream, had to be a dream but a part of me, a big part, knew it never was. I had been lying to myself. I pulled again at the power, begging it to answer to my call but even less came now. I could feel the small amount coalescing at my wounds, making them feel thick and tight like someone was trying to stretch them back together.

I grit my teeth at the pain and inspected my shoulder. Ever so slowly, my wound was closing. I could feel it pulling at the power I drew as fast as I could take it in. Tiny little amounts that immediately went to work leaving the rest of my body feeling drained. I could heal which I knew shouldn't be possible.

I looked up to see his face again and he struggled with what he was witnessing.

"You can heal, you don't know how to hold a sword, you have glowing eyes but you can talk..." he lowered his head while he continued to try and figure me out.

A movement caught my eyes and it was his companion stirring as he tried to slowly regain his feet. It was then, I knew I was going to lose if I didn't do something and fast. It's like the ball hog on the basketball team always says, sometimes the best defense is a strong offense.

I was clearly less than sufficient at defense but he said himself I was quick and I knew I could not afford to let his companion into this fight.

I flexed my stomach ever so slightly to test the wound. It wasn't fully healed but it would have to do. My shoulder still had a tightness in it but wasn't my dominant arm either way. I let the power I could get trickle in some more. He was talking as I did all this and I missed most of what he was saying.

"-dumb fool who's mastering the infinity code, is that it?"

I raced forward and swung with all my might for his neck. If he was caught off guard at all he didn't show it. He easily blocked my swing but when he moved to counter, I swung again. This one was blocked too so I changed directions, swinging again, and again, and again, faster and faster while I continuously pulled at the power. My swings came quicker and quicker but were all met with steel that stopped or deflected my blows.

I didn't relent. Annoyance crossed his face followed by determination. Back and forth I chopped, left, right, left, down, up, trying to stay unpredictable, hoping he would make a mistake. Sweat started to bead up on his forehead and I could see him straining to keep up.

"Tad." he shouted while his friend stood with an arm on a tree to support him, trying to shake off his obvious concussion. "Get your ass in this fight."

Tad pulled out his sword and started to run towards us swaying. His eyes were still somewhat glazed and I could see he wasn't focusing on me properly.

The gangly man started to make his way around in a wide arc, most likely to try and attack from behind.

I pulled away from Scar and darted at him, knowing I couldn't let that happen and he was a far easier target in his current state. I swung at him with all my strength. He got his weapon up to block it but the blow knocked the sword away and set him off balance. As he fell, he managed to pull out a dagger and I swang again when he landed. He reacted without thinking and held the long knife up in defense. My sword crunched though his knuckles instead and he screamed. I knew Scar would be close behind so I didn't have time to think, just react. I kicked him in the face and he sprawled out on his back. I lept then with my sword tip out and spun in the air as I could hear the footsteps directly behind me. I landed with my sword thrust coming down directly into the screaming man's neck and the sound was replaced by a wet gurgling noise.

I spun to face Scar and pulled the weapon free but his eyes were locked on those of his partner. He slid to a halt, completely motionless as he let his sword tip fall to the ground. I could tell he wanted to come closer to help his friend but I was still a threat. "My little Tadpole..." he croaked out, then raised his eyes to meet mine. "Go." They were wild with all sorts of unknown emotions. "Our fight here is done. You can have the boy. Take him and leave but do it quickly."

After he had made this announcement Deffy came walking out awkwardly, strolled right past me and kept going.

I took a few steps backwards, still watching the pair. Tads body lay twitching and Scar quickly bent over him, trying to force him to take the sword.

This was the first time I'd ever killed anyone. The first life I had ever ended. I leaned to the side and heaved but nothing came up.

I didn't kill him. Not really. None of this is real right? I mean, this feels terrible. Is it normal to feel this way?

Silence.

I frowned at the silence and shook my head as I desperately tried to convince myself that this was all some sort of vivid nightmare but as fate would have it, I was wrong.

I caught up to the boy in a few long strides and glanced over my shoulder to watch Scar. He continued to crouch over his fallen comrade until they became too distant for me to make out any- thing further.

Deffy and I walked in our silence for a while as I tried to compile and organize my thoughts and questions.

Suddenly he stopped, turned to me, took a quick step over and hugged me. I was caught off guard and it only lasted a fraction of a second.

"Thanks for saving me." he spoke, starting to walk again while his eyes stared at his feet.

"It's no problem." I responded as I moved to rejoin him from our brief pause.

"I don't know what happens to me if you lose. So I think it was probably going to be bad."

He said this without a hint of emotion in his voice but his face seemed to stiffen for a half a second after he finished.

He wasn't sure if I would win or not. He must have been terrified the poor kid. I thought back to his comment about no family and couldn't imagine what that was like, especially since I came from an overly large one.

"Deffy as long as I'm here, I promise I'll do everything I can to keep you safe. All I ask in return is that we can be brothers... and best friends, does that sound ok?"

He turned his head to look at me, his face beaming and a smile spread from ear to ear as he nodded gleefully.

"Well it sounds good to me too." I agreed, trying to match his enthusiasm. "From here on out we're brothers."

I let the moment continue on for some time, the joy he felt clearly imprinted on his face. I didn't know how long he'd been held at that house or why but I doubt they let him have people visit. I doubt he'd ever even had a friend, that was why he was so elated. I couldn't bring myself to ask that question. The answer would probably rip my heart out. Instead, I decided that if I was his only friend, then I'd be the best even if this was a dream. It hit me, I had to find out above all else if it was a dream or not.

"Deffy, do you mind if I ask you some questions while we walk to help pass the time?" I offered this as politely as I could, knowing how he seemed to shy away at my previous attempts.

"If we're brothers and best friends, can you call me your buddy?" he asked with a quick sideways glance.

"Now that we're friends, yes I will call you that, or Bud for short, is that ok?" I emphasized Bud and he smiled at it happily. "Sure." he said with a nod and that was all the response I knew I would get.

I had to start with figuring out if this was a dream or not but had to be delicate as to not scare him too much with the truth of my origin.

"Ok, first, I want you to know something. I'm not from this world, or at least, I don't think I am." I contemplated telling him about the link to my body but figured it would be too much for him to grasp. "And to be honest, I don't even know where I'm at right now."

His response was immediate and short. "Heart." He smiled happily with himself, continuing to walk as he waited for the next question.

Heart? I've never heard of any place called Heart before. Was it the name of the planet?

"Ok..." I started, trying to think of more questions I could ask to get more productive answers. "Who is Immi and how does she know about me?"

He shrugged. "She is a Sovereign." then left it at that like it explained everything.

That was the same thing the other two had said about me but weren't Sovereigns rulers or something? And how was it she came to know about me like some sort of prophet or oracle? To be honest, I don't know the difference between the two but either way, she had some notion that I'd be here, a notion that apparently was accurate.

I didn't know if I wanted to meet her or not but was at a loss of how to get straight answers from the boy.

"Do you think I could talk to her? Would that be possible?" He smiled brightly as he replied, "That's where we are going."

Well that was a start. I hope she has some answers for me and not stupid riddles like you always see in the movies and on t.v. shows. "To go forward, you must turn back," or "There are no wrong paths, just the right destinations." That kind of nonsense always irked me. If she turned out to be something like that, I'd just turn around and walk away.

So figuring out more about this place could wait until then so

I decided to move my line of questioning to be more about me.

"Buddy, the guy I was fighting said I could do things I shouldn't be able to. He made comments about me being able to talk, having glowing eyes..." I ran a hand through my hair while I tried to remember all that had transpired. "I mean, my body healed itself and I had powers. That sort of thing doesn't happen where I come from."

He glanced at me with a puzzled expression. "Your body can't heal itself ?"

"Umm, that's not what I meant. It can but not fast like that or using some sort of other worldly ability. It takes a long time to heal and some injuries don't heal at all." I was at a loss of how to explain the differences any further.

"All healing uses essence. If your body can heal, it can use it. You just maybe have a lot less where you come from. That's probably why it's slower." He stared up at me, "Are you from a dying world?" He let his gaze fall back to the ground the second his question was out as he awaited my reply.

"No, my world's not dying... Well, actually it is with pollution and all but that's not it. It's just different. People don't have pow- ers. We can't just summon some magic and get stronger and faster-"

"You can't get stronger and faster in your world?" His face was a mix of unbelief and puzzlement.

"Well, you can but..." This conversation was going nowhere and fast and I decided to kill that line of questioning to take a different approach. "Can you try to explain what he meant by those comments maybe? Why he said those things?"

He took a quick breath and nodded. "All Enlightened have glowing eyes but I think only Sovereigns have blue ones so they can talk to people but they don't fight... The other Enlighteneds have glowing eyes but they don't care about people so they just fight them a lot... and they have powers too and can heal too and stuff like that." He flashed me a quick grin then returned to his steady pace, head down, watching his every step.

So Sovereigns can talk but don't fight and Enlightened can fight so they don't talk? So what was odd about me was the fact that I fought or that I could talk like them? Maybe it's just that english wasn't compatible with whatever they spoke here.

My mind reeled when I realized that I, in fact, wasn't even speaking english. I wasn't even thinking in english. To save time and effort I'll just sum up what I wouldn't figure out for a while yet. The language I was using was automatically translated from a sort of universal language. It's in all of us, everything alive, deep inside. Animals know it, bugs know it. You ever seen a flock of birds simultaneously turn on a dime? Or a group of ants suddenly converge on a piece of fallen food? Everything has its own language it taps into when it becomes a part of certain species. Also it would be explained to me that each species has its own way to add to it and make it unique and undecipherable to others. Birds chirp, dogs bark, people speak. Our version we added is with words. Here on Earth most of you have lost the ability to tap into this universal language. I knew I never had it. Not until this place anyway.

For lack of fully understanding it myself, I will tell you what it is at its core. When you project yourselves from your body, you automatically become more attuned to the All and receive a sort of 'knowing'. This knowing allows you to speak and understand all the languages of your specific species, and in some cases, even more than that.

I decided to move my questioning on again as it was getting borderline difficult. "What about you Bud? How old are you? Where are you from?" I watched him as I waited for a reaction.

His smile melted away and there was a slight hesitation in his step but other than that he didn't respond.

"Ok. You don't have to answer personal questions if you don't want and I won't ask any more if you don't like them." He bobbed his head in agreement without turning. I'd have to gain his trust more to ask questions like that. "How about this, we talked about the Favored Few earlier, what exactly do they do?"

His face scrunched up while he thought for a minute then tossed his head to the side to remove his bangs from his eyes. "Favored Few are just guards or slaves and servants for the Enlightened and they are the servants for Aam... I think." He paused. "That's why they are so good at fighting though."

So Enlightened were supposed to be these 'higher' beings above regular people but had slaves? How do you justify that?

"Aam? [Pronounced Aum or Om]" I asked, picturing someone sitting cross legged trying to meditate. "Is that supposed to be some sort of God?"

There was no doubt in Deffys immediate response. "Yup."

His answer caught me off guard. What did this mean? He was implying that this place had a God that walked and talked among them. I didn't know if I could believe that or not.

"Yuuuppp... what?" I asked slowly, hoping he would explain further.

"Yup it's God."

I chuckled to myself at his answer. I don't know what else I actually expected. I didn't think this place had a real God, maybe it was some super powerful being who everyone just called God. Or maybe it was the leader of those Enlightened so got the title of God.

"Well then what makes you think Aam is God?" I asked, shifting the sword from my left hip to my right. I'd never worn one before and walking was making me chafe.

Deffy shrugged, "Scar said Aam knows the infinity code." My mind shot back to something similar he had said to me,

"Some fool who was mastering the infinity code," while he was

trying to puzzle out what I was.

What in the world was the infinity code and why did knowing it make you a God in this place? Or did it make you a God everywhere? Isn't that what being a God was, being everywhere or was that just a concept we assume because God is absent on Earth unlike the one here supposedly wasn't.

I turned to him, doubting he knew what it was but figured I'd try. "What's the infinity code?"

His expression didn't change as he shrugged away my question. "I don't know. What does infinity mean?"

I laughed, deciding I'd answer one of his questions for a change. "The definition of it is an unlimited amount of space, time or quantity I believe but that's wrong. That's from the wrong point of view because it only suggests one dimension. It's more than that Bud and it's really hard to explain in a way people can understand." He glanced at me and I didn't want him to feel like it was anything to do with him so I decided to try and explain it in a way he could make sense of. "Infinity is a term used when something exists outside of our understanding. Something that has no beginning, no end, or both."

He frowned while he thought of this and let his head come up, staring at the sun. "Does light have infinity?"

"Well..." I paused, I'd never really thought of light as an infinity before and decided to consider it further. "Lets see. Infinity is the mark of the creator and everything the creator touches is designed to replicate that. So this means if it is, then the light would radiate away from its source in waves." A dream popped into my head that I had as a kid where my mother taught me the concept of infinity. I pushed it aside and continued. "But also it would have to be multidimensional, like having a length and width but I honestly doubt it stops there. So, if you observed it straight from its source it's a wave but if you observed it from a different angle, like maybe its reflection, it would probably look different, like seeing a wave from the side it would appear as choppy dots or particles." I turned to him, realizing he wasn't paying attention and I was rambling to myself. I laughed. "Yes Bud, I think light is a part of infinity but I think I'm going to save the rest of my questions for Immi, ok?"

He nodded and we let the conversation end.

CHAPTER 4

There are references to this link in more accounts than just that of the esoteric religions. The great Charles Lindbergh once spoke out about an extremely spiritual outer body experience- where he was only connected to his physical self by an unexplainable link. He risked fame for ridicule to share what he had done. To try and tell the world a truth that he'd found. A truth that I am here to prove.

We walked along at a casual pace and I noticed the land had started to change. There were still pine trees but they grew further and further apart, separated by lush white birches, their round leaves spinning in all directions as the wind tossed them about. Red and yellow ferns appeared more and more regularly through the patches of moss and even some clumps of grass could be seen coming up. The smell in the air changed and was no longer the overpowering pine smell. It was still there faintly but masked by the aroma only spring can produce, fresh flowers mixed with an earthy sweetness. It reminded me of my childhood when my parents would take us mushroom picking in the wilderness.

I decided to break the silence. "Any idea how far we have to go to reach her?" I asked, kicking a rock from the path.

He froze in mid stride, one hand slightly in front of the other, opposite foot just touching down as if suddenly turned to stone. I hesitated, watching him to where he stared off near the woodline.

"Deffy?" I followed his gaze to the trees and there, floating like a feather in the wind, was a large butterfly.

He was all action, jumping up with a laugh of delight then darting forward and down the path to where the bug fluttered.

"Hey wait!" he shouted, "Do you wanna play for a bit?" He held out a finger and the thing bobbed up and down lazily then came to rest on it like it had understood his request.

I stopped on the road nearest him, watching the display with wonderment. Either I was crazy or that thing had just done what he had asked.

"Ok." Deffy agreed enthusiastically. "You can come with us but just until we find you a flower."

It was large for a butterfly, nearly the size of his face I realized while he held it to his nose for closer inspection. Large blue wings with black dots at their tops turned into a shattered array of oranges, reds and yellows at the lower part and were slightly transparent, giving it the appearance of a stained glass window. Its thin body was covered in a brownish hair complete with a head holding two giant eyes and two long antennae. They flicked back and fourth as if trying to touch him.

"Riddles?" he pondered, returning to the path and walking past me like I wasn't there. "I know some riddles but I like jokes more."

I followed in quiet astonishment. Could he really talk to butterflys or was he just pretending like other kids his age might. Instead of interrupting to find out, I decided just to watch and let him have his fun if that is what it was. Being held captive in that place didn't help him develop socially I'm sure so if he wanted to have bugs for make believe friends, who was I to judge?

He giggled. "No you go first." pause, "Ok riddles then jokes though." another pause. "Deal." He smiled gleefully, then pushed his lips to one side of his face, furrowing his brow in thought.

After a moment he finally spoke, "This is a hard one... ready? How far can a rabbit run into the woods?"

I chuckled to myself at the silliness of the question. It made little sense and there would be multiple correct answers. A rabbit could run as far into the woods as it wanted to I guess. Or until it reached a field or the end of the woods or something. The intellectual capability of kids these days didn't surprise me. With all the new technology we have on Earth, it's a wonder they can even process their own thoughts.

Deffy giggled in amusement. "I don't know how far two hundred flaps is," he put his hand over his mouth, "but it's wrong." Now I paused, two hundred flaps sounded exactly like some-thing a butterfly would use to measure distance. If he was pretending, he was very convincing. I started to second guess my first assumption. With all the strange things that have been going on here, why would a kid talking to a bug be so far fetched to me? "Nope." he said again with a smile, a short pause, then another giggle. "Why would it run until it dies?" His eyes danced with delight at the game he was playing with his new found friend. "I told you it was hard, and not just for butterflies, for everything." he hesitated a second then looked towards me. "Ok I'll ask him." He opened his mouth to speak but stopped, "I don't know why his eyes are glowing blue but that doesn't make him dumb." He turned back to the butterfly that slowly flapped its wings on his finger. "Your wings are blue." he teased with a smile then a laugh. He finally turned back to face me, "Hey Buddy, how far can a rabbit run into the woods?" He smirked then quickly added. "It's a riddle."

I rubbed my chin like I was pondering the question deeply. In truth, I was still trying to process the exchange I had just wit-nessed. This boy didn't seem to be the type to pretend or lie or do anything at all to mislead you into anything other then the truth. He was as nice as a grandfather and as gentle as a kitten. I doubted he had an unkind bone in his body.

I decided to just guess. "All the way?"

His eyes lit up like I had just solved world hunger. "Good job!" he praised, "But that's not right either."

I laughed at his intentions. He wanted me to feel good about myself even though I was wrong.

"Your turn again." he informed the butterfly. "You give up?" he continued, then nodded and looked to me. "Your turn again if you want to?"

"No thank you." I declined. "Your riddles are way too hard for someone like me to figure out and like you said, this one is really hard."

He grinned triumphantly, "Ok. You guys ready?" I nodded and the butterflies antenna twitched. "A rabbit can only run into the woods halfway, cause then after that it's just running out of the woods." He beamed with a smile so big it touched his ears. I couldn't help but chuckle.

What kind of child could return to laughing and smiling only moments after his life was in jeopardy? Maybe that was it. Maybe it was because of his new found freedom he could so easily transition back into happiness. Or maybe the fact that he was still a kid and kids tended to be more resilient to the hardships that plague the everyday life of adults.

"Your turn for a riddle," he stated to the butterfly. There was a long pause then he frowned in disgust. "Butterfly riddles are strange." he observed, making a face like he was trying to swallow two week old milk. "Lets ask my brother that one."

And with that, the butterfly bounced through the air to where it floated in front of me. I stared at it blankly for a moment, assuming it was trying to communicate but nothing happened.

I shrugged, turning to Deffy as the boy spoke. "He asked you what loves her mate so much, she'd rather be dead, instead of sharing her mate with others, she takes off his head?"

I contemplated the riddle for a moment. It was sort of dark, not the kind you'd ask a kid but this was a butterfly. The fact that it was an insect and most likely only interacted with other insects made me assume the riddle would be based around that.

I came up with my answer. "Is it a praying mantis?" I asked.

Its wings danced rapidly and it flapped above my head.

"He said yes! You must be really good at riddles." Deffy remarked in astonishment.

I shrugged. "I don't do a lot of riddle solving. They're designed just to trick you and always use different tactics to do so. You have to figure out what kind of riddle it is before you can even attempt to solve it."

The boy just kept staring at me with a wide grin. "But do you like jokes though?"

His smile to me was always more than just a smile. It was infectious. Whenever he did it, a true smile of happiness or joy or love, no one he ever met could resist smiling back.

I laughed as I grinned back. "Everybody loves jokes, Bud." His face was still scrunched up in glee, eyes twinkling excitedly. "And if I had to guess, I'm going to like every joke you like."

With that, the three of us continued on our way. Deffys jokes either extremely innocent and boyish or way too adult for him to know. I assume these he must have eavesdropped from Tad and Scar. The butterflies were odd and somewhat dark like his riddle. Guts pouring out of a bee's backside after stinging a bear as a punch line wasn't really that humorous to me but Deffy laughed wholeheartedly at each and every one and it was as contagious as a virus. I laughed with him every time.

Eventually we came across a cropping of small orange flowers with fluffy looking pedals on a long green stem. They looked like paintbrushes to me and the butterfly couldn't resist. We said our farewells and were left alone once again.

"Bud," I asked after a few moments of silence, "How long until we get to Immi? Have you been there before?"

He shrugged and shook his head. "Nope. She just said to walk on the road until we got to town and she'd meet us there."

Damn her, I thought. No clear directions just making us rely on her weird ability that I wasn't sure if I believed in yet or not.

"Well," I continued slowly as I considered the lack of direction we were given. "What if she's not there?"

"She will be." he stated like it was obvious. "But how can you be so certain?"

"Because she said to just walk to town and she'd be waiting."

I bit my lip in frustration. "Did she say what time? Do we even know what time it is now or how far we have left to go?"

It didn't seem to be close to night time yet but I knew eventually we'd have to try and camp out if we didn't reach this place by then.

The boy stopped and held out both hands towards the sun and squinted. "Right now it's still about seven knuckles to dark. Scar and Tad go into town all the time and they say it takes about a knuckle to get there... So we must be about half way." He turned back and continued on down the path.

I strolled up beside him, glancing up at the sun to where it hung in the sky, trying to figure out how he just used knuckles as a figure of time. Knowing how he was with questions, I proceeded with caution.

"Buddy, where I come from we use hours and days and months, do you know any of these?" I looked at the back of my hand like he had, "We don't use knuckles to tell time. I don't even know how they're relevant."

He nodded at me then scrunched up his face, "Well some people say hours and some say knuckles too." He stopped and pointed at the sun then to the far east where what I assumed was a giant moon hung just on the edge of the tree line. It was huge, three times as big as the Earth's moon and of a swirling blue so deep it almost appeared as if it was sucking in the sky around it. "You hold your hands about..." he hesitated, searching for the word, "a foot?" he asked, holding his hand in front of his face and staring at me. The distance seemed about right so I nodded. He smiled proudly then continued, "In front of your face and count how many knuckles fit between them. That's how people tell time when they're traveling. It's still seven knuckles to dark."

He flashed me a quick grin then continued walking.

Time here was frustrating to grasp to say the least and so I decided to give up the pursuit of figuring it out. This place was so strange yet so familiar in an odd way. The best way to describe it would be like remembering a dream you once had a long time ago. I had never set foot here before but somehow it didn't feel out of place. Its rules, its time, its logic and having its own God, this was all strange indeed but everything else felt somewhat normal.

Deffy and I continued on in our silence for a long while, it only being broken with the occasional gasp at the sight of a bug or bird. He'd chase them, exchange a few words then return to the path. Most in a hurry to find food, a mate or return home and so he let them go reluctantly. And that's how our journey proceeded for the rest of our walk.

CHAPTER 5

There are others who've claimed to visit alternate realities like I have. Patton and Gandhi I believe were two, Gandhi even stating something along the lines of "I've been to other worlds and mingled with other beings." Bruce Lee also spoke of similar accounts about reaching a higher realm but I never found any mention of the link, something I tend to look for to add credibility to a person's story. What I did find was something else. You see, when a person projects themselves to other places, it is this link that allows them to return back to the place and time of their origin. If it should become severed, and this is only accomplished by a higher being, then they would be stuck in whatever dimension they were visiting and their body here would then rescind into a coma-like state or even perish. For me, this not only grants credibility to what I read, but it also solves the mystery surrounding his death.

"Look Red." the little boy whispered as he and his friend both crouched in a patch of raspberry bushes. "That's him sitting there. See I told ya it was him. Oh man Weasel ain't gonna believe us Red. He won't never believe us." The boy called Red was as still as a statue staring in wonder at the stranger on the stump. The man sat with his shirt off sharpening the edge of a sword with a schwick, schwick sound. It's soft thrumbing broke the silence around them like he was running a stone across a bell. His massive frame sat easily over six and a half feet tall and his muscles bulged with his movements.

Leaning near his side sat the unique strap and bedroll pack that marked who he was to the boys. That marked who he was to everyone. The leather holster consisted of several separate holdings for his weapons that stuck out at odd angles when carried across his back. The largest two stood straight up and down and consisted of a spear tucked behind an odd looking great sword that had a white cloth imprinted with a unique symbol tied just below its gemmed pommel. Two others sat at forty five degree angles to its left and right, an unstrung bow and an ax. Below these, two more swords hung upside down, buttoned by their handles to prevent them from falling. Lastly, sewn to the leather sheath at the base of the swords was a spot to carry a dagger.

The man froze, his grey eyes flicking up at his surroundings then back to his work. "Come have your questions." he announced to no one in particular. His voice was raspy and smooth like pouring gravel down a silk tube. "I'm talking to you two in the bushes." he called again, metal still ringing out at his work.

Red popped up nervously, wiping his hands on his pants. "H'lo sir." he squeeked. "Um, I'm Red and this here," he gestured his companion forward and he obeyed, stepping out with his head down like he'd just been caught stealing from the cookie jar. "This here's Rock. Well... we was just wondering... It's just... we seen your sword, uh, thing there and-"

Rock cut him off in a rush of words. "Everyone knows only Seven carries sumpin like that. And that's his symbol too. We was thinking you were him. Seven that is?... are you?"

Both boys stood anxiously while the man considered their words. He held the sword up in front of him inspecting its edge in the reflection of the sun then flipped it over and started on the other side.

He looked up at them, his grey eyes like deep pools of a storm. "It's true. People call me Seven."

The boys went wild with excitement. "Is it true you killed Targ the Terrible with his own sword?" Rock asked in a single breath. "And did you once fight six of the elite Favored Few at once and kill them all?"

"And your greatsword that shouldn't be possible, is it really made out of beryl?"

"Did you-"

Theys stopped when Seven raised his hand to cut them off. "I cannot answer your questions if you don't give me a chance to respond." he chided with a frown. "It's true. I fought Targ the Terrible in single combat and claimed his life."

The boy's excitement was plain as he continued. "It's not true about the six elite however..."

Red eyed Rock with an accusatory look, clearly it had been a story he had told him.

"There were seven." he continued, "One was hiding in ambush when I tried to leave."

Rock gave Red a smug grin and they turned back to him.

"I don't have much time, boys." He stopped sharpening the blade, rubbing his thumb along it's edge then returning it to his strap. "You can ask a few more questions or you can have a story. Whichever you like, choose it quickly.

The two children didn't hesitate and in unison chimed, "Tell us of Targ the Terrible."

Seven grunted with approval as he recalled the accomplishment. At the time they fought, there were lots of names that were famous throughout the lands and both of theirs were among the top. Targs skill with a sword was legendary amongst the giants but he was widely revered for his raids and butchering of entire towns, elderly, women and children included.

Seven cleared his throat then began. "I was on a journey near their lands is how it all started. As you may know he was a colonel of one of the giants most elite militia, the club and boulder. They had just attacked a small town on the edge of their border..." he considered his audience for a moment and decided to leave out as many details as possible. "Terrible things took place there and I happened to be close by when word had spread. So, I changed my plans and set a course to try my sword against not only a giant, but the worst giant. I soon found one of his scouts and slew him then walked into their ranks carrying his head."

He chose to leave out the research and planning he had done to figure out how to challenge Targ himself without having to try and fight his way through an entire army.

One of the boys made a disgusted face and the other seemed amused by the image.

"After I wandered through the camp for a while I saw his tent near the middle. "Targ the Terrible." I called out to him in a loud voice. "I offer you this token of death of one of your kin as a challenge for single combat." and then I threw the head to the ground in front of his entrance.

"When he finally stepped out I knew immediately the challenge I faced."

Rock interrupted in a voice of pure awe, "What did he look like?"

"He was almost eleven feet tall. He had old scars all across his body and tattoos down both of his arms and on his back. His muscles were huge but not too big as to make him slow, the kind that made him strong and fast. He was bald like most giants are but had a beard that was cut flat across. Well he looked at the head and then he looked at me and yelled, "Who are you that thinks to challenge me?" Now I knew he had his suspicions because I could hear it in the murmurs of the crowd of his men that were gathering. I stood up straight and said "People call me Seven," then I stared him straight in the eyes.

He accepted my challenge and we went to the edge of their camp where a fighting pit was already set up. We fought for nearly twenty minutes straight." He eyed the boys for a second. "If either of you ever grow up to use swords you'll understand when

I say it was the hardest fight I'd ever fought. After twenty minutes my sword felt like I was trying to lift a tree trunk. I could tell he was tired too but he was smart. I tried some of my best techniques on him but to no avail."

The boys stood motionless, every word of the story pulling them deeper into their trance-like state.

"I knew I couldn't beat him with just strength. I was quicker but was so tired, my moves were slow enough I could have explained what I was doing before I had time to do it. I only had one option left: I had to be smarter than him." He tapped his head with a finger. "So as we sat there, both of us grunting and gasping, trying to catch our breaths, covered in mud, sweat and blood from a dozen wounds, I came up with an idea. I grabbed my sword with two hands, held it back and jumped at him, swinging with all my might."

He stopped and looked at the boys, letting the excitement grow a little.

"What happened next?" Red gulped.

"What happened next was what Targ least expected. You see when someone swings at you with everything they got, you can't just block it with a sword, a shield maybe but with a sword you have to have enough force to stop the blow otherwise it'll just knock through yours and take a chunk out of you after. Targ was smart enough to know this and that was his mistake. He raised his sword and stiffened his muscles to defend against my blow. I let go of the sword at the last second, letting it fall away but kept my fists balled together, turning them into a two handed club that swung below his block easily and connected directly with his jaw. He staggered at this and dropped his sword... So I picked it up and that was the end of Targ the Terrible." Seven grabbed his things and then stood.

The two boys were a flurry of commotion. "How'd you do it though Seven? How'd you finally kill him?" Rock begged, hopping from foot to foot with glee.

"I gave him a quick death, through the heart. With all his men watching I didn't dare do anything else."

"And they just let you go?" Red asked incredulously.

He grunted. "More or less. They were in shock and I didn't exactly wait around. I grabbed my things and left the pit and the camp without so much as a glance or a word. I did find out a few days later that they went searching for me but I'm not the kind of man who thinks to take on an army. Let alone an army of giants." he spoke the last part and then gave them a sly wink.

The boys' conversation continued while they replayed the battle amongst themselves.

"That's all for now boys. I have some business to attend to." He strapped on his swords and started to walk around the inn, grabbing a wrapped bundle that leaned there as he passed.

They caught up to him quickly. "Business? You're a sword fighter. Are you going to fight someone, Seven?" Rock pressed in disbelief.

"Perhaps, now run along, you've had your story." He ushered them on with a look of finality. "Leave me to myself."

The two boys ran off and Seven watched as they ducked into some bushes just around the corner.

Seven walked up the road until he saw the spot where there was a small clearing with level ground and short grass suitable for a duel. He set his bundle down and unclasped his straps before going though his movements and stretches.

One of the reasons he was the best at what he did was because he was always prepared. People thought there was some hidden deep secret that made him better then other masters and in a sense there was but mostly it was just common sense.

If you took two fighters of the same size, strength, skill and speed, how is it that one of them could win 8 times out of ten? Preparation. When Seven fought he almost never just charged in with reckless abandon. He stretched, making sure every muscle was in tune, looking for possible signs of cramps or soreness then logging it away as a potential weakness. If he was still sore in his left bicep from a previous fight he'd know his blocks to that side would be a little slower, his cuts a little weaker and overuse could lead to cramping, altering his technique completely.

On top of this he would take time to consider his opponent and the terrain. Watch to see their dominant hand and foot. See if there were any bruises visible, old scars, a slight limp, even the offset of their eyes. Most people don't realize the significance of this but people with eyes further apart tend to have better depth perception and more accurate reflexes. This isn't always true of course but a large majority of the time he found it was.

Seven finished his stretching and inspected the clearing more keenly. He noticed some rocks that could be used to cause an opponent to stumble and the other side had a slight incline to offer higher ground.

He knew none of this should be necessary anyway, he doesn't lose fights, especially to someone who... how did that Sovereign put it? Who was as new to swords as a babe to the teet.

Sovereigns. He had heard enough about them to know to stay away whenever possible. Because of the fact that they were able to communicate with lesser beings, they seemed to do it whenever they wanted.

I should have walked the other way as soon as I saw her, he thought to himself. *What had she said? Find a clearing and wait. You'll know him when you see him. Challenge him to a duel using one weapon of your choosing and if he wins, take him as your pupil then come back to me. If not, I'll grant you a boon. I'll get my boon alright, damned woman.*

His thoughts cut off as he heard the distinct sound of footsteps on gravel. He leaned against a tree to watch as the pair approached.

The one on the left was a young boy walking casually wearing a brown robe and a white hempen belt. On the right was a tall man, nearly as tall as Seven himself, with a muscular frame and wearing the uniform of the Favored Few. The small tunic didn't cover his entire stomach and the kilt showed far too much leg, it was obviously stolen. His hair swayed lazily in the breeze while he stared into the woods on the opposite side of the road.

Nothing special about them. Neither of these two could be the one Immi was talking about.

The man on the rights gaze swung around and locked onto his. The blue of his eyes was unmistakable, like two glowing pieces of cobalt and he froze.

"Deffy stop." I urged, whispering to keep my voice low. "There's a man standing by that tree staring at us."

Deffy followed my eyes then waved innocently when he noticed the man. The stranger stepped out onto the path and returned the boy's wave as he approached him.

His attention focused back on me as he spoke. "What manner of Enlightened is this?" he asked aloud, his voice coming out like leather across a cheese grater. He inspected us a little more closely then turned back to Deffy.

"Boy, how is it you travel with this..." he struggled for a word. "Being? Surely it's not a true Enlightened?" His eyes squinted as he continued to look me up and down.

"Umm, we just walk and talk and stuff." Deffy offered with a shrug, eyes wandering, refusing to meet the tall mans directly.

"Well tell him I've been sent here to challenge him to a duel. If he wins I'm to make him my pupil." His eyes stopped on each of the bloodstains while he spoke and confusion crossed his features.

He's probably wondering why there's no wound in the middle of them, I thought to myself. By now I'd had plenty of time to heal and noticed not even a scar was left behind.

He said he'd take me as his pupil and I knew that could prove useful. I knew very well I didn't have the slightest clue how to fight... in any way... with anything. Also, I was fairly sure he didn't realize that I could understand him or that I could speak too. I decided to keep him in the dark for the time being.

"Only masters have pupils though." Deffy argued with a curious glance. "What are you the master of ?"

He looked back down at the boy with a straight face and no emotion in his tone as he responded. "I am the master of all seven."

Deffy's eyes went wide for the first time since I've known him and they locked onto his unblinking. "YOU'RE SEVEN?" He practically shouted the question. Seven nodded and the boy spun back to face me with an enthusiastic grin. "You have to duel him. You'll be famous just saying you did, even after you lose!"

The large man regarded the boy with a frown. "You just talk normal and he understands?"

"Well he doesn't understand much I think though." Deffy responded. "But he'll duel you. I know it."

They both looked to me and I made a puzzled expression like I was still trying to decipher their conversation.

After a moment I nodded and Seven turned and started to walk to a small clearing just off the road. "Tell him to follow me and to make any preparations he needs. Also tell him he can choose any of the weapons he sees laying out to duel with." he finished the last with a yell as he walked on ahead.

Deffy regarded it all with a puzzled face.

"He doesn't know I can talk." I whispered. "Let's try to keep it that way for now. Tell him I agree and I'll just bow when I'm ready."

We made our way over to the clearing after him and Deffy ran on ahead to relay the message.

I walked to where he had unwrapped a bundle on the ground and looked it over keenly. On the dark brown cloth sat an assortment of wooden weapons both big and small, the kind used for practicing or dueling I assumed. All the weapons that had blades on them were straight except the ax. It was curved and appeared to be made out of a cork instead of wood.

I picked up each in turn, carefully inspecting it, running a finger along its edge or balancing it on my palm in an attempt to find its center of gravity.

I moved from the swords onto the daggers next and repeated the process. These also had both long and short blades and I guessed some had to be for throwing.

All in all, I was clueless on which one to choose. The more the merrier I decided, taking each one from the bundle and sticking them between the sword belt and leather skirt I wore. I reached down again to grab the sword that felt the lightest thinking speed would be my best hope.

"The blade." I heard him inform Deffy as he pointed to where the real sword still swung at my hip.

I had completely forgotten it was there so with the wooden sword still in my right hand, I tried to pull it from its sheath with my left which is the side it was hanging from. If you've ever attempted to do something this idiotic then you'd know it's not a feat so easily accomplished.

Usually one hand grasps the sheath to hold it steady so the opposite hand can free it smoothly. If you don't use the opposite hand, or hold the sheath, friction prevents it from coming undone and you end up just tugging at your belt and the sword bends at odd angles.

Well this is what happened to me. I tugged and it pulled the belt from my hip just enough to cause one of the daggers I had put there to fall free, connecting directly with the knuckle of my big toe. I winced in pain, hopping on one foot and decided to change tactics. I regripped the sheath with my left and attempted to free the metal sword with my right, the proper way but I was still holding the wooden sword. What ended up happening was me crushing my pinky finger between the two and reflexively dropping it as I winced in pain.

It landed directly on the same toe and I became enraged.

I grasped it firmly with my left, tore it free with my right then flung it away, yelling in frustration. "Damn stupid thing!"

It twanged as it glanced off a tree and into a nearby bush. I turned back to face the pair and Deffy sat giggling, eyes wet with tears, hands over his mouth.

Seven stared for a brief second in disbelief. "You can talk?" he stated incredulously then let out a low rumbling laugh that sounded like an avalanche of marbles. "Today's the day I earn that boon all right." he realized, putting a hand on Deffys shoulder to steady himself. "Gods be good the boy here would likely put up a better fight then you." He ran his massive hands across his face in an attempt to regain composure. "I'll tell you what.

If any one of those weapons touches me anywhere on any of my exposed skin," he gestured to his torso. "then I'll concede the fight. I won't even arm myself. The duel ends when you say yield."

I looked at his bare arms thinking maybe I could exploit his phrasing but as I watched, he bent down and picked up two leather gauntlets, putting them on to where they covered his arms up past the elbows.

I frowned while I considered my options. The man was bigger, meaning he had a longer reach so hand to hand was out of the question. Only a fool would do that anyway when offered a blade against someone unarmed. If I swung a wooden sword at him he'd probably just grab it and wrench it free. I also assumed he was faster than me, more skilled than me, and more experienced than me, I had no possible advantages physically so the only thing I had left was to try and outsmart him but I honestly doubt I had him in that category either.

Maybe I could trick him? A memory came to me from a time when I was a kid. A tactic my brothers and I would always do to people especially in the winter with snowballs.

I picked up the remaining swords, leaving only the axe, then made sure the daggers were back in their original places. I held two of the swords in one hand and the third in the other. I've never been completely ambidextrous but close enough to where it's caught people by surprise before.

I bowed to him and told him I was ready and he smiled eagerly. "Witness little one?" he asked Deffy.

"He has to hit you anywhere on your skin to win or say yield to lose." Deffy repeated.

Seven nodded then crouched in a wrestlers pose, both arms held out, waiting for me to move first.

I only had one chance. I had to be accurate and I had to be fast. For a moment both of us sat motionless until he finally started to approach slowly.

I waited until he was a few steps closer before I made my

move. I flung the first two swords up in the air with the one hand, sending them end over end in a high arc that I hoped would bring them down directly on his head. With the other hand I swung horizontally, releasing the blade directly at his midsection. The hope was to get him to choose, block high or block low.

His eyes didn't look to either, instead they stared directly at me while he reacted. He caught the sword with a quick snap of his wrist and stepped to the side as the other two from above landed harmlessly where he just was.

He dropped the first to the ground with the others causing me to grimace. I pulled out the daggers, deciding to try the same tactic again. I flung only one up this time and launched the other two horizontally, one chest level the other at his stomach.

His hands were like lightning. They snapped out, plucking each from the air like two attacking snakes. He put one into his other hand to free it then held it out palm up while he stared me in the face. The final dagger landed in it with a soft thud and he smiled triumphantly now that I was unarmed.

"I suppose you'd prefer me not to beat you into submission? You can just yield before that part if you'd like." he asked in a smug tone.

My shoulders slumped and I lowered my eyes, one final desperate idea popping into my head.

"It looks like I lose," I admitted, avoiding actually accepting the loss or yielding but sounding both defeated and humiliated at the same time.

"Agreed." he announced with a nod, then turned to pick up the fallen swords.

The second his back was to me I acted, slowly putting a foot under the ax where it still lay on the cloth and flung it at him silently with a flick of my foot.

It smacked into his back with the dull sound only wood on-flesh can produce and he spun, eyes full of confusion.

"YOU WON! YOU WON!" Deffy came cheering into the opening, both hands held over his head, hopping with joy. "You get to be trained by Seven!" He wrapped both his arms around my waist with a hug and I patted him on the back.

"It would appear so Bud." I agreed, looking to where Seven stood flabbergasted.

"But you.. it was over... I didn't..." His confusion was replaced with anger and he snapped one of the swords over his knee like a twig. "Damn that woman!" he growled, storming off towards the road where his weird satchel still sat. "Damn her and her damn twisted words." he spat again, grabbing for his belongings without stopping or looking back.

Deffy and I stared at each other for a moment then hurried to follow after.

A few moments later we caught up and matched pace with him. Deffy all grins from ear to ear, Seven the polar opposite. His frown was pasted to his face like a paper cut out that had been glued.

"This... woman you speak so fondly of." I inquired, "Her name wouldn't happen to be Immi would it?"

His head whipped in my direction but he didn't break stride. "Damned insufferable Sovereign." he grumbled, adjusting the two straps that crossed his chest. "My first bit of advice to you, whenever you see a Sovereign, especially this Immi, you turn around and walk away before she can talk to you. Once she starts talking it's like poison and everything you do is for her design not yours."

I chuckled at his logic and how similar it was to mine. "If I were you, I'd recommend doing the opposite of whatever she suggests. That's what I'd do, or try to anyway." I thought back to the small pieces of advice she had given me through Deffy.

"Yeah? You think it's that easy?" he barked in irritation. "Well her advice to me was to have a duel using only ONE weapon of MY choosing!"

After a moment I realized what he had done was in fact the opposite of what she had said. Not only did he let me pick, he let me choose any or all. I didn't have the slightest chance with one weapon, I knew it, he knew it but he must have assumed there was some trick to her words.

"She must have her reasons for me getting a master" I went on. "I don't like being manipulated any more then anyone else but I did win and I plan on learning whatever I can." I had plenty of time to consider Deffys words and the odd conversation about light helped me to come up with a name. I held out my hand. "You can call me Fin."

He sighed and clasped it with a single shake. "Seven." he announced. "It's an odd day for me. I'm usually more... reserved. I thought for sure today I would be granted a boon." He trailed off and I could see his fist clench in frustration. "I was so damn relieved. I finally... well, you won." He turned a keen eye on me as if examining me again. "I've never had a pupil before, never wanted one. I don't even know where to begin." he spoke in a slow tone like talking was something he didn't much care for then straightened. "Today's the day for questions," he announced.

"Great." I replied quickly. "I have so many-"

"But not for you." he cut in. "And not right now. Right now I get answers from Immi. After, I get answers from you."

As he spoke I noticed a large building on the corner of an intersection that sat just off the side of our current path. It was two stories tall with a large flat roof and had tons of windows all equally spaced out along both sides of it. Its white siding showed every ding, dent and chip the place had ever taken. I'm not particularly good at guessing the ages of things or people for that matter but this place clearly had seen a long expanse of time.

Where the corner of the building closest to the road should have been was cut at an angle to make it flat. On it stood two large swinging double doors that resembled window shutters. To put it more clearly, it looked like something you'd see on a bar in an old western film. Above the door was a sign with three pictures on it. A mug, a drumstick and a bed but no words. Drinks, food and a place to sleep in a way everyone could understand.

Seven turned to me. "You'll wait out here. I'll go get my answers" There was no argument in his voice, just plain command

CHAPTER 11

The 'taint' is the reason I never picked any one specific religion. I could see both the good and the bad they contained and because of the open mind I always kept, I was able to more easily see God's influence. I realized that people will always encounter that which they expect. What's already in their hearts or what they already believe. So what happens to a person who has a spiritual encounter with no religion? No specific belief except in the fact that there is a God? Then they are blessed greatly for they get to see the truth. They get to see Aam.

"This plan is so genius I'm stupid for not having thought of it before." The man sat crouched behind some thick bushes and his green eyes twinkled behind his dirty face. He had a long jaw with jet black hair that was slicked back to his head with sweat after having worn a wide brimmed hat in the heat of the day. His coat was lined with pockets and when he stood, reached down to his ankles.

He pulled a flask from somewhere inside it and took a quick swallow.

"Stupid." His companion echoed in a voice that sounded both deep and high pitched at the same time.

He sat on the ground near his friend, legs making the shape of the number four in front of him as he picked at his toes. His bald head and round cheeks held a pair of stormy grey eyes above a wide nose. There was a large scar on the left side of his head that seemed to indent slightly and he wore a leather strap about six inches wide that ran diagonally from his left shoulder to his right hip. Sewn onto this about half way down was a broken piece of plate headgear from a war horse, just enough to cover the half of his chest where his heart was. Strung to the top of the strap to help it from shifting and offer his one shoulder protection was a wide lipped frying pan with many dents and no handle. Even in his sitting position he was as tall as his companion.

He stuck a finger into his belly button next and jammed it around in an exploratory manner.

"Nah Ma, not stupid. Now, do you understand your part?"

The larger man bobbed his head up and down lazily, a toothless grin from ear to ear spread across his face..

"Good. When he comes back out to the clearing, you do exactly what I told ya. I'll do my part and bam, it's two stones for one bird."

"Two birds." His companion corrected, inspecting the substance on the tip of his finger then popping it into his mouth. "Alright then, it's agreed. Mind you I'm doing the dangerous part so I don't want to hear no complaining if this goes south." "Complaining."

"Here he comes. Get yourself ready now," he whispered and his companion rolled onto his feet to await the signal while the smaller man crept away.

Today is an exciting day. Today's the day I'm going to become famous and prove myself useful to God at the same time.

He smiled happily at the thought, his glowing eyes twinkling excitedly as he did his work. Now normally labor like this was beneath him but finding a competent lesser being was hard. He didn't deal with them often, only in small tasks here and there.

His encounter with the last one went well enough. He was able to convey his need for fish heads somewhat thoroughly. After several minutes of lopping them off and putting them in a jar the man caught on. He produced another jaw that was empty and showed him a coin and the agreement was struck and the jar was filled within the hour.

He brought them back to his study to continue his expirements but by then most of the heads had lost the essence they held. That wouldn't do if he was going to create something technically alive but without life. To accomplish that he would need live fish, directly from the river.

He looked down and could see them in their large schools swimming frantically to fight the current. Well he couldn't see them exactly just the traces of essence that their bodies were harnessing. To his eyes it glowed, dim but visible like a glow worm at night.

He spun back to where the two men still sat in the bushes clearly hiding from him and contemplated trying to have them do the work but he was almost done and trying to explain things was tedious in itself. Oh how he hated manual labor. Why couldn't he just have someone to answer to his every need that was competent and able to speak.

He leaned over with a hand ready as one neared the large flat rock he hunted from and snatched it as it tried desperately to get away. He held it firmly and made his way back towards the clearing, noticing the smaller man starting to circle its edge in a hunched over position.

What in the world are these two idiots trying to accomplish? It didn't matter. The activities of the lesser denizens in this place seldom did.

He reached the large keg that he kept in the clearing in an attempt at not having to deal with the bears he seen in the river when he began. It was filled with fresh water and he plopped his latest catch inside with a sigh.

That's 8. Two more and that should be more than enough, he spoke to himself encouragingly at the thought of almost completing his mundane tasks.

He turned and started to walk back to the river but before he reached the edge of the clearing he heard a splash behind him. He spun around to see the giant man bent over his keg, arms darting back and forth quickly, then pulling out a large squirming fish..

What? Is this man... giant... whatever it is, insane? In all my life I've never seen a being so stupid as to try and steal from right in front of my face.

He held the fish to his chest with both arms in a bear hug and smiled, then walked back towards the river.

Wait, why isn't he running off ? If he was stealing it he would most likely run the other way so why is he heading this way? These creatures...

Curiosity beating out the anger he felt at the sight, he decided to follow the man instead. As they neared the river he watched the smaller one dart from the river's edge and dive head first into the bushes in an attempt to not be seen.

These have to be the two stupidest beings I've ever come across. I could probably kill them both with ease and they know it. What's their game here?

He watched the large one step up to the edge of the raging river, turn, look him dead in the eyes, then throw the fish out onto the large flat rock that neared its edge.

"WHAT?" He screamed at the thought of having to redo labor he'd already done.

He sprinted over to the rock in an attempt to catch the flopping fish before it could reach the safety of the waters. His first foot landed solidly but there was no friction and he found himself sliding and waving his arms frantically as he tried desperately to stop his momentum. He let himself drop to his belly as his body did a slow circle and he ended up facing the direction he came.

The last thing he saw before he was swept away by the raging current was the giant waving goodbye to him as it laughed.

"Bam, that's how it's done brother. I told ya it would work. Bloke couldn't even fly."

"Dangerous."

"Now don't take that tone with me. You didn't even have to push him like we planned, besides, my job was way more dangerous. I had to crawl out onto that rock in that there raging river to butter it up all nice and slippery. I coulda fallen in! I coulda drown! I don't even know if I can swim?"

The large man looked back to the river where the Enlightened had disappeared. "Swim?" He questioned.

"He's an Enlightened Ma. Who cares? He'll be fine. He coulda killed us if he wanted so good riddance." "Coulda."

"I know, I know. They're not all the same. I'm sure he'll be fine when he manages to pull himself out of that nasty current. Speaking of, we should probably take our spoils and be long from here when that happens."

They approached the barrel to watch the fish move in a giant mass like a bunch of scaley worms.

"There's at least 8 or nine in there Ma, we're set for days. Dump a little water out so it's easier for you to carry and I'll fix it onto your hook."

The one called Ma removed the strap from his shoulders and handed it off then tipped the keg, being careful not to spill out any fish.

The little man stepped around him and pulled a dagger from inside his coat, whittling a quick hole near the top of the barrel. He found the hook sewn to the back of his brother's strap and then stuck it through.

"Here, slip this back on. I'll go fetch your... rock. We can be a ways down before it gets dark and have fish cooking in no time. Keep your eyes peeled for some tear root. It'll go great with the fish."

"Fish," the large man replied with excitement and the two quickly made their way back down the path that led to the road.

The aroma of cooked fish slowly engulfed the pair as they sat transfixed by the fire's hypnotic dance. The flames licked at oily skin and the air was continuously filled with a succulent smell that only added to the pair's hunger.

"Gimme them tear roots now Ma. They cook quick so they needed to be added at the exact right time."

The larger man handed over the small white and green vegetables and the shorter man added them to the skewer.

"I'll give ya the entire head, except the cheeks of course. Fish cheeks always was me favorite and-"

"Cheeks." The voice rumbled in protest while he stared at the smaller man.

He rolled his eyes. "Fine, how about this. I'll give ya the head and the whole rest of the fish, minus one half of a filet of course, and I'll give ya three tear roots if I can have both cheeks." The other man sat quietly for a moment before he finally responded. "Fish."

"Excellent!" he agreed. Truth was, he couldn't even eat as much food as he had just bargained for and the larger man could have probably eaten twice as much as he was just offered.

He pulled a flask from his jacket, took a quick drink then returned it. He turned back to where his large companion was tipping the keg to his lips and gulping loudly.

"We'll have to change out their water if we plan on keeping them fresh as long as possible," he remarked, making a disgusted face at the sight. "And that's not helping. Now one of us is gonna have to run to the river tonight in the dark and I've got me this terrible night vision you see-"

"Hello." The big man bellowed after he finished and set the keg back down in the dirt.

There was a small crunch of dried grass and the little man spun, a dagger appearing in his hand as if from nowhere.

"Hello." Deffy replied back, walking up and dropping next to the fire with his legs crossed. "My names Deffy but my brother calls me Buddy... or sometimes just Bud," he added while he stared at the flames.

"The names Quill," the small man offered, watching the boy, unsure of how to proceed. "Look kid, I don't know why you're wandering about at night alone but don't go asking us to share the fish. It's all accounted for."

"Fish." The larger man offered with a smile, pointing at the keg.

"Oh I'm not alone though. I just like to run ahead and then I seen your fire in the woods."

Quill stood up quickly and stared back to the road. "Well kid, how many of them are you? Are there women or other kids? Anyone carrying any weapons or things like that?"

"Oh yeah, lots of weapons. My buddy is getting trained."

This put Quill on high alert and he turned to his large companion. "Get your rock Ma, code blue." He announced in a hushed tone then darted into the woods.

The one called Ma stood, grabbing his metal pole that was embedded into a large rock and held it with two hands like a giant mace. He looked to where his friend had just disappeared in the woods then back to Deffy and put a large finger the size of a cucumber over his lips with a smile. Deffy smiled back.

"Let me enter first," Seven ordered quietly as we approached the small clearing where the fire could be seen. "And pull your blindfold back down over your eyes."

I did as he asked and followed close behind as we entered. Deffy sat with his back to us on the ground and on the opposite side of the fire stood one of the largest men I had ever seen. He looked like he could be Andre the giant's father. Seven stood at about six foot six or seven by my best estimations and this man was at least three feet taller than that.

He held a weird metal pole with a rock at its end in two hands like it was a baseball bat. For all his menacing appearances his face was oddly blank, showing no emotion. He just stood there staring at us.

"Greetings stranger." Seven started as we approached the fire but the man made no response. "I see you met our young friend here. I'm sorry if he intruded."

The giant's eyes looked at me then back to Seven and still he didn't respond so I decided to join in.

"Deffy, did you ask this man for permission to sit at his fire? It's rude to just sit without asking." The boy sat staring into the fire without saying a word. "Hey Bud?" I tried again and could see him smiling as he watched me from the corner of his eyes as we stepped closer.

Seven came up on his left near a large barrel and peered in it then held both hands out in front of him in a calming gesture. "There's no need for weapons. We're not looking for a fight." He unshouldered his satchel and dropped it to the ground behind him but the big man still sat motionless as he watched Sevens every move.

"Can you speak?" I asked but he didn't answer. "Deffy did he speak to you?" But the boy just continued to smile and not say a word.

"What in the blue hell is going on here?" Seven questioned as we looked back and forth between Deffy and the giant man. "I don't have any clue. Maybe he can't talk and Deffys just mimicking him? He looks like a giant. Can giants talk?" I asked.

"Most giants are a little bigger than that. He must not be a pureblood and yes, giants can talk." He stared at him for another moment. "Maybe he's not right in the head?" then shrugged, peering back into the keg, trying to make out what it contained in its dark shadowy bottom.

Thwaang. A dagger sunk into the keg just inches from where Seven stood and we spun to see a small man in a round wide hat with what looked like an old brown trench coat approaching.

"The last person," he warned, pulling out another long dagger and spinning it in his hand with the ease only a skilled man would possess, "who called me brother 'not right in the head' didn't live to see the next day. I suggest you buckos grab your effects and carry on."

I was taken aback by his voice and accent. He looked and sounded strangely Australian.

Seven held his hands up again to show he meant no harm. "I meant no offense to you or your... brother." He spoke the last like he didn't fully believe the claim. "We were just trying to collect our young companion here and we'll be on our way... unless." He offered, gesturing with a nod towards the keg, "you want to try and make a trade. That smells like fish in there and if I'm right, I can offer you sheet wraps and coin if your interested?"

Quill eyed Seven for a minute then pointed at me with the tip of his dagger. "What's wrong with your friend here? Only someone not right in the head wears a blindfold at night." He watched Seven intently to see if his words had the desired effect.

"He's my pupil and under strict orders to never take it off."

"It's night?" I asked, trying to play the part of not being able to see.

"Pupil you say." Quill squinted at me, trying to make out the symbol on the front of my blindfold as he came to a stop near the fires edge. "And what weapon would you be the master of then?"

"I am the master of all seven." He answered in a flat tone.

Quill's eyes shot back up to him, then me, then the satchel, then back to Seven. "A bold claim bloke, trying to pass yourself off as 'the' Seven but everyone knows Seven don't take no pupils. What's that he's carryin? Longsword? I bet ya trained under some no name master to get his mark and are now trying to pass yourself off as the legendary Seven. Seems ya got this poor fool to fall for it."

"It matters not whether you believe me. I'm only interested in the fish, if you have any you can part with?"

Quill eyed him for another second then looked to his brother. "Yeah we might be able to part with one but it's gonna cost ya. A lot. You don't know what we had to go through to get these fish. My brother faced down an Enlightened while I outwitted the bloke. Either of you ever outwitted an Enlightened?"

The larger man's eyes narrowed at his companion in a furious glare. Clearly his lies had displeased him and I chuckled at the absurdity of his comments.

"What? You calling me a liar? Well then maybe I don't have no fish for sale."

"It's not that." Seven spoke. "Everyone claims their goods are hard to come by or rare beyond belief to drive up the price. We don't need to negotiate like this. I told you what I can offer now, name your price."

Quill stood silently for a moment before he finally responded. "One wrap and one gold coin will get you one fish."

Seven didn't react in the slightest while he answered. "A gold coin could buy an entire fish stand at the market... merchant, table and all."

The small man just smiled and shrugged. "But if you're the legendary Seven then I'd imagine you're probably rich to eh?"

"Actually fortune doesn't come with the fame," he informed, "but here's my counter offer. I'll give you a wrap and a gold coin, in return you'll give us two fish and a piece of fire to cook them on and keep us warm until the morning. Then we'll be on our way."

Quill's mischievous smile spread from ear to ear. "Sounds like a mighty fine bargain to me," he agreed and then bowed at the waist. "The names Quill and this here's me brother Matches."

The giant man dropped the weapon near the barrel and plopped to the ground with a thud. Deffy instantly ran to him to sit by his side.

"Your brother Matches?" I asked doubtfully.

"Yeah he's me brother, you calling me a liar?"

"Not at all." I admitted, thinking back to the comment Seven had made about him not being a pureblood.

"Good. Now lets see to this here agreement," he urged, watching Seven rummage through his pack until he produced one of the disgusting wraps.

He tossed it over and Quill caught it with ease and buried the tip of his dagger into it to inspect its contents. "And the coin?"

Seven looked to Deffy who sat talking with Matches. The giants eyes filling with delight at the sight of the small mouse in Deffys pocket. "Deffy my friend. Could you please be so kind as to make our host here one single gold coin?" He asked in his formal tone.

"Sure," the boy responded, plopping the mouse onto Matches's lap causing the giant to laugh with glee.

Deffy clapped his hands together and the world focused for a fraction of a second until he pulled them apart, holding a single gold coin.

He tossed it to Quill and it bounced off his cheek while the man sat motionless, completely dumbfounded by what he had just witnessed.

"He just...he is... "he stammered, turning to Seven. "He's a bloody yielder! I coulda asked for a fortune. He coulda made me rich enough to rule the world!"

"Not for two fish," Seven replied. "You got more then theywere worth and should be happy with that."

He looked back to where the two sat, Matches continuously clapping his hands together then opening them with a frown of disappointment when they came back empty.

Quill snatched the coin up with an irritated growl and it vanished inside his coat while he walked to the barrel.

"Well you lot are gettin the damn smallest two then. I feel as foolish as a man wearing his assless chaps on backwards."

I chuckled again at his comment, watching as he pulled the fish from the barrel and dropped them at Sevens feet.

"You can cook them yourself... and get your own skewer," he whined, making his way back to the fire and pulling his fish off.

Seven dug through his pack once again and produced a frying pan and a round purple vegetable that resembled an onion.

Quill watched him silently, pulling a dagger from inside his coat and carving the cheeks and one side of the fish out then plopping them down on a giant leaf he had set aside for a plate. One small blackened vegetable was plucked off then he handed the entire spit to Matches who quickly sank his teeth into the head ripping out a chunk with loud smacking noises.

Seven reached back to his things and pulled out the dagger, the master's mark clearly visible in the light of the fire as he set to cleaning the fish.

Quill's eyes squinted. "That would be master Thunders mark then. They say he got his name cause he's always as angry and unpredictable as a storm. Mind if I have a look then?"

It was Sevens turn to eye him back before he wiped the blade clean on the grass. "They are fools. Anyone who knows master Thunder knows he got his name because his strikes always hit you before you ever even hear him move... like lightning before the thunder." He flipped the knife in the air a half turn and caught it by its tip then flung it towards Quill with a casual flick of the wrist. It stuck to his fish, pinning it to the leaf.

Quill eyed him with suspicion then pulled the blade out for inspection. He turned it about, back and forth, running a finger over the mark to see if it was fake or not.

"How did you get this? It almost seems real," he observed in a slightly disbelieving tone. "He puts a little dot just below the point of the lightning bolt that only a pupil would know to look for." He balanced it on one finger, testing its weight before mimicking Seven by rotating it in the air then hurling it back in one deft motion.

It sank into the fishes eye and Matches frowned at the sight as a mouse nibbled some food from his hand.

Seven didn't move but simply sat staring at Quill. "It was a gift after I refused to design a different mark for each weapon I mastered. Now how did you come by this information?" He wondered in an accusatory tone.

Quill reached into the opposite side of his coat and slowly produced another dagger. This one pure white with the same bolt and cloud mark etched on the base of its blade. It had tons of notches up one side and almost none on the other. The butt of it was an odd round shape with small hairline cracks and it had a black leather grip. It's crossguard was a row of teeth I realized ashe flicked it towards Seven and it sunk into the fish's other eye. Matches growled.

It's made of pure bone, I marveled to myself and watched as Seven grabbed it quickly and stood.

"How did you come by this blade?" he demanded, turning it about and examining its every detail.

"I earned it," Quill smirked in a flat tone, rising to his feet as well.

"Impossible," Seven snapped back, "I'll ask again, how did you come by this blade?"

Quill reached back into his coat slowly and I noticed Sevens muscles tense. "Careful friend," he warned, pulling a flask out and unscrewing the top, "It almost sounds like you're calling me a liar?" He took a pull. "Two sure ways to the grave there is. Messing with me brother and calling me a liar."

The two eyed each other for a long moment, the tension building.

Finally seven spoke. "Thunder was my master and my friend and I only ever heard him speak of one pupil with potential enough to earn his blade," he speculated slowly. "And his name wasn't Quill. I'm not calling you a liar, I'm just trying to get more information."

I watched the small man pick up his leaf of food and sprinkle some of the flasks contents on it before popping a piece in his mouth, staring at Seven as he chewed.

"I have no clue what's going on here," I announced to Seven. He continued his glare across the fire as he answered me. "That dagger belonged to my master. The only way to earn it as our friend here claims is to kill him and take it off his body dis- honorably or challenge him on his testing day and win. It signifies the pupil is more advanced than the master meaning he's unfit to teach, it strips him of the title and blade."

Quill's smile was smug as he listened, chewing on another bite as the silence returned. He finished it with a swallow and wiped his face with a handkerchief then put it back in his pocket.

"I earned that blade," he said, drawing out the word to let Seven challenge it, "by beating master Thunder on my testing day. I had no choice. He shamed me and I had to shame him back.

What better way then to take the only thing he held dear?" Sevens lips curled in anger. "You... I searched for you. You changed your name," he growled, his gravelly voice coming out
full of menace.

"If you really are the Seven you claim to be then you'll know just as I do that a famous name brings more trouble than it does good. Especially that name," e snickered with a grin.

"Say it," Seven spat out furiously and Quill just smiled. "Say it? But it's so obvious you already know it."

"SAY IT!" Seven yelled, his voice louder and full of rage.

Quill rubbed his chin casually as if uneffected or unconcerned by the display Seven was showing.

"Lets see, I suppose back then people called me... Lit Wick." He spoke it like he was proud. "Yup, wherever you found Lit Wick and Matches, you kept your distance."

Sevens head snapped down to the giant and then back up like something had just clicked. He bent down and grabbed both daggers then stormed to the other side of the fire, pushing Quills back into his hand and sticking his into the ground, tip first. He took a step back as Quill laughed.

"Umm, Seven," I warned, "are you sure this is a good idea?"

He ignored me, a smile slowly spreading across his face that looked extremely out of place.

"If you'd like some motivation," he offered, eerily calm. "Then I should tell you about a time when Thunder came to me asking for advice. You see, he had this one student who was always causing him trouble and he wasn't sure what to do. He said he'd listened to this pupils story and it was full of rage and anger and hatred but at his core was a goodness too great to be ignored. Against his better judgment he decided to give the boy a chance where no one else would."

Quill's grin oozed sarcasm but he didn't interrupt.

"This student turned out to show more potential than all of his other students combined. But he disobeyed constantly and started using his teachings to duel others without permission. So he asked me what should be done."

The smile on Quill's face slowly melted away and Sevens grew even wider.

"I said if it was me, I'd give him a lesson in humility. Make him an offer that he could either accept or refuse and end his training."

Anger started to bubble up onto Quill's face and I could tell Seven was hitting a nerve.

"So I asked him, what's the one thing on every young man's mind? Who is he trying to impress with all his showboating and arrogance? Why, the ladies of course. What better way to end all that by ordering him to wear only dresses for the remainder of his trainings... If he still wished to pursue it." Seven went straight faced as he finished. "It wasn't him that caused you that, it was me."

Quill sank his dagger into the ground next to Sevens and spat. "I'm gonna make you regret that," he snapped, removing his coat and hat in a huff.

"Don't speak to me of regret. He accepted you as a pupil against his better judgment and how did you repay him? Not only did you dishonor him by leading an army against your own kind in the only human on human war in the last several centuries but you also stripped him of being a master!" Seven pulled out a second dagger from his pack and tossed it from hand to hand as he stretched. "I have to say, I'm going to enjoy-"

He cut off as Matches stomped his way over and kicked both blades free and into the grass. He loomed over his brother like a monument.

"No." He growled.

"Ma, you stay out of this now, it's-"

"NO!" He shouted and Quil took a step back at his brother's sudden rage. "Friend!" He bellowed, pointing to Deffy who sat staring in the fire with tears filling his eyes.

I noticed this and ran over to his side, kneeling down quickly. "Hey Buddy, it's ok," I tried to sooth, rubbing his back.

He didn't look up at me, instead just sat solemnly. "I just got a second new best friend," he whimpered, trying to fight off the tears, "And if Seven wins, he won't have a brother and he'll be sad. And if his brother wins, we can't go help Aam like we were supposed to." He stuck his head down between his knees and began to sob quietly.

I put my hand on the back of his head and turned to Seven who sat motionless staring at nothing and refusing to meet anyones eyes.

Matches watched his new friend with tears on his face as Quill took a long swallow from his flask. The giant man turned back to his small brother and held up one finger.

"Friend," he informed then pointed to Quill. He held up a second finger, "friend," he repeated then pointed to Deffy. He held up his third finger and wiggled it, shaking his head to emphasize his point.

Quill's head sank at the implication. "I know Ma. You're one ahead of me now." He took another drink and held the flask in his hand as he thought. "I'm not one to ruin it for me brother." He walked over and picked up his dagger and it disappeared into his coat. "I withdraw my acceptance due to unforeseen circumstances."

He spoke the last like he was talking to no one in particular and then made his way just outside the edge of the campfire's light, plopping to the ground. He tipped his hat over his face, crossing his hands behind his head as he laid back.

Deffys head lifted up at the news and him and Matches smiled at each other gratefully. The big man moved back over and sat beside him, giggling as the mouse ran back onto his lap.

I turned to Seven who still sat motionless. "I'll go get the dagger," I offered and went to find it.

After a minute of silence he went back to cleaning the fish and soon after that they were cooked and we ate. Deffy sat sharing some of his with not only all his pets but with his new found friend as well.

I sat there watching everyone get ready to sleep. Seven curling up on his side, facing away from the fire, staying perfectly silent throughout it all.

Deffy fell asleep on Matches shoulder and the big man gently laid him down, pulling his blanket tight around him then walking to check on his brother.

He stood over him for a long minute while Quill snored softly. His arm was outstretched to where an empty flask lay just out of it's reach. His hat was on the ground to his side and the coat was still in a jumbled ball. He picked up the coat and pulled it up over his brother and then made his way back towards the fire. Instead of laying down I watched as he grabbed a fish and returned to where Quill lay, tucking the dead creature under his brother's head with a mischievous grin before going back and finally laying near Deffy. In minutes he was asleep and I was left alone with my thoughts.

I shook my head at the oddity of it all. I knew I couldn't sleep. I knew I didn't need to sleep. Technically wherever my true body was it was sleeping. Any prolonged period of my eyes being shut only made it's pull on my conscience that much more hard to resist and this proved that to me.

I rolled onto my back and stared up at what I had noticed earlier but didn't have the time to appreciate.

After a long discussion I'd end up having with Seven at a future time, it was explained to me like this. They had seasons where days were long and seasons where days were short. They also had seasons where it would change in patterns, short day once or a long day, cold day then a hot day because this planet, actually none of the six planets orbited their sun like ours did. They moved in patterns according to how hot the sun was and would form or borrow moons to help shape their patterns. Eclipses were considered night time as the faces of the planets never moved like they were magnetized in one direction. Instead, they remained balanced with something I could only compare to as a gyroscopic inertia.

Even after staring at it I still never fully understood how these eclipses worked but the beauty was breathtaking. Instead of a starry night, I looked up to a universe filled with giant colorful planets and moons that hung like giant Christmas bulbs. It was mind altering.

For hours I just sat there, contemplating everything I ever knew. What was real and what wasn't to me had changed drastically. What wasn't possible on Earth may be possible here. It was a lot to take in and I needed to take my mind off of things. I ended the night with another slow circuit of the cheim.

CHAPTER 12

Belief is the foundation of this reality. The world may not quite be ready to hear that or even fully understand it yet but I say it anyway. This statement gets proven more and more every day throughout your lives, in your societies, your religions and in your sciences. Unfortunately, you've always been told what to believe and have always believed what you've been told.

The sun finally started to peek out and Quill sat up with a silent groan. His hair was matted to his head, his eyes only opening into tiny slits while he scanned his surroundings.

His eyes rested on me for a brief minute and then they found his flask. He took a drink as he touched his hair. It shifted on his head like it was all glued together and he brought up the other hand up in a desperate attempt to untangle it. He searched around in confusion until he noticed the fish and a smile crossed his face.

He stood, put his coat on, returned the flask to a hidden pocket, grabbed the fish and then made his way over. Not sleeping all night had left me plenty of time and motivation to keep the fire burning brightly.

He eyed it and then me, "not much for sleeping then eh?"

I shrugged and Seven sat upright at the sound of a voice. He did a quick survey himself before finally stopping on me. "Cheim," he ordered flatly.

"Just got done," I replied.

He didn't respond, instead he removed his great sword and started to do it himself. When he did it, it looked like it was the most natural thing in the world. Like the sword was a part of him and it was a dance with a lover. I knew I had a ways to go before I could ever do it with that much grace and fluidity.

I noticed Quill watching from the corner of his eyes while he gutted a fish. "If it ain't too much to ask bucko. You think it's possible, I mean with your blindfold and all, that you can find a few apples in the woods there? I'll add 'em to breakfast and even share with you and the little one for your efforts if ya do."

I noticed Seven wasn't mentioned but I knew what an apple was so I agreed. "Yeah, the blindfold is actually see through so it shouldn't be too hard."

It took some time to locate one but eventually I found a tree and picked as many apples as I could fit in the fold of my shirt. I arrived back at camp to find everyone fully awake and sitting around the fire.

The sun was still barely half way out and it gave off a weird vibe, like a room only half lit. They were all oddly silent as I approached.

"Only need four," Quill pointed out, grabbing them from where I held out my shirt.

He stuck them on the spit with the two fish and I brought the remaining ones over to Seven. He stuffed them into his bag with the exception of one that he bit into as he sat back down.

"As soon as you two are done eating we leave," he informed behind a mouthful of crunching. "I want to be on the road before full sun."

Deffy stood at the news and faced him with his head hung low, eyes facing the ground. "Master Seven," he spoke in a quiet voice. "I told my best friend Matches about Aam and he said he wants to help. He wants to come with us too though."

Quill stood slowly, staring at the pair. "What's this now? Ma told ya that did he?" Deffy bobbed his head up and down without lifting his eyes. "This true Ma?" Quill asked, addressing his brother next.

The giant man sat petting the mouse delicately with one finger. "Friend," he confirmed.

"Deffy, I don't think that's a good idea," Seven remarked after a moment and Deffy turned back to Matches.

"Going," his rumbling voice carried easily across the camp and Deffy nodded.

"Well we decided either way that we're sticking together and if Aam needs help then we will need all the help we can get. And you said we need people to lead armies and Mr. Quill has led armies"

"But Quill's not a good person, not the kind that would help us without a price or betraying us. That army was against his own kind. He brought shame to his own master."

Quill glared daggers at Seven. "Don't pretend to know me having heard two stories. I can list some things I've heard about you that makes you no peach either," he shot back, the tension between the two building once again.

Deffy interrupted. "But if you didn't suggest it to your master then I doubt he would have done that. I think you're just as much at fault as Mr. Quill." A frown appeared on Sevens face at the observation. "And plus, if your master said he seen something good in him don't you trust in your master's judgment?"

Everyone sat quietly while we awaited Sevens response. "You have a lot of wisdom for one so young," he acknowledged with a sigh. "And apparently listen to our conversations more than I was aware of. So I will say this, for now, we are an open party. Any who wish to join, can, as long as they clear it with me first." He glanced at Quill briefly and then sat to finish his apple.

Deffy and Matches cheered. The giant man addressing Seven directly. "Go friend?" he asked, clapping Deffy on the back.

"Very well," Seven responded and the big man turned to Quill. "It will be a cold day in hell before I ask that man anything."

He cautioned, "I'm not part of your little group here but I am my brother's protector and as such will accompany him wherever he goes."

Seven didn't react to this in the slightest so Deffy shrugged happily. "We are going to save Aam!" he cheered and Matches clapped happily.

We finished our meal, put out the fire and were on the road as the sun finally freed itself from the eclipse.

"I think we should start trying to come up with ideas on how to reach Aam." Seven flicked at his stubble covered chin as he spoke to me.

"I did put some thought into that last night actually," I replied and he raised an eyebrow. "I would assume that because it's a present God we are talking about in this place, that this Aam is known and beloved by all?"

"Used to be present. Everyone here is aware of Aams absence as of late but yes, beloved by all. Where is this going?"

"And this includes giants, Enlightened, all the other beings?" He inclined his head and I continued. "Then I think it should be obvious. If we just made what we know public, that Aam is trapped in the tower by a being of unknown power and intentions and that we need help at a rescue attempt people would volunteer by the thousands. I bet if we just set up a time and place to join us, we'd have armies from everywhere of all kinds show up."

"Problem is," Quill interjected from behind, "if you have a huge number of supporters show, of all different types like you said, then they'd just end up fighting each other. There's always armies forming for one reason or another, but when giants see human armies, hatred consumes them and they attack."

"No one asked for your opinion," Seven remarked with an intense glare before he turned to me. "However, he's right."

Quill smiled smugly and winked and I couldn't help but smile back. I didn't have a quarrel with him. Honestly, if I'd been forced to wear a dress in order to complete my training I may have reacted in the same way.

"But if we get them to meet near each other, close enough to coordinate attacks but far enough to keep them from our throats, then we could at least use them as a distraction and try to sneak you in." He stared up at the sun as he continued to think. "We'd need to have a contact in each army, meaning a giant or preferably a Sovereign or even an Enlightened, whatever we can get. Well at least it's the start of a plan. We can start spreading the word at the next town to get the armies forming. We can have them meet at the fields closest to the tower for now, making sure to keep giants and humans apart. We will tell them we are looking for people with experience or leadership to help assemble and we'll start to ask around about those prophecies as well. Maybe we can even have someone inform the Enlightened about our cause, you never know."

"I would assume if this Immi knows then the Enlightened would too? Our problem would be getting them to show up and actually coordinate with us right?"

Seven shrugged. "I doubt little if any would concern themselves with anything we do. We can only hope for at least one Sovereign to show up and help bridge the gap in communications in case any do."

Bits of gravel went bouncing away as Quill quickened his step to come up alongside me. He stared at me with eyes squinted as if unsure what he was seeing.

"Pardon me chum but can I have a quick word when you're done?"

I turned to Seven and he nodded. "I'll see if the boy is hungry yet." Then he walked ahead to where Deffy sat about twelve feet in the air as Matches carried him on his shoulders. They were swatting at the bottoms of the overhanging branches, looking for signs of life as they passed and then laughing excitedly when they found it.

I turned back to Quill. "What's on your mind bucko?" I asked pleasantly and he snickered.

"What makes you so different friend?" he wondered, staring at me like a man trying to figure out a puzzle.

I realized he suspected something and so I tried to play it off. "What do you mean?"

He looked to make sure the others were out of ear shot. "Don't play games here. You guys need me. Everything you just said you were looking for, is me, but before I decide if I wanna join or not, there's some things that just aren't adding up and you're at the center of it all... bucko." He mimicked the way I had said it and I smiled.

I thought about what possible excuses I could use but not knowing much about this place yet, I didn't know which ones would work or not. I tried to buy more time.

"What makes you think you're what we're looking for?" I insisted, trying to appear unaffected.

"I'm the best dagger master, most likely in the world, I've commanded armies and I have an 'in' with the giants."

I watched to where Matches held Deffy upright to 'rescue' some poor creature that probably didn't want rescuing. It was obviously true, how had we not seen it before?

"My brother has never had a friend in his life, save me, and I'm not going to take that away from him, not for anything but if you guys want my help, I have three requests."

He was right. He was going to be with us no matter what and if his claims were true, it was a huge step in the right direction.

"I guess it depends on your requests then," I offered with a shrug.

"First," he started, "explain to me why, if that really is the legendary Seven, he has chosen to take a pupil, something he has never done before?"

I put on the most mischievous grin I could, trying to replicate the one he always did. "That's easy, I beat him in a duel."

Quill's eyes widened in disbelief that was instantly replaced by confusion. "If that was true, you wouldn't need him as a master?"

I laughed at his expression. "I never said I beat him fairly... or even with honor for that matter."

It was Quill's turn to laugh and he clapped me on the back. "We're gonna get along juuuust fine." He reached into his coat and produced a flask, offering it to me.

I briefly wondered if I could even get drunk in this place, accepting it with a shrug then taking a drink.

The liquid blazed down my throat like molten metal through a tube and my eyes watered so much my vision blurred. I coughed and he slapped me on the back.

"What the hell is this? Rubbing alcohol?" I guessed, wiping at my mouth.

"What the deuce is rubbing alcohol? Sounds like a bloody waste to me if that's what you're doing with it." He still smiled slightly as he watched me from the corner of his eye. "You see, you're different. The way you talk, the things you say, calling Aam 'our' God and the such. But what really twists me testicals is that Seven said he wanted to sneak YOU in to reach Aam." He watched me carefully, trying to get a reaction. "The great Seven, the man who's supposed to be a better fighter than any single being on this planet, including Enlightened when he's got his karma stone, wants to sneak you in... My second request is to explain this to me, what makes you so special friend?" He took a drink himself and popped it back into an inside pocket as he waited.

We needed this guy. I knew it, Seven wouldn't like it or even agree to it but we needed him. He was going to be with us anyway as there was clearly no separating him from Matches, Matches from Deffy or me from Deffy. We were all glued together by unbreakable bonds.

"Show him your eyes," a tiny voice that sounded like a violin sounded near my right ear.

I snapped my head around to confront it but there was no one and nothing there. I looked around in confusion to find Quill with a similar expression.

"You ok bucko?" he questioned, widening the distance between us like I was crazy.

"Did you just hear a voice?" I asked and he shook his head slowly.

I looked ahead to where Deffy and Matches were staring at me and laughing. Deffy held his palm upright in front of him and a tiny black dot sat at its center.

He leaned forward and spoke something to it. "It's just me Buddy," the voice came again into the same ear.

I turned once more and there was still nothing there. It didn't sound like his voice but as his lips moved I could see it reflected what he was saying only with a slight delay.

"I'm using the way this bug talks so I can talk to you." I watched him pause for a second then continued. "He's my friend so don't squish him. He's in your hair."

I watched him giggle and an eerie screeching noise not unlike a laugh was emitted. I reached up carefully and pulled the bug from my hair, holding him out for inspection. It looked like some sort of weird cricket and I frowned.

"Can you hear me?" I whispered to it and then cocked my head to the side to wait for the reply.

As I did this I noticed Quill staring at me in horror. "Remind me to never give you a drink again, friend. It does not do you good."

I chuckled at his comment and put a finger to my lips to silence him. "Yeah I can hear you. If you keep it with you then we can talk wherever we go even if we get separated. They can talk to each other from anywhere." The voice came back and I looked to Deffy who sat smiling proudly.

At the time, I was completely baffled by how it was happening. Later, I'd find out that some insects and species can communicate at any distance especially migratory ones and some with antennas on their heads. When Deffy spoke to his, it relayed the sounds it heard perfectly to the one I had, mimicking them flawlessly and reproducing the voices it heard. No doubt this is how Deffy was listening in to our previous conversations.

"Does he have to be in my hair all the time?" I pleaded in a whisper.

"No, I'll tell him to stay with me but every time you go out of sight he's going to fly to you and back into your hair though... Now show him your eyes."

"That's fair enough," I agreed and the tiny insect jumped and flew off towards Deffy. I looked back at Quill who's face showed a mix of emotions I couldn't help but smile at.

"Apparently my young friend has found a way to talk to me through bugs." He watched where it landed on Deffys head then turned back to me. "There's a lot that's not going to make sense to you. So you should probably brace yourself for this next part." I looked to Seven and then Matches before I continued. I didn't know anything about Quill except one thing, he cared for his brother immensely.

"Swear to me over your brother's life that you'll keep secret what I'm about to reveal to you."

He frowned at the thought. "That's no good bucko. I'd never-"

"It's that or nothing," I ordered flatly. "He's the only thing that I know for certain you care about."

He stared at me for a moment then finally agreed. "I swear over me brothers life to keep secret whatever it is you're about to reveal to me."

"And try not to overreact," I stated then pulled the blindfold up to my forehead.

He reeled back, one hand reaching up his sleeve for a half a second then freezing, not even continuing to walk.

I grabbed his shoulder to urge him forward and he shied away from me like I was infected with the plague.

I rolled my eyes. "Keep moving," I urged pulling the blindfold back down.

He produced his flask and stared at it. "You're talking to bugs and I'm seeing glowing eyes. What did that wench put in this?" He contemplated it for another second as he finally started to walk. After a moment he shrugged and took another drink anyway.

I snorted. "You're not crazy. Apparently I'm an unshackled."

He frowned at me, waiting to see if I was lying. "Unshackled are just stories people made up bucko. They're not real. Can you offer more proof than glowing eyes?"

I thought for a moment. "Umm, I can heal, use essence and Immi the Sovereign is the one who compared me to an unshackled."

He took another pull, this time screwing the top back on and putting it away. "Unshackled are fictional and supposed to be capable of things one step only below a God. There has to be something you can do?"

I shrugged. "I haven't really tried anything yet. We've been concentrating on my training with a sword."

Quills eyes darted around while he thought of ideas. "I've seen them form shields of essence that can block anything, form swords of pure essence that slice through anything except the most strongest of metals. They can shoot that light right out of their hands like an arrow and burn a hole right through ya or make it explode and blow everything up. It's always different. Hell, even some of the really powerful ones can fly," he stared at me expectantly.

"Don't get your hopes up. I can't fly. Or do any of those things actually. But there's no better time than the present to try... I should probably ask for permission first, that is, if Seven even lets you join us."

The frown returned to his face as he spoke. "That's my last request. I refuse to ask that man permission. You want me in, you convince him. Leave me out of it."

I was wedged between their feud like a cobblestone on a path. I decided to just call Seven back over and get it done with along with asking for permission to explore my abilities.

Sevens face was grim as he considered everything I had just told him. "In a moment we are going to stop to eat. After you run through the cheim I agree that it's time you start trying to experiment with what all you're capable of. But carefully and under my supervision." He looked up at the sun, holding his hand out in front of him to calculate the time. "If we don't stop we'll make it to the next city in time for a late dinner. As for the first matter, my answer is no"

I let out a puff of air in frustration. "Seven, I know you two have a lot of animosity towards each other but he's right. He's the best man for this job. I think we were very lucky to have met him like this." Seven didn't respond as he continued to walk. "If this is about your masters honor, then I think you're just as much at fault as he is." He glared at me with a look that could have sent statues running. "It's true. That was a pretty humiliating thing you told your master to do."

"I don't care about your opinion on the subject. My point is he attacked and killed his own kind. We give him an army and who's to say he doesn't betray us again? Who's to say he doesn't have some secret pact with the giants against humans? That's why he has an in with them and that's why his companion so clearly is one."

I looked to Quill and his face was red with anger but he didn't react or speak out in any way. A flask tilted to his lips out of nowhere and he took a long swallow. I turned back to Seven who raised an eyebrow as if saying I told you so.

I decided against any further arguments and let the conversation die as we continued our walk.

The trees here were different then what I was used to on Earth. Most had tall white trunks with black stripes like a zebras but instead of lush green leaves they were a brilliant orange. I'd later find they were named Divine Judgements.

Back in the history of this place if you were accused of a crime like murder they'd put a noose around your neck and hang you from one of its branches. A branch could be full of leaves and appear perfectly healthy but snap off anyway. No one knew why some were like this while others could hold the weight of a horse. They associated it with divine judgment and that's how it got its name.

I watched them sway like dancers at a ball as a breeze ran through them. The scent it carried was sweet and filled my mind with memories of home and my childhood.

"Blueberries?" I observed out loud, more of a question than a statement.

Seven looked around and sniffed at the air. "I smell them too. Let's find some and take our lunch there."

We set Deffy and Matches to the task and they took to it eagerly and within no time, we were all kneeling in a patch eating berries as fast as we could pick them.

After we were done I went through a circuit of the cheim while Seven continued his verbal lessons and then it was finally time to experiment with the essence.

I noticed Quill inching his way closer as we made to start. "Any ideas on what I should try?" I asked Seven.

"If you're supposed to become more powerful than the En- lightened than the first step is mastering what they can do. Not only so you know what to expect so you can figure out ways to go beyond it. I've put a lot of time and effort into trying to replicate the way they fight but the only thing I ever halfway had success at was producing one of their shields.

Seven pulled out his greatsword and I could feel his body fill- ing with the power. There was no vividness, no clarity to the world like when Deffy or I did it, only the shade of the karma stone changed slightly.

"I discovered this on accident," he informed casually while he walked nearer to me. "I was trying to find a way to shoot one of their beams like they do but instead, I ended up creating a very small, and very useless shield. Now, hold your hand out like this, fingers apart and try to push the essence into a spot just in front of your hand about a foot or so." After he said this a tiny shield popped into existence about the size of a softball just in front of his outstretched palm.

I nodded then began to pull in some essence and Quill's eyes widened a little as the world's focus sharpened. I pushed the es- sence into my arm and could feel it tightening my muscles, increasing their strength and speed like before but wasn't sure how to get it to form outside of my hand like Sevens.

I looked back to his display and realized it was a lot easier to see the essence when I was holding some myself. Tiny amounts of it trickled from his fingers to form the small circle of concentrated essence but most of it ran out of the tips in lazy waves and dissipated shortly after.

I knew immediately he was doing it wrong and a better way to do it. "I think I see but you're doing it wrong." I guessed and he stared at me doubtfully.

I pushed all my fingertips together to let the essence flow to a point just beyond my hand, similar to his and let the shield start to take shape for a half a heartbeat and then opened them once the flows had synchronized.

A bright shield of brilliant light about the size of a coffee table sprang alive in front of me. Quill fell backwards and Seven stared at me in wonder.

"Did you see how I did that?" I asked. "Start with your fingertips pressed together, this helps distribute the flow more evenly and should produce a bigger shield."

He nodded and immediately started trying to learn this new technique.

Quill scrambled over "Teach me," he begged, face a mix of awe and determination. "I believe you now, beyond a doubt. I'll be your pupil, you my master. Please just teach me what you just taught him."

I turned back to Seven who was holding a shield about the size of a basketball steady in front of him, an improvement but his face still showed disappointment.

Deffy clapped triumphantly for Seven as the other two walked back to join us and I let mine vanish.

"Do you have a karma stone?" I asked him.

"Umm, well sorta." He answered with a confused face. "It doesn't have a reservoir. It just transfers the essence directly into me." Seven and I stared at him with puzzled expressions. "Yeah, it's not very effective if you need to battle Enlightened unless they're weak. A man can only hold small amounts in slow flows. One large blast and he's cooked."

I searched him over but didn't see one on him. "Why don't you keep it visible? Seven said they absorb blasts as long as they're in the open."

Quill shook his head. "Nah, that only works successfully if it has a reservoir. Meaning it needs to be on me and visible. I'd rather just save it as a sort of hidden trick for emergency situations only."

He reached in his coat and pulled out a golden armband that spiraled around a clear circular stone and handed it to me.

I flipped it around. "There is no second stone. That's odd."

Quill shrugged. "As far as I can tell it never had one. I just assume it's a flawed design."

I handed it back and Deffy decided to join our conversation. "Hey Buddy, I can make him one that works if you want?"

Everyone froze, staring at him in disbelief.

"You can... MAKE a karma stone?" Seven finally asked.

Deffy smiled and nodded. "I made one before. For Scar. I can make it again if you want?"

Seven walked to his pack and grabbed the dagger with the gem I had previously broken. He handed it to Deffy.

"Can you fix this?"

Deffy turned it about in his hand, inspecting it carefully. "Sure. You have to pop out the broken one first though. That's all that needs to get fixed."

Seven took it back and went and got a second dagger to pop the stone out.

Deffy reached for it after he did, looking it over then tossing it aside. He clapped his hands together but this time they stayed there. The world focused and I watched the essence rush to him. More and more of it flowing to a point between his two hands, slowly taking shape.

A moment later he pulled his hands apart and in them sat an exact replica of the one he had just discarded. He handed it to Seven.

"Here you go." He yawned and his head started to sag.

"That took a lot out of you. Why don't we rest for a bit." Seven offered in amazement and Deffy sat down and leaned his head onto Matches.

The new stone was popped into the empty spot on his dagger and then he handed it to me. "See if it fills please?"

I grabbed it and pressed my thumb to it, watching the colors swirl as my reservoir was instantly drained. I continued to fill it until it was a deep purple then handed it back.

Quill stepped in front of me, eyes pleading. "Please. I'll do anything if he can make me one later. You've got to-"

"I forbid it." Seven cut in, twirling the dagger around to make sure the weight of the stone was the same as the one before.

"I'm sorry. I didn't mean to interrupt you before you started talking!" Quill spat. "Besides, that's not something you can forbid. If a master is also a pupil, his master cannot influence or affect his pupils other students. They are completely separate and you know it."

"That may be, but my pupil is no master."

Quill's face flushed with anger but he was determined. "Enlightened are not considered masters in title but in the fact that they are the only ones who can do what they do, yet most of the Favored Few are considered pupils. He is the ONLY of his kind and therefore a master by implication. You have no say. In fact, he's also to be your master if you want to learn from him so cannot tell him how to proceed where it has to do with me!" He emphasized the last with a look that dared him to challenge the words and I could see they had made an impact on Seven.

He shook his head in annoyance. "He's right. I want you as a master in this as well so cannot influence your decisions on what you do or who you teach." He turned back to me and his face cleared as he lowered his head. "What I mean to say is, will you accept me as your pupil in the training of everything and anything that you are capable of teaching and I'm capable of learning?"

I chuckled slightly, "you're always so formal. Of course I will." He bowed in thanks and Quill stepped back in front of me.

"Master Fin, will you accept me as your pupil as well in the training of everything and anything that you're capable of teaching and I'm capable of learning," he pleaded, desperation plastered on his face.

I shook my head and watched his shoulders sag. "If you've had a master before then you know it's not right to accept without knowing each other's stories, am I correct in this?" He nodded and so did Seven. "I already know his story and he knows mine. If you want me as a master I need to know your story. And if I even suspect you left out something or lied in anyway my answer will be no."

Seven smiled proudly and Quill just stared ahead unresponsive.

"But then you'll also hear mine. Those are my stipulations. And as the only master I will keep nothing apart like your previous masters. We will work at this in unity."

"I'll... need some time." Quill stated then put a flask to his lips, not stopping until it was empty.

We gathered up some more blueberries, put our things back on and continued our journey onward.

"I can't see its flow like you can," Seven was saying. I was trying to help him improve his shield but was having difficulty explaining how to relay how I saw it work.

"I think it's easier for us to perceive the essence flowing in straight lines from our fingertips like when you point at something. When you were first doing it, I watched as most of your essence was lost and only a small amount of it actually went into your shield."

Seven thought on this then put his hands out in another attempt but instead, ran into Matches who stood wide eyed, holding a still sleeping Deffy outstretched in his hands towards me.

"Hide friend," he pleaded with me. "What?" I asked in confusion.

He plopped Deffy into my arms anyway and reached behind his back to grab his metal pole and rock combination. Seven had explained to me that it used to be a signpost, the rock sunk into the ground to hold it there and they had most likely stolen it.

He spun back to face further down the road. A man stood there. One leg propped up on the keg we had discarded earlier, hand on his hip.

Our eyes locked as he inspected our party and my breath caught. They were a vibrant shade of glowing yellow. We all sat there staring until Quill finally stumbled forward to see what the holdup was, the contents of his flasks clearly affecting him.

"What do you think you're doing Ma?"

I contemplated waking Deffy but figured it would be best he didn't see anything happen if it ended up going poorly. I laid him at the base of a tree off the side of the road then made my way back to join the others.

The Enlightened pointed at Quill and then Matches and then at his keg, a scowl on his face.

"I think he wants us to get in the bucket Ma," Quill groaned, his words drawn out and slightly slurred.

"Fish," Matches chimed back.

"Nonsense. He's clearly mad we stole his fish now he wants to use us in place of whatever fate those poor bass had."

"Wait. Your claims of taking the fish from an Enlightened were true?" Seven marveled in disbelief. "No one's that stupid."

"I told ya, ya don't know nothing about me," Quill mumbled walking forward to the Enlightened. "Stupids me middle name." He grabbed the keg by its rim and stood it back up, trying to lift a leg over to get in but instead his foot caught the top and he tumbled in head first, just his feet protruding from the top.

Matches roared in a laughter so high pitched only dogs could hear it and I shook my head in amusement.

The Enlightened stood staring at the two straight faced then emitted a sound that was like a harmony of music and singing blended together. I realized instantly I could understand what he was saying.

"These have to be the two dumbest creatures I've ever come across."

I smiled at his comment but didn't intend to show him I could understand him.

"They're probably too stupid to realize they're from two different warring races." He eyed Seven and I for a quick second. "Guilty by association. I think I'll take the two idiots to catch me more fish. These two-" he cut off when Seven pulled off his pack, revealing the array of weapons and set it behind him in anticipation.

The Enlightened stared at it for a moment. "Incredible," he remarked.

Seven didn't take his eyes off the being while he spoke to me. "I don't suppose you can understand what he's saying?"

I didn't want to talk yet so I just nodded. Quill's feet disappeared the rest of the way into the barrel with a thump and a groan, producing even more laughter from Matches which was now starting to resemble a hyenas mating call.

The large man took a huge step forward and tipped the keg onto its side where Quill could be seen trying desperately to turn himself around to crawl out.

"Thanks Ma-" but he stopped when he saw Matches' face. "Ma don't you do-"

His voice was cut off as Matches put an oversized boot to its side and sent the thing flying down the road in a roll, Quill screaming the whole while. The giant man fell to the ground laughing hysterically and I shook my head. Clearly these two were on the edge of sanity.

The Enlightened cocked his head, staring at them dumbfounded. "No. They're not worth the time," he muttered. "And the punishment for stealing from me is death." He looked back to Seven. "Better do it quickly in case that is the legendary Alcinous."

The name puzzled me but I moved closer, knowing he was planning something but not sure what.

I watched him raise his hand at the giant man. Enlightened always held essence in their bodies and only ever needed to draw more when they've used a bunch or were about to.

I watched as it flowed through his arm and out of his hand but instead of his finger tips, it went out of the flat of his palm. It didn't slow and solidify like with a shield, instead it was condensed to one spot and made more and more active. Not only did I know immediately that this was one of the beams they referred to, I knew I could do it. The whole process took him less than a second but I was ready.

I leapt forward, fingers pinched together and then opened them, a large shield spinning up between him and Matches. His attack deflected off it harmlessly and he stared at it in disbelief.

"What manner of creature walks and talks with the lesser beings and can produce a shield? And why are his eyes hidden?" He raised an eyebrow. "So there is another. It's the only logical explanation. If he can talk, then so can you, can't you?"

I knew my charade was up so I nodded. "He knows what I am," I informed Seven.

"It's extremely hard to outwit an Enlightened." He pointed out, watching Quill.

The beings yellow eyes stared at me. "What's the point of your little, um, party here?"

I decided to tell him the truth. If we were going to help Aam we would need all the help we could get.

"We are going to help your God but need assistance." I knew instantly my voice had changed when I spoke. Instead of words broken up by short pauses, it was now one long continuous flow that changed in pitch and tempo. That's the best way I can describe it. "We need a contact amongst your kind. Someone to pass the word around that we're forming armies of all the different races to do what we can to help."

He shook his head. "Can't be done. No one knows what the being really is. The abilities and powers it possesses are unfathomable. It killed hundreds of our kind with one flick of its wrist.

I wouldn't be surprised if it could destroy all your little armies you gather with a sneeze. So you see how pointless it is?"

"No. You're overlooking one thing." He cocked an eyebrow at me. "I was told that I could become that powerful. That my abilities have no limits and with time I will be that strong."

"Your plan is like a rabbit attacking a wolf. Just because you're both animals doesn't put you on even grounds. I'm not going to help you but I'm not going to stop you either."

"The reason it's more powerful than I am," I growled, "is that I've only been training for ten minutes. You'll find I'm a fast learner."

I outstretched my arm and a beam shot into the air. He stared at me with a puzzled expression and Seven's eyes lit up in amazement.

"So someone taught you to shoot a puny essence beam. Am I supposed to be impressed?"

I smiled a half smile. "Not someone... you."

He frowned for a moment until he realized what I had implacated. He brought one of his hands forward and I watched as the essence flowed into his palm again, this time it formed solidly in layers upon itself, each layer adding form to the next, the outermost one smoothing and from its top came one single layer, razor thin. The whole thing continued to layer upon itself and grow upward until it finally came to an end in a sharp point. A sword made of pure essence. I sat fascinated then held my hand out like his and ever so slowly, duplicated the process. I gripped the final product in my hand and waved it back and forth. It had no weight and no wind resistance no matter what angle I held it at.

He nodded in appreciation. "If you can truly learn this fast... I will inform my master. He may be able, um, to provide you with a teacher at least. Or maybe help in his own way." He stared down the road to where Quill sat on all fours puking while Matches stood over him laughing. "Tell them two stealing from me was punishable by death but you've spared them that fate. As for you, where will these armies be meeting? I will relay to my master this information."

"As of now we're telling them to meet up at Targog Field," I informed, remembering what Quill had called it earlier. "That's all we have for now."

"Well then he will be informed." He spun and sprang into the air. I watched as his essence exploded downward to his feet sending him soaring in an arc that carried him a long ways down the road before he landed and jumped again.

We sat watching him go until Seven finally spoke. "Not powerful enough to fly," he observed. "What all did he have to say?"

I relayed the conversation to him while Quill rejoined us along with Matches who picked up a still sleeping Deffy.

"It's worse than we thought," Seven uttered, reshouldering his satchel as we made our way down the road once again.

"At least he's relaying everything to his master and he also said he may have someone who can train me. That could be huge. Not only could I mimic them but I would know what to expect and how to counter."

"We," Seven added. "I plan on being a big part of this strategy."

"We," Quill added with a stagger and a crooked smile that only touched one of his eyes.

I stared at him. "Not yet. Not for you. You know my stipulations."

Quill put a flask to his mouth to find it empty. It disappeared into his coat and another similar one appeared. He shook it triumphantly when its contents splashed around inside then took a drink.

"Ma, ya think you can do a code blue with your little pal there?"

Matches bobbed his head and started lumbering forward at a faster pace, scanning the woodlines for unknown foes. "What's a code blue?" I asked, watching his brother closely.

"It makes him feel important. He goes on ahead to scout for food or danger or water and it gives me time to talk business... or to talk to a lady friend. Usually the latter, can't keep their hands off me them lady folk." He tried to wink at me but one eye was already shut and the whole thing ended up looking awkward.

"I take it you don't want your brother to hear the truth about you?" Seven accused.

"Nah bucko," Quill spoke solemnly, "I don't want him to hear the truth about him."

I frowned as Seven walked away to leave us to our privacy knowing Quill was preparing to start his story. This is that account, the story of Quill and Matches.

CHAPTER 13

There are stories you've probably all heard at some point in your lives about visitors to this little corner of the universe and those of you who dare to believe, assume they only come from within this universe, within this time. I've heard about a man popping up with a passport from a country that doesn't exist. A time traveler who tried to scam the stock market. A caveman who defied logic. There are many accounts like this and although some of them are surely untrue, do you think all of them are? Beings popping up randomly as if from nowhere then vanishing without a trace is an ability I'm all too familiar with.

"This may come as a shock to you but Matches is not me real brother." If he was expecting a reaction he didn't get one. I just stared at him flatly so he continued. "I was about seven years old when I first met him. He came to our plantation with a convoy of all sorts of beings. That was common enough. There was always convoys coming and going. Faces changed, beds empty one day, filled the next.

I was to young at the time to understand any of it but I always spent my time with... our guests, as much as I could. I never had any real brothers or sisters. Just a mother who never talked and a father who beat us if the wind blew the wrong way. I considered 'them' me friends, however brief our time together may have been. Sometimes a few months, others a few hours, until they day they brought me Matches.

He never talked, only exercised and trained. Ruthless he was, always looking for a fight and even though we was about the same age, he was twice the size of me.

We'd scoff constantly, first he would start it out of anger but as my determination grew he started to respect me more. It started to turn into lessons and sparring. By the time I turned nine we was inseparable. I knew there was something special about him but I didn't know what and for some reason he never left like the others.

So I asked him where he came from and he said he'd tell me if I would tell him where I constantly got the black eyes and bruises that I never talked about. So I told him. I told him about me father who used me and me mother like punching dummies. I told him how he never let me talk to anyone or ever have friends and that's why I spent all my time with him cause me father never cared about the friends I had in the visitors quarters, or so he called them.

I told him about my hatred I had for me father but the story he told me... changed me forever. He was the great grandson of the mighty giant Eurymedon but was born of rape from his father. This is common among their kind however and his real mother died giving birth and so his father kept him. Amongst giants kin is most important above all else, rape baby or not. So his father had others raise him in her stead. He was trained to read, write and fight as soon as he could walk and talk. Destined to lead one of his fathers smaller armies, mostly because he was considered short to the rest of his kin on the account of his half breed mother.

But he was determined to prove his worthiness so at the age of only 8 he went into the woods alone to try and get his first kill.

He planned on it being something small like a fox or a badger but vicious enough to bring honor to his father.

Instead, what he found was my father and all his men. You see, my father ran the biggest slave trade in the world and I never knew it. When he saw Matches in the woods alone they grabbed him up, intending to hold him ransom knowing the importance of kin. It wasn't until after my father realized who his real father and grandfather were did he see his predicament.

So he hid him. He kept him in separate quarters away from the others, too afraid to release him and have word spread about what he'd done and end up with an army at his door. Even more afraid to kill him and lose the only bargaining chip he held for his life.

One day another captive giant had spotted him and recognized who he was but Ma denied it, making up the name Matches instead. When I asked him why he would do that he told me that one night me father found out we were friends and had came to him to hold it over his head. He threatened him, saying if he ever told anyone who he really was then he'd kill me.

Me hatred for me father grew to new levels that day and I decided to focus it for a good use. We started training and planning every day. Matches came up with the brilliant idea to fake our own deaths and escape.

The whole time this was going on I seen me father in a new light. He treated beings like livestock. Have sex with any of the ones he wanted or force them to have sex with each other to create halfbreeds that were worth more. Giants, humans, halfmen, blien, all kinds forced to breed like sheep. You didn't obey, you were killed. You were too old or sick, you got killed. Mother gone or no one to care for you, killed. Too young, too weak, too slow... killed. Like they were nothing but numbers.

It was near time to complete our plan. We had a body that was the size of Matches and was waiting on one that would pass for me and as we waited, to kill time we started helping others escape. Word of this had got back to me father and I sat in Matches room that night waiting for the consequences.

I listened to Matches talk while we waited. He told me about what he would do if he ever got free. He said the first thing he would do was to get an army and come back and wipe this evil land off the face of Heart. Nothing scared him. He was so brave and so smart. He was the only friend I ever had."

I watched Quill silently and was surprised to see tears forming in his eyes as he spoke.

"When he finally came for us, he had all his men with him and all the slaves were lined up to watch. He pulled us both to the center of the yard where he beat me to within an inch of me life. Too afraid to touch Matches still and too much of a coward to kill me himself.

He pointed to a large man with a sledgey to finish me, yelling, "If I'd kill me own son, what would I do to anyone else who conspires to try and escape from me?"

The man lifted the sledgey but Matches stepped forward, pleading for me life saying me death served no one and he had made his point. Me father didn't listen and told the man to finish the work.

Matches charged the man but his hands were still bound behind his back from when they grabbed us. The man didn't think, he just reacted, swinging hard and caving in Matches head like it was a melon.

Me father was so overcome with anger and fear thinking Matches was dead that he executed the man on the spot. He sent all the slaves back to their quarters and went to hold a council with all his plantation leaders on how they could get out of this without starting a war.

As soon as they walked away a man brought a horse over to dispose of our bodies but he didn't know I was still alive. He loaded us onto a blanket and went back to get some more things. The second he was out of sight I smacked the horse on the rump and dove back onto that blanket, holding onto it and Matches for dear life.

It ran aimlessly through the woods and luckily for us a huge storm hit and wiped away all our tracks. We made it to a small town the next day where I stole food, water and everything I needed to nurse him back to health. We survived but he was never the same and remembered nothing. I had to convince him he was me brother so he wouldn't wander off. I also had to keep him hidden for fear of someone recognizing him and telling me father.

I did everything in my power to protect him, keep him healthy and keep him happy. It was the real reason I was doing all those duels during me tutorship. We were homeless and needed the money to survive without having to beg, steal or murder for it.

I told master Thunder the story I just told you. I told him that I would use what he taught me to kill if it meant protecting me brother. What I didn't tell him was about my plan to see through Matches final wishes of that night. To get an army and go back to me father. I used me skills to give me father a slow death for what he did, not only to me but to Matches and me mother. I regret what I did to master Thunder. I was a boy full of stupid ideals. I needed me training above all else to protect me brother. I'd do anything for him." He took another drink and wiped his face. "That's all you get outta me for now. Make your decision so we can get to it or I can be on my way."

I could see the conflict Seven had explained about master Thunders' decision. He openly admitted his sole purpose was to use violence but at the same time it was to protect. I knew before his story even began I was going to accept him. I was no one to judge, believe me, I just wanted him to make the effort.

"You're in," I shrugged and he breathed a sigh of relief. "Now I'll tell you mine then you can accept if you still wish."

"Fella you could be Impendioam himself in disguise, here to end the world and I'd still agree. Even so, let's get on with it then."

I watched Deffy wake up and start to walk on his own again. He and Matches quickly darting back and forth across the path to chase a bug or harass some poor animal, all thoughts of the cold blue completely forgotten about as I started my story.

Between our conversations we had talked away a majority of the distance to the next city. Quill's head cocked to the side and he stared at me through one slitted eye.

"We're a couple of pieces of corn in a load of shit ain't we?"

I smiled at the comment. "I have no clue what that's supposed to mean."

"It means," he explained slowly, watching Matches approach with his hands hidden behind his back. "Where we came from didn't affect how we turned out as much as it probably should have." He eyed his brother suspiciously. "What ya got there Ma?" Deffy came up beside him giggling while the big man held out a giant mushroom covered in a red colored sap of some sort.

Smiling, his voice rumbled out excitedly, "Look." Then he pointed at a small speck at its center.

Quill shrank back. "I don't wanna look. I hate mushrooms. I hate their taste, their smell, their friends. This ain't funny Ma." Matches rolled his eyes then pointed to the speck again.

"Looook." He drew out the word this time, gesturing with his finger more insistently.

Quill hesitated for a second more then reluctantly leaned forward, not sure if he should trust his brother or not.

Matches's thumb popped up from where it held the stem, launching the large circular cap directly into Quill's face with a splat.

The giant held his belly and roared with laughter as the smaller man bent over gagging, trying to wipe the substance from his face.

"That's it Ma... hmmph... I'm not joking this time... hmmph... the barrel and now... a mushroom... hmmph... lines have been crossed."

The big man jogged off still laughing, signaling for Deffy to follow.

"I just taught him that," the boy announced proudly then ran after his friend.

When he was cleaned up, Quill stared at his handkerchief for a second before balling it up and tossing it to the side and I couldn't help but smile.

"Why are you two always doing things like that to each other?" I asked.

After a long pull Quill splashed some of the liquid from his flask onto his hands then rubbed it on his face like it was aftershave, muttering to himself. "Rubbing alcohol eh?"

His eyes opened all the way for the first time that day as the liquor burned his skin.

"What damned fool came up with..." He glanced at me then started rummaging through his pockets for his handkerchief then realized he had thrown it out.

He grit his teeth, trying to ignore the pain as he spoke. "Them first few years held little joy for us. We was kids..." He took a slow breath, starting to relax a bit. "One day, I was running from a farmer's wife after stealing a pie and stepped on a rake. It was a small rake and took me square in the rounds. It was the first time I'd seen him happy in ages. When the old biddy caught up to me, I stood and tried to yield, offering her the pie back. She took the pie and kicked me for my efforts, finishing the edgework on me rounds. Matches laughed clear into the next day. Ever since it's sort of become our thing. A way to enjoy life. It's the only way I could ever come up with to get him to laugh or smile, until that boy there came along."

He rubbed his sleeve across his cheeks in an attempt to help sooth the irritation.

"Well we'll have Deffy make you a weapon with a karma stone later. It seems to drain a lot out of him and he just woke up."

Seven must have realized we were done with our stories and he walked back up. "If I estimate correctly, we're not far now. We should probably find whatever inn is most popular as we will need to find out more information and spread the word about Aam. Also, not too far from Targog field is Darmon plain. We should have every race except the giants meet there. The giants have history at Targog field and I believe they gave it its name so they can have it as a base camp. We can have any other beings with leadership or command experience station themselves on the path between the two fields to seperate them, keep order, coordinate strategies and run messages from this more centralized location."

Quill spoke up. "Move the Skane with the giants." His voice was slurring even more heavily now after the long drink he had taken and he walked with a noticeable stagger. "They may not have history there but there's a lot of bad blood between them and the halfmen lately. Plus, they're large enough to keep the giants in check."

Seven thought on it for a second. "Agreed."

Quill had nothing further to add so I turned back to him. "Quill, do you ever get too drunk?"

He stared at me like I had just told him air wasn't for breathing. "If such a state exists, I'm certain..." He held a fist to his lips to fight back what I hoped was a burp. "I have yet to discover it." He pulled out a flask. "But let me check at the bottom of this here," he winked and wiggled the flask back and forth.

I smiled at him as I chuckled. "What I mean is, if you get to the point where you can no longer walk, we'll leave you on the road."

"Walking you say? That's not too drunk to keep going. We just did that yesterday." He pulled off his coat and pointed to a metal hoop between his shoulder blades on his back. It was sewn on the back of one of his straps of daggers he kept concealed around his chest. He smiled at me stupidly like it explained everything.

"Not only do I have no clue what you just said was supposed to mean, I have no clue why there's a metal hoop on your back." The smile stayed plastered to his face and his eyebrows bounced up and down. "I will demonstrate with this... demonstration." He slurred then turned back to face down the path, speaking loudly. "Ma! I'm afraid we have a code black."

Matches turned an annoyed look at his brother then came lumbering back over. He grabbed Quills jacket from him and helped him put it on backwards. Then he spun him around and put a finger through the metal hoop, removed his rock on a pole weapon from his back, and plopped his brother in its place where he hung like dirty laundry.

"Wake me up when we get to that inn. And pick one that has a big tavern full of big women with big... mugs of ale." He grinned showing all his teeth then tipped his hat down over his face while Matches hurried back to catch up with Deffy.

I stared at the pair as they went off in bewilderment. "You know sometimes I have difficulty telling which one of them has more brains," I speculated loudly and a rare smile spread across Sevens face.

"Agreed."

CHAPTER 14

The world is slowly realizing that we may not be alone in this universe. How life evolves is always changing and there are many different climates in which it can exist. Here on Earth your bodies are developed specifically to sustain you on this planet so you tend to believe it's the only way. You look for and expect any other evolved life forms to be similar to yours. To need water, to need oxygen, or even to be carbon based. This belief is only centered around your sciences, your reality. A single point of view from a single world, from a single universe. I'll tell you this now, not only are you not alone in this universe, yours is not the only universe.

It was a new day for Weniban the halfman. Today his luck would finally change for the better. After yesterday's events he decided staying in town was no longer a good idea and it was time to venture forth into the world and all its vast possibilities of endless fortunes.

That and the fact someone was trying to kill him. Well not someone, his girlfriend's husband to be exact. What was the deal with husbands anyway? It's not like they own their wives. Wives are their own people too. Free to do anything they wanted, including dashing young halfmen like himself.

Weniban was tall for his kind at a towering five feet, well depending on what boots he was wearing. He had long black hair and dark eyes. Tattoos covered one of his arms of all sorts of places he's visited, women he's been with and treasures he's stolen.

And there were a lot of them. There was the chalice of Au Tau. Getting that had been easy. Alice was so starved for affection she practically dragged him to her bedroom. After, it had been only a short search and a quick pick of a lock and presto, he was one hundred gold pieces richer. The chalice had been worth a lot more than that of course but quick sales are usually best in his line of work.

Next there was the red arrow of the unsung hero. That one was a little harder. Charlene was completely devoted to her husband so gaining access to the estate was difficult at first until he discovered she enjoyed the company of winkers. Men who preferred to spend time with women at social events but to be alone with other men. Impersonating one was as easy as a limp wrist and an over-embellished accent. No, the hard part was getting the arrow out. It seemed so genius at the time to take down the bow display and shoot it out an open window far off into the woods… until he had to try and find it. It took nearly three months and the recruitment of nearly two dozen children to climb trees and search with him before one of them located it at the top of a spruce and by then he nearly lost his buyer.

So how did this one go so wrong? He ran a finger down his arms knowing why. He delayed too long and it had cost him. How anyone could ignore a beauty like TerriAnne was baffling. She tried to resist his charm, they all do at first but his nice clothes and cool humor always mixed well with his bad boy attitude.

He'd show up on their doorstep selling some new exotic perfume, or clothing or whatever his previous spying had discovered they had a fondness for and they'd practically ask him to move in.

But TerriAnne was different. She made him laugh and feel good and he developed feelings for her. He kept visiting and delaying and ended up blowing the sale. The two hundred gold the buyer had offered for the crystal skull gone, and all he had to show for it was a husband and a group of his thugs chasing him, a heavy heart, and an apple he stole on the way out the back.

He bit into it. No point saving it. Yes, today would be different. He'd sit on the side of the road in his nice clothes and sweet talk his way into joining the next people that passed by on their way into town. Then when they slept, he'd make off with their... provisions, to help start him out on his new journey.

He listened from where he hid to the group that slowly approached. He fixed his hair and straightened the wrinkles from his pricey overcoat, first appearances were important after all.

He was a rich traveling merchant who had just stopped to relieve himself and would ask if they'd like some company. They'd have to camp soon unless they planned on arriving in town well after dark which was completely foolish. No they'd accept him in like a dear old friend for sure. Who ever expected to get robbed by someone who was so obviously rich after all?

He smiled to himself at the geniusness of his plan. Yes, today his luck was changing and for the better he surmised, stepping out from where he hid behind the large tree just in time to see a fist the size of a pumpkin connecting with his face.

"Code blue!" Matches yelled and spun, trying to wake Quill to show him his accomplishment.

"What's this now?" Quill eyed the well dressed man who laid sprawled out on the ground unconscious, a dribble of blood running from his lips.

"You actually snuck up on someone during a code blue? That's... amazing! This man must be the dumbest bloke on this half of Heart. I mean... not to say you're not the stealthiest person I know, about as stealthy as a fireworks display at a funeral if I'm being honest but good job Ma. Let me down and let's have a look at him."

The giant man lowered Quill to the ground and the smaller man immediately set to searching through the sprawled out half-mens pockets.

"Are you really robbing him?" I accused as Seven and I finally caught up.

"Nah, poor guy's broker then the back of the last horse Matches climbed onto. Besides I was just looking for something to see what he was all about." He pulled out a piece of paper from one of the pockets and scanned it quickly before returning it where he found it.

"A bee just told us he was hiding there waiting for us so we snuck up on him. I didn't know Matches was going to punch him though."

"You guys did well," Seven praised. "Most people don't hide on travelers without deceit in mind."

Quill softly smacked the man in the face a few times. "Aye fella. Time to get up. Hop hop."

Weniban opened his eyes with several rapid blinks while he waited for the world to come into focus. He sat up, putting a hand to his head and looking at the small group that encircled him.

The man who had punched him was the size of a small church and sat between a young boy and a man with a crooked hat. And a crooked smile for that matter. Behind them stood two tall men, one with an array of weapons sticking out randomly from the pack he carried and the other wearing a blindfold like they didn't want him to know where they were leading him. If they all stood in a row they could represent the time flow of evolution.

"I think ya punched him too hard Ma. He's just staring at us like we're a bunch of turd burglars."

The plan suddenly popped into his head and he hopped up, dusting himself off. "Your pardons gentlemen. The name's Merry." He bowed slightly. "People call me that because I'm always cheerful and full of goodwill towards others. I'm a traveling merchant of great wealth and I'm on my way into the city here to fetch my horse and cart. I was hoping to find some gracious travelers like yourselfs to spend the night with until the mourn. It's nearly dark and no place for a rich and well known man such as I to be traveling alone. Wouldn't want to get robbed in the middle of the night. What do you's say?"

Seven opened his mouth to speak but Quill cut him off with a gesture. "Merry the wealthy merchant are you? Well known everywhere I suppose?" Weniban inclined his head. "Well then Merry it's your lucky day! You won't have to worry one bit about gettin robbed all alone in the middle of the night."

"Oh thank you kind fellows so much-"

"Because we're gonna rob you right here, right now, in broad daylight." Quill flashed a toothy grin and pulled a dagger from his sleeve.

"What..what's this?" Weniban questioned, scooting back away from the man.

"You heard me. Let's see all them riches you was talking about then Weniban."

His hands fumbled through his pockets as his mind raced but he knew they were empty. "I, uh, don't exactly have them all on me per say..."

"Well we'll just take what ya do. We ain't greedy." Deffy giggled as Quill finished and winked at him.

"Actually, if I'm being honest, I don't have any on me right now. It's all with my cart," he stammered out while Quill spun the dagger endlessly on the palm of his hand.

"Well if you're being honest, why would a man with no coin be afraid of being robbed?"

"It's, uh, funny you should ask... I'm sorry but did you call me Weniban?"

Quill smiled brightly, "I assumed it was your name unless it's actually 'my loving Weniban' but I ain't calling you that. Not without a proper meal and drink first."

"You went through my pockets? You really are thieves. Well then as you well know I have nothing on me so robbing me is pointless."

"Nah bucko, what I'm more interested in now is why all the lies? Why the fake story and the hiding behind a tree? Unless of course you thought to lull us into a state of trust, hoping we'd think rich people don't rob then when we was fast asleep, maybe do a little robbin of your own?"

He swallowed hard at the accuracy of the observation. "Of course not! I don't rob people, that's absurd. My name is Weniban and I really am well known and well liked and if you guys harmed me in any way I have lots of powerful connections. You'd be hunted men!"

Seven finally decided to step in on Quill's fun. "Actually that's exactly what we're looking for. A well known man with powerful connections." Quill walked away and the dagger vanished up a sleeve. "How would you like to make more gold than you've ever seen in your life?"

Weniban looked around hesitantly as he stood. "Err, how would... what would be required of me?"

Seven motioned for us to keep moving and so we did. He put a hand on the halfman's shoulder, walking him along. "You see, it's obvious your intentions weren't the best at first so I'll let bygones be bygones and pay you a fortune. All you have to do is go talk to these powerful friends of yours and have them spread the word that Aam needs help and we're forming armies to do just that. Have them send any and every able bodied fighter they can to meet at Darmon plain at their earliest convenience. By then we should be there to set up and organize them. When you show up, we'll give you a payment in accordance to how many people you've reached out to. Sound fair?"

Weniban rubbed at his chin. Oh man, he was the least popular person in every town he went to. He was positive there were at least a few people in each place that were actively trying to hunt him down for less than honorable reasons. But most of them were overreacting. And what was this about Aam needing help? He had heard a crazy man preaching about it in the streets a few days back but no one paid him any attention. Maybe these people were just having fun with him. Either way, he was NOT going back into this city.

"As appealing as that all sounds, I'm afraid I have pressing business that I must attend to. I can be of no help."

Seven frowned at the tiny man. "That's really too bad. Would you like some help clearing it up?" Weniban stared at him with a confused look. "Maybe you've heard of me. People call me Seven."

The halfman's eyes went wide, flicking to his weapons and then back to his face. "And the previous offer is no longer on the table. You see, I think you've lied to us before and are still lying to us. In fact, I'm certain you planned on robbing us while we slept and I'm rarely wrong. Now normally I don't waste my time with petty thieves but for you I'd make an exception. So here's my final offer. You're going to accompany us into town. When we get there you're going to go to every bar, every inn, every business and building to tell them that Seven is forming an army to help Aam who has put out a call for aid. Tell them all to spread the word and to meet at Darmon plain as soon as possible and when it's all over they'll get paid for their services. That's where you will be and you will now only receive the same pay as them. If for any reason I think the numbers aren't impressive or you didn't try hard enough or you simply disappear and ignore my generous offer." He leaned down to come face to face with the halfmen. "And if I even suspect you of lying to me again, I'll put out a contract on you. I'll offer up an apprenticeship to any being who brings you back to me, dead or alive. Now how does that sound?"

Wenibans eyes darted around frantically while he tried to find a way out of his situation.

"Not so pressing any more is it? This business of yours eh?" Quill guessed, winking at the small man.

How in the world was he supposed to move around to spread the word without being found? A disguise? No, he'd have to come clean.

"I don't think you want me to do this. I left the city with a lynch mob searching for me."

"This city ahead or the one beyond it?" Seven inquired. "Umm, technically both," he answered with a nervous shrug and Seven stared at him. "I have a thing for wealthy married women."

"HAH!" Quill laughed loudly. "Maybe you should have it removed!"

I laughed with him at the remark and Weniban flushed angrily. Seven had no reaction while he rummaged through his pack, producing a small cloth with his master's mark on it.

"If you wear this on your wrist it will not only help prove the errand I'm having you run, it may offer you protection, at least from masters. If you tell others you're under my protection my name alone should scare off anyone else." He paused for a second. "But if not, maybe pick a different hobby besides bedding noblemen's wives."

Weniban grabbed it with an annoyed sigh and tied it around his wrist as Seven reshouldered his satchel.

"You don't have a choice. Consider it atonement for your ill intentions."

"Very well," Weniban replied in defeat. "Are we stopping soon? I could use some time to gather my thoughts before I face down a lynch mob."

"No. We're not stopping until we find a suitable place in the city to stay."

"Preferably one with lots of women and err... people to help spread the word," Quill added, popping a flask out of his pocket. Seven continued, "You can stay with us for the night so I can confirm with people your protection and your purpose. Also if this mob is around, I will speak with them."

A relaxed look spread over Wenibans face and he turned to Quill. "You'd probably want the Sovereign's Peace. It will be packed tonight. Sway herself is there and is offering an answer for the winner of the poetry contest it's having."

"Sounds perfect," Quill stated, taking one last sip. "What's an answer?" I whispered to Seven.

"It means you can ask her any question not related to the future that you want and she'll answer it for you."

"I don't get it?" I acknowledged, not sure how having a question answered was that valuable.

"Sway isn't like Immi. Immi can see futures and make predictions and prophecies and such. But Sway can access the vortex of the Alls' knowledge. She can see the past." He stared at me for a second then continued before I had to ask. "The vortex of the Alls' knowledge is a connection of all things that have ever been known. Not just from people but from anything. It connects all living things to each other. Animals and other creatures can use certain small pieces of it. How do you think they know to fear a hunter when they've never seen one before? Or how to crack open a nut?"

"I understand that. But how is this useful to us? Are we going to be fighting an acorn tree?"

Quill smiled at my joke but Seven just shook his head. "Think about it from our point of view. Who killed my brother? Where's the closest lost karma stone weapon?" He raised an eyebrow. "What are the prophecies given by Immi?"

I finally saw its value. "Oh wow. That could be huge for us. We have to win or at least try to."

"And how do you suppose we would be able to win a poetry contest?"

I rubbed the back of my head as I thought. "Hmm, well who are the judges?" I asked, turning towards Weniban. "Is it Sway or a panel?"

"Usually it's narrowed down to three by the host and then the crowd cheers its favorite in turn." He offered.

I smiled as the idea formed in my head. "Then the solution is easy. All we would need is someone they already know and love. Someone who's famous. Someone all the ladies wouldn't be able to keep their eyes off of."

We all looked to Seven and his head went back and forth as he caught on. "No. Absolutely not. I don't do poetry."

"You don't have to write it. I'm not terrible at it. I'll write, you read."

"Yeah bucko. I can write poetry meself too," Quill added cheerfully.

"Actually you just read one writing due to the large crowds. Otherwise it would go on for days," Weniban added.

"Well I'll write one anyway and we'll see who's is better."

"No need Quill. I think I should be proficient enough on my own. With Sevens fame and looks I think we should have a fair shot at it."

"I'm writing one!" he protested in a huff. "I happen to like poetry. The ladies swoon over it."

I turned back to Seven. "What do you say? You're our only real chance?"

He let out a breath, shaking his head in defeat. "Agreed."

I clapped him on the shoulder in appreciation. "Hey Bud," I yelled to where Deffy walked and he turned to me, walking back. "Could you make me some paper, something to write with and something to write on please?"

"Double that order if you would me boy." Quill added with a grin.

Deffy looked to me for permission and I shrugged. "Sure," he answered and clapped his hands together.

After he finished I started brainstorming to come up with ideas for a poem and turned to Weniban for help.

He walked with a dumbfounded expression, staring at the boy. "You guys really could have given me a fortune," he whined in disbelief.

"Yup. Should've been honest. Anyway, I need a topic for my poem but am having trouble. Who's my target audience and what's popular amongst them?"

Weniban pulled himself out of his fit and thought for a moment. "Most people that go to these poetry contests are couples, not rich but not poor either because there's a cover charge at the door. That would be a majority of the crowd, say maybe two thirds? The other third would be single women and the men who chase them I suppose." He scratched at his ear while he thought. "And what's popular among middle class couples and singles

in the city? Anything besides poetry they'd have in common?"
"Hmm, let's see. Dancing, drinking, boating, anything with

horses, they're rare and expensive or anything to do with en-
ter- tainment itself. Comedy is usually a big hit."

I nodded, not exactly what I was hoping for but I had enough.
"I'll just try to come up with something that covers it all."

"And I'll do the opposite. That way we can see both sides of
the maid without her spinning," Quill announced and I didn't
even bother trying to figure out what he meant.

With the help of Weniban and Seven I finished the poem just
before dark. "Give this a quick once over to make sure you don't
have any questions and it makes sense," I said, handing it to Sev-
en.

He grabbed it and scanned the page quickly. "Not bad... for
poetry," he concluded. "I don't like the part where you said 'you
don't dare cross words with Seven or his swords', it makes me
look too aggressive but other then that... I don't have to memo-
rize this, do I?" He asked, turning towards Weniban.

"No that's not necessary. Most people read off the page but
some either remember it beforehand or just make it up on the
spot as they go."

Seven shook his head. "Poetry. Never seen the usefulness in
rhyming words." He folded the paper up and held it in his hand.
"The contest is probably starting right now," Weniban specu- lat-
ed as he watched one of the giant planets start its slow alignment to form the eclipse. "You'd just be a late entry to the contest but that's common too. I think it's a copper fee to enter the

bar plus five more to enter the contest."
Seven nodded to the news. "Shouldn't be a problem. I'll have
Deffy make some spending money for food, drinks and rooms."

The boy perked up at his name. "How much though?"

"If you would please. Can you make us a coin pouch with say
forty copper, twenty silver and five gold coins? That won't tire
you too much will it?"

"Nope. Only a few things make me really tired. Money is easy."
He grinned from ear to ear.

"Many thanks young friend," Seven replied.

Within a few minutes he handed over the pouch and Seven handed it to me. "I'm going to keep some on me but I want you to carry the rest on you. You'll have Deffy and be in charge of paying for rooms and food if I'm... elsewhere," he complained. "Hold on me buckos," Quill waved a page in the air. "Right here's the winning poem and it's only fair I get some spending coin too as I'll be the reason we win this contest, by a landslide we will."

Seven stared at him with a blank expression. "We already have a poem and if you want room, drink or food then I suggest breaking that gold coin you have in your pocket."

Quill squinted at him for a moment then offered me the poem instead. "You read it and see if it isn't the queen's teets."

I chuckled. "It's dark and I'm wearing a blindfold that makes things even darker. Without a fire or something I won't be able to see a single word on that page."

He let his hands drop to his sides with a deflated frown. "So that's how it is then? Guy writes a masterpiece the whole world should hear and no one will even look at it." He crammed it into his pocket and pulled out his flask with the other hand. "Oh you're gonna read it and you're gonna love it. I don't care if I gotta prop your eyes open with toothpicks and nail it to your foreheads!"

"I'll read it when we get to the inn." He took a pull but didn't respond as our small party moved along in silence.

Some time later I was trying to explain to Quill and Seven how to replicate the shield I could produce when I heard a tiny voice in my ear.

"There's lights up ahead." The bug chirped silently and I smiled.

"Thanks Bud." Seven's eyebrows furrowed at my comment. "Deffy said there's lights up ahead. I assume it's the city."

"That would be Gargot Bridge. They keep it lit up at night. The city sits just on the other side of it," the halfman offered.

"Weniban what's the quickest route to the inn?"

"Actually it's just a straight shot. Just stay on this path and it's a few blocks down on our left." He wiped his hands on his trousers, a clear sign he was getting nervous.

"Deffy can you still hear me?" I asked, not sure if the bug was still around or not.

"Yup."

"I would like for the two of you to let us catch up. We should stick together now that we're so close."

"Ok we'll stop and wait."

"Thanks again Bud," I replied and caught Seven's still puzzled expression.

"How..." he began to say and I chuckled.

"Believe it or not, a bug." He shook his head at the comment but made no argument against it.

The bridge was large and its white color glowed faintly in the darkness. It had small lamps along its edge periodically and there were a few couples gazing out over the water. As we came to its center the city started to unfold before us.

There were dots of light as far as the eye could see. Some in straight lines symbolizing roads, others large, like windows or open doors. What struck me as odd was the lack of height the city had. It stretched out in every direction but up. The tallest building from where I was appeared to only be three stories tall and that dwarfed the ones around it.

"That's it up ahead," Weniban pointed while we made our way down the poorly lit city streets.

Seven counted out some copper into his hand. "Entrance for everyone who didn't get paid a gold." He instructed and Quill mumbled something under his breath. "We'll see about rooms first and then find a table to get some food and drink. Assuming I'm not called upon right away."

"Oh man." Weniban announced, slapping his forehead. "Do you guys have a screamer?"

Seven thought for a second. "Is that one of those devices guards use to direct people?"

"Exactly. People use them or you'll never get heard over the crowd. Sometimes they have them here but they sell out quickly."

"Either way, if we get a room I can just ask Deffy to make one."

Deffy turned eagerly. "I can make the best ones. I made one before that you can adjust to make it louder and louder."

I rubbed his head proudly. "That sounds perfect, Bud. Wait until we get into the room though so no one else sees ok?" And he bobbed his head up and down enthusiastically.

We approached the door to a large burly man with a long beard and a gruff voice. He looked us over. "Seven then?" He asked as Seven stepped forward.

"Yes, five please."

The bouncer stared at him and then tried to recount in confusion. "Is it seven or five?"

"My pardons. I thought you were saying my name. I'll be paying for five of us. The homeless man with the silly hat is not part of our group."

The man gave a start at his words. "You're... Seven?" He asked in bewilderment.

"Correct," he replied, putting the coins into the man's hand. "How do I go about entering the poetry contest?"

"You're going to enter a poetry contest?" he asked again but this time like he didn't believe the claim.

"If you would stop answering all my questions with questions I'd have an easier time with it but as of now yes. That's the plan."

"It's, uh, you're my idol," he admitted, rolling up a sleeve to show Seven a tattoo on his arm. "Can, I mean, would you punch me in the face? or something? Maybe cut me on the arm so it scars? The story alone would mean so much to me."

"Answer his damn question and I promise ya a kick in the sack," Quill ordered impatiently.

"Um, in the lobby by the doors to the bar is the sign up desk. No weapons beyond that so check them in or if you get a room leave them there."

"Many thanks," Seven replied and patted the man on the shoulder.

He grimaced in anticipation but Seven just walked past saying that's all he'd get.

"That's not what I was expecting though," the big man fretted then suddenly folded over, collapsing with a grunt after Quill's foot landed between his legs.

"Is that what you were expecting?" he snickered with a wink and tip of his hat. "Glad to be of some help," then dropped a coin on the man as he passed.

I helped him to his feet. "Sorry about him, it's just that... he's an asshole," I stated plainly.

The doorman stared at my blindfold. "You're his pupil then?" I nodded to him, walking past, making my way to the lobby.

The sound of music and laughing filled the air and people-could be seen dancing and drinking in the next room over.

In anticipation of the event the inn had tripled its rates and lucky for us hadn't filled up yet. We took two rooms with double beds as I didn't sleep and Quill, still refusing to break his gold piece, decided to try and share a bed with Matches.

After our stuff was all situated we made our way back down to the sign up desk.

"One entry please," Seven stated with little emotion.

The woman looked up at him. "You must be the one Wedge was talking about. Seven is it?" He nodded. "Would you like an introduction as well? It's an extra copper."

"Is that common?"

"Yeah. Lots of people do it. Most of its bullshit though. Poor man lost his wife and kids or some other sob story to gain favor. If you're really 'the' Seven, you should definitely get introduced."

I agreed with her and he paid the extra copper.

"Tell Thas, the man in the top hat and suit how you want to be introduced. Or write it down for him before you get called up. There's still a few dozen names left in the bowl so it's a good chance you won't go on for a while but don't dilly dally."

We thanked her and made our way inside. All the tables near the front of the stage were packed full and so we found an empty one near the back. No sooner had we been seated then a serving maid approached us.

"What can I get ya's?"

"We'll take five plates of whatever's hot and I'll have a mug of ale."

The rest agreed along with Deffys cider and she turned to Quill next who sat with a questioning look.

"Do ya's do flask fills?" She nodded. "How much for a flask fill of your finest?"

"Five coppers."

He puzzled out some quick math then growled, producing the gold coin. "I'll take five and a mug of ale and something hot to eat," he ordered, plopping the coin down on her tray.

"Five what?" she asked in confusion.

He reached into his coat and pulled out a flask, plopping it on the tray then repeated the process with another and another and another. He pulled out the fifth one and held up a finger while he downed the rest of its contents then dropped it with the rest. "And a round of slammers for the table," he announced with a wink.

She fluttered her eyelashes at him in a way that oozed sarcasm and walked away.

He looked back to the rest of us. "I gotta feeling tonights a night that's gonna be worth celebratin."

"Do you have the poem and screamer?" I asked Seven.

"The boy is carrying it for me until it's time. I think I should probably go talk to the man in the top hat."

"Do you know what you're going to ask him to say?"

"No. I'll just see what he knows about me and go from there."

"That should work. Have him emphasize on your calm, cool and serious attitude. It'll tie in better with the poem."

"Agreed." He stood and walked to where the man sat on a stool near the stage.

By the time he returned, our meals and drinks had already arrived. "Apparently there's much anticipation of my poem so they're going to rig the drawing so my name is called as soon as we're done eating and our plates are cleared. Normally it's random but they wanted to make an exception for me."

"Well here's to you then." Quill raised the shot he had referred to as a slammer above his head, gesturing for us to do the same.

Seven eyed his suspiciously. "You bought me one? What did you do to it?"

"Whaaaat? Nothing of course," Quill acted taken aback by the accusation. "Haven't even touched it. Ask them. I just like people having to owe me one and since you go out of your way to do nothing for me, I decided to be the bigger man. Plus, you'll need it to calm your nerves. Gonna take a lot of balls to do what you gotta do up there and we only get this 'one' chance."

I thought it was odd how genuine Quill's smile was but Seven picked up his slammer and downed it anyway and we joined him. No one spoke as we waited, instead we all sat listening to the poems. A man recited one about having lost his love to a rival writer followed by a woman who wrote about wild horses.

In no time at all we had finished our meals and the man in the top hat came over quickly. "You'll be next then," he announced, more of a question than a statement and Seven nodded.

He slammed the rest of his drink and held his hand out to Deffy who promptly placed the folded page and screamer into it. It was the first time I'd seen one and it wasn't very remarkable.

It was made of brass and had a swivel that gave it the appearance of a trumpet with the exception the spot you would blow on was wider and easier to talk into.

"Keep it on three," Deffy explained. "I think anything higher is too loud for in here though."

"And good luck Seven. Just remember all that's on the line if we win. That should help give you motivation."

He nodded to this and put on a stern face as he blew out a breath then followed Thas to the stage.

Seven found himself stretching as he waited for Thas to announce him, something he usually only did before a fight or duel but he did find it helped calm his nerves.

One shot. One shot for Aam. I can do this. One minute worth of reading is all it takes.

He found himself chanting this over and over, not sure how he could always stay so calm in the face of danger but reading a poem to a crowd had his stomach tied in knots.

"Our next participant you may have heard of before," Thas announced and the crowd stilled in anticipation of who they knew he was about to introduce. "He has more winning knicks on one sword then most garrisons have combined. He has mastered more weapons than any other living being known. World famous for his calm and cool demeanor in battle. Crossing him is as serious and deadly as a scorpion sting, slayer of Targ the Terrible, the blademaster himself... SEVEN!"

The crowd erupted into a deafening cheer. People whistled and hollered while he climbed up the stairs and onto the stage.

Keep calm, they're just words. He unfolded the paper and checked the screamer was still on three. They're just words. Read them and win to help Aam. One shot.

He raised the screamer to his lips and the crowd fell into a silence so deep you could have heard a moth's wings beat.

He started to read. "I really wish I was a little girl." He froze.

Somewhere in the back of the room a hyena began to screech.

What the hell is this? This is not the poem I read before. It must have been switched.

His cheeks flushed as he realized what Quill had done. He scanned the page and the poem rhymed and was actually a poem, something he had no notion of how to accomplish.

He looked up at the crowd who sat in frozen bewilderment.

I only have this one shot, he told himself then swallowed before he continued.

"I really wish I was a little girl, with long eyelashes and hair that curls. I'd tie it up in a bright pink bow, and if boys were around I'd let it hang low. I'd dance around in my sunday dress, cause it's the one the boys like best. Being a girl is my one true wish, well that and little Jimmy giving me a kiss."

The hyena fell off its stool with a loud crash.

There was more but he had all he could take, scanning to the bottom of the page to where in parentheses was written 'blow kiss to crowd'. He crumbled up the page and dropped it as he moved to walk off the stage.

The laughter and applause that exploded from the crowd nearly blew the roof off. He hesitated for a second to make an awkward bow then continued on as they started to chant his name.

"SEVEN! SEVEN! SEVEN!"

Thas met him at the bottom of the steps wiping at his eyes. "I can't tell if that was the worst or most genius approach to poetry I've ever heard."

He ignored him. Eyes staring forward as he moved back towards the table and Quill.

CHAPTER 15

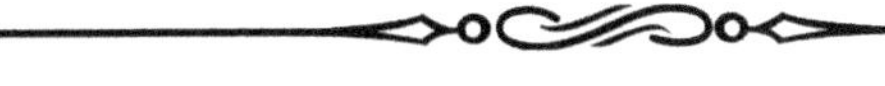

Not only is your universe not the only universe, your dimension isn't the only dimension. There are 'pockets' scattered throughout this reality where other realities press against yours. Each with its own physics, its own laws, its own time. Think of it like this; you live in a bubble that's inside a bubble that's inside a bubble. But also there are bubbles clustered in yours, sharing your space and even some of your time. They press against each other as they expand and contract endlessly. Except it's not that small. The bubbles are infinite and layered. Universes within realities and realities within dimensions, one after another, on and on, forever, infinitely, with a single dimension above them all. A dimension without time. It's where God resides and if you were to think upon this with an open mind, you'd see that all life, all creation and all time is nothing but a twinkle in the eye of the creator.

I wiped the tears from my eyes in a mix of emotions. Matches lay on the floor where he had fallen, still holding his stomach in laughter, struggling for breath. Quill sat up straight and put on his best smile as Seven approached like a raging bull, bowling chairs and patrons alike to the side.

"I'm going to kill you," he snarled, his voice low and serious. "Outside now." He loomed over Quill like a giant oak.

"What's the matter, bucko? Don't like tasting your own medicine? Not too fun having to be made to look like a girl in front of your peers is it?"

Sevens chest heaved in anger but he didn't respond and the short pause allowed Matches time enough to regain his chair. He wiped at his face with a hand the size of a mitt as their standoff escalated, trying to control himself as best he could in an attempt not to add to the tension further.

"Maybe the timing was a bit off but let me make it up to you. I know just the thing" he offered with a mischievous smile but still got no response. "I can introduce ya to little Jimmy," Quill offered.

Matches threw his head back in a howl of laughter and the legs of his chair shattered with the strain, sending him crashing to the floor once again.

I tried my best to hide my laughs while I stood up to intervene. "Seven I know it was embarrassing but honestly I think my poem would never have been this successful. Look around, people are still cheering and laughing so hard they had to take an intermission from the contest."

Seven didn't look around. In fact he didn't do anything at all. He simply stood staring for a long minute at Quill breathing heavily with the look of death in his eyes.

This gave the rest of us some time to calm ourselves and Matches slowly regained his composure, coming to his knees with only his elbows and head resting on the table.

"Seven," I tried again, "It took guts to do that and I think you did a great job," I offered, trying to help him see the lighter side of the situation.

"I don't care. I felt like a monkey trying to play the trumpet with his asshole."

Matches's head jerked up and his eyes went wide as he pictured the statement in his head then crashed back to the floor in another fit of laughter as Seven continued.

"Me and him, we are going outside now. Everyone else can stay in here, the boy included," then he gestured towards the door.

"Actually," I cut in, "You told me it's forbidden to fight or duel without your master's permission. If you do this you'll be doing the exact same things he did. The same things that you hold against him."

This finally got through to him and he turned to me, face a flush of emotions. "I ask for permission to defend my honor and-"

"Denied," I interrupted. "It serves no point to our purposes."

He kicked a chair and it exploded into kindling. "When this is over," he threatened with a growl and an extended finger in Quill's direction. "Me and you... are going."

He spun and stormed off further into the back of the tavern to take a seat at one of the booths by himself.

"Going where?" Quill shouted after him, then turned to me. "I hope it's dress shopping."

Matches squealed again happily as he rolled onto his stomach and pulled an empty chair closer to help him stand. He pushed it nearer the table and finally had calmed enough to rejoin us properly.

"I can always count on you to appreciate me genius Ma. The others will come around."

"It actually was," Weniban agreed. "I think Fin's poem was good and with Sevens fame may have even made it to the final three. Maybe. But the ridiculousness of it all gave it the extra edge it needed. I wouldn't be surprised if he wins this thing by a landslide now."

"I don't doubt you're right, and if we would have told Seven about it there's no way he would have agreed beforehand. It still seems wrong to have done that to him."

Weniban chuckled. "Quill just may be the genius he claims. Now if he could solve my problem about spreading the word faster, I'd be forever in his debt."

A toothy grin appeared on Quill's face. "Easy. When Seven gets called back up on stage, have him announce it himself.

Straight from the horse's mouth is best to cut away any rumors or doubts." Weniban nodded in bewilderment at not having thought of that. "Any other problems you'd like me to solve? World hunger? The infinity code? I got all the answers."

"Weniban don't think you're getting out of anything," I added, seeing the look on his face like he was finally free from his task. "We still need you. It needs to reach the other cities and as fast as possible, remember?"

His grin melted away and he spoke in a low tone. "If I live that long. Say Quill, here's a problem, what do you do when the man who wants to kill you is standing in the door with a group of almost a dozen men staring at you?"

"That's easy too. The best way to get someone to stop staring is to pick your nose. If that don't work, get naked. And if that don't work then I think he's got more planned for ya then just killin ya and you really shouldn't have took off your clothes." He chuckled at his own joke as I followed Wenibans gaze towards the door.

A middle aged man stood at the front of a group of men who were all armed. The looks he was giving the halfmen were of pure malice as the bouncer blocked their path, gesturing towards their weapons.

He pointed a finger at Weniban then used the same finger to gesture him over.

"What do I do? I'm not much use to you guys if I'm dead?" he whined and Quill eyed the men like a cat watching mice.

"You have Sevens band. I doubt they'll do anything with you wearing it. Besides, we'll just tell him. He did say he would speak to them...." I let my words cut off as we turned to look but found his booth now empty and him nowhere around.

"Oh man, where is he? A piece of cloth isn't going to stop them. You have to help me. They're going to kill me," he pleaded, voice getting frantic. "Can't you fight them?"

I thought about it for a second. I'm not supposed to without Seven's permission but he did say to use my head if he wasn't around," I offered, continuing to scan the crowd but finding no signs of him. "I am his apprentice though so I'll talk to them and see-"

"I'm not a eunuch at a whorehouse," Quill interrupted.

"Um, am I supposed to constantly guess at what your little sayings mean?" I asked him.

"It means this, Master, may I have permission to deal with these men on behalf of our tiny friend here and if it comes to it, handle them accordingly when they want to fight?"

I stared at him for a minute, not doubting he was a blademaster himself but questioning how inebriated he was. "Are you sure you're not too drunk?"

"If such a thing was possible, the world would be a terrible place. Besides, I'm always drunk during all me fights. It's when I'm at me best."

I didn't doubt the truth of his words so I shrugged. "Granted."

"Excellent!" He stood, finishing his mug then slamming it down onto the table. "Let's have some fun."

A giant hand gripped him by the shoulder. "Help?" Matches offered with a raised eyebrow.

"Nah. I need you to keep the little one occupied. He don't need to see what's about to happen."

Matches nodded and turned back to Deffy.

"IF Quill, IF it needs to be done," I emphasized and he shrugged heading towards the door.

"Yeah yeah, if 's what I meant."

I shared a concerned glance with Weniban and then we all moved to follow after him.

Quill walked with an unconcerned swagger towards the group of men, addressing the bouncer first as he approached.

"What seems to be the trouble here boss?"

Wedge turned and saw us, his eyes resting on Weniban. "They're here for him," he announced, "and are refusing to un-arm themselves."

"No worries boss. They can stay armed. We were all just about to go outside anyway, right me buckos?" Quill winked at the agitated leader.

He hesitated for a second then agreed. "Right."

"Then lead on me lovely," Quill insisted and smacked the man on the rump as he turned to walk away.

He spun on Quill, nostrils flaring.

"Hop hop little bunny. I don't have all night. I've got beers to kiss and ladies to drink so let's get the road on the show."

The man took several hesitant steps backwards, watching Quill closely before finally turning and walking outside.

We stopped under one of the weird street lamps that emitted some sort of intense white glow and lit up the area around it like a tiny star. I hadn't noticed this before so I stared at it now with a keen interest.

It wasn't a bulb, it wasn't fire, it was just a bright light illuminating from within a square glass box like someone had recreated or captured a miniature sun.

Quill's words interrupted my temporary observations.

"Here's what I know," he pulled out a flask and took a quick drink. "You fine young ladies have a problem with me friend here," he gestured behind him to Weniban. "But you see, we need him to run some errands for us so we can't have him harmed in any way. He's got some very important people to visit and I'd like him presentable and not all dinged up or scratched like I'm guessing you guys have planned."

"Nah. I just want to kill him. But rearranging his face first does sound awful tempting," he snorted and a few of the men chuckled.

Quill smiled too. "I'll tell ya's what. Hows about instead, you challenge me. If you ladies can beat me in a fight then I'll give ya my word we'll hand our little friend here over and no one else will try and stop ya. What say ya's?"

The big man grinned like he'd just won the lottery and I knew I had to try and do something before people got hurt. I didn't know how good Quill was but the odds he could beat all these armed men seemed slim.

"Actually," I spoke up, "the man you want is under the protection of Seven and if you guys interfere I'm sure you wouldn't like him hunting you down like you did to Weniban. Besides, I'm his apprentice, I'd be forced to intervene on my masters behalf." Not knowing if my threat had any weight to it or not I decided to give it a shot.

The men stared at me for a minute and then the leader stepped forward, addressing Quill. "Who is he to you?" he asked, pointing at me.

"Him? Why he's me master in a different field. And he's already gave me permission to handle you blokes," Quill smiled happily.

The leader thought on this for a minute then mirrored Quills expression. "So you agree to an unfair fight, you have permission, and you gave your word no one else will interfere or try to stop us including this man and supposedly Seven himself ?"

Quill nodded, the smile plastered on his face was so full of excitement it was getting ridiculous. I let out a sigh at knowing exactly what was going to come next.

"Then we agree," he confirmed, pulling out his sword and sticking it tip first into the ground. "Anyone else?"

All but two of the men stepped forward and one by one put their swords into the ground with his, chuckling to themselves at the lopsided fight.

"Witnesses?" Quill asked, pulling out a silver dagger that showed his specific master's mark on a green band and sticking it near theirs in acceptance.

The men hesitated at the sight of a master's mark, giving each other worried glances before grabbing their swords and shuffling back nervously, waiting for Quill to grab his dagger.

"Witness" Weniban and one of the other men who didn't accept spoke almost simultaneously and then they repeated the terms.

Quill tucked his coat behind the sheaths on his hips, revealing two separate rows of throwing knives then walked and plucked his first one from the ground.

"This is how this is gonna work," he started, walking to the side and dragging a heel across the center of the gravel road seperating the two sides. "When someone crosses this line, they die so I suggest trying to rush me, those are your best odds. Also that way I can kill yas faster and get back to me drinking."

One of the men spoke up. "So that's a masters mark then? You didn't say you were a master. Who was your teacher?"

"You didn't ask. Besides, you all challenged me, remember? Unfair fight, lopsided odds, I'm drunk and you're all so awfully... loyal to die for a friend like this."

"Nah, I was paid to help him find and kill someone. We assumed he may find help on his own but never this."

The big leader finally cut in. "And you already took the coin and are now engaged with plenty of witnesses. It's one man, one drunk man. Master or not this will be a cake walk."

The man who had just spoken shrugged, "after you then boss." The leader looked at the line on the ground then back up to Quill. "Put your off hands over your heart. Scrunch your shoulders to protect your neck, head down. I'm sure we've all had cuts before. Protect your vitals and he doesn't have a chance," he paused for a second then added. "Double the payment for the first three men to cross that line and double it again for any wounds taken while helping me defend my honor."

This seemed to give confidence to the group and they stepped forward cautiously, protecting themselves like he suggested.

A man in the middle of the first three to step forward stopped just in front of the line. "When I say when, I want you to go left and-"

Quill's hands flashed in a blur and three daggers flew through the air. They connected with a loud thwick, thwick, thwick into the left eye of each man.

They fell dead without a sound.

The big leader stared down in disbelief. "What the hell was that? They didn't even cross the line yet!"

Quill beamed wickedly. "Close enough. If I remember correctly, we agreed on an unfair fight, yes? You see... those are me favorite kind."

His hands flashed again and more daggers streaked through the air like bullets. The first two hit their marks solidly with another thwick, thwick, dropping the pair before they could even move and the remaining men burst into motion.

Two of them ducked to the right, trying to cover their sides and faces as best they could while another two mimicked this running to the left, leaving the leader crunched down in a tiny ball holding his coat out in front of him like a cloth shield.

Quill didn't slow, he threw a dagger into the legs of the two men on the left, then waited for them to react. They did, reaching down to pull them free as they howled in pain. The first man fell with a dagger to his throat, gurgling out his final breath. The second man took one directly in the chest where it must have pierced his heart because he crumbled like a sack of potatoes.

Quill spun quickly, only managing to fling a single dagger into the other two men as they closed the gap between them. It struck the man in the stomach but wasn't enough to slow his momentum as he tackled Quill to the ground.

Daggers and flasks flew everywhere as they tumbled and he fought desperately to climb on top of Quill but was getting cut repeatedly for his efforts.

The other man didn't hesitate, jumping into the air and stabbing down hard through the back of his own companion. The blade slammed through his chest completely and into Quill's shoulder, pinning him to the ground and causing him to scream out in pain.

The cowardly man left the sword where it was, holding Quill in place with the dead man on top of him.

He stepped back triumphantly. "I believe we just won, and I was one one of the first three across the line so that's double."

The leader, not wanting to argue with his own help, nodded his agreement. He let his coat fall a little and stood, walking to where Quill struggled as he drew his sword to finish the job.

"It ain't over until I'm dead," he grunted, heaving with all his might, using the corpse as a pry bar to free him from his predicament.

He rolled backwards further away and up onto his knees. There was blood soaked all along his neck, chest and stomach but not all of it was his.

He stared at the man who had stabbed him through the shoulder with a murderous glare. "Where's your sword friend? Wouldn't be fair of me to kill an unarmed man... oh right. Unfair fight and all."

The unarmed man stared back in horror, putting both hands out in front of him in surrender. "Now listen, I-"

Thwick. A dagger buried itself into his eye, dropping him where he stood and Quill turned back to the leader who was crouching behind his coat shield once again.

"And now for me grand finale," Quill beamed and spun the last two daggers from his straps up onto his palms then flicked them into the air, catching them by their tips. "Tell ya what I'm going to do. I've only got these two left you see. I'm gonna throw this first one right into the knuckles of your hand that's holding the coat. If you can manage to keep it there you might actually have a shot. But I'm willing to bet you expose something. Something vital and that's how I end this. What do ya say?"

The leader stared at his hand and his eyes darted wildly while he struggled to come up with a better defense.

Quill's wrist snapped and the dagger shot forward, plunging into the man's fist with a solid crack. He screamed in pain but managed to keep the coat up in front of him, blocking all angles from a second attack.

"Well I'll be..." Quill breathed out in surprise. "How long you thinkin you can hold it up like that?"

The man continued to fight back fits of pain and the coat shook visibly. "Long enough to let you bleed out," he spat.

Quill eyed his wound and then looked back to the man. "Yeah I think you're right. I gotta make me move soon."

He stood slowly and either the blood loss or the alcohol caused him to sway noticeably. "Here's nothing," he pointed with one finger to where the man crouched and closed one eye, taking aim, then flung the dagger.

It glanced off the top of the man's head leaving a deep gash that would scar but had no other effect besides producing a yelp.

Quill collapsed back to his rump with an exhausted sigh. The leader peered at him from behind his coat and seen all of Quill's holdings were now empty and it gave him confidence. He stood slowly and took a few cautious steps forward as Quill just sat puffing for air.

The man relaxed enough to breathe out an exhilarated laugh of relief. "Not a bad showing but it seems you're all out of tricks and all out of daggers."

Quill shrugged, "it appears bloody so."

The leader jerked the dagger from his knuckles and stifled another scream, wrapping it quickly with a kerchief from his pocket.

He brought his head up as soon as he was done, staring at Quill. "Best be done with this quickly," he said, picking up his sword and moving towards the downed man with haste.

"Of course," Quill started as the man drew back his sword to run him through. "Things ain't always as they seem."

His hands reached behind his back and then short forward in one deft motion. A white blur streaked the air and embedded itself into the man's neck.

He grasped at it desperately while he gurgled for air and fell to his knees.

"You see that one's not for throwing. It's balanced for hand to hand and with me good arm shot, I had to consider I was only accurate with it at a few paces. Thanks for helping me out by coming closer."

Quill rolled back and let himself collapse to the ground as one of the two men who hadn't accepted made his way forward to where the leader lay dying.

He bent near him, sorrow and anger flashed in his eyes and he stared at Quill with hatred. "He was my brother," the man snarled. "You're no great fighter. You're a trickster and a coward. A coward who doesn't fight fair... and a coward who's out of weapons," he noted with realization and glanced towards where Weniban and I sat off to the side, too far away to intervene.

"Now don't you try anything you'd regret bucko. You're flirting with a code two," he warned loudly and the man stood.

Quill sprawled out onto his stomach and made a lunge for something behind him.

The other man moved quickly, pulling a sword free as he approached. "Good, now you're armed," he said, getting closer and holding his brother's coat out in front of him with one hand and the sword with the other.

Quill rolled onto his back showing what he had dove for and it was one of his flasks. He popped the lid off and took a long drink.

The man paused, lowering the coat with a laugh. "What kind of idiot dives for a flask when he's about to die?"

"The best kind?" Quill answered like he was solving a riddle.

The man shook his head. "It wasn't meant to be a riddle." He started to take the last few steps forward but Quill kept speaking.

"I got one. What do you do to avoid flying trees?"

The man didn't slow as he answered. "There's no such thing as flying trees," then drew back his sword as he came to a stop over Quill.

"I wood duck," Quill answered and his eyebrows bounced up and down gleefully at his pun.

The man barely had time to turn when he noticed the large projectile and a tree trunk the size of a small canoe clobbered him in the face causing his neck to bend at an angle it clearly shouldn't have. He crumpled to the ground dead.

"Oh yeah and just a head's up, me brother doesn't fight fair neither." He looked at me nodding his head happily. "Get it? Heads up, because he.. bah, nevermind."

I turned to look where the thing had come from and saw Matches crouching back in the grass near Deffy who was completely oblivious to everything that was happening.

Weniban and I walked over to Quill and I offered him a hand up, "how's the wound?"

He took it with a grunt. "I've had worse."

Weniban shook his head, "worse than being ran through completely with a sword that pinned you to the ground? I doubt it or you wouldn't be standing here right now."

"You calling me a liar? I once had me whole arm cut clean off. Stitched it back on meself."

The halfman stared at him blankly. "No. I'm not calling you a liar, it's just... inconceivable."

"Well conceive it. I reckon you owe me one after this. We ain't gotta worry about any more lynch mobs coming for ya?"

"No. Not in this town anyway."

"Good enough for me. Gather me effects and let's go find Seven so I can borrow one of them karma stones and start to healing before I bleed out in the streets."

I wrapped his good arm around my neck, crouching low to help support him but as we turned to go, the other witness finally spoke up.

"Umm, they didn't say what to do in the event they lost."

I looked at the man and he seemed to be stricken and sorrowful. "Who was he to you?" I asked.

"He was just an employer. I worked his grounds. But that one was my brother." He pointed to the man who got stabbed from behind in an act of cowardice and betrayal.

I was at a loss of how to react to this. It was a new and awkward situation for me so I reached into my pouch with one hand and pulled out a gold coin. I knew horses were expensive but didn't know how much.

"Is this enough to rent a horse and wagon?" I asked Quill and he nodded.

"Thrice more then enough but for that much, he can load them on Matches and I'll-"

I stopped him with a gesture and flipped the coin over to the man. "Get a horse and wagon and load these men. Take them back to their families and keep the rest of the money with my condolences," I paused, "I'm sorry for your loss." I didn't think it meant much coming from me as I was holding the man that had stabbed his brother but he nodded solemnly and set to his work.

We turned back to head towards the inn and called for Deffy and Matches to join us. The crowd parted once we made our way inside, the bouncer who had watched the whole thing offered Quill a wide berth with a new found respect for the man.

I tried to talk Quill into heading straight to the rooms but he insisted he'd be fine and the wound and blood was like the flames to the ladies' moths.

I asked the bouncer for permission to use a karma stone dagger and he agreed as long as it was returned immediately after. I sent Deffy to fetch it as we took our seats and Quill set to ordering another round of drinks.

I scanned the crowd again in an attempt to locate Seven. After Deffy had come and went with the dagger and Quill was mostly healed he was finally seen exiting a small door to the left of the stage followed by a woman I had no doubt was the Sovereign Sway.

She took a seat far off to the side as Seven made his way back and our eyes met as he came closer. He looked at us all with a puzzled expression, taking in Quill's blood soaked shirt.

"What did I miss?"

"Wenibans friends showed up. Quill handled them but got stabbed for his efforts. I'll give you more details later."

He nodded to this and rejoined us at the table. Apparently he had calmed down enough from the rage he felt before.

"Ain't no woman worth dying for if ya ask me," Quill was saying to the halfman.

"Well, you've never been with a rich woman then," Weniban responded. "They smell like flowers. Their lips taste like wine. They shower you with gifts and," he cut off, looking to where Deffy and Matches sat. "They're eager to be, umm, satisfied let's say."

"You my friend, just described a silver maid," Quill joked, taking a drink from his mug. "Except the showering you with gifts part. But also no husbands trying to hunt you down and kill you to protect his honor." Quill laughed and Weniban put some serious thought into what he had said.

"It's different though. Having to pay someone and having someone genuinely want you. You can't-"

I cut in. "That's enough on that," I stated, noticing Deffy who sat uncomfortably during the talk. "And Quill, as your master I order you to be more cautious of the way you talk in front of him. Lead by example and all."

His head bobbled back and forth as he mocked me playfully. "Yes mommy." He teased and Deffy and I shared a grin.

CHAPTER 16

There is no physical aspect to the spirit world. Not the way you can perceive it anyway. You are simply an awareness in an ocean of energy and light. There are others like you there and you can interact by entering them through their psyche, sharing with each other your knowledge and experiences you've gained throughout your lives. There are also higher beings who wait, to help you transition into what's next or to enlighten you and send you back. It is this enlighten-ment that I will give to save you all.

As the night progressed I filled Seven in on all the details of the fight but he had no outward reaction to the accomplishment, calling it dumb luck and I watched Quills face go stern.

"Let's not forget I beat you with dumb luck. Those men agreed to an unfair fight. We can't blame him for their stupidity. But anyway, I'd rather talk about what happened between you and Sway?"

"Not much that was useful to us in any way unless I win. She wanted to confirm that I was still going to gather armies and you were still intending on going to see Aam. What she was really interested in though was you. She said when this was all over she was hoping to talk to you alone but you're not going to like this next part. She's refusing to talk about or reveal to us any pieces of prophecy that have to do with Immi and for the exact reason you said. If a person or place is written about in a prophecy and then you tell them about it, it's the same thing as giving them the antidote. They are immediately freed from it. I think you should still talk to her and see if you can figure out anything else of use to us. Find her as soon as this contest is done.

Quill smiled cheerfully and smacked the table with a laugh. "Hah! This is great news!"

I eyed him suspiciously. "Yes... it is."

"Oh not that part. The part about Svenlanna here getting up in front of an audience with all his deepest and darkest secrets and it was all for nothing!" He raised his drink. "I'll cheers to that. Anyone else?" Seven stared at him with a suppressed rage he could barely contain. "No one? Oh well." Then he finished his mug and reached for another.

"What if you win?" I continued. "She would have to honor the agreement. You could still ask for the prophecy or maybe where to find one to exclude her?"

He shook his head. "I could but she warned me against it. The prophecy was given for only a select few to understand and carry out. She even admitted that Aam... influences it to an out- come we are too insignificant to understand and if we interfered we could change the design of that outcome."

I thought on what all Seven had implied and Weniban chimed in. "Well then that means Aam knows about you being here and must also have known about this other being coming here and let it. Maybe she wanted it to come and you too?"

We all looked at each other as the words started to make sense and Seven bobbed his head up and down slowly before he spoke. "Immi herself said Aam requested you personally. This means you are expected and for a reason. Aam must have seen this other being coming and immediately set things in motion to bring you here, knowing you could... or would be strong enough to help.”

“So me being here...”

“Is a sign we will succeed,” he finished. “If anything, I’m even more certain of that now then I was before. For now how- ever, we continue as planned. When this contest is over and you talk to her we will see what all you have learned and then if nec- essary, change plans accordingly or keep them the same.”

I nodded my agreement. “What are you going to ask if you win then?”

He wiped some foam from his lips and set his mug down. “I’m not sure yet. I may ask something personal now that we can no longer ask after the prophecies. Sway only deals in the past and I have a lot of questions about mine if there is no objection?”

“I won it for us and I’d like a say on what gets asked,” Quill added, sitting up in his chair and looking to me for confirmation. “No. You tried to embarrass Seven, that was your only goal and you did it at the risk of us losing our chance to talk to Sway. I know things have changed but I think Seven should be able to ask a question of his own choice if he wins. After what he just did, I’d say he deserves it.”

Quill sat back mumbling to himself as he took another drink and Seven gave me a look of appreciation.

“There is one last thing I don’t want to forget about. Quill had the idea to have you announce your call for aid directly if you get pulled up on stage again and I agreed.”

His eyes narrowed. “Why don’t you order him to take the stage and do it himself ?”

“Well it’s best coming from you directly like I said. Besides, you want me to have Quill go up on a stage? God only knows the things he does when nobody is watching for his own amusement, imagine what he’d do in front of a crowd?”

Matches clapped excitedly to this with a smile from ear to ear but Seven shook his head reluctantly. “Agreed.”

Another round was ordered and we turned our attention back to the contest as it carried on. A few of the other contes- tants at seeing the success Seven had, changed their tactics hastily and it showed. What ended up following was a night full of dry jokes and dropped punch lines. One guy even went as far as to do a poem very similar to Sevens but he came out in a full dress and red wig. This produced several scattered chuckles through- out the room with the exception of Matches. He laughed so hard he broke another chair.

Eventually it came to an end and the host in the top hat took the stage once more.

"Ladies and gentlemen, after much debate we have narrowed it down to our final three. If I call your name please join me on the stage." Silence washed over the crowd like a breeze through a field. "Our first selection is Miss Fann and her lovely poem about rain in the desert."

The crowd applauded and a few people who must have known her personally even hooted and hollered.

"Our next selection is no new face to this stage as he's won a handful of different poetry contests here before. Hesiod and his emotional and inspiring poem about personal growth. Would you please take the stage with us?"

An older gentleman made his way up and the crowd cheered loudly, clapping their hands and stomping their feet while he slowly climbed up the stairs.

Thas held his hand up for silence. "Our last selection is no stranger either. New to the stage but not our ears, Seven and his poem about, umm, secret wishes." He announced with a wink. "Please join us on stage."

The laughter and cheering that erupted was immense. I watched as Seven's face flushed red and he stood, making his way over and onto the stage.

The cheering lasted a lot longer than it had for the previous two and it took Thas several minutes to get them quiet enough to where he could be heard again.

"I'm sure most of you know how this works but for those of you that are new I'll explain. I will hold my hand over a contes- tants head, when I do you cheer if you think that contestant had the best poem and should win. The loudest response received marks the contest's winner. Now let's begin."

He walked to Miss Fann and held his hand above her curly black locks. The response was similar to before with people clapping and only a few cheering. He moved down one and held it over Hesiod's head. His response was slightly less than it was before but everyone clapped and there were still a few cheers but not nearly as loud.

Thas laughed as he moved to Seven. "I think we all see where this is going," then held his hand up as close as he could to Sevens head.

The crowd exploded into cheers, this time standing, stomping and clapping. People threw roses and coins as they showered him with gifts. One person even threw a doll onto the stage which caused even more laughter.

Thas presented Seven with a carved slate that stated his achievement and asked if he would like to give a speech.

Seven shared a quick word about our quest to help Aam that was straight to the point and left the crowd in disbelieving murmurs. Then he was led off the stage and back into the room where Sway awaited him for his answer.

I turned back to the others now that the night's events were over. "I think you guys should turn in for the night. We are most likely going to have an early start and should be well rested just in case."

Deffy and Matches agreed and instantly set off to their room but Weniban eyed me suspiciously. "What about you? I've listened to how they talk about you and it's obvious you're different but I can't put my finger on it."

I shrugged, not willing to lie but also not willing to tell him the truth. "I don't sleep," was all I offered and he stared at me, not sure what to make of the statement. "Quill, you need some help?" I asked, avoiding the conversation.

"No shure. Itsh moshtly healed by... now." He swayed heavily as he stood and his eyes held the thousand yard stare of a blackout.

"I wasn't referring to your wound..." I cut off as he started to stagger after his brother, bowling over chairs and tables and miraculously staying on his feet.

Weniban stood but hesitated for a second. "I really am the worst person for this task. I don't know as many important people as you think and the ones that I do, want me dead."

"Just do your best. I know there's nothing keeping you from disappearing the second we're gone but if you had any care at all, you'd do it for Aam, not for us."

He nodded his head in acceptance, "I will. Do my best that is. I can't promise success but I will try, for Aam."

"Goodnight Weniban." And with that he followed after Quill and I was left alone.

People started filing out almost as soon as the contest was over and the large bar was now only half full. Musicians took the stage and people began to dance and mingle freely.

I watched them all for a while behind my blindfold until I felt someone touch my arm to grab my attention.

"No one wants to be alone on a cold night like this big guy. You got a room?"

I turned to find a woman standing beside me who wore a black dress that was so tight it revealed every curve her perfect body made. Her brunette hair was pinned up showing her two large gold hoop earrings and on her face from cheekbone to chin was a large scar that looked like it had never healed properly. Her slightly glazed blue eyes looked me over and she wore an expression that appeared both relaxed and like she was expecting me to blow her off.

"I do, but no bed. It's complicated," I explained not knowing how to say it without revealing to her I don't sleep. She rolled her eyes and turned to walk away. "But you're welcome to join me. Let me buy you a drink?"

She turned back and stared, trying to decide on my intentions for a second then shrugged. "What the hell. I've been striking out left and right all night anyway. Free drink would be nice." She took the seat next to me. "The names Lynnay and I'll have a red wine if you're offering."

"You can call me Fin and I'm sorry but did you say you've been striking out all night?"

"Yup." She offered, watching the waitress approach and ordering the drink herself. "I've been reduced to a last resort on account of my-" She was gesturing to her face but her words cut off as she looked at my blindfold. "Nevermind."

I frowned as I tried to grasp everything she was implying. "So that was you... flirting with me?" I asked with a chuckle. "Kind of straight to the point wasn't it?"

She stared at the stage as she responded. "Darling in my line of work you have to be straight to the point if you plan on making any money." The rest of the pieces clicked into place and I blushed. She must have noticed so she leaned closer with a warm smile. "You couldn't have guessed? You been living under a rock?"

I laughed awkwardly and took a drink to try and hide it. "More like on a different rock," I muttered under my breath. "What's that?"

"I was just realizing that's why you were disappointed I didn't have a bed," I replied changing the subject. "I do have a room here but all the beds are accounted for. It's no big deal, I don't sleep much anyway."

She drummed her fingers on the table staring at me "There's something different about you. I almost find myself believing your no bed story."

"I get that a lot," I offered, taking another drink.

"So what's the deal with the blindfold?" She asked. "And whose symbol is that?" Her eyes widened and she leaned closer. "Is that Sevens symbol? Are you his pupil?" she asked in a tone that was clearly impressed.

"I am actually. And under strict orders to never take it off."

She seemed to perk up at this and began to look around the room. "Hey is he umm, for hire? Can someone buy his services?"

"I'm not really sure." I answered honestly not knowing the truth. "I think so. I know he said he's done it in the past but now he's a master so I don't know if that changes things."

"Where is he?" she asked and I could see she was getting excited.

"He's in that room over there asking his question of Sway. He won tonight's contest."

"How much longer do you think he'll be in there?"

I shrugged. "I have no clue. Could be a while I guess depending on his question."

"I think I have time to run back first," she said, but I didn't think she was talking to me. "If he happens to come out while I'm gone can you please tell him that I want to talk to him and that I'm looking to buy his protection?"

"I will."

She stood and slammed her wine then turned to go but stopped. "Please don't let him go without talking to me. This may be the only opportunity I ever get."

I smiled at her and nodded. "I promise."

That seemed to put her at ease and she spun, leaving the tavern in a rush.

I watched her leave and then turned back to my ale, taking a long swallow before setting it down and turning my attention back to the stage. No sooner had I done this did Seven walk out and head my way.

"How did it go?" I asked, noticing the look on his face like he just found out his favorite pet had died. Or maybe in his case, bent his favorite sword.

"It was... shocking. I may have to change my plans slightly. We will talk of this further once I've made up my mind. As for right now, you shouldn't keep a Sovereign waiting."

I nodded to him. "Hey Seven I was just talking to a girl who wanted to buy some protection with you. She had to run somewhere real quick but she should be back shortly. I promised her you'd wait and at least hear her out."

"We don't have time and now-"

"I know," I agreed. "But I already promised so just wait and listen please. She has a huge scar on her cheek that goes to her chin. You can't miss her."

"Very well," he replied and took a seat at the table to wait.

I walked over to the doorway and took a deep breath then pushed it open. The room beyond glowed faintly with a soft blue light that hung from the ceiling. It was similar to the lamp from the street in every way but color. At a small round table sat a woman in a blue dress with a white shawl tied loosely around her neck. She had on a necklace of white pearls and her hair was up in a bun. Her large glowing blue eyes took me in as she gestured to the chair next to her.

"Please have a seat."

I did so and she leaned over and gave me a soft peck directly on the lips. My mind raced, thinking this was some weird custom I didn't know about and wondered if I was supposed to kiss her back or not.

"Umm, thank you," I greeted awkwardly.

"A bet in the future with us is already lost in the past."

I frowned at her not knowing what the comment meant and she laughed slightly at my expression.

When she laughed it was kind and gentle like a mothers or grandmothers. She was still a very beautiful woman but compared to the only other Sovereign I met, different in a lot of ways. Where Immi was all attraction and beauty, this Sovereign was elegance and grace.

"You don't have to be shy around me. I'm not going to bite."

"It's not that. You're just so different from Immi. Not that I have much to go off, I only met her that once."

"There are lots of ways her and I are different. She doesn't always consider the emotions of lesser beings as long as the end produces results and that is why she rarely deals with them. That's more my area of expertise. I find them and their emotions... preferable. It helps to keep them predictable like love, loyalty and maybe a little obedience." She smiled fondly at me. "I assume this place confuses you a lot?" she asked, gesturing with her hands and I knew she wasn't referring to the room.

"It does but I'm starting to catch on."

"Good. Then you must have questions. I'll help where I can." I scratched the back of my head trying to decide what question I should ask or if I even got more than one. "How many questions do I get?"

She let out a soft chuckle. "Well since I invited you here I think it would be rude of me not to answer as many as I could but there are some I cannot answer."

"Why are there some you cannot answer?" I didn't think before I asked. I just blurted it out then regretted it instantly. I tried to take it back but she stopped me with an upraised hand.

"That is a fair and important question although difficult to explain. I find it helps to use a story a person can relate to or compare to the subject at hand. That being said, you agree there is a gap between your current level of understanding and mine yes?" I agreed and she paused for a second. "You consider yourself more advanced than the dung beetle, yes?"

I laughed at this one. "I sure hope so."

She smiled fondly and continued. "Now say one day you met a dung beetle that developed its conscience just like you have and it started to ask you questions about its existence. What do you think it would do if it understood what you knew about it? That it rolled around and ate feces all day? Maybe it would become depressed at the thought and end its own life? Or maybe it would spread the news to all the other dung beetles and the entire species would collapse. They'd refuse to eat or do what they were designed for and they'd die out one by one. They'd lose sight of the bigger picture and give up, affecting everything above and below them, understand?" she gave me a hopeful look.

"I think so," I offered, "But we're a little more advanced than a dung beetle." My conversation with Immi and the groundhogs popped into my head and I couldn't help but notice the similarities.

"Yes but that doesn't mean you'll handle understanding things you aren't ready to comprehend yet." I huffed at her remark, doubting the words. "You're all so caught up in life to look further than it, or even before it and figure out what you really are."

"What are we?" I asked quickly, again without thinking. "Technically you're the end result of what happens when

higher beings play God," she shook her head to stop herself. "I think that's enough on that. Let's get back to questions more relevant to the here and now shall we?"

I had so many more questions I wanted to ask but decided against pressing the issue. Obedience was one of the things she listed after all and when it came to Sovereigns you always felt an absurd amount of willingness to please.

I thought back to the conversation with Seven. "So I can't ask about the prophecies either?"

She nodded. "I would refuse to answer, that's right."

"Then I can assume what Seven and I are trying to do is in them?"

Her head fell to the side slightly like she thought I was trying to get one by her and maybe I was. "I wouldn't tell you that no matter what the answer was. That's the exact sort of thing that could alter it."

I bit my lip for a second and then sat up. "Well what about Earth's prophecy? Does it have one from God too?"

"Of course."

I stared at her waiting for her to continue but she didn't. "Well what is it?"

Her smile returned and she shook her head gently. "I'm not going to tell you something you already know. Besides, you're not nearly at the right step to understand it yet."

I decided to give up on that too and moved back to the here and now. "Well can you at least tell me if Aam really asked for me personally?"

"Of course. Why else do you think I'm helping you? The best way for you to understand all of this, especially where it concerns prophecy, is to just pretend like it doesn't exist or won't affect you either way. The future is a complex web and extremely difficult for people to grasp, even me, that's why I prefer to deal in the past."

"I see," I said, trying to adjust my line of questioning more specifically towards the past and still be helpful to our cause. "Has anyone ever made it past the guards and into the tower to reach Aam?"

"Of course," she responded. "He's there right now."

The unknown being popped into my head and I realized my own stupidity as she chuckled softly at my expression.

"Just that one time?" I asked in disbelief. "How did he do it?" She squinted at me like she wasn't sure if she wanted to answer or not. "He simply walked in uncontested."

This went against everything Seven had told me and it made no sense whatsoever. "How is that possible?"

She gave me a knowing shrug and cocked her head to one side. "Maybe once you've solved more of the infinity code you can figure that one out yourself."

We stared at each other and she started to chuckle, knowing exactly what my next question was going to be without having to see the future. "What's the infinity code?" I asked.

Her hand came to rest on my shoulder as her mirth turned into laughter. "You don't know how naive that question sounds. It's not something you can just ask of someone and they tell you. It's something you have to figure out on your own. It is the secret to everything, only found in tiny pieces and each piece must be decoded before it can be understood and then once it's understood it will bring you enlightenment and a new level of understanding where there's even more infinity code to be found and understood onward and upward forever."

I smiled with her but only because her mirth was becoming contagious. "So you don't know it?"

She cupped my cheek. "No my dear, not yet. But I am further up the ladder than most beings. There are many ways to figure it out and it's not easy, especially the higher up you get. Let's just say I have the right pieces, the right equations, I just need to understand them."

"What are the equations?"

She laughed again but this time with a little more compassion for my ignorance. "I will try to simplify it into layman's terms. The infinity code is a series of steps each living thing goes through one at a time. Each step must be learned, understood, then mastered and then the next step is achieved. When this happens you get a sort of promotion."

"Promotion to what?"

"And from what? Life starts small. As tiny specs invisible to the naked eye but as they learn and understand they get promoted again and again, into bugs, into rodents or animals, onward and upward."

"Into humans?"

"Eventually, yes but do you think it stops there?" I paused to think on it but she continued without waiting for me. "It doesn't. Being human is an extremely difficult step, a final step or test as most see it, the one that earns you a soul once you've succeeded."

"What makes it so hard?"

She sipped from her cup and then set it back down. "Well the only simple way I can put it is like this. It's the final step of your physical existence and the first step of your souls. You need to gain it, or earn it back in some cases because you can't proceed without it."

I sat up a little straighter, the conversation intriguing me. "How do you do that and what happens if you don't?"

She chuckled. "These are the biggest questions there are and I'm afraid I can only give tiny answers." She spun her cup as she thought. "It's different for most people because not everyone is on the exact same step even though they are living in the same world. For most of them they need to attune to the All, to find God, to find their soul and believe to make it their own. Not everyone will get into Heaven and not everyone gets a soul, their free will lets them decide. So if they fail to do any of this, they get sent back down, over and over. Some even regress a step until the time comes when they succeed… If they succeed."

I frowned at this, "If?"

She nodded. "Eventually time runs out. Then I'm afraid if they haven't earned a soul, or if they don't believe in souls, then they simply cease to exist. Not really dying but no longer a singular consciousness."

"How is that possible?"

"There are two things that are always constant, essence and knowledge. The essence that made up their life dissipates and the knowledge they held simply returns into the All, which is why Seven referred to it as the Alls vortex of knowledge."

I sat back in my chair and opened my mouth to ask but she stopped me with a hand as she smiled merrily.

"You don't have to ask. You're far too easy to read. The vortex is a sort of knowing that all life is automatically attuned in different ways until it reaches the final step… or test… humans."

"Seven said animals have it? That was kind of hard to believe." "Is it? Have you ever heard of the cuckoo?" I nodded. "It is a bird who's species survives by tricking other birds into hatching their young by sneaking their eggs in place of the others in an occupied nest. So you see, it is born and raised without ever having witnessed this task yet when it matures it will repeat this process.

Engraved into their specific species DNA is a piece directly from the vortex."

"So you access the past through the Alls vortex?"

She nodded at me proudly. "All pasts. Even if they're part of this place's future. You see, you're from a place and time where the All is far more advanced than the one we have here and I can see it's past through you." She smiled again. "If I could, I'd pick you up and put you in my pocket for the rest of your life but I'm afraid you're needed elsewhere. So for now, let's explore it together shall we?"

Her comments showed me how excited she was and they made me feel good so I nodded and smiled. This conversation would end up being one of the most informative ones I'd ever had and I'm going to leave most of it out.

One thing I can say that she told me ended up being one of the most important things I'd ever heard. She offered it as a piece of advice and it stuck with me forever. "Stop trying to improve on things others have already done, instead be original and step outside the box completely."

That little tidbit of help would come back to me so much throughout my life that I feel like it's extremely important to mention it here.

From there we moved on to talking about how to reach Aam but all she would say on that was it had to be my choice because it was my story.

She did inform me that she spoke with the other Enlightened on his way through and sent word with him to recruit his masters aide directly and that she would show up personally to help us herself.

At the end of the night we said our goodbyes and I walked out to a completely empty bar with the exception of Thas who stood hastily as we approached.

Sway spoke with him softly as I scanned the room. I watched a bartender come from the back to finish some last second errands then I accompanied Sway outside to where a carriage awaited her. "I'll keep my word to spread the call amongst all the races." she assured, waving her farewells.

"Thank you." I replied as she climbed in and the door swung shut.

Her head popped out the window. "Stay out of trouble if you can and I'll see you again at Darmon plain."

I waved to her once more and she waved back as the carriage rolled away and I once again found myself alone, standing in the streets.

CHAPTER 17

*T*rue *enlightenment cannot be obtained until you've removed a certain influence entirely. Some of you have already done this but most of you unwittingly share it, with a select few having lost all control completely. He will take whatever control he can get, it's how he wins souls. You've all heard stories about someone on death row with all the evidence against them, including DNA, still falsely trying to claim innocence with their last breath. He is the reason that person was unable to change. He is the reason and origin behind all evil in this world. He is the reason I never realized what I was until he was gone and you must hear this with an open mind... He is TRULY the father of lies.*

I stood first staring one direction down the street and then the other, deciding a walk would be a great way to kill some time. My only alternative being sitting in a room full of sleeping people and staring at a wall.

I chose the walk.

I thought it best not to leave the main road not only to prevent getting lost, but it was lit slightly better then the others and I was still wearing my blindfold.

I passed a few people in my stroll and they went by in a hurry with their eyes down so conversations weren't likely but I was fine with that. Besides the occasional pet, I had the city to myself. I looked through the windows of little shops and marveled at the things they could create with their bare hands. The attention to detail was unlike anything machines from Earth could produce.

After a while the shops faded away and it turned into more inns, bars, and what I could only assume was a brothel.

The Maids Mirror, it read. As I made my way past it a low sob caught my ear and I turned in the direction it had come from. To the side of the building on a bench, a woman sat hunched over, her head in her lap and she was crying.

I sat motionless, my soul wanting me to go and console her and make her feel better but my mind told me it wasn't my business and to keep my nose to myself.

The decision was made for me when she suddenly looked up and stared directly in my direction.

"You!" She stood and made her way towards me hastily. "You promised me!"

I furrowed my brow. "Lynnay? I told Seven that you were searching for him, did he not find you?"

She let her eyes fall to the ground. "I must have been too late. When I got back they were clearing the bar and both of you were gone. I didn't mean to take that long, it's just that... well.. Bottles caught me walking out with my savings and didn't really like the idea of me leaving without permission so he took it as an apology for my... disobedience."

I watched her from where she stood just inside the shadow from the street light and noticed one eye had a slightly darker shade then the other and one lip was puffed out as well.

"What happened? Did he hit you?" I demanded, anger washing over me.

"Bottles hits all his women. Either way it's my fault. I knew it was a stupid idea and I should never have gotten my hopes up."

"It's never ok to hit a woman.," I told her. "Why don't you just leave? Work for someone else or go to a new place? Get a job in a different... area of work perhaps?"

"Look at me!" she snapped, her emotions flaring up easily. "Take off your blindfold and look at me!"

"Lynnay... I can see. The blindfold is see through."

"Then you can see I've got a face only a butcher could appreciate." She shook her head in defeat. "Besides, what do you think I was trying to do? Even if I could escape this place then what? I can't read. I can't write. I have no skills. I have nothing to offer any man in a marriage. The only thing I have is a young slender body that arouses the drunk and the desperate as long as they don't have to stare me in the face." She wiped at her eyes, trying to hold back the tears that were flowing freely. "And now I have no savings. Bottles was the only work I could find but no one in their right mind would pick me inside this place, not when they could have any of the other women. So he sends me to the people too fat or too crippled to travel. Or if there's none of them, he makes me go from bar to bar and inn to inn." She shook her head and let it fall back so she was staring at the sky. "The things he lets them do to me they pay heftily for. I'm too valuable and now I can't leave even if I wanted," she turned and faced me once again. "I thought the blindfold made you an easy target. If you couldn't see me, then maybe..."

My heart sank for her and everything she was going through and I pulled out the coin purse. "I can give you this. It should help you enough to at least try again. Or at least have that hope anyway."

She eyed it inquisitively, contemplating my offer. "No. No I realize after today I will never escape this place. He called me an irreplaceable one of a kind that he'd have Choice hunt to the ends of the world just to bring back. He's why I needed Seven."

"Choice is the reason not Bottles?" I asked, slightly confused by this. "Who's Choice?"

"Bottles run's this place but Choice owns it. He is the master of three different weapons. I once watched him duel four other masters in a row and not even get touched, not once. That's why I needed Seven." She stuck her hand out in acceptance of my gift. "I'll take your money but I have lost all my hope."

I pulled it back to my chest. "Come with us," I suggested and her eyes snapped up. "I'm serious. Come with us and I can personally guarantee if this Choice comes after you, I can have Seven handle him for you."

She laughed like I had lost my mind. "Oh you'll have him handle Choice for me? What kind of student thinks he can order his master around?" The doubt was plain on her face as she awaited my response.

"Our situation is... complicated. Seven is my master but I'm his too in a different area. If I ordered him to protect you I'm betting he would. Either way, I could probably do a fair job of it myself I'd bet."

"Is that so? And what exactly are you the master of ? What could you do or teach to the legendary Seven that he doesn't already know himself ?"

I smiled at her, trying to ease her from her doubts. "It's complicated like I said. But if you come with us I offer you Sevens protection and mine... and this coin."

I tossed it to her then and she snatched it from the air giving me a quizzical look before she fumbled through its contents.

Her eyes went wide at the sight of the gold. "For this much money I'd follow you on a short walk off a long cliff. You sure you ain't lost all your marbles? You're not just going to take me down the road and butcher me up and take all your money back or something?"

I chuckled at her assumptions. "No. I can promise that too if you wish. Besides, have you ever heard of Seven letting something like that happen?" She thought for a second and then shook her head no. "I didn't think so. So what do you say? Want to come with us?"

She stared down at the coin again then back to me, a smile spreading on her face. "Fine. I'll join ya. But for this much coin at least let me take ya inside and roll around in the bedsheets a few times. You already said you don't sleep much."

I was thankful it was dark because I can't imagine the shade of red my face must have turned. "Nah that's ok. But thanks for the offer." I stared down the road like I was trying to find something.

"Is it my face?" she asked in a calm level voice.

"What? No it's not that. Your face is beautiful. The scar does nothing to diminish that. If anything it gives it a... uniqueness that adds to your appeal," I stammered out, feeling caught between a rock and a hard place.

"So it's my body? Or are you a winker?"

By now my face could have been used as a stop light. It wasn't that I was shy around women because I wasn't. I just wasn't used to having one be so blatantly straight forward with me and I was constantly caught off guard by it.

"Are you kidding? Your bodies perfect... and I'm no winker, believe me I'm not, it's just-"

She pushed her hip out and propped a hand on it as she cocked her head. "Listen, you're young. I'm young. We both have needs. Fat old cripples don't help me with that. Now you either give me one good reason why not or we go inside and you prove to me you're no winker."

She stared at me hard, waiting for my response but I just sat there frozen.

"Yup. That's what I thought." And with that she grabbed me by the hand and led me inside.

I will refrain from the details but I will say this, it is a very different feeling entirely when you're away from your body and experience any sort of physical contact, whether it be pleasure or pain.

We made our way back to the inn just before the sun started to peep out. We found Seven sitting in the common room talking with Weniban and they stood when they noticed us approaching.

"This is her I presume?" he asked and I nodded.

"I invited her along but we'll get into that in a second. Are we saying our farewells to Weniban?"

"I was going over some final instructions, yes," he turned back to the halfman who was placing a folded piece of paper into his pocket.

"We decided it would be better to not only have written proof of Sevens protection along with his masters mark but also a written request for assistance from him. I'm going to copy and post these around the cities I travel to."

I nodded to this and he stuck out his hand to Seven and I as we said our goodbyes. "And please let master Quill know I am forever in his debt and to thank him for his services last night.

"I'm sure he already knows.," I told him with a friendly smile and with that Weniban the halfman bowed slightly and walked out of the inn and out of our lives.

I turned back to Seven. "Now, Seven this is Lynnay, the girl I was talking about last night."

Seven offered her his hand and she smiled politely as she took it.

"Like I said before," I continued, "she will be coming with us." I noticed Seven looking her over carefully, no doubt making the assumption of what her occupation was. "Also, I gave her my word on the both of us protecting her. Since I couldn't offer myself without your permission, I offered your protection with mine but wanted to run it by you to confirm."

"That may be difficult as I may need to deviate from our plans temporarily at some point to deal with a... situation. Who may I ask, does she need protection from?"

"An employer who has difficulty accepting her departure. Let's just leave it at that for now. Her business is her own. Now what's this about you having to seperate? Does it have to do with what Sway said?"

Sevens' eyes lost focus slightly as he went into a deep contemplation for a second then responded with a nod. "It does. But I haven't made up my mind yet on my exact course of action nor do I care to go into the details until I have."

"That's fair enough, I didn't ask for any. Just let me know when you decide so we can plan accordingly."

"Agreed." He turned to Lynnay next. "Ma'am, as long as you are in our company I will protect you from those who think to pursue you. I also grant my pupil these same privileges in the event I'm not around."

"Thank you ever so much Seven," she beamed earnestly like a weight had just been lifted from her shoulders. "But I think I should warn you about master Choice. He's a blademaster of three but he doesn't like people talking about him. He doesn't want the fame and said it causes people to never underestimate him and that you..." she gestured towards Seven, "were a fool for letting your fame spread. It makes you a bigger target and no one will ever take you lightly."

He stared at her for a moment. "His words are true. I didn't want the fame but we don't always get to choose our fates."

"There's more," I added and turned back to Lynnay.

"Oh yeah. I once watched him duel four different masters in a row and not even one of them touched him. He's very fast and very good and I really don't want you to underestimate him at all."

Seven cracked a rare grin. "I won't. In fact, I eagerly look forward to meeting this... master Choice." He enunciated the name slowly as if tasting it to see what all he could learn. He glanced between us. "You will go into more detail about him later." He instructed her then turned to me. "Anything else?"

"Just the conversation with Sway comes to mind but we can talk about that on the road. There wasn't much that was useful either way."

He nodded. "I'm going to go fetch a few items for our trip. Go and wake the others and have them outside and ready in a few minutes. I'll meet you all out front."

I opened the door to find the prearranged sleeping order had been changed. Matches and Deffy shared a bed with each other, heads on opposite sides and Quill had somehow swindled his way into a bed for himself.

Deffys eyes popped open before I even made a sound and I smiled. "Time to go Buddy. Wake Matches and get your things together."

He hopped up and roused his sleeping friend. Matches sat forward groggily and wiped at his face in an attempt to remove the sleep.

"Quill," I whispered, shaking his leg but he didn't move." Quill." I spoke a little louder this time and he made a soft grunting noise but remained unresponsive.

Matches walked over with a mischievous grin and started rubbing his hands together, eyeing Quill's backside.

"I think he's still too drunk to even feel that," I stated. "He probably doesn't even remember how he got here."

Lynnay smiled at Matches' intentions but put a hand up to stop him. "I got one better," she smirked then removed her dress to reveal her undergarments.

The faces of the other two both went crimson and they tried to avert their eyes. She sat on the bed, unconcerned with her audience as she slipped her leg under Quills, then turned back to them. "Stand over there," she whispered, then scooted closer to him and wrapped him in an embrace.

I chuckled and joined them as she started to kiss his cheek and his forehead. "Oh Quill. My dearest Quill, won't you wake with me? I can't wait to start planning our future together."

Matches made a confused face while we all watched her continue.

"Quill," she soothed, pinching his bottom.

"What's this now?" One of his eyelids popped open and he gave her a quick once over, his eyes widening slightly at the sight of her lack of clothes.

"I'm just so happy. I can't wait to tell my parents we're married."

"Matches slapped a hand over his mouth to stifle a laugh and Deffy and I both grinned.

Confusion spread across Quill's face and she kissed his cheeks again to prevent him from sitting up. "I know you were drunk but... I told you I'd never been with a man before. I was saving myself for marriage so you proposed and I said yes!" she let out a long sigh. "Should I call you Quill still or husband?"

He lifted his head a bit, clearly struggling with everything that was happening. "Listen here, doll face. I don't know what you're prattling on about but I don't remember no wedding... or no consummation of one neither."

She made a face like she was shocked and then it turned pouty like she was about to cry. "Don't say that. You can't take back a marriage or what we did. Master Seven himself did the ceremony. Masters can officiate such things ya know."

Quill sat up at this. "That bastard," he growled, eyes darting back and forth as he tried to connect the imaginary dots in his head. "Who witnessed? No one in their right mind would let me marry if I was that drunk," he protested.

I pointed towards Matches.

"Umm, a big man. A really big man I'd say. Oh," she gasped and pulled the blankets up to cover herself like she just now noticed us. "Him," she announced with a wink and gestured towards Matches.

Quill's head snapped around to where he finally saw us. We burst into laughter and started to gather our things to get ready to leave, thinking the farse over.

"You let me get married!" he yelled at Matches.

The giant man only hesitated for a second before responding. "Looovvveee," then laughed in his high pitched cackle only he could do.

Quill turned back to her. "We have to undo this! You don't want a husband like me! I'll never settle down! Or give you kids!" She rolled her eyes at his gullibility and stood, throwing on her dress. "That my dearest, is exactly why I said yes and I've already got permission to come with you so let's go."

He turned to me and I bobbed my head in agreement. His shoulders slumped and he visibly deflated as he tried to speak. "But... I didn't... I mean, I don't..."

"Get your stuff together. We have to meet Seven outside and head off soon."

He rolled onto his feet and sat with his head in his hands for a minute before finally grabbing his things. "Where's our marriage writ then?" Quill asked desperately, still trying to find a way out. "Master Seven has it still. Enough chat, you wouldn't want to piss your old lady off on your first day together would ya?" she asked in an annoyed voice, not even trying to keep up with her charade.

He snorted at her but didn't respond as he followed Matches and Deffy out the door.

She turned back to me and we shared a smile. "You got lucky naming Seven as doing the ceremony and holding the writ. They don't get along so it's probably the only reason he still believes you."

"I planned on ending it right away but he fell for it so easily," she mused, shaking her head. "No one's that stupid. How long do you think I can keep it up? Wanna make a wager?"

"You're going to bet the money I just gave you against me?" I asked accusingly.

"No. I was thinking more along the lines of what I gave you last night." I swallowed, feeling the heat return to my cheeks and she must have noticed because she laughed. "For every meal I make it through with him being none the wiser, you owe me some... alone time we'll call it. If I can't keep it going until at least lunch then you can do whatever you want to me."

I laughed. Like I said I was never shy around women but her straight forwardness was intriguing to me. I was usually the one pursuing not being pursued.

"That's fair enough," I agreed and she slapped me on the bottom as she walked by.

"Then let's get moving. I aim to be as far from here as possible by lunch."

I rubbed at the stinging as I followed her out.

We came outside to the sunshine beating down on us and warming everything it touched. With the sun always near its peak in the sky, it gave the feeling of midday. I should say it's not that the sun stayed in the same position in the sky. It moved in circles most likely from the rotation of the planet but I honestly don't know.

Seven noticed us approaching and I watched his lips move and a cheer erupted from Deffy as he and Matches shot down the road.

"Not wasting any time I see," I pointed out as we drew nearer. "No point. I have everything we need plus Deffy should anything else arise and I thought it best to be away from any would be pursuers as soon as possible." He offered eyeing Lynnay and she nodded her agreement.

"Pursuers? What's this now? I took care of Wenibans pursuers already," Quill declared, slowly rotating his shoulder to test it out as we all started to walk.

Seven went to answer but Lynnay beat him to it. "Well my dearest. Apparently you don't remember I was being courted. I had a date last night and you challenged him in front of everyone. He was so embarrassed, no doubt he's gathering a posse right now to help him extract his revenge." She batted her eyelashes at him with exaggerated admiration. "My hero."

Quill grimaced and turned to stare at Seven. "You may have won this round but you stepped into my world now. Childish pranks? I reign here! You'll see! You crossed the line!" he snarled then picked up his pace to walk with his brother and Deffy instead.

Seven stared blankly then opened his mouth to yell something but Lynnay stopped him. "Never argue with someone that stupid," she suggested. "He'll just bring you down to his level and then beat you with experience."

I laughed at her advice and put my hand on Sevens shoulder. "To fill you in, our lovely Miss Lynnay has convinced Quill that during a drunken stupor last night they got married with you as the officiator and keeper of the writ, consummated the marriage and are now traveling off together as happy as two mice in a wheel of cheese." She nudged me playfully. "Oh and more recently, are now being pursued by her previous date who he embarrassed publicly." The unamused look stayed on Seven's face so I decided to change the subject. "Speaking of pursuers, I think maybe we should arm Lynnay and perhaps teach her the basics. Not with a sword or anything like that, I was thinking more along the lines of a crossbow. Maybe one with a crank, smaller and easier to carry."

"Crossbows are a useless weapon," Seven stated while he contemplated my suggestion. "Unless your opponent is wearing heavy mail which almost no one does. Or if he's so far away any shot you put up would be a prayer anyway and better done with a bow. I can release about a dozen arrows with a bow before a man with a crossbow gets off his second shot."

"That may be for you but she's not as skilled or as strong as you and I doubt we have that much time to teach her. A smaller crossbow would be easier for her to carry and she could crank it back. Then the only thing she would need to learn would be how to aim. Besides, I have some design ideas where she could get off four shots before she'd even have to reload. With two smaller ones she could shoot 8 times to defend herself if we ever somehow got separated."

Seven stroked his chin looking from her to me before he finally nodded. "Agreed. Your logic is sound. It's always best to be prepared for anything. Especially with her possibly being pursued."

"I did come up with one more thing," I added with a bit of enthusiasm, "that I think could be extremely powerful but I don't see how no one has thought of it yet?"

He eyed me suspiciously. Intrigue and curiosity plastered to his face. "Well? Continue for Aams sake!"

I chuckled to myself. "Ok now it might be hard for the little guy so we'll see about one at first and if it works go from there. So what if we had Deffy make a crossbow bolt with a karma stone tip? If you shot it at an Enlightened it would automatically drain them of all their powers and they wouldn't be able to heal. That could be a game changer even if it only gave us a few seconds. Do you agree or has something like this already been thought of before?"

Sevens eyes danced while he considered the idea. "I've never heard of such a thing. This could be an enormous advantage for us if it works out. It may even work on the being holding Aam."

My eyes went wide as I hadn't considered that. "How has no one thought of this before?" I asked incredulously.

"For the most part, yielders are kept by the Enlightened so they're not going to try and think of ways to kill themselves. I'd guess only two or three ever have been outside their reach or directly worked for someone who was so there's been very limited opportunities. On top of that they are not as useful to the Enlightened as they are to the common folk. If they lose that usefulness or disobey or become an inconvenience in any way they are just as likely to kill them. They'd rather them be dead then return back to us where they could gain power and influence."

Lynnay cut in then, disbelief and amazement both in her tone. "Are you guys implying that young boy there is a yielder?"

"His name is Deffy," I spoke softly, "and please keep it to yourself."

"Of course," she assured us, staring at him in a new light for a moment before finally returning to our conversation. "Let's do it. I'd love to learn to shoot a crossbow. If I'm here, I want to help," she smiled at me and hugged my arm.

"Careful," I teased, "Wouldn't want your husband to see and spoil the bet."

She released my arm and bumped me playfully with her hips. Seven interrupted unintentionally as he continued to ponder the idea while his eyes were down. "I think the crossbow dart would be the most effective way. If we make it smaller to where it can't be pulled out it would basically make them powerless. Also I think it would be easier for Deffy to create seeing how the last time he was completely exhausted."

He continued to rant for a while, going over daggers, detachable arrow heads and all sorts of other weapons that we could attach a karma stone to but the crossbow bolt was still our best option. Quill even came back and joined us, offering up the idea of barbs to prevent it from being pulled back out.

By lunch we had smoothed out the plans and decided to call Deffy over and run the idea by him. "Sure friends," was the extent of his response while he fed the mouse a nibble of his bread. "Would it take a lot out of you though Bud?" I asked, knowing his communication skills weren't always at par with ours. "Oh umm, yeah probably lots. But I can still do it though." "That's great," I praised, rustling his hair. "For now let's see if

you can just do one small crossbow and some bolts for it so we can start training her. I don't think we'll have need of one made with a karma stone for a while. Whenever you feel up to it."

He nodded at me, "It's usually best to do those before I go to bed. They put me to sleep anyway. Also if you want more then just one I should wait a long time between cause it makes me tireder and tireder and hard to walk a lot."

I smiled at him and patted his back. "Like I said Bud, whenever you're comfortable with it. For now just the regular ones will do. The karma stone dart and Quills dagger can wait until you're ready."

He asked a few more questions, pointed out some flaws in my designs and even added a few tips himself. By the end of the meal he was confident that he could make a working four shot crank crossbow with a lever to switch between its multiple arrow chambers, causing the trigger to only affect one at a time and a fail proof safety pin so Lynnay could walk around with it fully loaded, not having to worry about it misfiring.

She sat forward intently to watch and I followed suit by pulling in a little essence of my own to watch closer as he slapped his hands together and the world shimmered. I watched as he first pushed the essence itself into the shapes he was creating but not between his hands, in them and outside of them as well. When the essence passed through his hand it transformed from just being invisible essence into taking form and shape like he controlled the particles themselves with just a thought. Wood and metal imprinted themselves in my mind as he called for the essence to change like he could speak to the universe itself and it listened.

His hands separated completely and one perfectly crafted crossbow plopped down onto his outstretched palm. He handed it to me and I looked it over in appreciation. He slapped his hands together and did the darts next then handed them over as well.

"Deffy this looks amazing. Great work Bud, you are truly gifted beyond description."

He beamed with pride at my words as I wound the crank to pull the drawstrings back and test the small weapon.

I loaded a dart into each of the four chambers and stood to look for something to shoot at. Matches instantly pointed to Quill with a giggle but Seven tossed an apple down at the base of a small hill.

"Stand back a bit so the bolt doesn't bury itself in the ground." I did so then released the safety pin and took aim.

Thwop. The bolt shot out in a small streak and struck the apple directly, severing it into two giant chunks. I flicked my thumb to activate the next chamber and repeated the process until it was empty.

"It's perfect," I observed, handing it over to Seven next. "The top chamber is accurate and we just have to remember to adjust our aim for the bottom three. That's the only flaw I can find."

We spent far too long playing with the thing and Lynnay had just fired her final shots when she finally spoke up. "I think we should be on the road now. If we are being pursued he's had plenty of time to catch up."

"Damn," Quill spat, taking a drink from a flask. "Wasn't sure if you was serious about that or not. I don't know what to believe." He tugged his hat lower towards his eyes. "I know there's no chance this bloke will annul our marriage but believe me, soons I find someone who can, I'll have that writ and be rid of ya. Let's go Ma," he ordered and Matches and Deffy both moved to follow.

Lynnay let out a fake wail and threw her arms around me pretending to cry. Quill gave a quick look back but didn't slow or stop his pace.

"Is he looking?" she whispered between exaggerated sobs. "Nope." I stroked her hair acting concerned.

"Good," she nipped at my ear. "That's one ya owe me," she teased, thrusting her body inappropriately against mine and Seven pretended to look elsewhere as he began to walk.

"It sure as hell ain't happening now," I laughed, gently removing her arms from my neck. "Come on. Let's catch up."

She cocked her head at me as we started to follow. "I like the blindfold," she concluded in a casual tone. "It hides your eyes. Most people I meet spend all their time trying to stare at my scar and it tends to wear on me but it's different with you. I feel like even if I could see your eyes they'd be looking into mine and not at my... flaws."

I smiled at her. "What flaws? I already told you, you're unique and desirable if you ask me."

She blushed for the first time and tucked some of her hair behind an ear. "So what color are they? Can I see them?"

"Let's save that for a special occasion," I suggested, trying to avoid the topic and not wanting her to press further.

"Oh I see." She tried to pinch my bottom again subtly but I saw it coming and stepped away.

"Please ma'am. You're a married woman. None of that until after the annulment," I declared, doing my best to act aghast.

She rolled her eyes at me as we continued on, only stopping a few times throughout the day to go through the cheim and eat. We started working on sword thrusts and parrying and that shifted back into creating shields and what they could do to improve theirs. Lynnay never asked any questions about our weird abilities and we never had to explain. Deffy made the other crossbow along with more bolts. Night Time came and went and we had just had our breakfast and were hitting the road when the sound of a horse could be heard slowly approaching.

Lynnay's eyes went wide with horror as the man pulled on his reins to look us over. "That's him," she gasped. "That's Choice."

CHAPTER 18

*K*arma *is something else you must work on as much as you can but most of you don't understand it. You think if you go around simply giving things away that the universe will give them back immediately but that's not always how it works. Your energy has to align with your intent. Your purposes selfless. The goal to never get repaid for your deeds, that way, when you enter Heaven you are rewarded in soul.*

The man jumped off the horse with the grace and agility only a few people possess. His hair was salt and pepper and tied behind his head in a ponytail. His tight white button up shirt showed all his bulging muscles while he removed his riding gloves and set them on the saddle. He turned to face us, placing hands on his hips as his small dark eyes took us all in.

"Hello," Deffy offered warmly and the man smiled, showing a set of perfectly aligned teeth with the exception of one being gold.

"Hello young one," he spoke in mock pleasure. "Who are your friends here?" he asked, looking at all of us in turn. His eyes started with Lynnay, then me, taking in my blindfold, its mark, then quickly moving to Seven where he paused for a minute, his smile growing. He gave a quick glance to Quill and Matches before finally returning his attention to Deffy.

"Umm, I'm Deffy and these are my friends Matches, Quill and Seven." He pointed to me, "that's my brother and my friend and..." He hesitated when he reached Lynnay. "Well I think she's my friend but I don't remember her name."

"That's ok little one. I already know it," he jested with a wink. "My name is Choice and you see, she belongs to me so I'm here to take her back."

Quill stepped forward at this and put out a hand to calm the man. "Now listen here bucko. I don't remember what I said to ya last night but trust me, you don't want no trouble here. I married the girl and we have the writ to prove it so you best just be on your way. Now hand it over." He held his other hand towards Seven and snapped his fingers before opening it, palm up as he waited but Seven didn't budge. He just sat eyeing the newcomer with a keen eye.

"Well I got to four at least. It was a good run," Lynnay whispered into my ear.

The man turned all his attention towards Quill with a frown. "There's two problems with what you just said... bucko." He spat the word like it was dirt in his mouth. "I've never met you in my life and no one in their right mind would ever marry a whore with a scarred up face."

Anger washed over me at the vulgarness of his words and Quill just looked around in confusion.

Lynnay clued him in with a shrug. "Seemed funny at the time."

Matches laughed loudly at his brothers expense and slapped him on the back.

"Why you sneaky grasshoppers... No matter, bloke here likes insults does he? I bet he's so queer, he's tried riding the saddle on the underside of his horse more then once."

Matches threw his head back to laugh at this but Seven stepped forward to interrupt, addressing Choice himself.

"You have implied that the young lady here belongs to you. I should have you know it is illegal to own someone or hold them against their will. Furthermore, I have offered her protection from any and all would be pursuers who intend to do anything that directly conflicts with her current plans. As of now those plans are to accompany us and until those plans change this will continue. In the event she decides to return to your employ, I will bring her to you myself. In the meantime, any objections or complaints can be taken up with me directly." The formality to his declaration was overshadowed greatly by the air of challenge he was displaying as he grit his teeth in a grin.

Choice returned the grin casually, "And you are?" he asked, like he hadn't just heard Deffy say it.

"They call me Seven," was the only response he got.

"Never heard of you," he lied in a mocking tone as if testing him. "And why do they call you that?"

"Why do they call you Choice?" Seven interjected, knowing the man already knew the answer.

Choice paused from where he stood fixing his hair and the two stared at each other, the tension growing.

"I suppose that's fair. It's because I put out three different blades and let my opponent choose which one he would like to use." His split his hair in two then tugged in opposite directions, tightening the binding that held it more securely to his skull then tucked it all into his shirt. "I don't see any need to know the bow. It's a coward's weapon and shooting it takes very little to master. The spear is for infantry with only peasants stooping to that level and daggers and axes are for halfmen and kids." He moved to the pack at the side of his horse and unfastened the strap that held some various weapons. "I assume if we fought, you'd want a choice like everyone else?"

Sevens smile was so big and filled with excitement it almost wrapped around his head. "On the contrary. I'd rather extend you your own courtesies and let you pick. I'd hate to accidentally choose the one you were least skilled with and have it said you weren't at your best when we fought."

Choice let out a hearty chuckle. "Excellent. Then by all means, I hear you're an absolute brute with the long sword. Let's use those shall we? Who is to witness and what are the terms offered?" he asked, pulling a pair of arm bracers out and some fingerless fighting gloves.

Seven gestured towards me, starting to slowly stretch as he eyed the man more closely. "My pupil will witness. My terms offered are, if you win you may take the sum of one hundred gold and leave unmolested but the girl still stays. The witness will care for my body."

Choice hesitated slightly at the offer of gold but then shook his head as he took a few test swings with his sword to loosen up his arms.

"Even if you somehow convinced me you had twice as much gold to offer, the girl here will make me far more than that during her employ. She's a rare find indeed. And besides, it's about the principle of the matter. Change the gold you offered to the girl and I still leave uncontested. In return my offer is to leave the rest of your little party here unharmed as well. In the event I actually lose, just put my body on the horse and smack its rump. It will return me home."

Quill mumbled something about it being drunkard trained under his breath but I ignored him, concentrating on my new responsibilities.

"Do you want this written down?" I asked Seven, not exactly sure what I was doing but Choice answered.

"That's not necessary. Just repeat it aloud if he accepts."

We all looked to Seven who turned to Lynnay for confirmation.

"I suppose if you can't beat him no one can and I wouldn't have a choice either way," she offered, moving closer to stand by me.

Seven turned back to Choice. "Terms accepted," then stuck his sword into the ground tip first.

"Terms accepted," Choice repeated and then did the same.

I cleared my throat. "In the event of Master Choices victory, Lynnay will escort him back to the city leaving the rest of our party unmolested. In the event master Seven wins... we are just to load the body up and put it on the horse and smack its rump. Umm, longswords have been chosen as the weapon, no disadvantages named." I leaned closer to Quill and spoke quietly. "Did I do that right?"

He nodded, not taking his eyes from the two as they finished a few of their rituals and then freed their swords, taking a quick step back.

Seven gestured us away to give them a wide berth as Choice eyed his horse. "Lady, go eat," he commanded and the horse cantered off into the grass.

Seven held his weapon out point first and Choice mirrored this, their tips coming together with a gentle ting to signal the contests start.

I was expecting them to feel each other out, maybe do a few test jabs and parrys, that's how it always started in the movies but Choice had a different strategy.

The moment the tips met there was a burst of motion. He swung his sword up hard and fast, lifting Sevens into the air then lunged forward, fist balled and swung to where it would have connected solidly with Sevens face but he saw it coming and tucked his chin down, letting the blow land on top of his head.

He took a step back and Choice lunged with a knee in the same motion. Seven lifted his leg and stopped the attack short then grabbed Choices hand before he could attempt another punch. Both swords were locked above their heads, arms grasped, faces only inches apart.

Choice grit his teeth and it was returned with a toothy grin as they both pushed away from each other in unison.

Seven eyed him carefully and repositioned his grip on the handle of his sword. Choice noticed this then immediately changed his as well as he smiled. Sevens hands moved again and again Choices did the same which in turn lead Seven to follow suit once more. As Choice moved into a two handed grip I shook my head in confusion. This wasn't sword fighting to me.

"What am I watching here?" I asked Quill as their hands constantly moved and changed as they regripped and repositioned the swords over and over.

"Each grip on the sword, like the ones you've been learning, has its best counter both offensively and defensively. They both have so many I don't even know half of them or if they're just making them up as they go."

Choice flipped the sword to his other hand and grasped it in reverse with a smile. Seven stared for a second like he wasn't sure if Choice was bluffing at the technique or was in fact just trying to make one up in an attempt at confusion.

Seven chuckled as he shook his head confidently. "There's two problems with what you're doing. The first is you're showing me the extent of your techniques and knowledge. Now granted I did bait you into it but you're not on my level so you can hardly be held accountable." Choice raised an eyebrow but he made no move to change his current grip or position. "The second, and far worse mistake, is that you're showing me at all."

He flung his sword into the air and then leapt forward. Doubt washed over Choices face and he froze, not knowing whether or not to watch the sword or the man.

Sevens hand shot up, snatching the sword from the sky at the last second and a flurry of swings followed. The air rang with the sound of steel on steel as his attacks were all parried but the other man's eyes darted around frantically, he was clearly caught off guard.

"Genius," Quill whispered.

"What is?" I asked, not sure what he was talking about.

"Aside from the amount of confidence and skill it takes to pull off that little sword flip trick to himself, the genius part is now Choice has no clue what grip he's using and in return, had to switch to a completely defensive tactic just to try and survive the onslaught. Also if you notice, it's causing his eyes to dart around which is never a good sign, especially if you're trying to match someone as renowned as Seven."

I frowned. "I find it impressive that he can follow the swings at all. They're so fast."

Quill didn't respond as Seven pivoted, shifting his grip but not allowing Choice to catch the subtle move.

"When you're fighting an opponent who is much faster or more skilled... your eyes darting around could be your death," he continued again slowly as he watched intently.

I considered his words as I felt Lynnay step closer to put her face right near my ear. "He's faking," she said under her breath. "I've seen him fight too many times. He's letting Seven think he has the advantage. He's much better than this, he's only acting... You have to tell him," desperation crept into her voice.

"Even if that was true. Telling him would be considered interfering. He would automatically concede the fight and declare it a loss and Choices terms would be granted." Her breath caught and I felt her grip my arm.

"Bloody hell she's right," Quill remarked in disbelief. "He's so good, he's able to feign desperation but perfectly block every attack without leaving room for an opening or making a single mistake. It looks like he's just waiting for Seven to tire or maybe make a mistake of his own."

The barrage of offense Seven was performing did appear to be overwhelming to me. I couldn't see what Lynnay had guessed at or Quill could see so I ever so slowly pulled in some essence. After a moment it was enough to enhance my abilities and reaction time enough to understand what was happening. Not only was Choice moving slower then he really could, he was timing his sloppy looking defenses perfectly so that each block and parry was at precisely the right time.

This man is a true master. I thought to myself and noticed I was holding my breath.

Left, right, kick, thrust, thrust. Seven executed each with perfection and I could see the motions of the cheim in his movements as I watched.

Block, block, sidestep, parry, parry Choice met each attack with a clumsiness so perfectly acted out that Deffy and Matches clapped happily at how well they thought Seven was doing.

It happened in a flash so quick I doubt anyone caught what truly happened besides me. Seven had just swung down so hard it appeared to have knocked Choice off balance. As he planted his foot to pivot and reverse his swing, Choices foot, whose legs flailed as he pretended to stumble, caught Sevens on the inside of the knee and caused his weight to buckle under him.

He fell and Choice planted his foot solidly and spun, his other foot lashing out parallel to the ground where it connected with a loud thwack on Sevens head, sending him sprawling backwards.

He used the momentum to roll into a somersault and attempted to come to his feet but Choice was on him in an instant.

Swing after swing in a downward motion prevented him from being able to rise and forced him to defend from a seated position as he scooted away desperately.

In the middle of one of his spike driving like swings Choice shifted his grip and pulled the tip of his sword in to miss Sevens defense and it buried itself into his boot after it passed.

Seven growled in anger as Choice clutched it with both hands, trying to put all his weight on it and pin Seven to the ground. Seven saw this coming and prevented it with a solid kick to the chest from his good foot that caused Choice to fly backwards and take his sword with him, freeing Seven as he did.

They both stood slowly, eyeing each other as they prepared to face off once again.

"Oops," Choice apologized with mock sincerity, starting to slowly shuffle to his side.

Seven shifted to his right with a slight but visible limp and Choice grinned when he noticed.

"That's going to make it very hard to swing from the left now that you can't put weight or pivot from that side. Don't you agree?"

Sevens facial expression didn't change as he responded. "Come find out."

The gold tooth in the other man's mouth twinkled as he flashed a triumphant smile. "I think I will." Then he sprang forward.

His sword cuts came in flashes, his movements like a cheetahs as he darted in and out, constantly circling to the side to keep Sevens weight and pivots on his bad foot. Again and again his blade lashed out, most barely blocked and some even slicing a leather guard or nicking the skin.

The limp started to become more prominent the more he was forced to keep his weight on it and Choice noticed this. He started to put more arch into his blows, sacrificing speed for power in an effort to cause Seven to stumble.

When he finally did, there was no hesitation. Choice leapt forward, sword held high as Sevens weight appeared to buckle under him as he tried to hold it with his bad foot. His arms went wide in an attempt to keep his balance as he crumbled down.

Lynnay's nails dug into my skin as she gasped but a smirk appeared on Sevens face that gave us pause.

He waited until Choice was directly over top of him and then planted his foot solidly, like it had never been hurt at all. He sprang up like a fish out of water directly beneath Choices' attack and his forehead smashed into the other man's nose with a satisfying crunch that only breaking bones can produce.

Choices nose exploded in a spray of blood and he flew backwards, rolling to the ground and then instantly springing back to his feet in case he was being pursued.

Seven just stood there like he wasn't even winded let alone wounded. He rested the tip of his sword on the ground as he spoke. "Are you ready to take me seriously yet?" he asked, apparently seeing through the other man's ruse.

Choice wiped his face with a rag from his back pocket then stuck his thumb to one nostril and shot out a clot of blood then wiped again. "It would seem I must," he surmised, snapping his nose back into place with a quick jerking motion and cracking sound.

Matches and Deffy both winced at the sight and Seven continued. "You can go on and on with your charade if you'd like but I'd prefer if you try a different tactic. Maybe show me what you're truly capable of instead of this game of charades."

Choice cracked his neck and then rolled his shoulders back and forth like he was just now preparing for the fight. "You should be careful what you wish for. Don't think I can't tell you have a few tricks up your sleeve but I'm much too fast for you to even comprehend how outclassed you are." He admitted with a shrug.

"If you think that because you had speed enough to block while pretending to be slow that you somehow have me outclassed I'd love to disappoint. Even if that display was only half of your true speed, technique always prevails."

"Technique or tricks?" Choice mocked, walking closer to his horse and pulling something out of the pack as the intermission continued.

"They are one and the same. I only need to know one technique that you don't and your speed counts for nothing," Seven squinted as he finished, watching Choices moves carefully.

The other man was placing the pommel of a broken sword back into the pack as he turned to face Seven again, pulling his glove back on.

"Your nose is no longer bleeding. You used the essence to heal," he accused.

The other man shrugged. "It was your pupil that said no dissadvantages named and it was agreed upon. Besides, you used it to heal your foot."

"No. I used years of meditation and mental fortitude to block out the pain. I will however use some now." He gestured towards his pack and I grabbed his karma stone dagger and tossed it to him.

He held it for a moment and then threw it back, rocking his weight from foot to foot to test it out.

I put the dagger back as Lynnay spoke up softly. "So he knew all along about Choices ruse?"

"It looks like it," I answered, not sure what all they were just pretending or actually capable of. There were so many layers to sword fighting at this level and I was way out of my league.

"Not only that," Quill added to our conversation without turning. "But I think Seven has been pretending too. I wouldn't be surprised if he was actually much much faster than he seems to be now."

"Do you think it will be fast enough?" Lynnay wondered aloud but no one answered as we watched the two creep towards each other with careful steps.

Seven paused for a second and then lept in, blade low, tip scraping the ground in an upward swing that sprayed gravel as it went. Choice reacted in a flurry and countered with a parallel cut of his own as the sound of battle once again rang through the air but this time, with a tempo much faster and deadlier than before.

Blow after blow was deflected and countered. Seven managed to kick a boot out or swing his fist but Choice was too fast and dodged easily.

"He's truly a master," Quill observed, mesmerized by their dance of death.

"You're talking about Seven I hope."

"Yeah but I'll deny it," he snorted. "Choice seems much faster than he was before but Seven... is the far superior fighter." I watched but I didn't know what I was looking for, Quill continued. "If I was going to swing a sword at your head what would you do?"

"Block it?" I offered skeptically, knowing there was more to the question.

"Exactly," Quill agreed, never taking his eyes from the fight. "But you're a beginner so to you it's as simple as putting your sword in the path to block his. But it appears Seven is outmatched in speed and he knows it. Now watch his blocks."

I squinted to see if I could notice what Quill was. Choice sliced in and Seven blocked easily, swords connecting just above the crossguard. He countered with a low sweep but Choice caught it mid blade and countered with a straight thrust. Seven deflected it, this time, the base of his blade hitting the tip sending it just wide of his torso and he countered with a thrust of his own.

"Sevens moves look more...short and choppy. But I have no clue why."

Quill nodded his head. "It's because they are. He's taking the shortest route to block the path of the blade, not sparing an inch. If you noticed, he just blocked near the base of buckos swing, that cut the reaction time down and blocked the swing before it could gain momentum. And the thrust, he knocked it off by its tip, sending it just wide. A gamble indeed but it's a shorter motion and takes less time to pull off if you know what you're doing."

It was starting to make sense to me and I looked at the contest in a new light. Choice did quick fluid motions that covered a wide variety of ranges whereas Sevens short jerky motions were just as effective and required less speed. I was awestruck.

Frustration began to show on Choices face as he struggled to comprehend how his speed wasn't overwhelming his opponent and he made the first mistake. He went in for a thrust that he had grown accustomed to Seven parrying but it didn't come. Instead he mirrored his attack and turned sideways, causing Choices thrust to miss. The man tried to reel back at his error but not in time. Sevens blade bit deeply into his side and blood gushed out as he hopped back.

Rage washed over him and he assessed the wound. Seven stuck the blade into the grass, cleaning it then crouched again in anticipation.

It came with a shout of pure anger and fury. Choice bursted forward, his style completely different then it was before. No longer was he just swinging his sword, it was a series of thrusts and spins, leaping from side to side, crouching, standing, never in the same spot for more than a heartbeat as his sword struck out again and again.

I stood motionless at the spectacle, not knowing how a person could move with such speed and agility. It wasn't until I heard Lynnay gasp that I noticed the line of blood on Seven's cheek.

Then another sprouted up on his shoulder, followed by one on his leg.

"He's... losing," I muttered in disbelief.

Excitement twinkled in Choices eyes and he picked up the pace. Seven who no longer had time to counter the quick short jabs did all he could to defend the bombardment.

In the middle of landing and spinning, Choice changed directions, shooting forward instead of sideways and into a surprised face, pummeling Sevens cheek with the butt of his sword then grabbing Sevens as he did, wrenching it free while he fell backwards.

Choice laughed maniacally, twirling both swords around in triumph while Seven rolled back and up onto one knee, a blank look on his face.

The two stared at each other for a moment then Choice looked down at Sevens weapon. "I think I'll keep that one," he stated, then tossed it into the ditch near where his horse grazed.

The rest of us stood motionless, not believing what we were seeing.

Lynnay began to shake her head in denial. "I'll shoot him. I'll shoot him the second he turns his back on me."

I took a hesitant step forward but the glare I received from Seven froze me in my tracks.

"You know, I wasn't completely forthcoming about how I got my name," Choice admitted with a wicked smile. "I sometimes give people the choice of how they wish to die."

Seven lowered his head to the ground as if asking for a quick death and Choice nodded appreciatively. "That's fair," then stepped to the side, gripping his sword in two hands. "What was that saying you told me earlier? You only needed one trick I didn't know?" he laughed and raised his sword over his head and swung down.

Sevens fist shot out, his fingers spreading wide and a large essence shield exploded into existence, deflecting the blow and leaving Choice completely off balance and confused.

Seven stood and spun so fast he looked like a blur. In one motion he grabbed the sword, wrenched it free and continued his spin to end up behind Choice, facing the opposite way as he slammed the sword in a backwards motion. It entered through Choices back and protruded from his chest as he was left staring at us in shock, blood bubbling from his lips as he fell to his knees. "I only need one technique that you don't know and your speed counts for nothing," Seven responded as the other man fell face forward to the ground dead.

Lynnay jumped and cheered, running out to hug Seven as Matches and Deffy clapped gleefully then turned to walk down the road in pursuit of other entertainment.

"Like finding a pair in her panties I did NOT see that coming," Quill observed in amazement.

I walked over to Seven who was quickly following through with Choices wishes, loading him onto the horse and sending it on its way.

"Did you watch closely? Did you learn?" Seven asked in a serious tone.

"I did but Quill had to point out what was going on so I could follow it better."

He nodded to this. "So you knew I could have won at anytime?"

I frowned, "Umm, I didn't know you would win until you won if I'm being honest."

The look he shot me was full of disappointment. "My original strategy was to go slower, using moves from the cheim to allow him to use as many different varieties of techniques as he had in his retinue so you could learn. I let him stab my foot to show you the power of mental fortitude and to always expect the unexpected. It wasn't until he pointed out your little misspoken term that I realized I could also use this as an opportunity to learn as well and try out my new technique. It was risky, I had to let him knick me a few times but I was much faster than him even without the essence. Once I was allowed to draw some in he had sealed his fate."

He stared at me and realization dawned on me. "So you were hiding your true speed the entire time! We had our suspicions but weren't sure. But thank you. I did learn a lot."

He clapped my shoulder as if congratulating me on some accomplishment even though he had just won the sword fight. "But never do what I just did. Always try to end it as quickly as possible, expect anything, and never gloat over a victory you have not yet earned." He shook his head. "I gladly put a few notches on my blade because of that.. personal pet peeve of mine. Arrogance serves no purpose but to make us fall harder when we do." He gave me another knowing look. "And at some point we all do."

I nodded to his words as he continued to go on about certain things I should have noticed and why he did them and what I should do if I encounter something similar. I listened intently as we continued on our journey.

CHAPTER 19

Faith is also important but for me I had no specific religion to claim so instead decided to create my own personal holy trinity of mind, body, and soul. Everyday I read, write and study. The mind is the cockpit of the soul. The more technology I can give it, the further it can go. I also eat healthy and exercise. If life is a test, I want as much time as possible to succeed and grow. Lastly, I meditate and pray. Meditation is an excellent way to expel negative energies and praying is great for your faith. The more you talk to God, the more responses you're likely to get.

The weeks came and went as our quest went on, only stopping at small towns to get a good night's sleep and spread the word. My training moved along quickly as Seven realized I was a fast learner. Quill got his karma stone dagger and both of their shield creating abilities improved vastly but he was particularly good at shifting the essence from limb to limb as quick as a thought. But it didn't matter how much I tried and demonstrated, neither could replicate the attacks I could do. They simply could not see or feel the flows like I could.

I paid off my debt to Lynnay plus interest and found myself growing very fond of her. I knew my place wasn't here. I knew nothing could ever really come of it but we cannot control what we desire and I was as weak as an infant on its birthday when it came to her.

We had just stopped for the night, her on the ground next to me, head on my lap as the fires spasms and crackles mesmerized us into a state of revery.

"Yeah, we have symbols and things like that surrounding our births too. Umm, lets see, one of mine is the sixty nine symbol, like the yin and yang. And then there's my astrological symbol, the crab. And I do technically have three different nationalities which is crazy and shouldn't be possible. That's the only thing that comes to mind that would really make me different then anyone else I know I guess." I finished explaining to Lynnay who was drilling me for answers on my origins to see what set me apart from others.

"Well you're not like anyone I've ever met," she whispered, finally giving up on the pursuit and turning back to face the flames. "There's something completely different about you I can... feel it. And you treat me like I'm the same as anyone else. Like I had a normal job or have a normal face. Usually there's an awkwardness when people talk to me. They treat me differently because of how I dress and how I look," she paused and I took the time to speak as I fidgeted with her hair.

"We are all people. Some of us had very different lives and came from different places. Some of us have cracks and some of us are shattered but nobodys perfect. I think... Well what if we all came from the same soul? Continuously put back into life as someone new. So that guy who just stole from you, he was you in a different life, raised differently, taught differently, treated differently, different looks, different brain. All these things affected who he was and how he behaves and that's the only reason he's different then me. That means if I was in his shoes, I'd do the exact same thing. Make the exact same choices because we are all just different versions of the same soul. We are all just... people. Does any of this make sense?"

She hugged my leg tightly but didn't look up. "No. Not really but what about men and women? Can you be both?"

"Yes, that's my point exactly! It has to be obvious there's not actually different sexes in the afterlife right? It's probably just a sort of polarity between the masculine and feminine and they can enter in as either, not just the one they line up with. Masculine souls in female bodies and feminine souls in male bodies. Gender is just another variable to test who we are. Am I losing you still?"

"Not completely," she answered slowly in contemplation. "But what about the fact that some people are just born the way they are before any influences at all?"

"I think if you do something wrong at a higher level or maybe if you didn't learn or accomplish whatever it is you were supposed to in this life then you get sent back. Like reincarnation. That could explain how a kid is born knowing how to play the piano or is extremely advanced at math or stuff like that." My conversation with the Sovereign popped into my head. "Or maybe they're just more attuned to the Alls' vortex of knowledge. The variables are almost infinite." I shook my head, not completely confident in what I was saying. "It's just a theory though."

She chuckled at me. "It's ok to be unsure. Nobody knows for certain. I just thought you treating me differently in my head. Maybe it was because I couldn't see your eyes..." She trailed off as she turned to look up at me and into my blindfold. "Your eyes," she said again and this time with a bit of shock and wonder. "Take off your blindfold!" she commanded and moved to do it herself.

I caught her hands, "Lynnay... I."

"They're glowing," she snapped, "and it looks like their colors... shifting. Somethings wrong! I need-"

I patted her hand and shook my head, pulling away slightly. "There's nothing wrong. I need to tell you something then I'll show you my eyes," I reassured her while she sat back in confusion. I struggled with where to start so decided to just start with the worst of it. "Lynnay, I don't think we can be together, you and I."

Her head jerked back like she got slapped, tears forming in the corners of her eyes as she tried to play it off. "What makes you think I'd want to be with you anyway? And what the hell does that have to do with your eyes?" She stood and pulled out of my grip as anger bubbled to the surface to hide her true feelings.

"No. It's not like that." I shook my head in frustration and grabbed for her hands, taking them and pulling them to my lips for a kiss. "Let me start over. Pretend like I didn't just say that ok?" She nodded and some of the anger left her face. "I have feelings for you... umm, strong feelings but I'm not from this place... or this planet. I'm not from here like you. I'm from a place called Earth. I still have a body there and everything. I can feel it... tugging me back when I close my eyes. It's why I never sleep. Or need sleep for that matter because my real body is sleeping in a different world right now. The world I'm really from."

"I've heard some doozies before but this takes the cake. If you don't want to be-" she cut off with a gasp when I removed the blindfold.

"I was told your kind calls me an unshackled," I explained softly. "Sooner or later... I will have to return to my body so you see... we can't... I mean..."

"How long?" she asked and I knew what she meant.

"I don't know how much longer I have. I've already been here for so long and I feel no different but I think... what if my body is unresponsive? Like in a coma and time is moving there like it is here? My family would be worried or maybe... maybe they'd pull the plug." I spoke hesitantly, at this point in my life I wasn't sure if that was even a bad thing or not but this place made it different. I tried to reassure myself that I would feel slaps to the face or know when someone was talking to me and it just hasn't happened yet. Her face didn't change as she continued to wait for a straight answer. "If I had to guess, not long. But if you'll take me, I promise you every second I have in this place."

She bent down and put her face a few inches away from mine, her eyes searching mine as she spoke. "That's more than anyone else has ever offered me. Of course I will," then she kissed me. "Buddy," Deffy interrupted from nowhere, startling us both. "I'm ready to make that crossbow arrow now." Lynnay sat back down on the ground next to me and we both stared at him where he stood, face down, eyes watching the fire. "I can't fall asleep anyway and I think it will help though."

"Ok Bud. If you're ready, come sit over here and I will walk you through what we were thinking."

He came over and sat cross legged by Lynnay. She wrapped her arms around him holding his head to her chest like she was holding her own son as I rummaged through the pack to find my drawing then showed it to him.

"You see how it looks very similar to a regular one? Except notice the stone is only visible at the tip and I put these barbs here about halfway down the shaft. Hopefully this will prevent it from going all the way through or being pulled out easily."

He didn't move his head from her embrace as his eyes darted around the paper. "The stone stops at the barb and thins out?" he questioned.

"The hope is that if someone tries to pull it out, it just breaks instead, leaving the karma stone inside and basically making them powerless. Does this look like something you could do?"

He stared at it for a few more seconds then bobbed his head cheerfully. "Sure. Do you want it to say anything though?"

"No. I don't think that's-"

Lynnay cut me off. "Deffy it's for me and if it's going to be the first of its kind then I would like something on it. Something so that generations to follow will always know who it was made for." She batted her eyelashes at me sarcastically then laughed. "I've got it, how about, 'With all my love, Lynnay.'"

"It's for you so sure," Deffy responded happily. "But can you put me in bed when I'm done though? I'll probably be really tired."

"Of course Bud. You don't even have to ask."

He smiled and the world's clarity intensified the second he slapped his hands together. His eyes shut and pure concentration washed over his face while he worked. I heard his call again to the essence and realized it wasn't almost like he was talking to the universe itself, he actually was. Metal, gem, wood and ink were demanded of the particles in the essence and they shifted to align with their masters intent. The whole process took less than a minute which is longer than I've ever seen it take him, other karma stone weapons included. When he finished his head sagged into his chest and Lynnay gripped him, pulling him back to her chest. I grabbed the dart and set it aside while I lifted him from her and brought him back to his bedroll near Matches.

When I returned, Lynnay held the dart out in front of her as she inspected it. "You know," she started. "This is the only of its kind. I could probably buy a kingdom for how much this would be worth. I honestly doubt there is anything in the world that would ever make me want to shoot it at someone."

I laughed at her honesty and she handed it over. "Hopefully you never have to then. That way, when this is all over, you can sell it and buy your kingdom," I agreed as I inspected it carefully, spinning it between two fingers to where it read 'WITH ALL MY LOVE, LYNNAY' and smiled. "Queen Lynnay does have a nice ring to it," I agreed, handing it back.

"Not as good as Empress Lynnay," she offered, loading the dart into her crossbow's bottom chamber and then setting it back with our things.

"How about Lady Lynnay? Is that a title royalty gets?" I wondered aloud, my lack of knowledge with it all as plain as day on my face.

She smiled seductively at me that pulled me closer. "Only if she's married," she warned, raising an eyebrow. "But right now the only word I want to hear before my name is oh," then she started to kiss my neck.

"Oh Lynnay?" I asked and realization dawned on me as I laughed awkwardly.

"Yeah, kind of like that but let's put a little more passion into it shall we?" she asked, grabbing her bedroll and heading towards the privacy of the trees.

Time was distorted to me here. I could count the days and weeks but perceived them differently then the rest of the people I was with. It's hard to explain what I myself couldn't grasp and even though I knew a week had passed to me it felt like a month and the oddity of it all caused me to stop keeping track. I was assured daily when I shut my eyes that I still had a body to return to and that is all that kept me going.

It wasn't until we came to an intersection that Seven finally spoke up about what Sway had told him. I was staring down its cobblestoned path marked on both sides with posts and ropes, officially making it the best maintained road we've seen yet.

"I need help with my decision," he finally offered as the others made their way to a nearby clearing for lunch.

Quill had come back from the river with a goose and two fish so it was aiming to be a relative feast.

"I don't always have the right answers but I'm always here to try," I said in earnest.

"That is all I request. It's about my conversation with the Sovereign," he stated flatly, staring down the same road. "She informed me that my brother rules now and that my father passed some time back." He cut off and an awkward silence fell over us. I knew his father had tried to kill him and the torment he endured by his brother at constantly being forced to play that evil game had caused him so many scars, both internally and externally. But they were still his family.

"Seven, I'm sorry..." I stuttered out, unsure of exactly how he was feeling and what to say.

He waved my comment away. "I feel nothing for my father nor brother anymore. The problem is, he's a problem. A big problem. He deals with Enlightened in slavery now. He rules with fear and constantly makes public showings of executions to anyone who opposes him or even angers him in any way. But that's not the worst of it," he added and I seen sorrow in his eyes causing me to realize the seriousness of the choice he must have. "My..." he swallowed and started again. "My younger brother has gone missing. I think Victor may have done something to him but it wasn't included in my question so Sway wouldn't tell me. She said I had to find that answer on my own." He let his head sag backwards, turning his eyes to the sky to prevent the tears from forming. "What if he's still alive? What if he needs me?" he cut off when I put my hand on his shoulder.

"I don't think a God can die. I'm sure Aam can wait a while longer for you to do what needs to be done." He turned to face me and I nodded. "And this DOES need to be done," I reassured him.

He nodded back, determination now on his face. "If I remember correctly it should only be a day or so if I'm quick. I will go there, save Able, deal with Victor and head back the second I'm done." He paused for a second to think. "Give me four days. If I'm not back by then, leave and continue on with the quest as planned. I will catch up."

"Won't you have lunch with us first?" I asked, gesturing to where Quill sat plucking the goose.

He shook his head. "I think not. I want this done as fast as possible."

I smiled at him and offered a hand. "Good luck my friend and safe travels."

He shook it with a grip like iron. "Many thanks. Continue your training and be sure to keep your blindfold down as much as possible." I laughed, realizing I hadn't done that since the night I took it off for Lynnay. "At least during the day. We aren't too far off yet and people are going to start trickling in from all directions soon."

"That's fair enough," I agreed, securing it back in place.

He nodded to me and spun on his heel, moving into a jog quickly as he made his way off.

I was watching him disappear into the distance as Quill walked up. "Where's our silver tongued poet gone off to?" he asked, still plucking at the goose.

"He has some personal matters that require immediate attention," I replied, heading back to the others. "He'll be gone for four days and if he takes longer, we are to proceed as planned without him."

Quill didn't seem too displeased with this news at all. "Well good riddance. More for us," he smirked, holding up his prize with a toothy smile.

I laughed and bent to start the fire for Lynnay who was just bringing up another bundle of wood as I relayed to the others everything that had just happened.

CHAPTER 20

*F*ate is a concept not everyone subscribes to but it's real. Whether you believe in it or not it affects us all, some in only little ways, others in monumental proportions. Think of it like this, you are all in cars driving towards your destinations. Some of you are behind the wheel, switching lanes, speeding up, slowing down or even turning onto new paths as God helps you guide yourselves. Others go through life with the seat reclined, feet out the window, music blaring, oblivious and uncaring to their purposes in life. They have no clue where they're going and rarely do they like where they end up. It is these people, like me, who have let fate take the wheel.

"Father please!" his daughter begged in desperation. "If Lord Victor finds out he'll kill you! Then what are we supposed to do?" Wheels furrowed his brow in determination, refusing to meet his daughters eyes while he hefted his sack onto his shoulder. "Now Lilly, I gone and already said I would and ain't nobody gonna

say that Wheels was a liar. I won't have that on my name."

"But father-" she tried to respond but he cut her off with a look.

"If helping people's a crime then I reckon I'm an outlaw." His face softened when she started to cry and he put a gentle hand on the back of her head, pulling her into an embrace. "Besides, today he's on the opposite side of town at one of those fancy parties he's always having. I'll be in and out afore I ever get seen." She hugged him tightly and he kissed her forehead. "Me brothers one of them. Your own uncle. He's as innocent as the rest I reckon. It's not right, them starving to death like that for no good reason for sumfin they ain't never done."

He pulled out of the embrace and pushed her aside with one arm and headed away.

"I'll be back by suppertime," he shouted over his shoulder. "And what if you ain't?" came the reply and he missed a step,

not knowing how to respond.

'Then you be a good lass an look after your youngers,' he instructed and disappeared down the hill before she could say more.

Wheels approached the pit where the prisoners were kept. It was a large circular hole dug into the ground with its floor dirt and its walls a smooth edgeless concrete of some sort most likely to prevent climbing. The occupants all sat along its edges where they were chained to the wall by their necks.

He walked around to the ladder that sat at its rim and spun it over, lowering it quietly then dropping his sack down beside it. He hefted his leg over then started to make his descent. About halfway down the ladder buckled in the middle under his weight and he fell to the ground with a crash.

"Wheels? Wheels is that you brother?" a voice asked a few shackles down.

He sat up and clutched at his ankle. If it wasn't broken it was surely sprained and badly judging by the amount of pain he was in. "It be me," he acknowledged with a wince, trying to stand but finding it too unbearable.

"What are you doing here? You have a family to be looking after."

"That I do. I already lost my rose and I won't be losing a brother too," he declared, rolling onto one knee and trying to figure a way to best maneuver.

"It was cut almost all the way through in the middle," the man chained closest to him observed. "Sorry friend, but this was a booby trap." He inspected the piece of ladder he held for another moment then offered it over. "For a crutch," he suggested and Wheels grabbed it.

He pushed himself to his feet, propping one of the broken steps under his arm and tested his weight on it. It held so he hobbled his way over to his sack and opened it.

"There's plenty for everyone now," he spoke loudly as he started to pull out some loaves of bread and hand them out. People started to notice and an excited murmur began to spread. "I've brought plenty of water too," he added and made his way over to his brother.

They hugged and his brother held him at arm's length for a moment, completely baffled. "Wheels you old fool. You damned yourself just to give us a meal?"

He stuck his chin out. "It ain't right. A mans gotta have morals I suppose. I ain't gonna let happen to my brother what happened to my Rose." He fought back the emotions when he remembered hearing the news his wife had starved to death while she awaited trial. She was charged with conspiracy to start a rebellion over a comment she had made on the new taxation laws.

He slipped some jerked meat out and handed it over with some bread. "I'm here now and there ain't no turning back. You'll eat and so will everyone else."

He started to do a slow circle of the other prisoners, handing them some food and letting them take a drink one at a time. He stopped when he came up to a young boy and asked him what he was accused of.

"I told my friend someday I was going to kill Lord Victor for killing my Pa and now I'm to be tried for plotting a murder and treason," he whimpered with eyes full of tears. "I miss my Mum."

Wheels handed him a piece of the meat and patted the lad on the shoulder. "Don't give up hope just yet," was all he could think to say.

When he was finished, he plopped back down to the ground in front of his brother, sending the rest of the water and food out to each side to be passed around.

The two stared at each, not knowing how to proceed now that they most likely shared similar fates. "Harvest was good this year," Wheels offered.

"Really? Even with so little rain?"

"A dozen barrels of wheat alone. That's why I can afford to spare a few loaves."

His brother nodded his head appreciatively to this. "Then it was a good year. Is it that air-agaition system you copied from that Sovereign's garden?"

His eyes twinkled at his brother as he responded. "Aye, it be just that."

"Pa?" a voice called from the top of the ledge. "Pa why are down there? What happened to just dropping it over the edge?" Lilly's voice sounded frantic. "And is that the ladder all busted up?" Fear spread throughout her and she began to search around wildly.

"Now Lilly I came down here to have a meal and chat with my brother just in case it was my last chance. Now get on home and mind your youngers. I'll be home shortly." He tried to be re-assuring but the lie caught in his throat as he tried to force it out.

She stared at him disbelievingly. "And how do you plan to get out? The ladders no better than kindling."

"Never you mind. Now get on home afore I get myself into a fit with ya!" he warned, trying not to be too loud.

"She set her jaw in determination as their gazes locked. "No," she stated plainly, defiance in her eyes.

"Now Lilly-" he started but she walked off before he could continue. "Fool girl," he mumbled. "As stubborn as..."

"As her father," his brother chuckled gently and took a drink.

A moment later she returned to the lip with a long rope in one hand and flung one end of it over. "Other ends tied to a wagon. Should hold just fine," her voice was smug with her success.

Wheels shook his head. "Lilly please. It ain't no use. I can't climb that rope. I busted up my ankle pretty bad in the fall. I'm beggin ya Lilly bug, go home and mind your siblings for yer Pa." Tears flowed freely down her cheeks at the news. "Not with- out you!" she vowed. "Tie it around your waist and I'll pull ya up."

"Lil..."

"Then I'll find someone who can! Please Pa! Please!"

Wheels stared up at his daughter and fear froze him in place as two soldiers walked up behind her. One grabbed her by the hair and wrenched her head back as they surveyed everything that was going on.

"What have we here?" the one with the beard asked. The other looked to the rope, the broken ladder, the prisoners who all sat eating and then lastly at Wheels, taking it all in with a frown.

"Reckon it's a prison break. Feller here went down with food, no doubt to get their strength up before they left. Probably trying to pick the shackles that's the only reason someone would go into the hole ya think?"

"I reckon," the other agreed.

"They didn't count on the ladder to be rigged up," he chuckled. "Ropes rigged up too but I doubt they noticed that yet." He shoved the girl over the edge and she screamed. "You can stay in there until Lord Victor hears of this." He turned to his companion. "Fetch him at once. Everyone knows attempting to escape before the trial is the same as a confession of guilt." He smiled down at the helpless people. "And we just had ourselves a mass confession. Reckon that makes it execution day," as cries and exclamations erupted in the pit.

Wheels held Lilly's hand tightly as they were marched to the edge of the fighting square which was now used as the execution grounds. Lord Victor stood statuesquely, hands clasped behind his back while he watched the prisoners being marched in.

His dark eyes squinted in the sun and the brown hair that curled to his shoulders swayed gently in the breeze. His elegant long shirt was of a fine red velvet and offset his white pants that were tucked into his polished boots.

"Pa," Lilly whispered, pulling his father out of his glare. "Daisy and Spins are just over yonder watching," she pointed out, gesturing with her head to where the two sat at the edge of the stands.

It took Wheels a moment of searching over the large crowd that had gathered before he finally saw them. Their eyes met and Daisy pointed to the bushes just behind them.

"Pa," a whisper came from tall shrubbery. "We're ascared Pa. We don't know what to do." The fear in the voice of his second oldest caused tears to well up in his eyes.

"Get yerselves on over to old Gems place. She'll take ya's in. Tell her she can have the farm and that there's enough harvest to last out the year and then some," he whispered gruffly.

"But Pa," the voice came back frantic and desperate.

"I love you son. Maken sure your brothers and sisters know that too. Now get going afore you end up in line with us.``

There was a rustling sound and a few minutes later Axles' face appeared next to those of his siblings. Lilly stared at them.

"Go," she mouthed silently and Daisy shook her head defiantly. "They ain't leavin Pa."

He watched them with a heart full of sorrow. "I see that. Ain't nothing good gonna come from them watching this but there ain't nothing we can do."

"I love you Pa. I'm sorry I-"

"None of that. You ain't got nothing to be sorry for." He squeezed her hand. "I love you too Lilly bug."

Their conversation was cut off by a loud voice amplified by a screamer. "Ladies and gentlemen, quiet down," Lord Victor commanded in a tone that didn't leave any other option. "Before us we have sixteen prisoners who were awaiting judgment. During this time it was brought to my attention that today these people were caught in the act of trying to escape, a crime that forgoes trial and admits guilt, the penalty of which is immediate death," he informed flatly. Cries rose up in the crowd, slowly building in anger and frequency. "IF," he shouted, "anyone would like to join them by all means speak up now and I'll gladly add you to the line." The crowd went as silent as an empty church. "No one?" he waited for a moment. "Then I shall continue. Two others have been brought up also as leaders of this attempted prison break and their trial shall be held here and now."

He made a gesture and a guard shoved them into the square. Wheels propped himself on his daughter and hobbled his way over to stand in front of his Lord.

Victor's eyes first looked at his ankle then burrowed into his, full of spite. They held a sort of self centered wildness only found in someone who was always accustomed to getting their way their entire life.

He kept his gaze locked onto Wheels and addressed him first. "These crimes were witnessed by none other than my trusted guards. They stated they found you in the pit supplying drink and food to the prisoners. Do you deny this?"

"No," Wheels answered loudly and the crowd murmured.

He turned to Lilly next. "And you were found securing a rope to help after the ladder was broken. Do you deny this?"

"No," she answered truthfully.

"The pair of you were clearly attempting to help prisoners escape. Do you deny this?"

Wheels stopped Lilly with a gesture. "We do," he protested, producing another slightly louder response from the crowd.

"You do?" Victor marveled in surprise. "And why is this?"

Wheels straightened and tried to hold back his anger while he spoke. "I've seen how you treat the people in those pits. You let my wife starve to death down there while she awaited a trial for bogus charges she didn't do." His voice was getting louder and more venomous as he went but he tried to conceal his rage. "I wasn't going to let something happen to those others or my brother. It happens too much to too many innocent people."

The ruckus grew even louder as the crowd voiced their agreements. Lilly flew through the air after the backhand connected solidly with the side of her face and Wheels crumbled at the sudden loss of his human crutch.

"I always hit where it hurts the most," Victor snarled, standing over him in a rage. "Now watch what your defiance has earned you." He beckoned a guard over. "This man's entire family is to be brought up on charges of treason. Find them all and bring them here at once. Men, women and children," he commanded and the guard saluted then ran off to do as he was told.

"Please no," Wheels croaked as Lilly scooted back over to try and help him. "I have no other family."

"If that was so you wouldn't be so upset with the order." Victor stood and anger washed over him as the crowd's banter continued to build the longer it went unchecked.

He raised the screamer back to his lips and screamed at the top of his lungs. "SILENCE! Do you not agree with my proceedings? Do you not like the way I'm running my kingdom?" He walked to the center of the arena, chest heaving with a fury he couldn't contain as he searched for someone to release it on.

"Well? Is there none amongst you brave enough to be heard?" He put a hand to his ear as if waiting and the crowd fell dead silent as their Lord threw another one of his famous tantrums.

He was the best sword fighter in the land and everyone knew it. He made sure they did by holding public displays of his accomplishments at every opportunity he got. Balls, luncheons, holiday parties, they all ended up with someone dead and sometimes even mutilated beyond recognition depending on his mood.

One man had almost beat him when Victor stumbled, far too drunk to be fighting and ended up taking a sword through the shoulder. He ended up killing the man then having his entire family executed with him.

He stomped his way to the center of the ring and planted his sword tip first in the ground then made his way over to it's edge, trying to find someone to make an example of, to show them his skills and power as he offered them the challenge no one ever took anymore.

"What other Lord is there who makes offers like this? Is there none among you who will accept my challenge? No rules, no counter terms or stipulations. Beat me with a sword and it's all yours. Beat me with a sword and you can be Lord." He stared at the men in the front row one by one hoping one of them was stupid enough to accept his terms. "Or are all of you a bunch of worthless cowards?" he spat.

A large man stepped out of the crowd and onto the sands. His pack held an array of different weapons that stuck out at odd angles. He lowered it to the ground as he pulled out a giant great sword made of beryl that flew his masters mark at its base, signifying who he was to the crowd.

"I'll play sticks for blood brother" Seven announced and Victor's eyes went wide with fear and shock.

"I accept those terms," Seven announced, sticking the tip of his sword into the ground near his brothers, sealing the agreement. "Witnesses?" he bellowed and the crowd erupted as every single one of them tried to claim the responsibility.

"You!" Victor shouted, voice frantic. "You're supposed to be dead."

Seven pulled his blade out and took a step back, the crowd going silent in an attempt to hear what was being said. "I killed only the name," he pointed out, stretching each leg, eyes watching his brother closely. "I have a new one now or have you not yet heard it?"

Victor grabbed his sword with a quick jerk and stepped back also. "Yes, yes, everyone hears the heroic deeds of Seven, master of all weapons. Had I known it was you, I'd have sent my army for your head long ago." Victor swung his sword in giant arching loops back and forth as the two started to inch closer to each other. "The way I see it, you wasted time learning those other weapons. Time I spent mastering just this one beyond what you can ever even dream of."

"We shall see brother." Seven lunged with a quick thrust that was easily defended then stepped back once again.

"Don't call me that. You're no brother of mine," Victor hesitated then stood straighter, a smile appearing on his face. "You still don't know, do you?" he asked in realization, then let out a laugh of pure glee. "Oh I've always wanted to be the one to tell you this. You're a bastard born of rape. That's why father hated you. That's why I hate you, Able hates you and even poor mother. She tried so hard to love you but looking at you only ever reminded her of that nightmare and who you really are."

Sevens blood went cold as the words hit their mark and so much of it made sense to why he was treated the way he was. But Able too? Something stuck him, he had said hates, as in still does. He's alive!

"Where is Able?' he demanded, voice low and threatening.

Victor glared at him. "He's exactly where he needs to be to cure the insanity that has overcome him."

"If he's hurt, so help me I'll make you beg for death."

Victor laughed openly at the threat. "Come now. While you played hero I trained everyday." He took a tentative step forward, gaining confidence. "I am not so easily fooled by your tricks as last time. Sticks for blood!" he screamed, jumping forward with a high arcing blow and Seven caught it easily, signifying the true start to their contest and the crowd erupted as steel on steel began to ring in the air.

The amount of skill and dexterity Victor possessed truly astonished him. There was no exaggeration in his boast about practicing daily with the same weapon, he no longer had any doubt in the truth of that.

He watched his brother carefully, always looking for an opening or a mistake he could exploit but none came. His thrusts struck out with perfect precision, his blocks and parries were exactly at the right spot at the right time for an easy counter.

Victor slashed parallel to the ground from the right, leading tip first so Seven had to hold his sword wide to block. He did and his brother pivoted in a blur with the exact same attack but this time from the left. He blocked again. The same attack came again but now from the right where it had started and Seven immediately saw the pattern.

Left, right, left, right, the same blow over and over coming perfectly executed and lightening fast with no chance for a counter. Seven thought, trying to figure out the strategy and it hit him. Each swing is causing him to block at the furthest point from both his left and his right, maximizing the range between the two movements. He's using my great sword's weight against me perfectly. At this rate my stamina will be depleted in a mere matter of moments.

He narrowed his brow as he tried to think of a viable strategy to get himself out of it. He hopped back and his brother moved with him, only a half a heartbeat behind.

"Do you see now? Do you see the folly of your ways?" Victor cackled gleefully with a mix of maniacal rage. "You are already starting to slow. Fitting you picked my fathers heirloom to fight me with. It betrays you and the false blood that runs in your veins."

Seven swept a foot out during a block and his brother hopped over it with the grace and agility of a cat, never missing a beat with the timing of his swings.

"A child's trick," he laughed again. "A blind man in a cave could have seen that coming."

Seven could feel the strength leaving his arms at the constant left and right motion he was stuck in. The crowd must have noticed his predicament and they started to murmur as their hopes dwindled.

Seven hopped back and again his brother was right behind him, his swings never relenting. Another hop, another follow. Seven smiled and his brother raised an eyebrow.

"Oh did you find an opening? A mistake perhaps? Let's see shall we."

"Sometimes in the game of chess, if your opponent is completely dependent on his queen, the best strategy is to trade them. This way, you gain the greater advantage."

His brother frowned, still contemplating the words as Seven hopped back once more. Victor followed instantly but this time Seven made no effort to block. Instead, he thrust his sword forward, straight out and into the meat of his brother's left arm. His dominant arm, producing a surprised yelp as Victor's blade bit deeply into his own left shoulder.

He stifled a yell of his own as they pulled away from each other to survey the damage.

Victor must have realized his disadvantage against a larger foe, larger sword and only his off hand for defense. "Coward!" he spat out. "Your tricks won't save you here. You'll see I'm just as fast with my right as I ever was with my left."

Seven stuck the sword into the ground as his brother spoke, shaking his arm out and giving it precious time to relax and recover.

"That could be possible... either way... maybe now we're both about even in speed but my reach and strength are far greater. Speed isn't everything... brother." He antagonized and Victor's eyes narrowed in rage. "Or," Seven continued before the other man charged. "It could be.. that I'm just just... stalling for time. Allowing my arm to recover and taking away yet another advantage you may have had."

Victor looked to where his arm swung freely at his side and the sword in the ground. He sucked in a deep breath in a fit of anger and charged wildly, the sound of steel once again ringing out loudly.

Weariness shown on both the men's faces as the fight continued. The blood loss they both suffered only added to the exhaustion each now felt.

"You truly are a master of the sword my brother," Seven praised honestly, finding the level of skill he now faced remarkable. "If only you had mastered your mind as well."

"What is that supposed to mean?" Victor laughed, the two slowly circling each other as they waited for some strength to return.

"It means if you weren't so corrupt I wouldn't have to kill you now." He shook his head. "You could have helped us tremendously on our quest."

"To hell with your quest and to hell with you! This fight is not over until you're dead!"

"No brother," Seven speculated, stepping back to put his right elbow up level with his head and placing his blade on the leather guard of his bad arm. Victor made a confused face. "I suppose it's only logical you don't recognize this stance. Spearmen are so far beneath your station you never took the time to study them."

His brother laughed at the words. "You think using a greatsword like a spear will give you an advantage? It's only basic sweeps and thrusts. Easily defended and easily countered against."

Seven shook his head, a grin spreading across his face. "That may be so... but I'm not holding a spear. I'm holding a sword, an exercise I've practiced often to blend the two into one unique and unseen offense that is quite effective."

Victor bared his teeth at the claim and growled, "let's see it then. Let's see a technique so rare only the almighty Seven himself is its master."

Seven paused, "I forgive you brother," he whispered then shot forward like a flash.

He thrust the sword across his guard like a spear and Victor knocked it away. He used that momentum to swing it low, causing his brother to leap. He let the blade hit the ground and yanked it back up, using it as a deflection. It sliced through his brother's shin and he yelped.

Seven jumped back and reset the sword on his arm. He leapt forward with another thrust but this one was a feign, only executing it halfway to force Victor to try and block. His brother's parry met nothing but air as it swung by and Seven sat motionless, patiently waiting for the mistake he knew would come. As soon as it had cleared the tip he finished his thrust forward.

The maniacal man's eyes went wide when his sword missed and he tried to roll away but the great sword bit deeply into his side. He stumbled back but Seven was on him.

He pulled back and thrust again and again and again as his brother struggled, trying to block and parry and retreat from an offense he had no clue how to counter.

The last thrust Seven let get deflected but he pushed his hand forward anyway then yanked the blade back across his brother's wrist.

Victor screamed, dropping his sword to the ground and a deafening roar came from the crowd as Seven held the tip of his sword to the other man's throat. He stood over him just staring as the crowd's cheers turned into a chant.

"SEVEN! SEVEN! SEVEN!"

Victor's eyes narrowed as he sat on the ground with two useless limbs and he screamed to be heard, "guards! Shoot him!"

A few of them stood where the prisoners were held, stunned expressions on their faces. One held a crossbow on his back and he snapped out of his shock, bringing it around to the front and taking aim.

Seven extended his hand towards him, fingers pressed together as he pulled in some essence from the sword. They opened and a giant shield loomed into life between him and the man.

The guard fired anyway but the bolt was deflected harmlessly away as Seven stared at the other man to let it all sink in.

Victor's eyes went wide with rage when he realized he was only being toyed with. "With those powers you could have killed me at any point!"

Seven bent lower as his wounds were slowly closing from the essence he held. "I wanted you to go to the next life knowing when we fought I gave you the greater advantage and you still lost," he admitted then plunged the sword into his chest, watching the madness drain from his once brother's eyes as his life faded away.

The noise from the onlookers was louder than anything he'd ever heard as he strolled over to pick up the screamer and address the crowd.

One of the men congratulated Seven, telling him he was going to be the best leader this kingdom had ever known.

Seven shook his head at the comment. "I cannot be your leader. I have other matters of more importance to attend to," he spoke loudly into the screamer and the crowd murmured in confusion. "Aam needs our help. I'm forming armies and looking for any and all willing to help."

"I'll go," a man yelled from the line of prisoners. "If you free me."

Seven waved a hand at the comment. "Yes, yes, as of now any of the prisoners who haven't actually physically committed a crime are to be set free."

There were cries and cheers of joy as the guards set to removing the chains and families rushed to embrace one another.

"Who will lead us then? How is this kingdom supposed to survive without a leader?" someone shouted.

Seven held the horn back up to his mouth. "Where is my brother Able? He can lead you. He is the rightful heir."

A guard stepped forward, eyes down as he spoke solemnly. "M'lord, I was ordered to put Master Able in the Tower of Tears."

Memories flooded back to Seven from when he was a youth and heard stories of the place. It was a cell at the very top of a turret that had triangle spikes on its floor and a ledge around the entirety of the ceiling that held oil and was always burning, both of these to inhibit sleep. The prisoner was thrown in naked and only given one meal a day until he went crazy. It's said the only people to have lasted longer than a few months had gone so mad they were found gleefully eating their own feces or talking to drawings they had made with it on the walls.

"M'lord," the guard repeated and Seven pulled out of his thoughts. "That was nearly a year ago."

Seven froze, his heart sinking at the implications. "Take me there now!" he commanded and they spun in unison.

The guard turned the key in the lock and Seven pushed him aside as the door slowly swung open. The room blazed brightly and there was a naked man huddled in the corner mumbling to himself.

Another guard came hustling up and held out the bundle of clothes Seven had ordered him to fetch.

"The food and drink?" he asked.

"It's on its way M'lord," the guard responded with a bow and Seven nodded, turning back to his brother and taking a cautious step forward.

"One bite, two bites, and one more is three. There's a cake for you and a pie for me. Let's eat it all down before the cook does see. One bite, two bites and one more is three," his brother sang gleefully in his madness as he fingered at a groove in the brick without turning.

The song hit a soft spot with Seven when he remembered where he had heard it before. Able used to sing it when they'd trade stolen sweets with one another. It was the closest thing to poetry he'd ever cared to learn.

And now his brother recited it in his delusions.

The big man shook his head sorrowfully as he recalled the next line, speaking it softly. "One bite, two bites and one more is three. I got a butterscotch and a mint stick for free, but would you trade your cake for all this candy? One bite, two bites and one more is three."

His brother whirled and their eyes locked, neither speaking as they assessed each other. Seven noticed his hair hung shoulder length and stuck out in every direction, matching his unkempt beard. His body was thin but still somewhat muscular which was odd with him only getting one meal a day.

He stared intently at his brother's green eyes as the mad man spoke to him. "Who are you?" Able demanded.

"I am the one you taught that song to long ago," he responded regretfully and held the clothes out to his brother.

Able made no move to grab them. "What game is this? How do you know those words? The only man that knows those words is long dead." He shrunk back to the ground and put his face in his hands. "Oh no. I really am going mad now. I knew it was only a matter of time." He mumbled to himself as tears formed in his eyes.

So he thinks he's not mad yet Seven speculated to himself, unsure exactly how to handle his younger brother's fragile mind. "Able... it is me. The real me. You're not crazy... about that part anyway but..." His brother stood back up, unsure if he believed the words or not. "Who else have you taught that song to? We only sang it together when we stole... well, when I stole. You were quite young and only ever stole anything for me a hand- ful of times.," he recalled with a gentle frown. "Now please put these on. It's time to go home."

"Home? To Victor? I'd rather die!" Able spat. "The murder-ous-"

Seven took a step forward and held his hands out to calm his brother's emotions. "Victors... dead," he announced, trying his best to be reassuring. "I killed him in a fight for the kingdom."

Able glanced at the blood on Sevens shoulder and then back up. "You expect me to believe you killed Victor in a fight?" he laughed. "Only the legendary Seven himself could pull off some-thing like that and I don't see him anywhere do you?" He shook his head. "And I'm supposed to be the one who's mad. You-"

"Abe?" A feminine voice called from back by the stairway. "Abe are you freed yet?" It came again but this time a lot closer.

He took a step back, confusion plastered on his face. "What's the meaning of all this?"

A tiny slip of a girl came flying around the corner and crashed into him with an embrace and a kiss. "Oh Abe we did it! You're finally free. This man killed him Abe. He killed Victor and now he's the ruler. He said you're his brother Abe, but you never told me that Seven was your brother. It's him, Abe. He's 'the' Seven from all the stories and I ain't never seen no one fight like that, no never. He's like an Enlightened and.." she babbled excitedly as she reigned kisses onto the baffled man as he stared in stunned bewilderment at the news.

"Summer... I... he... Please." He begged, gently pushing her off in an effort to speak.

"Get dressed so we can get out of here Abe," she suggested, handing him the clothes then turning to grab the food on the tray the man behind her was carrying.

He pulled the pants up and threw the shirt on as he continued to stare at his long lost brother.

"So it's true? The reason we could never find you is because you hid in plain sight? Just under a different name?" he shook his head.

Seven gave him a curious look as he responded. "How is it that you seem so well? You should be mad?"

Able laughed and slapped his brother on the shoulder. "We have a lot of catching up to do but first, let us leave this place and never come back."

A rare smile appeared on Sevens face. "Agreed."

They separated to wash themselves up and met in the dining hall where a very small banquet had been set up. His younger brother looked like a new man when he sat at the table, freshly shaven, hair tied back and smelling of soap and spices.

"I have so many questions," he greeted with excitement. Seven met his eyes, "As do I."

Able grinned and pulled a chair out as Summer took the seat next to him. "Seven this is my fiance Summer."

"A pleasure to meet you," he said and inclined his head. "Oh God, where is my etiquette "Lord" Seven?" He emphasized the word. "Please forgive my blunder."

Seven waved the comment way. "Think nothing of it. I plan on giving you the kingdom within the day so the title is not mine to claim but yours if you'll have it."

Summer gasped and Able froze in place. "You're... serious?"
"Of course. I have far more important matters at hand and have no inclination to rule a kingdom. I'm only here to find and end that lunatics reign." Seven noticed a slight flinch when he mentioned Victor. "I'm sorry for your loss."

"You truly are a remarkable man," Able praised, ignoring the apology. "I would gladly accept the kingdom if you'll give it but I won't let your acts go unforgotten. We'll make it a new kingdom with a newname and a new flag and your symbol will be at its center. I will erase everything that man was and did from this land if it's the last thing I do." He shook his head at the thought of all the things his brother had done and caused throughout the lands. "You have no idea how right you were. He was a lunatic. The last few years after father passed he slipped further and further into his insanity. He threw me into the place to 'cure my madness' he said when he found out I was to wed Summer, a girl of common birth." The two shared a look, a whirlwind of emotions passing between them as they did.

Seven cocked his head, "so how did you last that long without going mad?"

His younger brother looked back at him with a sly grin, placing a hand on his fiance's shoulder. "Summer here risked everything for me." He turned to face Seven more directly, voice getting serious. "The first few weeks were hell. That place... it's hard to explain. The continuum of time echoes off those walls turning yesterdays into tomorrows and nothing ever changed... it's like time stops completely." Summer squeezed his arm lovingly, bringing him back to focus. "I thought I was mad when I first heard something clicking on the rooftop until after a while an arrow flew in carrying pen, paper and jerked meat. From my view on the floor I didn't even notice the gap in the roof but it makes sense. Burning that much oil constantly you'd have to vent the place."

Seven turned to the girl with a surprised expression, "you can shoot a bow?"

She grinned around a mouthful of food. "Taught myself right quick I did. The first night they locked him up there I snuck over and climbed the big elm closest to it. When I got near its top I could see light coming from a hole along its side and knew what needed to be done" she cut off and took another bite, Able staring at her in adoration.

He turned back to Seven. "It progressed from there. One night I was scared and embarrassed out of my wits when an arrow came through with a note that simply stated. 'I'm climbing in. Hold this rope like the love of your life hung from its other end." She smiled at her own joke and he laughed. "It turned out she was small enough to fit through. She brought me food, blankets and umm, things to help with the smell," he stated uncomfortably. "She had thought of everything."

"Well it weren't nothing really," she admitted, wiping at her lips with a cloth. "Old smithy had built most of the brick work in these parts anyway so I asked him how big he thought the opening was and he told me they were all standard size, same as you'd find on any place burning torches. So I found one and crawled through it with ease. Soon thereafter they pulled the guard off except to bring his meal and my visits began," she boasted proudly

Able leaned over and kissed her cheek. "She really did think of everything. It was her idea to act mad if someone ever came in to check in hopes they'd see I lost my mind and free me. That's why I was singing." He ran a hand through this hair. "No one ever came though. To check. We were giving up hope and that place was wearing on my mind. Even with everything she was doing for me"

Seven finished chewing his food and swallowed, addressing his future sister in law. "My brother is truly a lucky man, you sound like a remarkable woman."

She blushed deeply, "thank you M'lord."

"Think nothing of it. Besides, this kingdom deserves a Lady of your moral character to help... think of everything," he winked at her.

"A lady?" she muttered softly then her eyes grew to the size of saucers. "Oh my God I'm to be a Lady!" she realized in shock and wonder.

Able chuckled at her. "It appears so my love. It appears so."

The dinner ended and the casual conversation and small talk turned into Seven telling Able about his mission to help Aam, about our party, me, the Sovereign, everything.

"You're still the Lord here. You can order the people of these lands to do as you command."

Seven shook his head. "I will do no such thing. What the peo ple and armies of this land do is your concern."

"Then I'll order them-"

"No." Seven cut him off. "Keeping people in line who don't want to be there is a burden I don't need and can't make time for.. I need willingness and loyalty to our cause. But I do have a yielder and will also accept mercenaries who need money."

Able put his hand to his chin and scratched it. "I won't order anyone but I can offer my pay plus yours to the army and I bet every last one of them would join. They should still be disciplined enough below their commanding officers to help keep others in line."

Seven didn't respond to this as he remembered something else, turning away to face the fire. "There is one more thing I forgot to ask you."

Able sat forward at his brother's sudden change in emotion. "Go ahead," he offered gently.

"Victor told me... I am a bastard. Born of rape on our mother."

Able let his head fall at the words. "I believe that to be true," he acknowledged. "For years I refused to give up on the search for you. They told me you had run away after trying to kill Victor and stole the heirloom and all sorts of other nonsense. When they first told me that, I assumed it was a lie like the rest but there were others... older friends of mine who I trusted... They were there when the caravan was raided and mother was taken. He kept her as a personal slave that he planned on killing once he had had his fun but she got pregnant very quickly and to giants, blood is blood above all else. So she was treated like royalty until one day she was able to escape." His eyes looked up, full of pain at having to bring him this bad news. "I never gave up on you brother. I didn't care what they called you or who your real father was. You were and still are, my family." He placed a hand on Sevens shoulder and the big man looked up at him.

"And who am I?" His voice came out flat as he tried to hide his emotions. "Who is my real father?"

Able shook his head at the name. "Your real father... is General Dag."

Sevens world spun as he tried to come to grips with this new turn his life had just taken. General Dag was one of the most powerful and ruthless leaders in the world of the giants. If he knew who Seven was he'd use his entire force to track him down and force him into servitude or death if he refused his blood rights.

The two stared at each other, neither one knowing how to proceed. There was a crash as the door burst open and a guard stood there huffing.

"M'lord," he announced frantically. "You may want to come see this."

The brothers addressed him at the same time. "See what?"

"Well M'lords, we don't right know. It's just that...somethings happening in the sky."

They glanced at each other in confusion then sprinted to the nearest balcony. They burst through the door and immediately saw what the guard was referring to.

The eclipse on the sun was just about to start as it cast its eerie glow on the world but that wasn't all that made it odd.

Able stepped up beside him, "what in God's name caused that?" he asked, completely dumbfounded.

Seven stared to where the clouds raced across the sky from all directions of the horizon to a single point, like a black hole was sucking them in. "I have no idea," he admitted aloud, the two completely puzzled as to what they were witnessing.

A small gust of wind tossed their clothes about then continued to increase, whipping up dust and small rocks as it gusted about.

"It's blowing with the clouds," Able shouted to be heard. "They're going the same direction."

Seven didn't respond, concern spread across his face while he tried to puzzle out what was happening. A tremor ran through the ground, small at first and then increasing in intensity the longer it went, forcing them to crouch to maintain their balance.

"Abe!" Summer yelled as she flew out to latch onto him. "What's going on?"

"I don't know." he shouted back, the three of them watching as the sky started to glow in the direction everything was feeding into.

Not a black hole, it's like a star is being born, Seven thought to himself as the shaking intensified further.

"What in the world could be doing that?" Able yelled again. "For Aam's sake what the hell is over there?"

The ground calmed and the wind and clouds stopped simultaneously, the far off area flashed so bright it looked like a sun exploded as everything returned to normal.

Seven sucked in a breath as he realized what direction they were facing and Able looked at him as he regained his footing.

He spun to face his brother. "That is the direction I came from," he announced in disbelief. "That is where I left the unshackled."

CHAPTER 21

Freewill is the greatest gift mankind never uses. You are under the impression because you are able to use basic logic to come to conclusions and make choices that this is your freewill. There is another thing on this Earth that shares these same qualities... A computer. Completely devoid of freewill a computer will always respond as it is programmed to. Its hardware wired in different ways to produce different results, different programming offers different experiences. And this is what you are as humans, biological computers programmed to grow, think, and respond in different ways as you interact endlessly with your environment and until a time you chose to be more than just a physical being, you will always be slaves to your bodies.

"Did you ever fight your brothers though?" Deffy asked, one eyebrow cocked inquisitively like he suspected I might lie to the question.

I laughed as I poked at the fire with a stick. Ever since I had told him he could be my family, be my brother, he's made a point of nearly every day asking me about what it's like. Now that we were halted and waiting for Seven, his curiosity had been relentless.

"Yes Bud, I have fought with my brothers." His other eyebrow raised in surprise. "But I'd never fight you. I promised to always protect you, remember?"

He frowned as he tried to figure it all out. "But why did you fight them though?"

I smiled. "All brothers are different and sometimes they do things to hurt you or embarrass you and you end up fighting. But they're still your brothers. You still love them." His face was still scrunched up and he stared at me in confusion. I looked around. "I got it. Pretend like your brother was Quill," I started to explain but he cut me off before I could finish.

"Oh, ok. It makes sense now," then he turned to walk back to Matches.

"Now wait just a bloody minute here," Quill complained, sitting up and taking offense at the conversation. "What was ya going to say?"

I held my hands up in protest. "Just how lucky Matches truly is," I suggested with a feigned look of innocence.

The giant laughed at his brother's expense and then plopped to the ground with a thud, sticking a giant toe in his mouth.

"Is he biting his nails?" Lynnay whispered into my ear.

I didn't look up from where I still sat poking at the fire in boredom. "Don't know. Don't care." "He is!" she exclaimed softly.

"Wanna go check the hooks?" Deffy asked him as he tapped the giant's shoulder. Matches shook his head as he continued his work. "I'm gonna go by myself then," he warned, trying to bait the other man into going but getting no response.

"I should go with him," I offered, "I don't like him near that raging river all by himself."

Lynnay wrapped her arms around my neck, holding me down in my seated position. "Or," she whispered, her tone becoming seductive, "we let him go. I'm sure Matches won't be far behind. Quills drunker than a clam in a wine barrel and most likely won't last but a few more minutes and we... can sneak off... for some alone time." She finished the offer by kissing my cheek repeatedly, slowly trying to make her way to my lips.

I kept staring forward as I watched Deffy. "Hey Bud," I yelled and he turned back to me, "Why don't you just wait for Ma?"

He shook his head. "I'm not afraid. I don't want the fish to have to suffer and I wanna do it before dark though."

I breathed out loudly, feeling guilty about knowing I should go with him. "Well be careful next to the water. You could be swept away before you ever had a chance to scream." He smiled and turned to walk away. "Promise?" I yelled before he got too far.

"Promise," he responded without looking back.

Lynnay's kisses started reigning in again. "I can't watch him... do that," she pressed, trying not to look at Matches. "It's ruining the moment. Let's just get out of here now please." She spoke this like it was more of a demand then a request then grabbed her bedroll and began to head in the opposite direction towards the trees. I shook my head then stood and followed after.

"It's just now touching the sun," Lynnay observed. "Not bad timing if you ask me."

I pulled my shirt back over my head. "Yeah well we're a great team, what can I say?" I replied, rolling the blanket back up then offering her my arm.

"Umm, Buddy can you hear me?" the small voice chirped in my ear and I nearly jumped.

"Deffy, is that you Bud?" I asked rhetorically, knowing it was but caught off guard by the boy.

"Yeah but I want to say thank you for being my brother." He sounded scared and I frowned in confusion.

"Of course Bud, what's this all-"

"I don't think I can be your brother no more cause Crest seems awful mad and I think he wants to kill me."

I froze in place, Lynnay following suit as her ear was close to mine as she eavesdropped on the conversation.

"Deffy no ones going to kill you," I tried to reassure him as I started to run back to the camp to make sure it wasn't a joke.

I entered the clearing to find Quill sound asleep and Matches still sitting at the fire, staring at it absently.

I moved faster and Lynnay started to fall behind as I sprinted past the pair making my way towards the river.

I evened out my speed in an attempt not to lose the bug to the wind as it whipped by. "Who's Crest and are you still at the river Bud? I'm on my way now."

"Crest is the Enlightened I just had to make stuff for. He's the one that took me."

Fear and anger both flooded through me and I found myself running faster. "Deffy try to get away. Run towards us," I offered, trying to think of ways he could stall.

Memories came back of all the conversations I'd had with Seven about the leaders of the Favored Few. They were very powerful Enlightened with almost no care for the beings below them. He also told me that they would usually rather kill any yielders they found than actually keep them and that Deffy was lucky to still be alive. He must have not displeased them yet.

It all clicked together and I was left with no doubt of who Crest was or what his intentions were.

"Deffy just stall him!" I screamed as I pulled in essence to move even faster.

There was some screeching sounds but they cut off as the bug was whipped from my hair by the speed at which I was now moving.

I reached the river and followed its bank towards the place we had put the hooks before. I stopped and searched frantically until I heard some voices coming from directly above me.

I spotted them floating in midair and I froze. It was the first time I'd ever seen a being with red eyes and the color caused fear and I doubted my abilities.

There were two of them and both of their eyes emitted a soft light that gave the impression of blood, swirling and glowing. They both wore similar clothes and had similar features. Straight jawlines and clean shaven faces. One of the only differences I noticed was the one who held Deffy was clearly upset.

The other one looked down and noticed me, then nudged his companion to do the same.

"Deffy I'm here Bud. It's going to be ok."

"I'm... ascared." was all I could hear from his reply.

My mind raced with what I could do. I pointed a finger at the two and felt my voice change again automatically as it had before. "Let him go. I'm the one that took him. Your quarrel is with me."

The one holding him shrugged, a sword of essence forming in his hand then he jammed it through Deffys chest and I heard his gasp.

I froze.

My heart dropped from my chest and tears filled my eyes as I watched him casually flick his wrist and send Deffys body into the raging waters where it quickly disappeared.

I took a few steps towards it, willing to risk it all and jump in but was cut off by the two Enlightened who lowered themselves into my path.

"If you're talking, I wonder what you're hiding behind that blindfold," one of them tried to inquire but I didn't have time for their questions.

"MOVE!" I screamed.

The Enlightened glanced back at the river then turned back to face me. "He could still be alive, you know," he grinned. "But not for long. What I want to know is why you care so much?"

My eyes burned behind the tear stains on the blindfold and my chest heaved. I felt helpless. I wanted to cry, I wanted to scream. I wanted to save Deffy and I wanted them to die. I didn't just want the power to kill them... I needed the power. ALL the power.

I sucked in with every fiber of my being and this time it answered me in a torrent. The essence flowed into me like a tempest, the amount beyond anything I'd ever done or felt before. I felt my body start to fill beyond its capacity and knew I was flirting with danger.

I didn't care.

I continued to call it in and started to focus it into one of the attacks I had learned from the Enlightened on the road.

The sphere instantly took shape and I continued to call as much as I could. I could feel my body burning away at the amount that flowed through me but it wasn't enough. I needed more. The world went dark as clouds whipped in, blocking out the light from the sun. I screamed in my madness and put another hand up to feed the attack with two hands, knowing it wasn't enough yet.

The wind whipped and I found myself in the eye of a tornado as the essence was ripped from the world around me to answer to my demands. The ground started to shake violently and I watched as the river splashed about, flooding the lands all around it as destruction enveloped everything.

I wasn't done.

I could hear crashing and rumbling but could no longer see anything but the blinding attack I held in front of me and the two beings it was intended for. They sat with arms covering their faces as they struggled not to be swept away by the tempest that was now encircling us. I was ripping the world around me in two with my anger but I didn't care.

I was ripped out of my chaos by the sound of a feminine scream and instantly realized my foolishness. I stopped calling the essence and released everything I had directly at the pair as I screamed out my wrath for their actions.

Two hasty shields popped into existence but they were far too puny and weak compared to the devastation of the attack I had just unleashed. The world reverberated with the explosion and the sky lit up with a light so bright it blinded me even with my eyes shut tightly.

I tried to calm myself, frantically searching as my vision cleared but there was no sign of the two beings. I suddenly realized I was suspended in the air but had no recollection of how I did it.

"Where's Deffy?" I heard Lynnay call from behind and I turned my head, watching her limp up visibly.

It was then my Earthen body tugged at me with a force like I had never felt before at this point in my life. My conscious grip slipped drastically and I felt myself falling from the sky as I desperately tried to fight it. I had to do everything in my power to resolidify my hold on this reality, I knew Deffy still needed me.

I crashed to the ground but the pain was distant. I forced myself to keep my eyes open, to keep my awareness in this place as long as I could for the sake of the boy.

I watched Lynnay fall to the ground beside me and gently try to lift my head. "No," I pleaded. "Leave me. Deffys in the river. Go."

"They threw him in the river!" Lynnay related to Quill and Matches who only nodded as they sprinted by, continuing on down the bank.

"Are you ok?" She asked, turning back to me.

I could hear genuine worry and concern in her voice but this wasn't the time. "I have to fight it. My real body... is pulling. I need you to go... help find him."

"I'm staying with you!" she tried to make it a demand. "PLEASE!" I screamed. "I need to concentrate."

She rocked back for a second then stood and ran off.

I leveled out my breathing and tried to will my heart rate to slow in an attempt to calm myself. I rolled onto my side and fought the sensation with everything I had while I listened to the sounds of my friends yelling grow more and more faint.

It was well past dark when I caught up to them. I had finally regained control enough to venture out and search but hadn't made it very far when they came walking back.

"I'm sorry," Lynnay whispered with a shake of her head at the hopeful look I had given her.

Quill came up beside us, "Ma won't stop looking. The boy could be anywhere with hows you shook the river right out of itself and all over the place. I even found fish scattered around in the woods."

I let my head fall backwards, staring at the sky. "We extend our wait by one more day to continue and search over every square inch of this place. This also allows Seven more time to catch up so it seems the only logical option."

The other two made no argument and we went and lit a fire to make torches with. The night went on as our search continued and I walked in a daze. All of this wasn't supposed to be real to me yet there was nothing fake about the emotions I felt for Deffy. I couldn't understand what I did wrong or why my promises always ended up broken.

I watched Matches as he ran to and fro, a pained look in his eye as he searched around desperately. Lynnay always stayed near me and Quill used some essence from his dagger to sprint ahead and cover more ground.

It was near noon the next day when Lynnay finally approached me, eyes down as she flicked her thumbnails together nervously. "We can't look forever," she spoke so softly it was almost inaudible, and I stopped. "Quill went to get Matches. We have to eat, to rest. We have to continue on."

I spun on her, the anger and frustration must have shown in my face because she took a step back. "I don't give a damn about the fate of some God who has lived a pampered life. I'm NOT abandoning the search for him."

I could feel the tears forming in my eyes and she stepped up to me, placing a hand on my jaw as her thumb brushed them away. "Whatever you choose, I'm with you. You know that... but Quill said he saw the blade pierce through his back.. we're not looking for Deffy, we're looking for his body."

Her eyes stared into mine as I no longer wore the blindfold during the search. I replayed it all in my head and knew Quills observations must be right.

"He also scouted down the river a ways. He said it branches off so many times we could never search them all. Some even look new, most likely a result from... your..."

I waved her comments away knowing she was at a loss of how to explain what I had done.

"Let's go eat and rest. I'll make up my mind by then."

Quill put a few of the fish he had found on the skewer and stuck them over the flames. They crackled and spit while our small party sat quietly in our mourning. Matches would randomly scream or beat his fists into the ground and Quill would have to go over and help calm him.

"It's ok Ma. He was young so he's going to go to a better place," he soothed, holding the giant's head to his chest. "Don't give up hope. Maybe in another life you'll meet him again."

The big man sniffed loudly, the words seeming to calm him. He looked up to his brother, a question in his eyes as he touched his forehead, lips and chest.

"Alright Ma. I'll lead a prayer." Quill stood and gestured for Lynnay and I to follow suit. "Ma would like me to lead a prayer for the boy. I'd like yall to speak with us." He put a hand to his forehead, "with my mind I will think for you." He touched his lips next, "with my mouth I will speak for you." He touched his chest last, "and with my heart I will love for you." He held out his hands to each side and Matches and Lynnay mimicked him so I did as well.

"Aam please share our words with the boy named Deffy who you have so recently received home. We offer up these words in hope that he will receive them and hear our final goodbyes." He shifted his weight from foot to foot then continued. "Deffy, it's me Quill. I know we didn't know each other all that well but you were like a brother to me brother and well, I guess that makes us brothers too. Take care young one. You've always got a place in me heart." He turned to Matches and the giant stood, wiping his eyes.

"Brother," he moaned, then sniffled, "Love brother!" he wailed again, this time more loudly then collapsed back to the ground and sobbed silently.

Quill put a hand on his shoulder and turned to us.

Lynnay spoke first. "Deffy... We've only known each other this short time but you were probably the most genuinely good kid I'd ever met. I wish I had more time with you. Good luck on whatever comes next for you." She stepped back and let me speak.

"Hey Bud," I started and my voice came out in a croak. "I'm sorry I didn't keep my promise. I didn't mean for it to happen..." I felt Lynnay rub my back and it helped me to continue. "Bud, if I can really do things like this, go from place to place or whatever I'm doing. I will find you. One way or another I will find you and give you the happiness you deserve. On my soul I promise this. I will never stop trying." I wiped my tears and we all sat at the fire. "Goodbye brother. Until we meet again," I whispered into the flames.

We ate our meal in silence, packed our stuff and decided it was best to continue on away from this place in case anything else came to investigate. We hit the road shortly after but at a much slower pace, trying our hardest to just make it closer to dark and return to a normal sleeping pattern. When we finally halted for dinner it was all they could do to stand and continuing was out of the question. I ordered them to rest and sat up by myself to tend to the fire.

That first night alone was terrible. Several times I had to talk myself out of turning around and going back to look. I pleaded to this God Aam a lot, hoping for an answer while I stared at the giant ring in the sky that only an eclipse of that size could produce.

I had convinced myself that I hated this Aam and decided it would give me all the answers I would demand from it when I reached it. What kind of God lets a boy who was so good and pure die so young and so tragically? What kind of God creates life and then refuses to interact with it or give it direction or purpose?

But that was then and my ignorance was massive. Like a toddler crying because his square peg didn't fit in the round hole, I wasn't advanced enough yet to see all the angles and like so many of yours are, my prayers were selfish and irrational. If you've ever found yourself losing sight of your goals, losing your religion or losing God because of unanswered prayers remember this; you are pleading to a being who can see through time and no matter how much you want that job, wish that person would notice you or don't want that loved one to die, the finish line is a soul and God's intention is to get everyone there. You have no clue what your future entails and I implore you to remain faithful.

But the funny thing is, sometimes your ignorant prayers are the ones that get answered first. The regret they will bring you can offer the best lessons and the greatest change.

CHAPTER 22

Freewill is your soul's ability to change your programming and nothing more. Making choices has always been based upon your physical self and the environment you were raised in. Tastes, allergies, promiscuity, hobbies, humor, anger, happiness, all of it. What foods you like, jokes you find funny, coordination, physical appearance, attractions, you respond to these exactly how you are programmed and when you do, your physical self rewards you. It pushes out certain chemicals causing a degree of ecstasy and this encourages you to repeat the process. It is this feeling that births addictions and anything can cause it, not just drugs. Sex, food, gambling, plastic surgeries, even adrenaline junkies and video games can cause this release and become overpowering. Addictions are demons of all sizes and truly I say to you, if you don't take the time to control them, they will take your time and control you.

More time passed and we drew nearer our destination. Travelers now filled the roads with every cross section and merge having a few different races and people on their way to heed the call to arms by Seven. I was forced to keep the blindfold on almost nonstop and was singled out as the leader of them all until my master arrived. A responsibility I had no care for but was left with no choice according to Quill, the symbol on my face marked me as the next in rank behind none other than Seven himself.

"It's not long now until we reach the fields," Quill was saying, his speech slurred with the amount of alcohol he'd had throughout the afternoon. "We should come up with an initial plan on how to proceed until Seven shows." As part of my new promotion, the first and only thing I did was make him a general and he took to it with purpose.

As he talked, I watched Matches trod along silently, head down, eyes full of hate. He hadn't taken Deffys death well and it was only a matter of time before he exploded. I could see it in the way he stared at the other travelers we encountered.

"We'll continue on with the initial plans but we probably shouldn't mention we no longer can pay as we have lost our yielder." I shook my head to fight the emotions that thinking of Deffy brought back to me. "For now, let's find some people with leadership or battle experience and start promoting them. We'll assign them each their own divisions of troops and then have them repeat the process until we have small little bite size sections. We'll keep the giants and Skane on Targog field and the rest on Darmon Plain."

Quill raised an eyebrow. "And you think the giants will listen to ya? I doubt they care much for that symbol."

"Well Sway said herself she was showing up and would most likely be bringing that other Enlighteneds master. She can bridge that gap if needed to keep them informed and in line."

"If not, we're going to war before we even want to and not with the right enemy," he stated in a flat tone, then took a sip from his flask.

"I could pretend to be one. An Enlightened. Show them my eyes and command them."

"Might work. We'll have to wait and see how that all plays out," he uttered, stumbling slightly but catching himself before he fell.

I snapped my fingers to grab the attention of one of the men who had joined us but struggled for his name. "Hey, my man, do you think you could have the scouts find a place large enough for us to break for lunch then pull everyone to it?"

"Yes sir," he shouted, snapping off a salute by pounding his fist to his chest, then spun and ran on ahead.

"And stop calling me sir!" I shouted back.

"Yes sir!" he answered again and I shook my head.

Lynnay chuckled. "What's so bad about leading men for a good cause?" she asked, resting her head on my shoulder.

"It's not me. I'd feel like... a hypocrite." She stared at me, not understanding and I let out a sigh. "I wasn't exactly the best kid. I always had a problem with authority. Most authorities anyway, I had like two people in my entire life who actually deserved their position and that I respected. I always hated how just because their station or title was above yours it somehow made them feel better than you. People are people. If you're a boss, teacher, officer, judge, regardless of age, race, looks, religion, anything. You have to remember that we are all just... people. Does that make sense?" She didn't look up from where her head rested and I felt her squeeze my arm slightly where she held me. "I knew you were different," she praised softly. "It makes perfect sense. That's why you're going to be such a good leader. You treat them like people, not subjects or whatever race they are. You treat them equally Seven may have a hard time taking over when he gets back if you keep it up," she swung her hips into mine as a gesture.

"Good God don't say that. Don't speak it into existence please," I warned with a laugh.

The same man that had run away before came running back a few minutes later eating a carrot. "Sir. We have found an area big enough to fit our entire retinue, including the new people who just joined. It's just ahead. Stacks would like me to inform you he has acquired more fish, geese, and wild vegetables, enough to make stew for everyone."

I kept a straight face as I stared at him through my blindfold, trying to recall his name. "Dog is it?"

"It's Mutt sir."

I shook my head, "Mutt, the next time you call me sir, I'm going to take that carrot from you and shove it somewhere it won't taste nearly as good."

He smiled from ear to ear. "I'll be sure to let my wife know sir," he offered in a sly voice.

"Let your wife know? What?" I asked in confusion. "About our date sir. She tends to get jealous."

I lunged for him but he hopped away laughing.

Lynnay snorted in amusement. "I told you they're starting to like you."

I bared my teeth at her menacingly, "I already warned you," I threatened, doing my best to act intimidating.

"Oooo, what ya going to do? You got a carrot hidden somewhere I don't know about?"

Stacks the halfman sat next to me by the fire. His small wiry frame gave him all the appearances of a child until you looked at his old wrinkly face with gold wired spectacles that sat at the end of his nose.

I had put him in charge of rations and gathering only after he volunteered for it, stating he owned a store and was good with numbers and such things.

He took to it with a passion.

"I ordered one of the new arrivals to the gathering party without your permission I'm afraid. He had a bow with him and knew how to use it and with our numbers growing, I felt it best."

I waved the comment away. "It's fine, Stacks. I only care about big decisions, not all decisions," I told him, repeating what I had already said to him before.

"As it is, I will let you know anyway."

"What are our numbers at? Or do you not have an accurate count still?"

"Accurate is no longer possible, instead it is now an estimate as people continue to pour in non stop from all directions. We'll need someone to be in charge of all new recruits. Find out where they best fit and send them there. For that matter, we'll need divisions to start forming, hunters, gatherers, arms swords, arms spears, bow and crossbowmen, females can cook and clean, youths can-"

"Stacks," I interrupted.

He looked up from where he had everything we could ever possibly need written down. He did take pride in his work, that much was evident.

"I only asked about our numbers."

He pushed his glasses up his nose and they slid right back down. "Well the last good estimation I recorded was just over four hundred people so far." I looked around and the number seemed a little high. "We are still waiting on the scouts, the hunters, the gathering parties and the messengers to return. For now I've just been mass grouping them until we start with the formations."

I looked around again and the number made a little more sense. "Well let's get this done with while the food is cooking shall we?" I stood up, "Dog! Here boy." I whistled loudly.

The man stood from the next fire over with his tongue out panting and I rolled my eyes. "It's Mutt sir," he corrected, then pounded fist to chest.

I stared at him. "Dog, will you grab two others and run to tell the stragglers to get a step on it. We are starting at once."

"Will do, sir." He saluted again and spun, pointing to two others and they all jogged away in different directions.

I addressed the rest of the camp. "Can I get your attention? I would like everyone to line up so we can go through you one at a time. If you know you're a spearman or a swordsman or whatever, please make your way to the areas we have designated. They are clearly marked." I gestured back to the areas I was referring to. "Everyone else, line up, let's get this over with so we can eat."

A few people cheered to that and with the help of Quill and Stacks, groups were split apart, people were promoted and divisions were formed. Quill gave them some tips about separating skilled with unskilled to help the learning curve and I made the decision not to seperate anyone because of their race or species. You were what you were regardless of anything else.

We had just finished and I was sitting to eat when a messenger came running up to Weeds, the man I put in charge of the new recruits. His face went ashen and then he turned to look at me, walking over instantly.

"Sir."

I sighed, no longer in the position to deny the silly designation. "What is it?"

"It's giants sir. They're here... to join. They're being brought forward as we speak."

I turned to Quil and he shrugged. A few moments later the two giants came lumbering up. They each stood over ten feet tall, had bald heads and round bellies making them look like twins. In fact, the only difference between them was one had a large tree branch with a broken and sharpened shield strapped to it forming an ax and the other had a giant sword as long and as wide as a man.

The terrified messenger that was leading them pointed to where Weeds and I sat and then went in the opposite direction.

They approached us in a few long strides and looked around at the camp. "Maybe this was a mistake," the one with the sword's voice rumbled out, low and deep. "None here can fight." His companion bobbed his head in agreement.

"You two are the first giants to join us," I informed them, trying to appear unaffected by their size.

They eyed me, one of them reaching into the pot and grabbing the giant spoon, bringing it to his nose to sniff at it.

"By all means have some. It's for all who gather to help Aam." I turned, "Dog, will you fetch us two... buckets?" I asked, trying not to insult them by offering them the tiny bowls the rest of us used.

"No," he grumbled, freezing Mutt where he stood. He bent down and picked up the entire pot from the fire then raised it to his lips.

"Don't!" I shouted, trying to use a tone that implied there would be consequences. "There are still people who need to eat. It's to be shared-"

"Make more," he suggested with a shrug and then began to raise it again.

"If you drink that directly from the pot, so help me I'll-" "You'll what?" the other asked with a mischievous smile on his face.

Matches stood slowly, anger bubbling on his face and he struggled to control it. The two giants showed surprise at this as they must not have seen him among us.

"Ma, now don't you-" Quill started but cut off as Matches palm gently engulfed his face and pushed him out of the way like a tall weed.

"Mixed blood," the one with the pot started as he watched him approach. "Who is father?"

Matches didn't respond as he stopped directly in front of them. He was only slightly shorter with his face about equal with their neck. I noticed as he reached out and gripped the pot with two hands and pulled it away, surprising the other giant before he bent and put it back on the fire.

"Who is father?" it repeated and Matches turned back, smiling from ear to ear, then hit him so hard with a right hook it sounded like a tree snapping. The giant fell to the ground like a crumpled shirt and Matches spun to face the other as the entire camp went silent to watch the confrontation.

"Cousin!" it yelled, looking at his comrade and then to Matches. He lept forward to crash into the smaller giant but Matches was ready. The two locked arms and amazingly, Matches held his own.

Quill stumbled forward, two daggers spinning into each hand as he made his way to help.

"Quill!" I shouted, stopping the man in his tracks.

He turned back to me. "Me brother-"

"Is getting out some frustration at having lost his best friend. And on two people who not only deserve it but are probably the only ones here who could handle it and live." The two tugged and heaved, locked in their embrace, throwing random kicks, punches and headbuts at every opening.

Quill stared at them, still not completely convinced. "They're not using weapons, stand down."

He stood for another moment and then the daggers disappeared back to wherever they came from.

The larger giant started to get the edge on Matches, his size slowly wearing his smaller opponent down. Matches let himself drop to the ground in a ball but stayed on his feet while the other giant moved to grapple him again. Matches exploded upwards, his entire body behind the attack, a fist the size of a small keg leading the way to where it crashed into the massive nose of the giant.

The thing rocked back in a daze and Matches wasted no time. He reached back like he was attempting to throw a rock over a mountain except he balled his fist. The punch landed with a sound like cannon fire and the giant spun two full circles before crashing to the ground.

He stood over him for a moment, chest heaving as he made sure his foe wasn't getting up.

"You done?" I asked and he turned to look at me. He gave an uncaring shrug then walked back to sit and finish his meal.

Weeds spoke up then. "Umm, sir, should we, um, have them removed?"

I looked at him like it was the dumbest thing I'd heard all day. "For now just bind them. When they wake make sure they're calm and then I want them given provisions and promoted."

"Promoted?" he asked in disbelief.

"Promoted," I repeated. "These are our only two Giants. Tell them to run ahead and form ranks on Targog field and then explain to them how. Tell them I'll send a messenger periodically for reports and instructions and not to interact with any other human except the one who calls himself Mutt."

There was an audible groan from my left that made me chuckle as he spoke. "Oh sure, now he gets it right." I heard him complain.

As time went on our ranks started to swell beyond even any good estimations as volunteers poured in in large groups. The roads were packed with all sorts of beings who had responded to our quest and I even met my first Blien.

Its tall slender body was completely hairless and of a dull bluish color. It held a head with an elongated skull and two gi- ant slightly slanted eyes. She wore skin tight pants and a tube top styled shirt that barely covered her chest.

She approached me with an elegant gate and a smile, batting her eyes at me as someone pointed her my way. I blushed and noticed Lynnays hands go to her hips from where she watched us from the side.

Her voice was soft and her words drawn out like she was sighing as she spoke. "I am Takka. Are you the one in charge?"

"It's Fin, and yes," I greeted, trying to act casual as Lynnays stare bored holes through the side of my head.

"Excellent. I have been sent to you to seek instructions. We Blien are already gathering on Darmon plain. There are others gathering there as well, including Skane, but we do not mix with the serpent scum."

I had heard Skane were one of the most ancient free thinking species in existence, half snake, half humanoid, but most were wicked beyond belief.

I nodded and gestured for her to walk with me, offering my arm. She took it and I could almost hear Lynnays eyes roll while she stormed away.

I chuckled and then started, "they are supposed to be at Targog field. I will send a messenger to clear that up." I tried to think of a way that would be possible and looked around for an idea. As I did I noticed Mutt go as white as a ghost and I laughed before I turned back to her. "Tell me, has anyone taken charge their yet?" "Yes, my husband Tattak is leading the Blien. I do not know the name of the ones leading the others but I do believe they each have one."

I nodded to this. "I will try to handle this myself. As of now, he will be promoted to General. I will send instructions on how

I want him to group up the troops by skills, rank, leadership, everything except race or species."

Her head turned and one side of her hairless brow raised, "there is a purpose to this?"

"Yes. From what I understand, giants and Skane in large groups are enough to put everyone else on edge. I don't want any more division apart from them. One massive army of all kinds should be enough to keep them somewhat... dissuaded from any irrational actions before our plan can be executed."

"And what is this plan?" she inquired softly, her hips gently swaying from side to side as we walked.

I shot a glance around hoping Lynnay didn't notice me noticing. "To be honest, it's not completely done yet. We are waiting to talk to Sway and see all she has to say and who all shows up then go from there. As of now, it's gathering armies and attacking the mythical beasts that are nearly impossible to kill." I purposely didn't mention the part about Seven and I trying to sneak in.

She rubbed a slender thumb against her thin lips in thought. "They are called the Timeless," she mentioned offhandedly.

I turned to her, "Why are they called that?" I asked, hoping to learn as much as I could about an enemy I knew nothing about.

"The Timeless are part of creation. They are the first things Aam made, sort of like mindless obeyers. They do not eat, they do not drink, they do not age, they simply obey. If a new world were created right now the first inhabitants would be them. To maintain order, build, destroy, whatever was required of them until the beings there could think on their own. Their power is immense, they are a very formidable foe indeed. Much of the Blien are excited at the thought of dying during this fight."

I frowned at this, "excited to die?"

She nodded, "yes, don't you see? Dying in the service of your God is the ultimate sacrifice. The rewards in the next life would be magnificent."

"Takka, you seem very knowledgeable. Thank you for everything. You're the first Blien I've met, are they all this smart?"

She beamed at my praise, "No, my husband is shaman and so it is my responsibility to be well informed when he asks for council. As for me being the first of my kind you've met, we live on the opposite side of the continent so I'm sure you will probably not see more until you've reached Darmon Plain."

I thought about this for a second, "then how did you guys find out about our call?"

"The rumors had arrived some time back but we were at a loss of what to believe. When my husband received a letter from a Sovereign, we spread the word and formed quickly to come. There are still armies upon armies marching in. We are just the first to arrive."

"I see," I responded, thankful for the aide I somehow knew had come from Sway. "I'm going to send you with a messenger to have a set of those instructions drawn up. I'll make a set for the Skane too, do you think it's possible you could find someone to deliver them for me?"

"I will do this myself," she offered, pride showing and she stood a little straighter.

"Very well," I replied, not wanting to question her judgment. I turned to where Mutt was walking and was surprised to see Lynnay clinging to his arm like Takka was to mine. Our eyes met and she stuck her tongue out at me, then turned back to the man with a laugh like whatever he had just said was the most interesting thing in the world.

"Dog," I called loudly and he broke away from her, approaching me with a salute.

"Yes sir?"

"Can you find Stacks and have him write up some instructions on how to form armies like we just did here please? I need two copies if you would."

"Yes sir."

"And Dog, one more thing," he hesitated and I glanced at Lynnay who had her arms across her chest in a tantrum at having lost her opportunity to make me feel jealous. "Spread the word that no one is to walk with or carry out any but the simplest of conversations with our beautiful Miss Lynnay here," I winked at him to let him know I was joking and he winked back.

"Great idea sir," he saluted again and then turned to wait for Takka.

"You!" Lynnay warned, storming her way over to me. "That's not fair."

I smiled innocently. "It's one of the perks of being in charge. You're the one that told me to take pride in it."

She turned to Takka next and the woman pulled off my arm. "It was nice meeting you Fin," she bowed, then made her way over to Mutt and the pair ran off.

"And you as well. Give my thanks to your husband and tell him I'll see him soon." I emphasized the word husband for Lynnay as we waved our farewells. I turned back to her. "Don't you think I'm a great leader still?" I gave her a toothy grin.

"No. You're the worst," she huffed out.

"But this way, I get you all to myself and I don't have to share."

She smiled and stepped closer, "Ok, I guess maybe you're not that bad."

"On the other hand, you were clearly trying to make me jealous and I can't have that added stress. I may have to make you travel with the women and children at the back."

Her eyes narrowed, "you wouldn't dare. You are the worst."

I laughed and offered her my arm in earnest and she took it with a warm smile. "That's what happens when people flirt with the woman I love," I teased.

"Love?" she gasped, then smiled from ear to ear and threw her arms around me. "I love you too! You are the best!"

I laughed as she kissed me. "I think you could be crazy. Your opinion of me seems to flip flop around like a fish out of water." She raised an eyebrow as if daring me to say something else negative. "But that just might be my fault," I added quickly.

The smile returned to her face, "Well lucky me. It looks like you are a fast learner," she smiled happily and we kissed again.

CHAPTER 23

Your programming contains more variables then you realize and there are some that are shared by everyone to some degree. Fear for instance, comes to you all in many different ways but the root of it is always the same. You think it's just the snakes, spiders, or germs that you fear. You even think it's death. The truth is, none of these things are what you really fear on their own because what you really fear is the unknown. What would that spider do if it got on you? What do the viruses that hide on that doorknob contain? What happens when you die? It is this uncertainty that enhances your fears and it's not alone. Not being able to understand something or someone can cause an even bigger problem then fear. When you fail to see things from outside you're own point of view, your own physical appearance, what you've experienced yourselves or what you believe, then this can bring you hatred. It is these two tyrants that are causing the downfall of men. Truly I say to you, understanding is the key to harnessing your freewill and evolving into something greater. You must realize that it is only uncertainty that brings your fear and it is ignorance that has birthed your hatreds.

There was still no sign of Seven as we continued on our quest. I found myself sneaking off at night while the army slept just for some time to practice with the essence. I also tried to replicate how I flew but no matter what I did or tried, I could not figure out what I was doing wrong. I just assumed it was because I didn't know how I did it in the first place.

I continued helping Lynnay shoot her crossbow as people poured in in scores. By the time Stacks had made a good estimation it was already time to do another.

I watched as gathering teams ravaged the land, cutting trees, harvesting fruit, picking herbs, vegetables and even flowers, leaving a wake of death behind us like a giant slug trail.

I found it quite unsettling when Mutt ran up to me one morning with the report that we'd arrive at Targog Field by just after lunch and that General Tattak awaited me with urgency.

I frowned at what could be wrong but Mutt continued. "General Tattak says to report to you dozens of other armies in the area but most are still a ways off. As of now there are only two that have arrived but they are of... unknown intent. One very large army made up entirely of the Favored Few is moving at a steady pace and should reach the tower at around noon today." I tried to think of what they could be doing there but he swallowed before he continued, like what he was about to say next was even harder to believe. "The other army is already setting up a base camp to launch its attack. It's made up completely of the Enlightened. He believes they are about to engage the timeless." We all froze in our tracks. "What the hell are they doing? Are they there to help?" I asked, turning to the others but no one offered up a response. "Maybe Sway has convinced them to join us?"

Mutt snapped out of it and pulled out a folded letter he had stored in his pocket. "She was there as you said she would be sir as well as Immi. Sway told me to give you this." He handed it over and I took it, opening it and reading quickly.

'Fin, I have assumed the role as translator between the armies for now as they await your arrival. I have brought the one Enlightened I told you I would bring and he assumed charge of the giants and Skane. The leaders here would like me to inform you that they all concur, an immediate attack coordinated with the other Enlightened is the army's best hope. If you agree please send them word with all haste.'

I lowered the paper and searched around as everyone await-ed me. "Quill?" I shouted, "Someone send me General Quill at once." Mutt turned to go, "not you." He turned back. "I want you to find your fastest runner and bring him to me at once." He saluted and ran off. "Stacks?"

"Yes M'lord?" he answered from only a few feet away.

"I would like you to see to the gatherers, hunters and scouts. Have them all recalled at once."

"Umm, yes M'lord but we've lost all communication with the rear scouts last night, I haven't had time-"

"Forget them. Just pull the rest here as I asked, please."

"What's this now bucko?" Quill questioned as he walked up. "General Quill," I spoke with all seriousness, hoping to drive home the extent of the situation. "Start the command. I want the entirety of this army armed, armored and battle ready completely and marching at double time as soon as possible."

His eyes went wide for a flash then clarity returned to them. "Aye sir," he snapped off a quick salute then ran into the men barking orders.

Mutt returned with his runner. "This is the best one we have sir."

I nodded. "He'll do." I turned to the youth directly, "I need you to make all haste to Targog Field. Tell General Tattak that I'm coming at double time with the entire army and they can consider us late reinforcements."

"Sir?" Mutt inquired, the men around us gasping as they worked out what I was implying.

"Have him ready his men and to initiate the attack at once."

General Tattaks' thinly muscled body towered over Immis while he paced back and forth at the entrance to her tent.

"We need to attack, and soon!" he announced, impatience oozing with his demeanor.

Immi eyed him carefully, "It will happen," she replied.

He spun on her, "It's not that I don't believe you, I just, I don't see why we all have to obey this... Fin? Just because he helped gather the armies doesn't mean he has the final say."

She frowned at him, "That is true but this is his story. It must all revolve around him for the outcome to work out the way it is intended."

He stopped his pacing to stare at her, "And by whose intentions would that be?"

"Come now Tattak, even you are smart enough to figure that one out."

"Sir," a man shouted, pulling up to a stop from his run. "Colonel Pile says all troops have finished preparing and are battle ready sir. They're awaiting your orders."

"Bah!" he spat, not answering the man but instead turning to glare at Immi once more.

Her expression didn't change, "Tattak, do you know the difference between coincidences and miracles?"

He frowned, "Coincidences and miracles? What kind of damned question-"

"Sir," another voice called and a second man ran up. "Yes soldier?"

"I'm from the scouting unit you had watching the Enlightened sir. They have initiated their attack on the timeless. They're drawing them from the sacred grounds."

"What!?" he asked, completely shocked by the report. "We need to act-"

"Sir!" a skinny youth came running up and Tattak spun again. "Yes?"

"I bring orders from Fin," he announced, dropping his hands to his knees to catch his breath, "You are to get all troops battle ready and commence the attack with all haste. He is marching his forces at double time and you should consider them late reinforcements."

"Take a break, soldier," he ordered then spun back to the other messenger, "Have all scouts and recon teams brought in ASAP and send for my wife." The man saluted and ran off. He turned back to the last messenger. "Tell the Colonel to initiate the attack the second those things are exposed."

"Yes sir," he saluted and then ran off and Tattak was left facing an unaffected Immi.

"Coincidences and miracles?" she asked again.

As we neared the plains it became evident a large army had been through the area. The hardwood trees had been felled in all directions leaving behind a thin wood that allowed very little cover or shelter for anyone or anything. The ground was trampled profusely and there were smoldering fire pits everywhere along with a few tents, bedrolls, and blankets. It looked very similar to what we had left behind us.

"Sir," Mutt yelled, slamming fist to chest.

"Yes?"

"Sovereign Immi would like a word with you. She has a blue tent set up ahead off the side of the road. She suggested you relinquish your command and let them continue on without you." I looked around and Quill nodded without me having to say anything. I turned back, "Dog, do you know the exact location
the armies are fighting?" I asked.

"Yes sir. It's a hard right up ahead past the fields and a little back tracking. Forgive me but I've already dispatched a messenger to the forward scouts to show them the way."

I raised my eyebrows, impressed with his decision to act without orders. "Well done. No reason for forgiveness," pride showed on his face and I winked. "When this is all over, maybe we'll have that date after all." He laughed out loud at that and Lynnay joined him. "Carry on Mutt," I ordered and he saluted then ran back to his duties.

I turned back to Quill and his brother. "Matches take care of my General. I'll catch up with you two just as soon as I can. I can't imagine her holding me up that long."

"It's all under control boss man," Quill assured me, straightening his back a little. Matches stuck up his middle finger and waved it around in my face. "No, no Ma! That's how we salute military personnel we DON'T like," Quill said then turned to me with a shrug, "It was funny at the time."

I smiled at him and Matches appeared to be embarrassed. I let them continue on as Lynnay and I broke off from them and made our way over to where the blue tent sat.

We entered to find Immi sitting at a small table, sipping at a cup. Her eyes were unfocused as if deep in thought as she stared absently. She motioned to the chairs next to her without looking up.

I pulled out one for Lynnay then sat in the other as I addressed her. "Hello again Immi. May I ask why you pulled me away from the army?"

She finally broke out of her contemplations and turned to me with a raised brow. "Why is that a concern? Do you plan on fighting with them?"

"Of course," I admitted. "I'm not going to lead them into a battle to watch and-"

"Did you forget it was supposed to be Seven gathering armies and Seven leading them into battle? A battle they cannot win?" Then she stared at me.

In my mind the plan was we would attack, win and then I would enter the tower like a conquering hero. I sat deflated, knowing she knew a lot more than I did about the outcome.

She waved away my frustrations, "I only asked you to go to Aam and now somehow the two tasks have merged into one." She pushed a cup over to Lynnay and gestured to the teapot. "But it matters not. This outcome was foreseen and your part in this side of the war is only the first step. The one you must take for now to get you to the right path."

Lynnay filled her cup and then poured one for me. She stirred in some honey and then sipped at it carefully with a smile of delight. I looked back to Immi as she continued.

"Your training, how far have you progressed?"

I shook my head, "Not very far. I'm more of a visual learner. If I could have seen more, then I probably could have learned more. As of now I can make a shield, a sword, and attack using the essence."

She propped her elbow on the table and then leaned on it as she stared at me.

"I'm... very strong and I even flew once but I don't know how I did it."

Lynnay tried to help emphasize my point and spoke up. "By strong he means he pulled in so much essence he caused the world to shake, blacked out the sun and killed two of them Enlightened with a single attack."

Immi's face didn't change as our testimonies failed to impress her. "You are... weak. I'm sorry but your strength right now is not that important. This first step was just to help you open your eyes. I once saw a being who was exactly like you but he was so powerful, I watched him suck the essence out of his victim with a thought and then blast him to pieces with a wave of the hand," she shook her head. "You are a bird amongst dragons but it is your story and if you want to fight alongside them then there's nothing I can do or say to stop you and we both know it." The words hurt but I knew they were true. "Won't this coordinated attack with the Enlightened and their armies give us a chance at least?"

She forced out a smile and took a sip of her tea before she finally spoke. "So precious is our ignorance while it is unbeknownst to us." She set her cup down and leaned forward, face going serious. "I am afraid you will find no allies amongst them or anyone for that matter by the day's end."

I stood outside the tent staring up at what this place called a sun. Its dull light drew me in once more as I often found myself mesmerized by the oddity of the thing. Our sun is much too powerful to stare at so I didn't take this one for granted.

Giant planets and moons hung in the air like frozen beach balls as I listened to the women softly talking inside. I had come out after Immi implied that everyone was going to turn on us.

Either that or she meant me personally but that made even less sense. I knew I should rejoin them but needed some more time to think and clear my head.

Lynnay stepped out and smiled, her hair fluttering in the wind and covering her face. She pulled it back and tucked it behind an ear and I noticed her eyes were puffy and red like she'd been crying.

"Come my Fin. We have been here long enough. Let's walk and talk and just forget about this war."

I frowned at the words and Immi stepped out behind her, pulling a cloak over her shoulders. I turned back to Lynnay and her smile was still forced as she stared at me but I couldn't read what it was all about.

"Why are you looking at me like that?" I asked. "Were you crying?"

She tried to keep the smile on her face but it did little to hide what she was truly feeling. "What is it about you that makes you so special?" she asked and this time I could see genuine curiosity in her question.

"Nothing. I'm the same as-"

Her laugh cut me off. "I don't know what you're like where you are really from but here you are like no one I have ever met and it's the reason you stole my heart. Here you can do what the Enlightened do. Here you are the most important piece on the board, win or lose. Here... even Aam has bent to your will."

The two stared at me and tears began to form in Lynnays eyes. I tried to form words to respond to what she had just said but what had Immi told her?

"Lynnay... Aam would never bend to my will. If that was true I'd end this all. I'd make everything right, bring Deffy back, I'd-"

"I know!" she laughed, shaking her head as she tried to make sense of it all. "I believe that too! It's just... Immis telling this time... it wasn't a vision. It was a message from Aam," she stated as if that clarified everything. I frowned and she threw up her hands in frustration. "You can't oppose the will of a God. No one can! It would be like trying to scoop a river with a rake. If

Aam says you're going to do something, you're going to do it, freewill or not, it happens. But you...you are given a choice..." She shook her head again to try and convince herself what she believed couldn't be true. Immi stepped over and put a hand on her shoulder in comfort as Lynnay calmed herself enough to finish. "And you destroy us all."

My veins went cold and numbness spread over me like a cold shower. "No!" I shouted, shaking my head. "That's not possible! You'll see! I won't!" Anger flushed over me as I looked between the two women. "Lynnay I promise I-"

She stepped forward and put a finger to my lips. "Please don't promise. You can't oppose Aam's will. If it's said it will happen, you can be sure it will happen."

Something bubbled up inside of me again and I struggled to control it. I refused to believe what they were telling me and found myself pulling at the essence without thinking.

I turned back to her. "If I go help them right now, this will prove that stupid message wrong wouldn't it?" I asked, gritting my teeth.

Lynnay shrugged, honestly not knowing the answer. "Go," she finally responded. "Go and help them. We will catch up."

As the essence continued to flow into me I noticed the ability to fly had returned. I let myself hover off the ground in an attempt to master what I was doing. I started moving slowly from side to side then completed a full spin, coming to a stop facing Lynnay again.

"Stay away from the battles. I will find you when it's done."

She nodded and I rose slowly into the air to get my bearings with exactly where I was at. I could feel large amounts of essence being pulled not far to the east and I exploded through the air towards it like a streak of light.

CHAPTER 24

Freewill can bring you understanding when you use it but there is an exception. You will never fully comprehend the meaning of infinity. It is simple to understand its definition but the definition of understanding is simply impossible to do when it comes to this. When you try to dissect anything infinite your understanding fails, it slides around this concept like butter on a frying pan. Take space for example, it's made up of almost all light and dark but this is a physical reality and everything physical has a beginning and an end. This means space isn't infinite, somewhere out there is an edge to this universe with nothing beyond it, but nothing is absolute and that's where you lose your understanding. Nothing being beyond the edge of your universe is both impossible and the only possibility. There is also an exception within this exception. Light and dark can both have a beginning or an end once you see the truth, that darkness is a deception created within the absence of light. Once you understand that you will realize that light can only exist if there's dark.

"Front lines fill those holes as fast as they open. I want a never ending solid wall on all fronts. You, find General Tattak and tell him I am to speak with him at once. You, take two battalions and try to push them further north, we need to clear a way in."

Men saluted and ran in all directions while Quill strolled-through them barking orders.

"Sir, the archers would like to engage but have no openings." "Tell them any skilled enough to shoot through the holes in the front line can. Tell them to stand several paces back and pick their targets carefully. Send the rest with the two battalions I just sent to push them north. If they catch on we're only trying to create an opening they may try and circle back. Have them ready." The man saluted and ran off to do what he was ordered.

Matches pounded his oversized weapon into his palm in anticipation. He had cut a square out of a keg he'd found and now wore it over his head like a helm.

Quill reguarded him, "Don't get any stupid ideas Ma. You are the entire personal guard of the only in charge General this army has."

His brother growled deep and low, never taking his eyes off the battle lines. War was a big part of a giant's nature and Quill could tell it was calling to him now.

He turned back to assess the lines himself, watching sprays of people fly through the air as explosions hit the ground, others were from the large swipes of the timeless.

"Them bastard Enlightened are blasting everything that moves," he observed out loud now that his army's lines were drawing nearer to where they engaged the timeless. "Are they stupid? We are supposed to be on the same side." He spun around frantically. "Mutt!"

The man came running over at once. "Yes sir?"

"Issue the commands. Have the men pull away from where them blasted Enlightened are engaging the timeless. They are to be avoided at all costs and are to be considered hostile." The man saluted and called for his messengers, sending them scurrying like roaches.

"General Quill," a voice came from behind and a tall Blien came running up.

"General Tattak I assume?" The slender man nodded and opened his mouth to speak but Quill beat him to it. "I've just ordered the men to consider the Enlightened hostile. Damn fools are killing everything that moves."

"Sir it's worse than that," Tattak finally spoke. "You need to have your men pull back at once and in a hurry. Call your reinforcements back too. I am already having my army do the same."

Quill stared in disbelief, "and abandon the cause? What sort of mutiness-"

"Sir," Tattak continued, "My scouts just reported the second army has changed its course and is now approaching directly from the south... the road you just arrived from."

Quill froze trying to puzzle out the strategy behind this maneuver. "That makes no sense? That would only give them a strategical advantage if..."

Tattak answered for him, "If they were going to attack us." The two stared at each other in shock. "Send the orders sir. At once. They're going to round that corner at any moment."

Quill snapped out of it, calling for men and sending orders out as fast as he could. "Damn. If I hadn't just ordered two battalions to the side, I could have sent them up on that ridge. It would have been a perfect spot for a counter," he realized, shaking his head. Tattak glanced at it then turned back, "It would have but I'm afraid it's too late. If they see us trying to move anyone there now

it would give us away and they would be prepared for it."

Quill spit in frustration and took a swig from his flask then offered some to the other General.

He stared at it for a moment then accepted it with a shrug. "We may all die today. Might as well do it with some warmth in my belly," he surmised, taking a drink then handing it back.

"I'll drink to that," Quill agreed, then took another of his own.

"Form lines. Bowman, I want two full volleys then pull back for a full attack," Quill shouted while he stood at their front.

They all stood in silent anticipation as the enemy army flowed around the corner like a mass of slow moving black tar. General Tattak stood at his side as a constant flow of messengers were always coming and going from the pair.

They looked over the men and where there was once determination and purpose now stood fear and despair. People rocked from foot to foot, nervous twitches as they constantly looked back and forth to each other for assurance.

"If even one of them decides to flee I think they just all might," Tattak whispered in disgust.

"Where's the apprentice?" someone shouted. "And where is Seven? Are we supposed to all get slaughtered while they hide?"

Quill ignored the man's inquiries as he wondered the same things himself.

BOOM, BOOM, BOOM, BADADADADA BOOM, BOOM, BOOM.

The enemy's war drums blasted through the air, spreading fear like ripples across a pond. Their front lines formed up and spears were lowered as they came to a trot.

"Well?" the man shouted again and this time people took up his call. "Are we to fight the battle for cowards?"

There was a collective gasp as every single face in the army turned to the sky. "What in the world?" Quill thought and the wind suddenly started to gust as if from nowhere.

Tattak followed the men's gazes as they gasped and pointed. From his point of view it looked like a piece of the sun had just broken off and its fiery fragment now plummeted towards the ground like a meteor.

"What in God's name?" he wondered in astonishment and Quill slapped him on the back.

"That my friend, is the one in charge. That's our secret weapon in all this," he announced as the fiery inferno crashed to the ground in an explosion right in the middle of the enemy army. Shields popped up in every direction and essence beams started to fire randomly, frying enemies like ants as they scattered from his onslaught.

"Who... is he?" Tattak asked in disbelief.

"That bucko is Fin the apprentice. He's our own personal un-shackled."

Tattaks eyes went wide at the comment. "Everything Immi said makes sense now. By God he's fighting an army all by himself."

"Oh God he's fighting an army all by himself," Quill repeated but not nearly as confident as Tattak. "Front ranks! Form lines! Prepare the attack!" he yelled and a few of the men actually moved to do as he ordered but hesitated when the one spoke up again.

"Why should we help an Enlightened?" And again others murmured their agreement.

"You fools!" Quill shouted at them. "No Enlightened fight like that! That is an unshackled! Don't you even recognize your own leader?"

They watched where the lone figure darted in and out of the air, sending men flying in all directions.

"It's him!" Mutt exclaimed in amazement. "Look! He's still wearing the blindfold!"

Others began to notice and a cheer slowly rose into the air as Quill shook his head. "And he needs us! Prepare at once for a full attack!"

They threw their weapons up and roared their agreement, the ground trembling with the pounding of their feet as they finally started the charge.

I stayed at the tops of the trees in an effort not to be noticed as I arrived. The sounds of battle could be heard all around me and I decided it was time to risk it so I could get a better sense of what was going on.

I let myself go higher and higher until I was far enough up to get a good view of everything around me. The first thing I noticed was a tower. Its tall massive size and obelisk shape jetted up from the world below it like someone's attempt at reaching the heavens themselves. There was a large valley encircling it that seemed to have no depths and only connected to the world around it at two points.

A battle raged at the point closest to me and I watched as blasts erupted from the Enlightened while they fought an enormous silverish grey enemy that was half humanoid and half beast. The Timeless, I realized, and noticed they fought on two fronts and that at the other battle line they engaged large snake like creatures and giants who seemed to be holding their own against the mythical things.

To the south two more armies were coming together as well. I watched as a slow moving black army rounded a corner and started its preparations to attack. The other stood as if in fear and I noticed the men at their front. One of them wore a crooked hat.

Quill! I realized, thinking to make my way directly to him.

BOOM, BOOM, BOOM, BADADADADA BOOM, BOOM, BOOM.

The army in all black blasted their war drums and lowered their spears as they started to advance on Quill and the men.

I felt anger wash over me again at the sight of them attacking us instead of helping and Immis words came to mind.

"I will not let them lose!" I screamed to myself and sucked in as much essence as I could, throwing myself down towards the center of the slowly advancing enemy mass.

"He's got shields! You can't hit him!" Quill shouted in an attempt to be heard over the sound of the army's charge. "Once they're in range fire at will. I want a constant stream of arrows in the air."

"Yes sir," the man replied and ran off.

"Tattak what we need is something big, like the damned giants and skane. Why have they not pulled back?"

"The Sovereign said an Enlightened has assumed charge over them. I thought that was a good thing until the rest seemed to turn. I don't know his intentions but I do know my wife is with Sway and them now."

"Send a runner to her and see what she can do for us." The other man did so and a few moments later the twangs of bows could be heard and a noise went up in the air like someone had kicked a hornets nest.

"Brace for impact. Spears up!" Tattak ordered and the front lines crashed together with a sound like thunder.

Quill stopped to assess the lines that instantly formed, listening as men hollered and screamed, metal clashed on metal and above it all was the distinct sound of... laughter?

Matches threw his head back in a full bellied laugh as the madness of his bloodlust consumed all rational thought. He raised his weapon high and screamed as he charged into the melee, ignoring his Generals protests.

"He's our leader," Mutt argued with the Captain at the front of the lines, men fighting all around them. "We have to try and cut a path directly to him. He can't keep this up forever."

The Captain took a few swipes at a soldier who was engaged with one of his men, the enemy falling with a gasp as he was cut down from both sides.

"Orders are to hold the line," he stated, searching for somewhere else to help. "That's what I intend to do."

Another man shot forward and took a swipe at Mutt, the messenger blocked easily and the Captain, trying the same tactic, came at him from behind. A different man jumped forward then cut him off and was soon joined by another and the man was quickly overwhelmed.

"Reinforcements!" he gasped, blocking and dodging as fast as he could but still taking several cuts. "Break off and get us help before they kill us all."

"KILL ALL!" A voice echoed back to him in laughter. Matches charged into the men swinging his makeshift mace like he was felling wheat. The two men flew a dozen feet before they crumbled to the ground. "KILL ALL!" He bellowed again and swung the mace the other way, dropping two more.

Mutt kicked his foe away and the Captain rammed his sword through his back the second the opening presented itself.

"Hey," Mutt yelled, not knowing the name of the quiet giant that the General referred to as his brother. "Hey big fella."

Matches finished pounding a mans head through his legs then turned to face the tiny messenger.

Mutt swallowed at the crazed look in the giant's eyes but continued, "he needs our help." Then pointed to where my attacks and shields were becoming less and less frequent and not as bright. Matches stared to where he had gestured. "He's not even flying anymore. We have to save him."

"Deffy brother?" he questioned, realizing the dire situation I was in. "DEFFY BROTHER!" He roared and charged forward, swinging his weapon to and fro like a sickle.

Mutt turned to the Captain as he ran past, following the frenzied giant. "It's now or never."

The Captain firmed his jaw. "8th unit full advance. Follow that giant. No one gets behind him." He ordered then limped off to help the two.

I hit the ground, sending out all the essence I had pulled in every direction. The results were as intended, people shooting through the air like a bomb had just detonated. I stopped trying to overthink everything and instead just let my mind react.

Shields.

They sprang up around me like I was enclosed in a soccer ball. I held both arms out and started forming and releasing blasts of the essence as fast as I could think. The men fell by the dozens but still were able to press in on my shields from all sides and started sticking their weapons through the gaps between.

I leapt into the air and crashed back down only a few dozen paces away, surprised looks appearing on the men who so recently considered themselves out of harm's way. I continued to blast and people continued to fall like dominos until I was left without an enemy within a few paces.

I jumped again, looking for a dense spot then crashed back down, pushing out essence and shooting beams rapidly as I spun. The weapons came again between the cracks and I reacted.

Spin.

My shields went into an orbit around me so fast it hummed, severing spears and limbs alike. I could hear a roar like a giant cheer going up and then the ground trembled. I ignored it, continuing my reign of death.

I saw a man shouting and pointing during one of my leaps and it was the last thing he ever did. Only someone in charge would point and yell, I decided and I changed my strategy. I lept again and saw another man shouting and I dropped on top of him, crushing him to the ground with a noise like snapping spaghetti. I lept again and saw another officer and blasted him through the face with a bar of light before I landed.

There was a hiss in the air then a crash like thunder but it was distant as I was noticing something wrong. The essence still flowed to me like a surging river but less and less was actually being harnessed, like my body was starting to reject it. I jumped anyway and noticed a drastic loss of the essence I could hold so let myself return down instantly to fight from the ground.

No more flying, I thought but let my shields continue to spin as I shot bars of light out randomly.

Pain blossomed in my shoulder and I spun. A man lay on the ground, an empty crossbow pointed at me. I formed an essence sword and stabbed him through the chest as I clutched at my wound. The bolt was lodged perfectly through my shoulder, the tip sticking out the front, its feathers out my back. I snapped off the feathers and pulled at the tip, screaming as the pain sent shockwaves through me. My Earthen body tugged at my conscious hard like a mother trying to protect her baby and it was all I could do to fight it. I fell to my knees, the spinning of the shields spraying up dirt and even slicing apart a man who was trying to crawl under like the other had. I forced myself to my feet and made a few jabs at the others who were all quickly trying to follow suit at seeing the weakness the first had exploited.

I watched in stunned disbelief as the men suddenly surged at me, dicing themselves apart on my vortex that encircled me like a deadly saw. I could feel the drain on my essence and had to let some of the shields wink out as I sat watching the ones behind push the ones in front to their deaths in stunned confusion.

My exhaustion was growing and the tug from my true body was getting stronger. I stumbled back to my knees, letting all but three of my shields wink out as I desperately fought the pull.

I suddenly realized why the men were pressing in on my shields and it wasn't to get to me, it was to get away from him. Matches swung hard and level, sending the ones closest to me hurtling through the air. He reversed his grip, holding the weapon like a baseball bat and swung again to defend his ground and three more men were smashed aside.

"Sir!" I seen Mutt pointing to me and I collapsed, the last of my shields winking out.

"Full circle. On the big man's flanks. No one gets through."

I heard the orders being barked as Mutt reached down to grab me under the shoulder and help me to my feet. I gripped his shoulder in return as the small group slowly circled us and prevented the enemy from advancing.

"Dog is it?" I teased, an exhausted smile on my face.

He smiled back. "It's Mutt sir," he replied and I finally stood on my own as some of my conscious grip returned.

"No, a mutt is something you'd refer to a stray dog as. But a dog? A dog is loyal to the very end."

He stood straighter at the words, pride radiating from him. "From this day on sir, it's Dog."

I clapped him on the back. "Is this a rescue attempt Dog? What's the next part?" I asked as I looked around.

His face went solemn, "I didn't even know if we would actually make it here. There was no plan... or escape plan sir."

I continued to scan as I realized the perilousness of our situation. The men fought hard and seemed to hold their own here in the middle but it was only a matter of time before we were crushed like an eggshell. They were being pressed in hard and our little circle was getting smaller and smaller as Matches swings were also forced to be held back.

"Spears!" one of the enemy officers shouted from the side. I want spearmen to the front. Let's take them-" He cut off, falling dead with a dagger through the eye that pierced his brain.

"Ma! Ma don't you... Ma get back here!" Quill watched his brother charging away in a fit of laughter and bloodlust. He stood there frozen, torn and not knowing what to do.

"Runners," he bellowed and a man jumped forward. "Yes sir?"

"Go to the supply cart and get me the throwing knives and I need them yesterday."

"How many sir?" the man asked.

"ALL THE THROWING KNIVES!" he screamed. "TAT-TAK!"

The other General lumbered over. "Sir?" "Did you get that order out?"

"Yes sir I did."

"Good. Are you familiar with the rolling tide technique?"

The slender Blien frowned for a second as he thought. "It's the maneuver to slice an army in two? A wedge drives at its center, the last men constantly charging to the front until they've breached through?"

"That's the one," Quill responded and took off his coat and dropped it to the ground. He eyed it for a moment, picked it back up and pulled out a flask. He drank deeply, then put it back inside then finally let it fall to the dirt.

"It's one of the worst tactics there are? It splits an army in two but leaves you sandwiched between them..."

Quill tugged at the strap of daggers he had across his chests to reposition them better. "We ain't trying to get all the way through. Just to the middle."

Tattak blinked in disbelief. "That would leave us completely surrounded... It would be suicide..."

Quill stopped and addressed the Blien seriously, "Me brothers out there and the closest thing I've ever had to a friend is with him. If it's suicide then I'll die happy."

Two men came running up holding armloads of leather straps all containing daggers.

"Start strapping them on anywhere they'll fit," Quill ordered, holding his arms out wide. He turned back to Tattak. "Besides, the unshackled is the only one who has a chance against that other being. Without him, we can't help Aam.

Tattak didn't argue. "As you command sir."

"Start the orders at once and don't look so worried bucko." Quill reassured him as he assessed the hundreds of daggers that were now strapped across his arms, chest and stomach. He pulled the one from his sheath that held the karma stone and drew some in then put it back. "Sometimes the best way to cut a wedge is with a dagger," he winked, "try and keep up." Then shot forward in a sprint.

"God I hope these men understand how to pull off the rolling tide," he muttered to himself then started barking orders instantly.

Dog and I spun in unison to see where the dagger had come from. Quill was as agile as a panther. He stood slicing wide, knife taking a man across his back then let himself drop under a spear thrust. He separated the man's Achilles tendon then rolled as another man moved to stand over him. His left hand shot out and a dagger sunk into the man's neck as he used his momentum to hop back to his feet, opening another enemy's stomach as he did. He spun and another dag flew out, hitting a man who wasn't paying attention behind the ear and then was lost to the crowd.

"Dog, relieve Matches of his post. Do your best to fill the gap." I turned to the giant. "Matches," I shouted, his head cocked but he didn't turn from the fighting. "You're being relieved."

Dog timed out the large man's swings and jumped in front of him with a spear thrust. "Close the gap," he ordered and men moved to stand shoulder to shoulder as Matches fell back.

He lumbered over and put his hands on his knees gulping for air as he eyed me.

"Catch your breath for a moment," I offered and he continued to breathe deeply.

Before I could speak again he noticed his brother fighting to the side, leaving a trail of wounded and dying as he darted in and out of the enemy force.

"Brother," Matches bellowed as he stared at Quill.

The smaller man smiled between attacks, his head popping in and out of random openings as he spoke "Roll tide... is coming... left flank... me right."

Matches nodded and pushed a man out of the way as he started up his giant sweeping swings.

"What the hell is roll tide?" I asked and the Captain answered. "It's a suicide move only used when trying to chop a larger opponent in two. Usually it's only done if you have reinforcements coming because it surrounds the wedge on all sides as it slowly rolls in on itself."

I sat speechless, mostly because I was still exhausted but partly because I didn't know how to process the information.

I heard more shouting and turned in the direction it came from. A large Blien was barking orders as his spear lashed in and out like a needle into cloth.

"Keep moving. You, take your men left. You, take your men right. I want a full continuous unending circle always rolling. Move, move, move!"

The army continued its flow and in no time at all our little party was completely cut off from the battle and gave the men some well deserved rest. I watched as they shifted themselves similar to my shields except when one man was tired or injured, he fell back and was immediately replaced by someone standing at the ready from behind.

Tattak approached with a salute then leaned on his spear heavily, "It's nice to finally meet you sir," he offered between breaths. "And you as well. You did a great job in such a short time." He nodded to me, "Aam is very important to us all."

Quill walked over huffing and stretching out an arm as his brother collapsed to the ground like a felled oak, chest heaving.

The smaller man stood a little straighter before he finally addressed me. "We sent for some giants and Skane and requested they attack from that direction when they come." He pointed to the far off distance where the other two races still engaged the timeless. "But I doubt they'll all respond. I honestly have no idea how many numbers, if any, we can expect."

"Could we continue this rolling movement and work towards that direction if they come? You know, meet up and hopefully join forces?"

Tattak stroked his chin. "No, I don't think we should fight too near them. But if we made to head in the opposite direction we may be able to reverse the circumstances, pin the enemy in the middle between us."

Quill stared at the Blien sideways. "That's genius if we can pull it off. And if they actually-"

"Sir," a man fell to the ground with a dozen wounds on his legs and arms, a piece of his ear was missing and he wore the black leather of the enemy. "Sir it's me," he protested, staring at Quill, hands held up defensively.

Tattak put a spear to the man's neck as Quill spoke. "I know lots of mes. None of them wear that uniform."

"I took it off a dead man," he replied, standing slowly. "It was the only way to make it through to you guys. I'm one of the messengers you sent to the Sovereign. I have news sir."

Quill stared at the man. "Yeah I think I remember ya. Make your report then and I swear to Aam if it ain't good news..." The man glanced at me and then froze. 'You're back? Should I report to-"

"Just report," I ordered and gestured for him to continue.

He stared at Tattak for a second nervously and then shook his head, "maybe in private?"

"Son, there is no private, just make your report," Quill ordered and the man nodded.

"I was outside the Sovereigns tent waiting while she spoke with some noble lady and the Enlightened in charge of the giants and Skane inside. Suddenly another Enlightened showed up and went inside with a piece of paper. We don't know what it said but suddenly everything went mad. The Enlightened ran out and tried to kill the Sovereign! We moved to stop him but he started attacking us too. He killed the Blien messenger and two others before we finally ran off," his eyes darted to Tattaks and back as the words sunk into the tall General.

His eyes filled with tears and his face turned to one of pure rage as he struggled to try and keep his composure so the man could continue.

"We all scattered and I ran into the woods and hid but was at a loss of what to do. I sat there just watching as he worked diligently to relay his orders to the giant and Skane messengers. He's ordering them to attack us! They are going to strike the first chance they get!"

I turned back to stare in the far distance where they were still engaged with the timeless but realized it was just a ruse. Most of them were organized and ready for a full retreat to turn on us the second the opening presented itself.

Tattak suddenly let out a scream of pure anguish and then charged into the front lines to release it on the enemy. The rest of us just sat stunned, not knowing how to proceed.

Quill shook his head and chuckled, "Well we can't live forever and I'd like to say I died by my friend and family if you'll allow it?"

"Of course," I insisted, shaking his hand when he offered it. "Friends."

"Friends." Matches agreed and pulled us into an embrace where my face splashed into his chest with the amount of sweat he was covered in.

We stepped back from each other. "At least if we die-" BA-ROOOOOOOO. BAROOOOOOOO.

A horn blasted from the top of the ridge and an army started to pour over its edge. Its battle charge echoed over the field causing both sides to hesitate in confusion.

"Who in God's name?"

"I'd know that horn anywhere," the messenger said as he frowned, "But it doesn't make sense. Why would Lord Victor ever help anyone but himself ?"

Nobody responded as we watched the army sweep down in perfect formation. A flag no one had ever seen before flapped violently at the forefront and at its center sat the unmistakable yellow triangle with the number seven.

CHAPTER 25

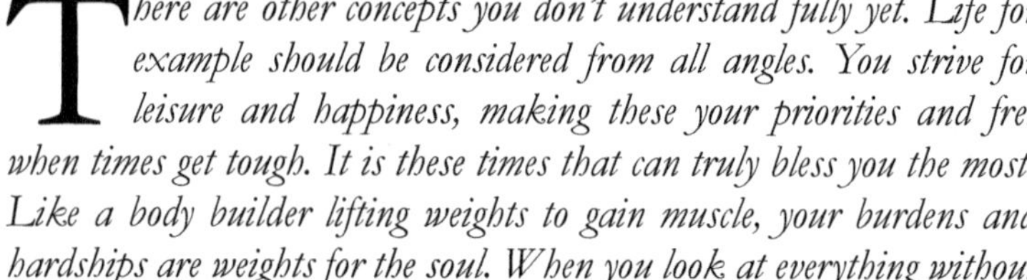

There are other concepts you don't understand fully yet. Life for example should be considered from all angles. You strive for leisure and happiness, making these your priorities and fret when times get tough. It is these times that can truly bless you the most. Like a body builder lifting weights to gain muscle, your burdens and hardships are weights for the soul. When you look at everything without a negative inflection you will always see the truth. The hard times and the struggles are only opportunity for the growth of your soul. Know that God never gives you more then you can handle. The harder it seems, the greater your potential.

"There's a faster route if you take this right up ahead. It doesn't lead to the fields but it does lead to a ridge directly above where the battles are being fought."

"That ridge could prove extremely beneficial if we were to go unnoticed. We'd have to march at full speed to make it in time to be of any use however," a plump officer called General Books offered, hiking up his trousers well above his waist line. "As long as these soldiers are certain of this report?"

The men eyed each other before one finally spoke. "I am certain of the ridge but don't remember the exact point we must turn off to find it."

"I think I do," another added, stepping forward, "But would have to see it again to know it for sure."

Seven looked between them. "As of now you are all under my command. I relieve you of your rear guard duties and reassign you to the front scouts. Find the path, find the ridge. Dismissed." They snapped off some salutes and then headed off to their new tasks. Able turned to his brother the second they were gone. "Should we send a runner to let them know we have absorbed their rear guard? And that we are coming up fast with an army and to expect us on the ridge?"

Books wiped at his brow with a kerchief, answering the question himself. "Yes. Coordinated attacks are most preferred and effective but they are marching at double time so we'll need to send an extremely good runner," Able snapped his fingers and a man saluted and ran off to find one. "We should have him try to draw the timeless out and expose their backs to the ridge. We can sweep down to form a solid wall and leave a path directly to the tower."

Seven nodded to this but didn't respond so Summer took the chance to come forward.

"My Lord," she spoke as she trotted up on her horse. A large bundle lay folded across her lap and she looked pleased with herself.

"You don't have to call me that... M'lady," Able replied, drawing it out in an attempt at mocking her.

She smiled back, "Unlike you I like my title." She offered the bundle over to him. "It's done," she announced proudly.

"Done?" he repeated in astonishment.

"Are you implying you don't believe me?" Summer asked, her lips in a thin line as she dared him to challenge her claim.

"No. Heavens no!" he chuckled, "I'm just beyond impressed. That's all."

"Good. It has our new symbol together at its right. The new symbol we made for our new land on its left and I put his," she gestured towards Seven, "at the center like you said."

"Summer that truly is amazing," he praised.

"It's what you can expect from me throughout our lives." She bit her lip, "But there is one small... tiny adjustment I decided to make." Able looked up at her and she smiled innocently. "I was... most proud of you, of us, and everything we now represent... so I doubled its size."

"Doubled?" He laughed and she nodded her head sheepishly. "You'll be able to see that from the moon," he observed.

"Well that was my hope anyway," and they laughed.

The young man kept his eyes down as he ran. His long skinny legs were always good at running but he wanted to fight. Being used as a messenger all the time was a great responsibility but never offered any chance at glory.

He stared at his new shortsword where it hung at his hip, swinging back and forth in timing with his long strides. All the countless hours he spent sparring with his brothers, working on his cuts and parries were useless if all he ever did was run. He knew he was more than an errand boy. He just needed the chance. His thoughts were cut off by the distinct sound of a sword fight. He came to the top of the hill and saw its source immediately. Two men in black leather fought one man wearing plain clothes. Hope washed away some of the desperation on the mans face when he noticed him coming down the road.

"Are you one of the rear guard? For Aams sakes help me!" he cried.

There was no hesitation at the command and the tall youth freed his shiny sword in one motion just as one of the men in black spun to face him directly.

"Another traitor!" he spat and their swords connected with a loud pang, the jolt rattling every bone in his body.

Nerves caused his limbs to feel heavy as he struggled to block desperately. The man in black swung again and he raised his sword to block. They clanged together and the realization dawned on him. He's slow? Slower than all my brothers, he thought and confidence started to replace his fears. He knocked the man's next swing aside easily and then lunged, plunging his sword through his chest and killing him instantly.

He quickly moved up behind the last one and the man noticed. With the circumstances completely reversed now, he made a desperate move and darted at his opponent, running him through the stomach as they toppled to the ground. The young messenger didn't hesitate, stabbing the enemy through the back the instant the opportunity presented itself. The black garbed enemy rolled over slowly and growled, "Traitors! We've been ordered to kill every last one of you. Even now our army is circling behind yours to wipe it off the face of Heart. You deserve the deaths you'll get for serving such a-"

His words cut off as the impaled adversary rammed a dagger into his heart. He pushed the corpse off of him then stared at the blade that had run him threw in shock. "Oh God I'm going to die." he moaned then moved to pull the weapon out.

The young messenger stopped him with a raised hand. "Pulling it out will only quicken your death. You need to trust me on that."

The man stopped, not knowing what to do as he stared down, watching his blood leak out slowly.

"Do you know who those two were?" the messenger asked and the man nodded his head.

"They were the Favored Few. They showed up to the fields with all the Enlightened. We figured they were there to help us attack the timeless but... he just called us traitors?" Blood bubbled from his mouth while he talked and he wiped it away with a trembling hand.

"So the Enlightened and Favored Few are all there but they are going to attack our side too?" The other man nodded. "And your army has no idea?"

He shook his head in confirmation. "And if they're circling around then that means they're blocking the path back. There's no way you could get word to them in time."

The messenger shut his eyes, not knowing exactly what he should do with all that transpired.

"I'm going to return to Seven. It's my only option." He stared down at the dying man. "I can end it quickly... if you'd like?"

The man didn't look up from where he sat, tears falling freely. "No. No, I don't think so. The pain isn't so bad now and I'd like to sit and just... remember." The messenger turned to go but the injured man spoke again. "One last thing. I'm from Hillbottom. If you're ever that way find a woman named Branch. Tell her... I loved her and I'm sorry I couldn't come home."

The other man gave him a comforting smile. "I'll tell her you killed two men saving my life." The other man looked up in disbelief, a smile coming to his face and he nodded at the words happily.

The messenger nodded in return and then spun, running in the direction he came from and refusing to look back.

A buzzing noise stretched across the field, slowly getting louder and louder as a rain of arrows descended like a swarm of angry birds. Screams of pain and agony erupted as the enemy fell dead from the barrage. Metal glinted as breastplates reflected the sun and spears were lowered, shields held forward.

"A real army," Quill breathed out in astonishment. "How in the world did that bastard get a real army?" I stared at the front-lines' perfect formations while its charge quickened, won- dering the same thing myself. "Alright fellas! If you plan on liv- ing start cutting a wedge towards that ridge. ROLLING TIDE!" Quill screamed and Tattak came jogging up, covered in blood and breathing heavily.

"Rolling tide! Same as before. Groups form," he stated, taking over for Quill easily.

I still stood exhausted, watching the army advance in a mesmerized daze. The arrows stopped falling and within one heartbeat the front ranks crashed into the enemy with the sound like a train wreck.

"That was perfectly timed out," I commented in amazement.

"You're just used to these... fine folk," Quill gestured and a few of the men glared at him as they passed. "What about you? Can you walk yet? Fight? Fly?"

I held the grip on my consciousness firmly now but couldn't take in anything smaller than a trickle of the essence. "I can move and fight... just not with the essence."

Quill nodded. "Good enough. Let's get a move on it. I'm on your right. Ma take his left."

Tattak was at wedge point and we relieved him within moments, Quill and Matches dropping the enemy like they were merely practice dummies.

We cut our way through them quite easily with the two out front and were just about to break through to Sevens army when I heard a sound like hissing directly from the direction we were heading.

An army of Skane charged in, their legless bodies flowing over the ground much faster than any man could move and they tore through Sevens armies exposed flanks like a hot knife through butter. I watched in stunned disbelief as beams of light suddenly started to burst forward from the center of their formations, a shield popped into existence and realization dawned on me. It was the traitor Enlightened Sway had recruited who was leading their charge.

"When do we attack? They have no time to prepare a proper counter. The army is nearly upon them!"

"Patience M'lord," Books suggested. "They need to be fully engaged and committed for us to be able to maximize our attack effectively. See look there," he pointed. "Armies are already being recalled and lined up between them. They have realized the betrayal."

"But is it in time?" Able continued as Seven continued to stare. "It should be but I doubt it will hold. Once the enemy lines merge they'll put every man they can behind their front to keep a solid wall. This will leave their sides and back exposed. That's when we strike."

Able scratched at his chin anxiously. "Is everyone ready?"

"All preparations have been made M'lord and await the signal. You'll find this is a well practiced and well disciplined army," he informed, letting the pride ooze into his tone.

"That's good to know," Able added and Seven leaned forward. "Where... is Fin?" he asked, scanning the field." He looked to where a man with a crooked hat stood near a tall Blien as men ran to and fro from the pair constantly. "He should be at their front but he's... nowhere?"

"The unshackled you spoke of ?" Able questioned.

"Yes," Seven confirmed as he continued to search over the men. "He should have assumed charge and that means he should be at their front but... he's not among them."

"Maybe he's trying to sneak in like you said?"

Seven adjusted his leather gauntlets, "Possibly but not likely. I think-"

BOOM, BOOM, BOOM BADADADADA BOOM, BOOM, BOOM.

"That would be the enemy signaling its attack," Books spoke and they all stared in silence. "It's nearly-"

His words were cut off immediately as they watched a ball of blazing fire fall from the sky and land in an explosion that sent men flying in every direction. Shields popped up engulfing the being and beams of light started to burst out randomly.

"Mother of God that's him isn't it?" Able marveled as everyone watched in stunned fascination.

"I believe it is," Seven speculated, "But he's... different. And stronger."

A roar sounded and the other army finally started its charge.

"Hold until the front lines are fully engaged!" Books commanded. "Await my signal."

The men continued to watch as a frenzied giant blasted through the front lines, swinging a weapon back and forth like he was sweeping the ground.

"What are they doing?"

Seven stared more closely. "Our unshackled is losing his grip on the essence. I believe that's a rescue attempt."

Able turned to Books. "They need us. How much longer."

"Well M'lord, they aren't reinforcing the fronts like they should be. That unshackled fellow and the large man are disrupting them quite effectively. If we attack now, I'm afraid they would have plenty of time to prepare and meet us head on."

Able shook his head and turned to Seven. "It's your call brother."

He snarled in frustration. "Damned fool. Who attacks an army from the center? It's suicide." He complained as they watched a small company surround me and my shields wink out. "Damn it all! We have no choice-"

"Speaking of suicide M'lord," Books cut in. "It appears the army is performing the rolling tide technique in an attempt to reach this... friend of yours. They're risking everything to save him."

Seven watched as a wedge cut through very close to where Matches had led his men, but this time, the entirety of the army rolled in on itself behind it.

"That must be one very important man for an entire army to sacrifice itself for him," Books offered, staring at Seven.

"It's his story," he muttered, thinking of Immis words. "Whatever that means. All I know is he's the only one with a chance at killing whatever the being is that has infiltrated the tower." He stood up and began to stretch. "Books, when they reach the middle and form their walls I want the attack signaled and not a second later." He pulled out his sword and checked its edge. "Enough of this sitting and waiting. I'm no bystander," he growled in irritation.

"At the ready!" Books commanded and the orders were relayed down the lines. He raised his arm to wait. One heartbeat went by, two, three, his arm descended and the horn blasted its death cry.

BAROOOOOOOO, BAROOOOOOOO.

"M'lord, Able requests your presence sir," the man informed as he approached Seven timidly. The tall man fell back and let some of the other soldiers fill in his gap. "He's in the middle with the honor guard still."

Seven trotted over to find his brother standing with a short female who had a scar across her cheek. "Lynnay?" he observed. "How did you get here?"

"Well since I couldn't make my way back to that army, I came here as soon as I realized you led this one," she offered.

"Yes, but how?"

"I was with the Sovereign. We found a dying man in the middle of the road and he told me of the betrayal so I ran on ahead to try and warn you guys. Seven it gets worse. I found out the other Enlightened with Sway has turned too. They all have. Everything on this battlefield is now actively trying to kill us. They're calling us the traitors." She let the words sink in and added, "and he's the one leading the giants and Skane."

"Why would anyone turn on the quest to save Aam?" he questioned in disgust. She shook her head to answer but there was a loud hiss and they all spun.

The large serpent-like bodies of the Skane crashed into their exposed flanks and men died with surprised looks on their faces at the betrayal. Essence beams started to blast from the front of the lines and a shield popped into existence.

Seven lowered his head in rage. "Able, stay away from the fighting. If we start to lose, order your honor guard to escort you to safety in a full retreat."

"I'd never be so cowardly," Able shot back aghast.

Seven ignored him, running to meet the Enlightened head on, pulling in essence as he ordered the troops aside.

The Enlightened saw him and raised a hand, a beam of light shooting out but Seven was ready. His off hand shot forward, fingers spreading apart and deflecting it harmlessly away into the air.

There was no hesitation as he slammed his shield into the other beings, using his size and momentum to his advantage and sending the Enlightened flying to the ground. The white helmet it was wearing flew off and exposed the back of his head as Seven lept high, coming down with a sword directly through the back of its skull and cutting off its weird form of shouting instantly.

Both armies stared at him and Seven took the opportunity to address the Skane. "Now who leads you? I will kill every one of you traitorous snakes one at a time if I must!"

"He told us you were the traitors," one of them hissed.

"He lied! We are trying to free Aam from the being you've all heard of. You've all been deceived! Stop and join us! To save Aam!"

"He sssaid Aam isss the biggessst traitor of all!" it shot back.

"More lies! Stop this fighting you know Aam is not capable of lying. How could you fall for this?"

The words hit their mark and the large green being addressed his men. "Ccceassse the attack! We have been decccieved!" it shouted and the orders echoed out as more and more took up the call.

"Attack the ones in black! They oppose all who try to help Aam!" Seven commanded and both armies turned at once to obey.

Matches was the first to breach the battlefront and make it to the safety of Sevens army, Quill and I a close second.

"You fight... like a cloud. No one could touch you and-"

Quill laughed at my praise, "Although I appreciate the comparison to literally the least threatening thing in all existence, save it. Here comes Captain Poetry."

I turned to see Seven striding over followed by a few others. Lynnays eyes locked on mine and she cheered, running forward. I caught her in an embrace and we kissed.

"What in the hell was that?" Seven demanded as he stomped his way over. "I ordered you to use your head in my absence. You don't attack an army from the center unless you have a death wish."

I shrugged, a relieved smile on my face. "I may have lost my temper," I admitted apologetically. "I guess I messed things up pretty badly."

"Actually, not nearly like you'd assume," a chubby man in an officers uniform informed me.

I stared at him as Seven spoke. "Fin this is General Books and the man to his right is my brother Able and his fiancée Summer." I greeted each in turn. "This is General Quill and his brother Matches," I offered, noticing Seven wasn't planning to.

"Shall we retire to the rear M'lords?" Books asked. "We should start formulating new plans as things here seem to be wrapping up quite nicely."

Able nodded and the group started to make its way back. "Quite nicely?" I asked.

"Yes. Your little distraction prevented them from ever reaching any semblance of organization . The giants and Skane are now making quick work of the ones that are left." He turned to one of his men. "Send out the orders to let any that try to retreat to do so. I want the entire army back here until we strategize a new timeless offensive." The man saluted then ran off and Quill repeated the orders to his men next.

I shook my head at the sudden change of events. "It all seemed so hopeless for a while there."

"We're not out of the woods yet. That was just a hiccup. We still need to find a way to not only pass the timeless, but now some hostile Enlightened as well."

I contemplated the new circumstances as Able ordered tables and chairs set up and we sat to formulate a new plan.

"If the plan is just to get you in," Lynnay started, "why not just put on one of their uniforms and try to sneak through? At least that way if the Enlightened see you they will think nothing of it and hopefully the timeless are too engaged to notice."

"Yes," Seven added, "They know he flipped and joined their cause but they don't know he's dead... yet, we'd need to move quickly."

Able snapped his fingers and a guard spun, speaking before he was commanded, "We'll fetch his outfit sir," the man pointed to another for help and the two sprinted off immediately.

"Can you pull in essence yet?" Quill asked and I nodded. The longer I went without using it, the more I could feel it returning. I stood, finally removing my pointless blindfold and several of the people around gasped. "Not enough to fly yet but if I circle around through the woodline it should give me plenty of time."

"So you'll be going alone?" Seven questioned. "You have my faith. I trust in you completely."

"Seven about that..." I started, my eyes falling to the ground. "Aam-"

Lynnay stepped in front of me, cutting off what I was about to say. "Faith is a good thing to have." She protested and I stopped, staring into her beautiful eyes.

"Sir! We have it." Came the voice of one of the men who went to fetch the outfit. They handed it to me and I threw it all on quickly except the helm. I held out my arms and spun. "How does it look? I can't see myself."

"You're a bit taller than him so try to stay crouched if you get seen," Seven offered.

"Yeah bucko. Who looks like a cloud now?" Quill teased at the color of my outfit as he threw his coat back on happily from where one of his men finally returned it to him.

"Use it only until you can find a black one and then try and change. They may figure out sooner or later that you aren't who you are pretending to be," Books offered and I agreed.

"Best of luck," the others started to offer and Lynnay stepped forward for one last kiss and then pushed the helmet down over my head.

"I don't know what's supposed to happen next but Immi said..." She shook her head. "Just be careful. I love you."

I ushered her towards the others and started to walk backwards as I stared at them while I spoke. "You guys are acting like it's the last time you'll ever see me. We'll meet again, you can count on that."

Lynnay's eyes shot wide in pure terror and Seven started to shout. I heard a soft thud on the grass behind me and spun. A being dressed in all black landed and cocked his head, a snarl on his face where I could only see his lips as his helm covered the rest of him.

I sucked in the essence but only half of what I could do before came to my call and I used it to form a hasty shield.

He reached his hand out as if grabbing a spiderweb and ripped the essence from my body, my shield winking out and leaving me completely defenseless. The blast took me through my right side and I spun with the force, landing face first on the ground.

I pushed myself to my knees, disoriented by the pain and the tug on my conscience. I looked down to where my shoulder used to be but noticed it was gone. Numbness crept over me and time slowed. I watched as Seven charged forward, freeing a sword from his pack. Quill's arms pumped like pistons and daggers flew. A shield appeared in front of me to stop them and I turned to Lynnay. She was aiming the crossbow, one eye closed as tears streamed her face.

I smiled.

I wonder if that damn bolt can pierce a shield? I thought as a sword of pure essence entered my neck.

The world went black and I found myself flying through a tunnel, my Earthly body finally getting its way

INTERLUDE

That was the first time I ever remembered projecting. In my research I found many people who have come close but not quite do exactly what I did or go to the realms I went to.

I was different. A body always manifested for me and I went to real worlds. I found myself doing it more and more with little consideration for what it was costing me or the people I affected. I was a living superman, blinded by my own brilliance and it made my real life dull in comparison.

Eventually, I found love and started a family but even that didn't stop me. I often think back to my wife and how she never noticed how some mornings I'd be glued to her side, excited to see her, to see the kids, excited to be back, no clue what day it was, what our plans were, everything was forgotten. It was a single night to them, but to me... sometimes it was years.

But I didn't care. It was fun and it made me happy so it was good. I'd soon learn that too much of a good thing can be bad. Everything has its price and we cannot escape our fates no matter how much we try.

My fate would play out for me in a few different ways. First, I would become a sinner. Not just the average everyday lord's name in vain kind of sinner. I am the worst. It consumed me, turned me into a monster. When I was handed a life I never wanted, a life I felt I didn't deserve, I refused to play by the rules. I became selfish. I took whatever I wanted from whoever I wanted because the world owed me. GOD owed me!... or so I told myself in my selfish tantrums. But we are none of us perfect because the truth is, life is hell. Earth is hell and sometimes you have to hit rock bottom to find out which way is up when you're drowning in a sea of loathing.

The second thing I found that always dictated my fates was a number. The number 8 to be exact. I would find it everywhere and in everything important throughout my life. I only ever had 8 real relationships and I married the 8th one. We were married for 8 years and the difference in age between my oldest and youngest is also 8 years. We owned 8 vehicles, lived in 8 different houses, I had 8 different jobs, and I could probably fill 8 more pages with examples and better examples but you'll see more of those later. For now, you should know I am an 8th born child. I kept all of it secret, trying to convince myself that it was just unusual coincidences... but I've since learned God speaks to us in coincidences, and shouts in miracles.

8 YEARS LATER

CHAPTER 26

"The beast that was, and is not, is himself also the eighth, and is of the seven, and is going to perdition." Revelation 17:11

Reality popped into existence without a sound, like turning on a light. With the amount of time that has passed from where my story began, the places I've visited and things I've seen or done were beyond count and affected my memory greatly. The human brain is not designed to withstand that amount of time and because of this, I'm afraid most have been lost to oblivion.

I looked around. The small circular opening where this places mindwarp was located was very similar to the more primitive ones I've encountered before with nothing to it but a round clearing cut into its surrounding forest.

Slightly more advanced civilizations would have stone slabs erected, mounds formed, a pattern of rocks and all sorts of other displays to welcome us extra dimensional beings who came to visit. Advanced civilizations would even have servants, food, clothes, decorations, everything you could want upon your arrival.

But this place wasn't completely void. It just had very little with nothing but a small path that led away from it.

Primitive, I decided so instead of taking its path I chose to continue my normal rituals when encountering something like this one that was less traveled to.

I pulled in the essence but just a trickle. I didn't know anything about this place and more than once have been met with hostility so going unnoticed was always a priority.

I watched the essence where it danced into me, it flowed through the trees, the moss and everything in small vibrant waves. I stopped pulling it in and instead just took a deep breath to enjoy it. It had been a while since my last projection and I missed its warmth. The way it felt to hold it was joy, love, life. It was purpose. I watched it flow through the air and saw a tiny amount get called not too far to the west, deciding I'd investigate that right after I finished everything else.

I bent my knees and jumped, attempting to push the essence I held to a point just in front of me. The body then becomes weightless as it tries to follow the energy that sustains its mass and this is the easiest technique I found for flying. I soared through the air and knew I only held enough of the power for a very quick flight but that was ok. My only goal was to get away from the very unwelcoming mindwarp.

There was a narrow road to the east and so I decided to go west and somewhat closer to where I noticed the essence being pulled to before. I landed in a small opening a mile or two away from where I started, thinking it was far enough off from everything to test the limits of this world.

I let my mind relax and grasped the essence firmly and then pulled at it with everything I had. The world went vivid and pure energy soared through everything to beckon to my call in a torrent of power. The few clouds in the sky at the time were sucked into the whirlwind I was creating and the ground began to tremble and then shake. I continued at this for several moments before I could finally feel the limits of my physical self fast approaching so I stopped, not needing to reach it, just seeing where it was.

I clapped my hands together, shifting the essence I held in them and focused my thoughts as I had once unknowingly learned from a young boy. I formed it in my mind first, seeing every detail in perfect clarity and what it was made of. A plain shirt, short sleeves, one front pocket.

Wool. I called to the universe and pulled my hands apart vertically to catch the thing after it was formed. The shirt fell into my palm and I continued this process, making underwear, socks, pants, boots, and a knife. I decided against any other sort of weapon for two reasons. First, I didn't want to stick out too much if I was seen. Primitive mind warps usually had primitive species so I doubted they had anything too advanced. The second, I could only call to the things I'd actually watched Deffy make personally and that was very limited. A few different types of cloths and leathers, one type of wood, one type of metal, and a karma stone. I finished dressing and felt exhausted at having pushed my body to its limits so fast and then creating things so soon after. It made my Earthen body tug at my conscience with its gentle invite. I decided to try a technique I had come up with as I lay dying in a place, fighting the call of my true self and remembering some advice the Sovereign Immi had once given to me that affected me a lot. I'd always considered myself a visual learner and could mimic the things I could see others do but she had once suggested to stop trying to improve what others have already done and step outside the box completely. And on that day, I did. I knew it wasn't really me laying there dying. It wasn't even my real body, it was just a projection my subconscious formed automatically in this place when I arrived. I let go of my body, as if succumbing to the Earthly ones pull, then instantly reinforced my consciousness back into its place. I called it blinking.

My body in this reality would vanish like it was going to return home and then reform again immediately, completely rested, healed and well. It was a difficult ability but I was beginning to master it the more I used it. I did it and was successful then turned in the direction the essence had been called and lept into the air.

For the next hour or so I flew in short little hops until I reached a tiny house in the dead center of a large field. Its small thatched roof had a rock chimney that smoke rose from lazily and its walls were made up of red logs, cut up and stacked very similar to the kind on Earth. It was one story high, had a few windows, a door and even a porch where an old lady sat rocking. Some children ran through the field chasing a dog and I landed at its edge, deciding to walk up.

The beings were common enough and so were their clothes so I let out a sigh of relief that I wouldn't have to change into anything drastic. The old lady didn't even slow in her rocking as I approached, her hands busy weaving a basket.

"Greetings," I offered with a smile and a wave to catch her attention.

"Greetings to you as well," she responded, her voice frail and cracking like being listened to on an old record player. She finally glanced up at me and then smiled from ear to ear as I froze.

Now I've already mentioned my memory was now almost completely shot and this was proof. When I noticed her two glowing purple eyes staring back at me, I instantly realized that mine were the exact same. There was no hiding what I was.

"What's wrong love? Cat got your tongue?" She chuckled and I smiled back.

"No, I've just never encountered a being with purple eyes before... I thought I was the only one. Usually I try to hide mine, it's just that I'm slowly becoming more and more-"

"Forgetful. I understand, believe me," she chuckled again. "So you've come here from Earth. I suppose that means you're on your next step."

I stared at her, sucking at my bottom lip as I thought, "How do you know so much about me?"

The smile on her face was genuine and she winked, "I know more about you then you. If you can believe that or not."

"I tend to believe that believing in itself is a belief formed from believing." She cocked an eyebrow and it was my turn to chuckle, "Sorry. It was part of a riddle a higher being once told me."

She let herself rock back in her chair, nodding her head, "They're not called higher beings here, they're called Ascendals. And they'd probably call you a Boundless."

I perked up at this. Any place where there were higher beings, there were bigger pieces of the infinity code to be found. "That's good to know. Thank you. But if I may, how did you know I was from Earth?"

She gave me a sly smile that suggested she knew far more than she was letting on. "As I said, I know more about you than you do. Besides, I'm from Earth too."

The comment caught me by surprise. I've met my fair share of beings who could do what I did, travel from place to place, universe to universe, but never from Earth and never old. Unless it was a disguise but with her eyes glowing purple I highly doubted that. You see when your mind projects itself to a physical reality, it always gives you a body at its peak form around my current age of twenty 8 or younger if you haven't aged that far yet. So I was at a complete loss as to why or how she was old.

She chuckled again softly at my silence. "You either don't believe me or you don't know why I'm old."

I shrugged in surrender. "It's... hard to believe. I've encountered beings before who could project themselves, just never with purple eyes, never from Earth, and never old... You're a triple anomaly."

She sat back with a laugh, tugging a strip of bark to tighten its weave more firmly in place then set it to the side and gestured to the seat next to her. I took it and was handed a cup of liquid that looked like tea and smelled of berries. I gladly accepted it, knowing how important it was to give the body sustenance early in these places.

"I think it's obvious I'm not exactly like you. My true name was Mary. I can tell you this because I know there's not a damn thing you can do with a true name."

I smiled at her honesty then returned it. "My names [Earthen Name Omitted] but when I travel, I prefer Fin," I greeted.

"Well Fin, one thing that makes me different," she started up again, stopping her rocking to turn and face me directly, "is that as fate would have it, I'm stuck here without a body to return to."

I knew this wasn't supposed to be possible but decided against pressing the issue until her account was done.

"The life I was destined for had I stayed there was set to be a doozy. Well one time when I slept and my soul returned to the spirit realm as, we know it does, someone... found me... and made me an offer I couldn't refuse." She stared at me for a second as she thought. "I was promised a different life away from all that and an enlightenment only a few beings truly ever obtain. I chose to come here, with help, and let my link to my Earthen body be severed, never to go back. After it was done, I was engulfed completely by this time and that is why, as you have noticed, this body now ages and I'm old."

"And you've been here the whole time?" I asked as I sipped my tea. Blueberry and apple mingled in a flavor that was delightful and it reminded me of sitting in a field with my grandma.

She set back to rocking. "Yup. Fell in love. Got married. Had kids. Had grandkids." There was fondness in her voice as she spoke, staring to the side.

I followed her gaze to where the two boys and the dog dashed in and out of the tall grass chasing some small rodent and laughing gleefully.

"Enough about me, tell me about you. How long have you been projecting?" she insisted, starting to rock in her chair once again.

"Hmm, the first projection I can remember was about 8 years ago to a place similar to this one. Since then I've done it countless times. I honestly couldn't even put a number on it."

She shook her head in disappointment, "Careful with that now. Time can bend the mind or even break it if we take on too much." I shrugged her comment away. "I'm careful enough but I do notice some of those effects. I used to be able to remember everything and people actually considered me smart. Now I'm lucky if I can remember what end the food goes in."

She laughed at my joke, "That happens, especially when we bite off more time then we can chew. The little ones usually keep us grounded and less... adventurous." She cocked an eyebrow and I knew what she was implying.

I smiled proudly, "I have three. Two of them are my own and yes, I find myself projecting less and less lately."

She accepted my words with a frown, "two are your own?" I finished off the tea and set the cup aside. "Yes, my girlfriend had one before we met."

Mary sat back with a sigh, "Poor woman. Gives you three kids, two of your own doing and all she gets in return is to be called girlfriend." She peered at me from the corner of her eyes, "something wrong with her or something? She don't treat you right?"

I put my hands up in protest, "No it's not that. I mean she does have her demons but they're so similar to mine I would never hold them against her. I'd be a hypocrite. Besides-"

"If you don't agree with her demons then why'd you get with her in the first place."

The question brought me back to a time and place where I had met a woman named Lynnay. "That's easy, there were too many reasons to ignore. She was exactly like someone I met before. She was also exactly like me and I asked for a sign from God and actually got one. It was the only time I'd ever actually got a response to any prayer I've ever made and that has to be a good omen. I knew God gave me that sign to finally give me a better life." I shook my head. "But I was trying to say-"

"So you love her?" she cut in again.

"Yes. More than anything-"

"Do you want to spend the rest of your life with her?"

"Yes if you would-"

"Does she want to get married?"

I laughed at the way this old lady was berating me and shook my head in defeat. "Yes she does. We do. If you'd-"

"Then do it or you might lose her. Would you be ok with that?"

The thought of not having her anymore made my heart sink. "I've been trying to tell you. We actually just got engaged. We are getting married, it's just that I'm not used to calling her fiancé yet."

She finally nodded to this and let the questioning continue on.

"That'll do. So what's got you to a place like this?"

"Well she left town and took the kids with her so I had the house to myself. It's easier to do it when she's gone because it gives me plenty of time to remember and figure out everything I was doing before she left. I literally keep pages and pages of reminders stored in my phone to help prevent arguments or explaining why something didn't get done," I added with a shrug. I stared at her and realized that wasn't the answer she was looking for. "Oh, the reason I do it is easy. Pursuit of the infinity code."

She nodded like this was a better reason. "Plenty of that here. This place is crawling with all sorts of Ascendals who are doing the same, a whole city of them actually. But fair warning, steer clear of the ones with the red eyes and don't let them figure out what you are or they'll try and kill ya. They hate anything that can kill them back so do everything they can to prevent that to keep them at the top of the pyramid. Death isn't common amongst their kind, it's their only fear. Drives them sideways. Just letting ya know."

"Thanks for the heads up. Higher beings have an extremely enlightened understanding of the infinity code and I'd hate to have my fun end before it even begins."

"Well if the code is your absolute priority then I have something else for you." She leaned forward like what she was about to say was beyond secretive. "This place also has... two Gods."

I sat back astonished, not knowing if I fully believed her or not but doubted she would lie. "Two? Are you certain?" I remembered going to a place where one God lived, a God named Aam but never actually encountered it. And this place had two?

She nodded. "I was instructed to never tell the inhabitants of this place as they wouldn't understand it but... well, you aren't from here so that means you don't count."

"Thank you! I've never met a God before. I could learn so much." I watched as she set back to rocking, pleased with herself at having given me such good news. "So, how do I get to them?" She shrugged, "don't know if you can but there was one being who found a way. Popped up in that city I was telling ya about and blew half the thing up before finally making off and gaining access. Can't really say how but if there's one place to find answers, it would be in that city."

"Well if that being could do it then so could I." I let the excitement edge my voice at the thought of learning from a God.

She eyed me suspiciously, "Think yourself that powerful do ya?"

I laughed, "I'm confident enough in my abilities."

A boy came running up just then and he was sobbing, "Gam Gam, it bit me again," he whined, holding up his hand to show where the blood dripped.

Her lips went pouty and there was an audible change in her tone as she spoke, "Come little one, let's fix it up one more time." I watched as she called the essence and brought it to her palm.

Her left hand pushed the essence into the wound and her right hand called it back out, the energy swirled and the wound slowly closed itself. I knew instantly I could do this.

She grabbed a rag and wiped the blood away and then kissed it. "All better?"

The boy wiped his eyes while he inspected it with a smile, "All better, he cheered, "Thanks Gam Gam!" then ran off happily. "Maybe you stop harassing those poor groundhogs and it won't keep happening!" The boy didn't respond as he disappeared back into the tall grass.

I sat puzzled, "how does that work? I mean, I watched you do it so now I know I can do it but I don't understand how?"

She went back to her basket work and her rocking, "I just sped up the healing process is all. It's what essence does."

I paused. That didn't go along with anything I understood about essence and how it worked. "You can use essence to alter time?"

She looked at me like I was joking then laughed when she realized I wasn't, "Oh son, you can't be as all powerful as you think if that confuses you." I still sat confused and she rolled her eyes then continued, "it's the reason we age. The reason you can do what you do. It's how I healed his bite. I think it's one of the oldest known ideals in the entire history of all creation!" I shook my head at a complete loss of what she was talking about. "Time is of the essence!"

We continued our talk for a short while after that and she gave me some pointers on how to reach the city and what to expect from the beings I encounter. We said our goodbyes and I went on my way. No real concrete plan except to reach the city and try to find a way to the Gods without giving away exactly what I was. I found myself growing excited at the prospect. I knew what I was capable of in places like this and its limits were nearly nonexistent. I could fight, fly, create, destroy and best of all, I couldn't die. Not really. A fatal blow here would just wake me up where my body slept. Here, I was an immortal. I continuously pulled at the essence while I flew, knowing I was moving much too fast for anything to catch me and investigate what I was.

I watched as the terrain below me went by in spurts. The lush green pines and tall leaved trees were thick at first but quickly transitioned into a more vibrant and colorful forest of all sorts of unknown plants. I turned to one side and noticed a desert in the distance that seemed to roll on for eternity. I looked the other way and found a mountain range, its peaks jetting up from the ground below it like the giant teeth of the world itself. I let my gaze fall back to the landscape below, watching hills, rivers, towns and even on occasion a city go by as I kept in the direction I was instructed to follow.

Eventually I got to what I was looking for that marked the outskirts of where I was going. The tall trees grew up into the clouds themselves like colossal broccoli and I stopped pulling in the essence, letting myself descend slowly as I looked for a spot without any signs of life.

I landed next to a tree whose base was about as thick around as a school bus and set to my tasks. I had decided that entering in on foot would be the best way to stay under the radar but would need to appear common. I focused my will, letting the essence drain from me until I held so little my eyes would appear their normal blue color then I clapped my hands together to make a coin purse and coins. Enough for emergencies but not enough to draw attention. I finished it all off by blinking again to refresh myself from the long flight and then made my way out to the road I had seen, whistling merrily as I went. I knew this projection was going to teach me more than I'd ever thought possible. To be the best one I would ever have and be one that I would always remember. What I didn't know was that only the latter would be true.

"I don't want to go back Pa. You know what it means. We ain't even citizens to them. They can't make us do nothing!"

"Cherry, you begged to go on the last trip and I caved. You caught an eye and now you've been requested. Don't go assuming the worst just cause you heard a horror story once. They have more slaves and servants then they know what to do with. Probably just want a lock of your hair or to study your eyes."

"Or to take my maidenhead or chop me up into little pieces to see what my insides look like."

"Cherry! That's enough of that. If I honestly thought they was going to do that do you think I'd bring you to em willingly?" The girl put her eyes down, ashamed she even suggested such a thing. "Don't be such a worrywart Cherr, just as likely a good thing they summoned you. Maybe they wanna pay you to dance for em? Lord knows you're beautiful enough. Every man with eyes knows that. Maybe one just wants to save your likeness in one of them fancy paintings you always see on their walls? Point is, we don't right know and it's not for us to understand them and their silly ways."

"I know Pa. I'm sorry. It's just that. I'm nervous is all. I hate not knowing."

He watched his daughter fidget with her dress while she sat on the seat of the wagon next to him. He was often summoned like this into the cities to pick up and drop off supplies between the neighboring towns. A work order usually arrived via messenger and stated what needed to be brought and what he could expect to return with and where it went. But this time was different. He got the same work order as before but at the bottom was a set of instructions that said to bring the same girl as before. That did make him nervous but what could he do? Say no and be out of a job?

He turned back to watch his mule clomping rhythmically down the road and noticed a man strolling along its edge, whistling a tune he'd never heard before.

"Howdy stranger. You headed into the city?"

I spun to see a man in plain brown pants and shirt. His dirty boots were propped up on a foot rest and to his side sat a girl in a light green dress and of unparalleled beauty. Her long curly red hair flowed down well past her shoulders and her high cheekbones were slightly freckled. I guessed her age to be at least in her early twenties as our eyes met. I noticed they were of such a light colored green they matched her dress and I smiled. She reminded me of Christmas.

I nodded to the man, "sure am. You offering up a ride?" I answered, trying to mimic his accent as best I could.

"Reckon so. Hop on. Cherr move closer and let the man ride up front." The girl did as she was told and I swung up gently without the wagon even having to slow. "The names Toad. This here's my daughter Cherry, on account of her hair if ya can see."

"It's nice to meet yas. You can call me Fin." I stared at the girl's hair for a moment. "And I can see," I pointed out with all politeness. "It's beautiful. Like flowing lava down a mountainside," I teased and her face took on the color of her hair as she blushed. There was an awkward silence and I realized I must have struck a nerve. "Someday she'll make someone lucky I'm sure but as for me, I'm spoken for. Three kids and done." I smiled at the two.

The father seemed to relax a bit, "little ones hey? They grow up quicker than a hair on a freckle they do. You can count on that. One day they're crying when they have to play with boys the next, they're crying when you won't let em. Enuff to drive a man mad it is." I laughed at this. "They're all loveable and easy until then!" He spit off into the grass and turned back to me. "What's got ya headin into town if you don't mind my askin?"

"I don't mind at all. I got some family in there who's starting to set up a shop. Kids are at their Gam Gams so I'm off to lend a hand," the backstory came out easily.

"A shop hey? That's mighty fortunate of them. Hard to get spots in that city or so I've heard."

"I heard the same. Was told they was awarded it on the account of some research they done. My sister's husband, that fellas a regular genius if ya ask me."

"Intellectual types." He spit again then replaced his wad, offering the tin to me after he was done. "Some leaf friend?"

I took it with a nod and stuck it in my gums like he had. My mouth went cold at the overpowering flavor of mint.

He smiled at my expression, "make it myself."

"It's great. Thank you."

He inclined his head, "What was I saying? Oh yeah, intellectual types. They're beyond me with that stuff. Thinkin on things no one else does. Potions and inventions. Worlds fine the way it is if I can say so."

"Well I like that sorta thing," Cherry spoke up. "Just the other day when I saw Fella, she had this awful smelling paste she bought. She put it in her hair for a time, now her hair color's blonde and it's as soft as a rabbit's tail."

"Cherry, if you stood Fella in a field on a windy day her ears would whistle. Someone probably got one over on her and-"
"Did not Pa. I seen it."

He waved her comment away and looked back to me. "Your first time visiting the city Fin?"

"Yes sir it is. I can't right lie. I'm a little nervous and excited."

He tugged at the reins to direct the mule around a pothole on the road. "Well then where ya headed? I've been in a few times now myself and can drop you off directly if you'd like?"

I kept my composure as I thought how to best continue with my charade. "Actually, I'll just get off wherever you guys are going if it ain't no problem. I'm a bit early and wouldn't mind doing some sightseeing."

"That'd be Main Street then. Gotta do a drop off of sorts there." I watched as his daughter looked up at him anxiously as he finished and decided to see if there was more to it.

"Awful light load you got here isn't it? Or do you have other business?"

"You're spot on. Usually my loads are fuller but we just came in and a few days ago with one. Well I brought Cherry here with me then and now she's been requested back."

I knew how some of the higher beings in physical dimensions worked. The same way everything else in existence did, with little to no care for the species below it. But can you blame them? Look how humans treat cows, chickens and what was probably likely in this lady's situation, lab rats. No wonder she looked so scared. Poor father was too dimwitted to realize or too scared to disobey.

I decided right then and there to use the girl as my pawn to infiltrate the Ascendals community.

"Y'all don't mind if I join? My brother in law has a lot of pull so I hear and if things go bad maybe I can drop his name and help out."

The two glanced at each other for a quick second then turned back to me, "much obliged that'd be." and, "that would be much appreciated sir." Their words coming out at nearly the same time. I decided to change the subject to help keep them at ease. "Now, what I really wanna know is the secret you're holding back about the flavor in this here leaf."

CHAPTER 27

Death is another thing you view completely wrong. It isn't until you look at it from the correct angle that you can see its truth. When you die, the soul rescinds back into the spirit realm but what you don't know is that before this life your soul existed there as well. This means your true origin is the spirit realm and you are just visitors to this world. It is a dream from Heaven, your dream. Death is only like waking up. Death is only going home.

Ameletas checked the math again. Seven thousand one hundred and fifty four. So seven plus one plus five plus four together makes seventeen. Subtract that from the original number then divide by nine. That would make it the seven hundred and ninety third multiger of nine. He rolled his eyes. They were supposed to be considered higher beings but the numerical system his dimwitted counterparts used was the same as the common folks. Sure it got the job done and could get you from point A to point B but so does a horse. Wouldn't you rather saddle it before you use it? They simply did not grasp the effectiveness of the three, six, nine tri numerical system.

There was a shuffle at the door and he looked up to see the pair he'd been waiting on walking in. He pushed the paperwork back into his pocket and stood.

"Finally. Evlosin and Thiesin, I've been waiting to talk to you two." He announced as they approached, "I heard a rumor that you two are planning the abduction of another common folk but this time for selfish or less then respectable motivations. I'd like to know if there is any truth to this?"

"Leave it alone Ameletas. No one put you in charge." Thiesin responded and Evlosin followed up.

"Besides, we're not being selfish. I may decide to take her as my wife and if not, then I will share her with the Loyamore." They chuckled and brushed him aside as easily as a hanging curtain as they passed. "Think of it Thiesin, an army of redheads."

Ameletas stared at the other two Ascendals, his glowing eyes boring holes into their backs. "Just because our God is occupied, doesn't mean there won't be consequences. What you are doing is way outside the gray with this one. There are rules that we need to follow if we are to remain in this place."

"There are no rules, only suggestions. I've been doing such a good job lately I felt it was time to reward myself."

"But your actions could affect us all." Ameletas pleaded as he followed behind. "We are permitted here for now but not for much longer if imbeciles like you can't advance beyond their primitive urges. Just because God doesn't stop something personally doesn't mean others won't step forward to do so."

This got their attention and they both spun on him. Evlosin stepped forward, his red eyes blazing like fire trapped inside two marbles. "Others like you?" he asked, daring the weaker being to accept his challenge.

Ameletas let his eyes fall. There was no point in challenging them. The red in their eyes was symbolism for what step of Enlightement they were on. They were the most dangerous and unpredictable of the Ascendals as they struggled to control and understand their purposes.

"What is the life of one female to you?" Thiesin asked. "I've heard stories of you ending the lives of the common folk. Surely that's worse than simply forcing her into marriage?"

He shook his head, "You two need to understand intent. I took lives to save lives. My intent was justified. You are taking her freedom, and for despicable reasons. Your intent is selfish. I care nothing for the girl's life or your choices until they affect me. If you do this I lose my wagon driver and-"

"I will personally get you a new one Ameletas. Why don't you stick around and at least see why I chose to get married again so soon after the last one's death. I promise, even you will feel a, how did you just say it? primitive urge." He laughed and Thiesen joined him.

Ameletas huffed. "Primitive urges indeed. You'll find I'm far beyond the pastimes of lesser-"

Thiesin cut him off with a snort, "women don't do it for ya? Is it men?"

They continued to laugh until Evlosiin finally grabbed his companions shoulder to get his attention, "it's neither. You ever wonder why all the pages of his research stick together?"

They doubled over in their fit, knocking a few items to the floor as they flailed around merrily.

Ameletas furrowed his brow in anger and turned to walk to the door but a being had just entered. He spoke out and the words sounded like it couldn't make up its mind between clearing his throat or sucking at his teeth.

He held up a drawing board with a picture of a wagon and a girl with red hair.

"Oh good they're here!" Thiesin pulled out a book that was used to help bridge the communication gap between them and pointed to a few symbols. The servant bowed and walked away hastily. "Now you have no choice. You have to stay. This female is the finest of her kind beyond a doubt and I won't let you deny this. You're coming with us."

He put his hand on Ameletas's shoulder to escort him to the courtyard where he instructed the servant to bring her.

As they entered, fond memories of his master and him cre-at-ing this place came back to mind. Ameletas stared at the red-stone path that zigzagged this way and that through its short blue grass. White flowers speckled it all like paint drops and there were carved wooden benches of the most elegant and complex de-signs he had ever seen. On the skirts of the abode were the bio crystalisk trees his mentor had once created himself.

Giving life where it was not natural was not allowed on the outside but in these walls the transparent orange and yellow trunks grew up into hundreds of branches, their leaves gently ringing against each other like a quiet symphony. Gemstone fruits changed shades from red to green before they fell and shattered into tiny explosions where they were then harvested for jewelry. He turned to his favorite part of it all. The bridge made of water. Not ice, but water held in its place. It still swayed and swirled as tiny bubbles ran through it but its surface tension was strength-ened tenfold to keep it solid, hold weight and resist tampering until it was formed. Under it flowed the river of liquid rock. Its multicolored mass of reds, oranges, browns and blacks splashed and flowed like a river should. He thought back to a time he had stuck his arm into it. The substance had no temperature and felt like someone was pulling a coarse leather sheet continuously around his skin.

There were many places like this around the city where they are permitted to play God, bending and breaking the rules of nature.

"Let's take this bench near the bridge," Evlosin spoke out, breaking off his daydreams. "I want her to be as awestruck as possible before we remove her from her father."

Thiesin opened his mouth to speak but noticed the servant ushering someone through the door. "Right on time," he stated, nudging his companion.

An older man walked in wringing an empty sack between his hands nervously like he was choking out a weasel. To his right walked a tall man of average looks and dull blue eyes who took in the garden with appreciation as if nothing else in the world \

mattered. Behind them walked a small timid female with long flowing red hair that blazed like it was made from the autumn sun itself. Her body curved exactly where and when it should and she had two green eyes evenly spaced apart above a tiny nose and two pink lips. There was not one noticeable flaw and even her freckles complemented her natural allure perfectly. For the first time he could remember in a long time, Ameletas found him struck by the beauty of one of the common folk.

"Look at Ameletas," Evlosin teased. "He's more mesmerized than you Thiesin."

The smaller Ascendal pulled out of it with a shake of his head. "I won't stand for this. You will not remove this woman from her father or do anything she doesn't agree to personally or I will report you myself. Misosin may look past your primitive urges but I doubt he'd risk God's displeasure so carelessly as you two."

This got their attention and they both stared at him. "My dear Ameletas, that almost sounded like... a threat? You wouldn't dare threaten two of the most powerful Sin at the same time would you? Thiesin what do you think?"

"I think he's trying his hardest to put a damper on your fun. Or earn an express ticket to his next life."

Evlosin nodded his agreement, "I think it's both."

The cornered Ascendal stood straighter, trying to hide his fright. "You wouldn't dare."

Evlosin took a step closer, a wicked grin spread across his face at the thought of violence. Ameletas found himself shrinking back and searching desperately for a way out. As he did this, he noticed the tall being with blue eyes whisper something to his companions. Their faces went white and then they slowly started to back themselves to the door as the being made his way over. He walked between them casually, like he was approaching old friends.

"You must listen and listen like your life depends on it," I instructed softly, leaning closer so only they could hear. "One of them plans on forcing Cherry into a marriage and I doubt that's a good thing. They are threatening to kill the small one because he refused to let them. I'm going to distract them, you two sneak out."

"How do you know-" Toad began but I cut him off with a gentle shove.

"Go!" I ordered, then turned and made my way over to the three Ascendals.

"Come now Ameletas. Put up a fight at least. Make it fun. Standing there like a helpless child isn't going to save you," Evlosin taunted.

"Fight back so you can say I attacked you first? I think not! If you're going to murder me then you're going to do it like the cowards you are."

He finished his sentence with a puzzled expression as I stepped between the two, an uncaring smile on my face. "Thiesin are you watching this?" Evlosin marveled in astonishment, "I think this one lost his wits."

"I am," the other answered, "Maybe you should see if you can knock some back into him?"

There was no hesitation as the first Ascendal let a back hand fly that would have sent a normal man soaring. I pulled my head back just enough to let his blow swing by in a rush of air.

Thiesin laughed from behind, "apparently you can't." He joked.

Evlosins eyes narrowed in anger, "Insolent fool," he muttered and then swung again, this time a back hand from the other side in an attempt to catch me off guard.

I moved away from it with a giant casual step to the side that brought their attention with me and away from the door where Cherry and her father were escaping.

"Oh my this one is electric," Thiesin appreciated with respect. His partner didn't share his observations as he growled in frustration.

"Oh you poor fool. Get out of here before they kill you," I heard the one called Ameletas mutter as he continued to cower behind me.

"I am past my graciousness," Evlosin spat. "Any lesser creatures who dare meddle in the affairs of beings far superior to them deserve death." His hand raised into the air and pointed directly at me. I watched him as he formed the essence into a ball in front of his palm and smiled as he released it directly at my chest.

The beam blasted through me in a hiss and where my rib cage and right lung used to be there was nothing left but a gaping hole. I continued to stand there smiling as they stared at me in stunned bewilderment.

I felt the immense tug of my Earthen body at the pain but was waiting for it. I succumbed to its call but only for a half a heart beat.

I blinked.

My body reformed solidly inside my clothes, the gaping wound now replaced by soft uninjured skin and Evlosins eyes went wide in confusion.

My hand shot out, gripping him by the wrist before he could pull it away. "You know," I started and there was a collective gasp at my words and the fact that they could understand them. "I've always held the belief that it is the responsibility of higher beings to protect the life below them, not take it. But..." I let a sly smile come over my face as he tugged at my wrist where I held him like a vice. "I think today I'll go by some new advice I just heard. How did you say it?" I cocked an eyebrow to see if he would respond but Evlosin just froze as he stared me in the eyes. "Any lesser creatures who dare meddle in the affairs of beings far superior to them deserve death." I raised my other arm level with his face, palm out like he had just done to me. It went ashen and he shook his head in denial. "You've been caught meddling" He threw up his other hand to either attack or defend but it didn't matter. I ripped the essence from his body, leaving him completely defenseless and formed it instantly into a ball then shot it back at him. A move I picked up 8 years before when it was used to kill me.

The beam exploded through his head with a sizzle and I let go of his wrist, his body slumping to the ground. His partner stared at me in wide eyed horror, looking from the corpse then back to me.

"Please, it was all him. I was just here to see what she looked like. He was the one that was going to keep her."

I turned to Ameletas, "what do you think? Wasn't he about to kill you?"

The small Ascendal shook his head to regain his senses. "That's very kind of you," he spoke as he stepped forward, "But I doubt this one has it in him."

"So we give him a second chance?" I asked, turning back to the red eyed being who still stood in shock.

"I believe it's the right choice. We are not as accepting of death as the inhabitants of this place."

I shrugged, "I believe in second chances. However, I have business here and can't have people knowing about me so I'll make you a deal. You ever heard of the game hide and seek?"

He rocked back in thought, "Is that one of the games played by the common folks children?"

"That's correct. As of right now me and you are playing hide and seek but to the death. If I see you again, or even hear a rumor that you're somewhere close by, I'll seek you out and kill you without a word. And I should warn you... I'm very good." Thiesin just stood, unsure of how he was supposed to respond, "now go hide," I commanded and shewed him away.

He pulled in essence and shot through the air like a streak without looking back once. I turned to the door to find it empty and was thankful Toad and Cherry were able to make their escape.

Ameletas walked forward then, still watching the other go. "I feel very sorry for the next being who earns his wrath. He is of the Sin. They do not forgive and they do not forget. I feel if you really did want to remain a secret in this place, it will not be for long."

I gave an uncaring shrug, "hopefully I don't need that long. I'm just here to find a way to meet the one you all call God."

"I'm afraid you're too late for that. We had a being come here a while back to do the same thing. It destroyed half the city and killed hundreds before it was able to gain access and even then no one knows how that was accomplished. It must still be there now as there has been no sign or word from our God since then."

I turned away from the door and went back to where the body lay on the ground. "This being will either let me in or I will kill it. As you can see I have no respect for the wicked."

"I can see," he stated, looking down at the body. "But if I may ask, why is meeting God so important to you?"

I bent down and grabbed the feet of the dead Ascendal and stood. "Two reasons, boredom and pursuit of the infinity code." He shook his head in disbelief. "What kind of being can do the things you've just done and show not even the slightest hesitation when told of a being strong enough to destroy half a city by itself ?"

I paused in what I was doing to watch him for a reaction as I spoke, "I was told that your kind would refer to me as a Boundless." His eyes went wide in amazement for a half a second but then he quickly composed himself.

"I've heard that Boundless are very unpredictable. Some as weak as the common folk and others powerful beyond our comprehension. It all depends on what step they are on. It is why we refer to them as Boundless. You must be very skilled indeed to control the color of your eyes... or are they naturally like that?" he questioned but I didn't plan on giving away too much so didn't respond. "Where are my manners? I'm Ameletas, an Ascendal of the fourth understanding as my green eyes may have given away," he bowed to me as he spoke.

"I am Fin. A human of... no understanding as my confused expression may have given away. If I may ask, how could I have known that based on your eye color? I've been to lots of places and always eye colors were hereditary except amongst the higher beings. Red, orange, yellow, green, purple, brown, all different, all glowing, but no one has ever explained to me why this is?" I of fered an awkward bow to his then went back to my work, feeding the essence into the corpse as I awaited his reply.

"Well you see, here in this place we have a God who every now and then, lets us know certain pieces of the infinity code…" he cut off as curiosity got the best of him while he tried to puzzle out what I was doing. "Can I ask what you're doing?"

I finished feeding the essence into the corpse, the massive amount it now held barely contained by its thin layer of skin. I planted my back foot and heaved with all my might, sending the thing flying into the air where it exploded into a vapor.

"Removing evidence. I don't like to leave a trail behind me. Please continue, I assure you I'm listening," I offered, swirling more essence into the bloodstain and slowly cooking it away.

He stared in disgust, "as I was saying, eyes and their color are always a representation of the soul, even among the lower beings. When they reach the final step, their current level of understanding is reflected in what color eyes they are born with. Certain souls can only go into certain bodies. After the test, if they fail, make no improvements, or even advance slightly, it may change in the next life accordingly. This will continue until they reach the next tier of the ladder, Ascendals."

I thought on this, "but Ascendals have more colors, why?" "This is true and easy to explain. They are now capable of experiencing different dimensions and have received more senses to help them progress their souls as they go. Once they've stepped off of the common beings ladder the souls change, the rules change and the progress they can now make is extended. Common beings have less colors because there's less they have to master. Once they reach the next tier, then they are required to do them all and they can start anywhere, it's always different but most get stuck at the bottom as it's the first step of this ladder and the hardest.``

"What are all the colors?" I asked standing as I finished.

"The same as the rainbow." He shook his head like he was talking to a child, "Red, orange, yellow, green, blue, indigo, violet.

I am of the fourth, which is why my eyes are green. Most of the others here are red, which is Wrath, and its balance mercy."

"All the colors are like this? About finding a balance?"

"A balance to the soul, yes but sometimes the completion of one requires much more understanding to balance its counter properly. All of our eye colors are based around this. Sloth and its balance vigor, pride and it's balance humbleness, greed and it's balance generosity, lust and it's balance-"

I waved his overly long explanation away. "I get that part. So that means beings with purple eyes are on the final step?" I asked, trying not to show my excitement by thinking I was about to reach another tier.

"No." I visibly deflated at his response. "As I said, you can start out anywhere and every color must be mastered before the next tier, and some colors require failure to proceed, from what I was led to understand. If lower beings can master all of them in one life I suppose it's possible at this tier too."

I tried to hide my disappointment, "Are there any other colors besides those? Maybe a different step or something?"

"Only one comes to mind."

I turned back to him with a disbelieving look, "There's one with different colored eyes outside the spectrum? Who?"

"No offense but your grasp on the infinity code is extremely deficient if I have to explain that to you," he stated as he stared at me with a look like I was cleaning my ears with a loaded crossbow. I shrugged as he rolled his eyes, "GOD!"

Realization spread across my face and I laughed at my own stupidity. "I could have guessed that I suppose." There was a commotion from the doorway and I heard shouting so I turned to face it as I continued, "and what color eyes does a God have?"

He turned to stare at the door with me as he responded slowly in an attempt to hear what was going on outside, "all of them and none of them."

I shot him a glance then started to move towards the door, "how is that possible?"

"That's simple, you should have learned this as a child I would have imagined-"

His words cut off as Cherry came crashing through the doorway. There were tears streaming down her face and she had blood on her arms and hands. She stumbled to the ground but got up quickly as I ran to meet her.

"They killed him! They killed my Pa!" she cried, fear and sadness causing her voice to crackle. "Please!" she stumbled again but I caught her in an embrace.

"What's going on?" Ameletas asked in confusion.

A man ran through the door behind her, a bloody sword in one hand and he had scratches all over his face. "We have our orders-" he cut off when he noticed the Ascendal and instead just froze.

Ameletas approached the man and pulled out a drawing pad and gestured to a few of the symbols. "They tried to leave without permission. The guards were ordered to not let them off the grounds under any circumstances," he spoke this like he was talking to himself but eyed me sideways as he did, "The poor fools were just doing what they were ordered. The old man must have tried to fight his way out and they killed him for it."

Cherry had her face buried in my chest and was sobbing uncontrollably as I stroked her hair in comfort. Anger and sorrow both washed over me at the loss of such a kindly old man who had helped me out without having to be asked.

"Go into the other room and make sure we aren't disturbed until he gives you further orders," I commanded and pointed to the door as I did.

"Sorry friend but I only take orders from the red eyed-" he cut off when Ameletas pointed and snapped his finger as well, not sure of how to proceed.

"I'd play it safe if I were you. He's not in any kind of mood," I added and the man finally saluted and walked out.

"It's amazing you can talk like them. What did you tell him?"

"Just to wait and guard the door to make sure no one comes in until you give him further orders. He was reluctant about the last part though, said you didn't have the right colored eyes."

Ameletas nodded. "They serve the Sin but aren't dumb enough to disobey any other Ascendals I'd assume."

I ignored him, prying Cherry back in an attempt to talk. "Cherry," I called softly and she lifted her eyes. "I want to help you. I feel like all of this is my fault."

"No it ain't! You gave us a chance. Those men out there told us what they were planning to do. Said if I wasn't a good wife they was going to let them have me in his stead. Pa didn't like that too much so we tried to run.. but Pa..." She started to cry again, trying desperately to regain her composure. "Pa wouldn't let them take me back to those evil things. I told him not to fight but he was so upset at himself for bringing me here..." she put her head back to my chest and began to cry in earnest.

"I know. I know," I soothed.

"They just left his body lying in the street. I just held him for a while and they let me but the second they turned their backs I decided to run and try to find you. We heard you, you can talk like them!"

I ignored the comment and instead addressed a different issue, "so your fathers just lying in the street? What do you want done with his body, I can help with that I'm sure."

She shook her head and it caused her curls to bounce back and forth. "When Ma died we started moving around a lot so I guess it doesn't matter." Her eyes went wide as she realized the extent of her situation. "What am I supposed to do now? I have nothing and no one! I don't know how to drive a wagon or nothing like that. I don't know how to work or-"

"Cherry," I said softly to interrupt her. "You said you had a friend, Fella? Could you stay with her?"

She shook her head. "I say she's my friend but we only seen each other a few different times. When you move as much as we did you don't get time to make a lot of friends. I don't even know where Fella lives. I just talk to her when she walks by."

"There has to be somewhere you can go or someone you can stay with?"

She pushed back from me to stare me directly in the eyes. "What about you? I can help your family at their shop. Tend to the kids, cook, clean. Help out your wife? I'll earn my keep' I promise."

I let my head drop, the lie coming back to sting me, "Cherry... I made all that up. I don't have a wife or kids here. There is no shop and I'm not even from... this planet."

"I don't understand? Why would you lie?" Her eyes searched mine as she awaited the response.

"I'm different. Like I said I'm not from this world but here I'm a being that's very powerful and I can talk like them." I pointed to where Ameletas watched us curiously. "That's how I knew what they planned to do with you. I killed the one that plotted it actually."

She wiped her eyes. "I believe you. I told you I heard you speak like them but you're powerful enough to kill them too?" she asked in amazement.

I gave her a gentle smile to try and calm her, "Yes, I am."

She finished wiping her tears and stood up straighter, a serious expression on her face, "Then I want to stay with you. I can cook, clean. I'll give you kids and be your wife but I'm never leaving your side."

I reeled back at the offer, her beauty would give any man pause. "Cherry, it's not that simple. I'm not from this world and that means I could leave at any time I wanted."

"I don't care. My mind is made up," she continued to stand with her back erect, not looking at me. "Even if you say no, I'll just follow you."

I laughed at her determination. "How about this, you can stay with me as long as I'm here but not as my wife. I feel like I at least owe you that much. Also, I'll be sure to try and leave you well off when I do have to leave," I said, emphasizing the words well off to make her feel better, "Is it a deal?"

She finally looked at me, "deal."

"Now, you don't mind if we stay in the city? I have business here I would like to attend to."

"You can stay anywhere you want as long as I'm there too."

"And the burial of your father?" I asked and she started to fight back tears again.

"Just somewhere close and quick I suppose. To get him out of the street."

I nodded to this and turned back to the Ascendal. "Is there a way I can tell the guard to do something and he would think it came from you?"

"What message would that be?" he questioned. "Just burial plans for her father."

"Simply tell them it's from me and I can give a signal confirming the order."

I called the guard back in and ordered him to have a plot dug and the body prepared for burial. He asked where he should send notice when it was done and I turned back to Ameletas.

"He wants to know where we'll be?"

"Oh we can retire to my place in the meantime," he offered, and showed the man the address of his residence.

"One more thing," I called to the guard before he turned to leave. "I want you to spread the word among all the other people in this city. If they see this woman here," I gestured to Cherry, "they are to treat her like a lady. From here on out all of their kind," I gestured to Ameletas next, "want her treated like she is royalty and any slights against her will go punished immediately." He turned back to the Ascendal and the being confirmed without knowing what he was even agreeing to.

The guard bowed and ran off to do as he was told and Cherry turned back to me. "Why would you say that?"

"I told you before," I said with a casual shrug, "and when I say well off, I mean well off." I offered her my arm and she took it with a sorrowful smile.

CHAPTER 28

ime is also viewed wrong and this is because you're under the wrong impression. Time going on forever is easy for you to comprehend as long as it continues to flow in the only direction that you know, forwards. It is only when you try to conceive it going backwards forever as well that your understanding fails you. Time having no beginning is also both impossible and the only possibility you can imagine. It isn't until you realize its truth that you can ever fully understand it. Time isn't a true infinite, it's just an illusion cast over your awareness. It is a perception and perceptions can be changed.

"God allows us to visit here or keep a residence, do our research, keep the peace, teach, that sort of thing. Ruling is prohibited and watched carefully but not unheard of. It's even commonplace in some areas."

"And you travel similar to the way I do but your body follows?"

"That is correct and yours doesn't. The laws of your reality are designed to keep you shackled within your own universe, your own time, which is why I don't believe in the Boundless and referred to you as an impossibility."

I smiled, "I've heard that before," I responded thinking back to my first projection. "But what does all this have to do with nuts?"

He chuckled to himself. "My apologies. I have a keen interest in knowledge, both the collection of and the passing on. There is a nut native to this world that has all the perfect combination of chemicals our bodies need to project themselves. That is why every other farm around this city grows them... and we still have to have them shipped in. You see when-"

"Oh my!" Cherry's gasp cut off his words as we rounded a corner. I lifted my head to see what had caused it and Ameletas filled us in.

"This is me then," he said, then gestured us through the gate.

We stood in front of a large structure very much like a house but unlike any kind I've encountered before. The yard didn't exist. In place of grass was a view of some sort of universe with millions of glimmering lights of various sizes, shapes and colors twinkling like tiny embers floating in a sea of tar. On top of it all floated some giant lily pads as a sort of stepping stone walk- way. This path was also lined with poles holding a brilliant blue flame that sputtered and popped as chunks of it fell in on itself like some sort of odd volcano. A fish jumped from the side and sent ripples throughout the illusion and what looked like a brilliant night sky only appeared to be the reflection of one, with the real sky above being a soft blue.

The house in its entirety floated about ten feet off the ground as if by magic. Its walls were made up of what I thought was painted trees in the fall until a breeze ran through them. I squinted as we stepped through the gate and noticed the pattern repeated itself after several seconds like it was a looping video. Its windows were all mirrors that I assumed were two way and its roof was an unending flow of water that cascaded to the side and disappeared silently into the void below.

Ameletas noticed our faces. "I could spend four lifetimes explaining everything you see in this place and how it worked but I won't. Instead as you know, I have a keen interest in all things knowledge so I will just say this," he started to point as he talked. "The abyss keeps people from trying to come into my yard, the anti-gravity on the house helps prevent them from breaking in, and the flowing water," he finished by pointing to the roof, "keeps bugs and leaves from collecting. Now come along. I assure you it's quite safe even if you fall in." He made his way down the lily pads and gestured for us to follow.

I walked behind him and stared at one of the weird torch light poles as I got closer. Its bluish substance popped like some sort of perpetual chemistry solution as it continuously fed itself to solidify, liquefy then run back down, feeding the bottom again and starting the process all over.

I shook my head, "It looks like ice." I was astonished, not knowing how else to explain it.

He glanced back, "what? Oh, it is... sort of. Temperature fuels it. Come along."

We got about half way and Cherry finally gave out, refusing to continue on and shutting her eyes as she buried her face in my chest. I tried to act comforting as I picked her up but she latched onto my neck like a frightened kitten. We made our way to the house and Ameletas pushed a tiny amount of essence into a lever on the last pole before the house. A whirring noise sounded and an enormous solid white slab that looked like marble descended and we stepped on it. We gently floated up and stepped off onto the front entryway that closely resembled a porch.

"Hidden door too?" I asked after noticing there wasn't one visible.

"I take extra precautions. The technologies I have collected here could alter too much too fast and would be extremely dangerous if it were to get out. That sort of thing could have consequences."

He pressed the wall with three fingers and a portion of the trees cut out and an opening appeared. We walked in, Cherry still clinging to my neck with her eyes shut tight.

The entryway was massive, about the same size as the house itself appeared from the outside and to my surprise, somewhat ordinary. Brown walls ran along its edges with doorways every few dozen feet or so. There was a giant chandelier that cast rainbows in all directions but where the light was originating from I couldn't tell.

I nudged Cherry as I moved to set her down and she peered around timidly.

"Ameletas, with all the precautions you take, how is the guard supposed to get us the message when he's done?"

He turned around to address me, "there's a box outside they can punch symbols into. It's not the best but he should be able to convey his reasons." He extended an arm to gesture us forward, "shall we head to the lounge? Goodness it's been ages since I've entertained an actual guest."

Cherry stood on her own now as she regained her confidence and a thought occurred to me. "The lounge isn't all... advanced like the outside is it? I think the lady here does not do well with that sort of thing."

He pushed his lips to one side as he eyed her. "I hadn't considered that. I forget how fragile underdeveloped minds can be. I'm afraid the lounge is designed to inspire and impress my colleagues. Common folk have never entered. It's very impressive indeed," he snapped his fingers. "I've got it. I'll just bring some tables and chairs here. She seems to be doing fine now and this way we can continue our discussions."

"That would be great, thank you."

He came back with a table, then two chairs, then one more chair and a tray of pastries and drinks. Cherry and I were already seated when he finished and sat with a sigh.

"Again, thank you," I offered.

He waved the comment away as he started to fill his cup, "Think nothing of it. You did save my life today. Or at least, saved me from a severe beating."

"Would he really have killed you?" I asked, offering Cherry the tray and watching her pick a small fluffy pastry covered in a red jelly. I took one similar to hers and put the tray back at the center.

"Hard to know. As I said before, we Ascendals do not usually kill our own kind as it gives cause for our deaths to be sought out as well. Death is something very serious and is a rare occurrence amongst us." He paused to take a sip before he spoke. "But things have been getting very odd lately. I doubt it of Thiesin, he usually directs his wrath towards things that can't kill him back but Evlosin, he has grown very bold as of late."

I took a bite as I listened and my tastebuds were instantly overwhelmed, like I was eating the world's most delicious sandwich. The fluffy donut-like food was filled with a nut flavored cream and topped with a jam that was similar to raspberry. It was beyond delicious and I turned to Cherry, watching her eyebrows go up in surprise and delight as she savored every bite.

Ameletas smiled proudly. "Knowledge in all things, even baking."

I nodded my agreement before I swallowed, then continued our conversation. "So things are odd. Does this have to do with the other being?" I took another bite and watched a second being walk out of one of the doorways and freeze.

His glowing yellow eyes taking everything in with a frown as he spoke. "Ameletas, why are, um, common beings being entertained in the entry room? What of the strict policy we enforce?" His eyes lingered on Cherry for a minute then moved back to me.

"My favorite pupil' Sepistomone. I sometimes don't even realize you're here. Have you been working this entire time?"

"Yes... but why are-"

Ameletas cut him off with a gesture. "This one here may have saved my life earlier so I'm offering him help."

The other Ascendals brows lowered in disbelief. "Um, saved your life? A common folk?"

"Yes. He killed Evlosin. It was actually quite spectacular. I went to investigate that rumor you told me about and-"

"A COMMON FOLK killed Evlosin?" The one called Sepistomone interrupted again, doubt heavy in his voice as he nearly shouted the words. "Ameletas, I think you've finally stepped outside your own mind."

"What? Oh yes. He's not common folk. He is one of the most powerful beings I've ever encountered. He is a Boundless."

I stood with a smile, swallowing the last of the delightful food and held out my hand. "The names Fin."

He reeled back from me with his arms clutched to his chest like I was contagious. "He can talk?"

"Yes, yes. Please catch up," Ameletas snapped, taking another sip from his cup and I sat back down with a shrug. "Now where were we? Oh yes, oddities. I'm afraid you're right. With the only thing ever keeping us in line being the presence of God who is now... absent, lines are being crossed more and more to say the least. All attempts at contacting Ananke have failed. Nothing goes in, nothing comes out."

"Why can't they get in?"

"Well the guards there do not permit any living creature access without permission. They will actually attack and kill anything that tries."

I cocked my head. "Then send in something without life?" I blurted out like it was the simplest solution then leaned forward, "or help me find a way in! You know I'm powerful enough to have a chance."

Ameletas shook his head. "I don't know if getting in has ever been done... but I do know of one that has tried, Misosin, the leader of the Sin. He's despicable enough to have tried it at least once that I know of. If anyones ever found a way in, it would be him." I watched the other Ascendals eyes dart frantically as he thought. They went wide for a second then he spun and left us without a word. Ameletas frowned at him, "Problem is, Misosin only holds council with his Generals. To gain an audience with him you'd have to join the Sin and obtain that rank and that could take years." He turned back to me with an inquisitive stare. "Assuming you somehow had red glowing eyes."

I didn't like the thought of it taking years but figured to meet a God, I'd probably wait an eternity. "Leave all that to me. I just needed to be pointed in the right direction and maybe... a place to stay."

He put a finger up to go deep into thought as he watched Cherry eat another pastry absently then slowly grabbed one of his own and took a bite.

The upraised finger snapped and he looked up to me proudly. "Assuming you have red eyes, I just came up with your plan. All you need to do is go down to NaoSin Hall. Say you're Evlosins kin and will be staying at his place as he's left town for a time and will be looking over his affairs. This way you get a place to stay that's not nearly as advanced as mine, a plausible reason to be there, a name to vouch for you and you're in with the Sin."

I rocked back in appreciation and we quickly started to smooth out the details. After a few moments the finished product was that Evlosin had obtained Cherry for me as my wife (they call them that but they are treated no better then slaves) as a welcoming gift. He had pressing business in the countryside, something he was known to do anyway, and there was no timetable for his return.

Ameletas continued to give me a rough walk through of everything else I needed to know and then some. We covered their communications boards, their background and history, common attire, common sayings and all sorts of other things I felt were a bit over the top but I listened anyway. He finished by giving me directions to our new place and when he finished I took the time to start putting our plan into effect.

I looked to Cherry and the blood and crumbs that covered her dress. "I suppose if you're going to be the wife of one of them beings, you're going to have to like the color red."

She cocked her head at me and I stood, clapping my hands together. The world went vivid as I recreated her a dress I'd once seen in a different world but changed its color to red. I gave it form and let it plop into my hand then offered it to her where she stared in stunned fascination.

"Put this on." She nodded slowly and took it, hiking her dress up as she did. I spun away. "A little heads up. I thought you'd want some privacy?"

She finished pulling the new dress down and straightened it as she talked. "His kind don't bother me and you're my husband remember?"

"Fake husband," I added, keeping my eyes averted. I thought back to what Evlosin had worn and decided to make the same thing. I clapped my hands together once more and formed the outfit one at a time, setting them on the table until I was finished. I glanced over at Cherry who now stood spinning gently, the bottom of the jagged dress fluttering with the motion, giving it the appearance of dancing flames. This new dress fit far better than the last one and I found myself staring. She was the most

beautiful woman I'd ever seen in any place ever.

She looked up and noticed me standing frozen, a surprised look on my face. "Is it that nice?" she asked, doing another twirl. "Yes. It's... You're beautiful." Her cheeks reddened slightly and she smiled. "Oh, and head ups, I'm changing now too." Her cheeks darkened further and she put her eyes down.

I finished dressing and checked myself over. "How is it?" I asked Ameletas who watched the whole thing with deep interest. "The things you can do are beyond comprehension."

"The outfit," I pointed out.

"Oh, of course. It's very good except for your eyes."

I laughed at my broken memory, "Yeah, I can't see them so I always forget." I relaxed my mind like before but this time pushed the essence back into them as I imagined blazing red coals glowing in a fire then used this to enforce my will and give them a new color. Shadows changed slightly but other than that I felt nothing but knew it had worked.

"You're amazing," Cherry muttered and Ameletas spoke up too.

"Remarkable. It's uncanny." Then he leaned forward.

I decided to blink to refresh myself after the removal of the body and now the new outfits. It didn't drain me a lot but I always felt it was best to play it safe. I did it then and instantly noticed a pain in one of my legs where it couldn't reform because of a pant leg in the way. Usually when I blinked it was too fast for the clothes to even move but apparently not this time. I pulled the pant leg up and watched the flesh reform, knowing instantly I could probably replicate this little trick if I tried. But that could wait, I turned back to the others and finally responded.

"Thank you." And then sat to await the messenger.

We continued our talk and decided to stay in touch, the Ascendal coming up with a way to stay under the radar by using the physicars shop he constantly worked out of as a middle man for our letters. Some time later the messenger came and we said our farewells. Cherry and I were led to a graveyard where we stood alone. With me not having any one specific religion I decided to just support her with whatever one she practiced.

Death was different here. It was still sad but not nearly as it is on Earth. They had an extremely enlightened way of viewing it. First, they knew it wasn't permanent and second they knew that if they did it right they went somewhere better. Maybe it was because they knew a God? Whatever it was, it was viewed as more of a see you later instead of a final goodbye.

She finished her thoughts and we made our way down the street towards the new address. I let her cling to my arm with her head on my shoulder as we walked and knew it wasn't a common sight. People stared and gawked in disbelief but I didn't care.

Eventually we found the place and made our way in. It was a massive stone building one step below a small castle, one step above a giant house. I waited patiently as Cherry handed the door servant the new instructions about me taking over in his old master's stead, about her to be treated like a Lady and that every order she gives is to be obeyed at punishment of death.

The servants and maids accepted this with indifference when I silently signaled my orders after she had finished.

"Now show me to the master's chambers at once," she commanded, trying her best to impersonate someone with authority. I held back a smile when it worked and we were led up some stairs to a bedroom the size of a small gym. Its enormous bed sat in the middle of the room against the wall under a window. It had red lace hanging around it and more pillows than anyone would ever need. To the left was a fireplace with two large soft chairs and to the right a large wardrobe and dresser with a mirror attached. The floor was covered in massive animal skin rugs of a kind I've never seen before. Their long silky hair a mix of red and oranges with a few spots of yellow. These beings clearly took pride in the color of their eyes.

I watched Cherry as she moved about the room, inspecting each thing in turn with a curious look. Had she not just lost her father I bet she would have been far more excited.

"What do you think?" I asked, following her from where she touched the rug to where she scratched at a large painting of an ocean at sunrise.

"It's amazing! And bigger than the whole barn we just rented out." She turned back to the bed. "Actually, that bed is about the size of the last house I lived in." She turned to face me, "What do you think? It's ours!" she stated, implying I'd be staying in it with her.

"No. It's yours. I don't sleep."

She clasped her hands behind her back and let her eyes fall to the ground, "but will you anyway? I don't want to be alone. If you really don't sleep then you can just lay in here with me until I do. This place, these people, they all scare me." I took a breath, contemplating how to answer. "I'll get better eventually. I am trying! You told me to change my clothes and I did without arguing. I've never done anything like that before. Undress in front of a man but I knew I couldn't be a burden. I have to help in any way I can and I'm supposed to be your wife so I need to prove to you I'm useful and that–"

"Cherr," I interrupted, walking forward as the tears started to stream down her face. "I'll stay here with you. I think it would be expected anyway if you're supposed to be my wife." She nodded but didn't respond. "How about this? I will do anything you ask of me to keep you happy as long as it doesn't interfere with my other plans. Sound good?"

She looked up into my eyes and they went back and forth slowly as she stared into each in turn. "Do you promise?"

I smiled, "I promise."

"Good. Then I want you to hold me until I fall asleep like my Pa used to when I was scared. There's something about you that reminds me of him, like when I'm around you I don't have to be afraid of anything."

"I guess I can do that," I agreed with a shrug.

She ordered some servants to prepare us a meal and draw a bath then blushed from head to toe when she noticed they only filled one. I told her she could bathe alone as blinking was far more effective then any bath ever could be.

She came out a few minutes later wearing nothing but a towel. "Um, can you make me some night clothes?"

I chuckled, realizing our small overlook. "Is that a question or a demand?" I teased.

"I'd never demand anything of you but will you?"

I clapped my hands together and formed some silk pajamas for her as I spoke. "It's ok to demand sometimes, if it's really important to you."

She looked at them sideways as I handed them over then walked away to get dressed. She came back staring at her legs and arms with her eyes wide in amazement, "This stuff feels wonderful!" She marveled and I noticed right away I forgot to make her a bra and underwear.

"Cherr, we forgot the bra and underwear. I can make-"

She shook her head, "If you wanna look you can look. I'm a woman of twenty years and am comfortable with who I am."

"It's not like it's a big deal. It will only-"

"It's fine. This stuff feels way too good and besides, I didn't sleep in them before, I ain't gonna start now." She hopped in the bed and pulled the covers up to her chest and then gestured to the spot next to her.

I walked over making sure to sit on top of the blankets before I scooted closer. "Tomorrow while I'm gone you can have the maids bring you anything and everything you need. Undergarments, clothes, dresses, shoes, all that sort of thing."

She lifted my arm and wrapped it around her neck, placing her head on my chest then spoke softly, "I'm coming with you." "Sorry but you can't. Not this time. I'm going to NaoSin Hall to join and that could be dangerous."

She glared at me as if to show how serious she was. "Well then I demand you always take me with you whenever you can. I ain't afraid of danger, or anyone or anything when I'm with you. Don't you ever leave me behind."

I let my head fall back and hit the pillow with a sigh, realizing how much trouble this girl was going to cause me.

"Fine. I'll never leave you behind." "Promise?"

"I promise."

CHAPTER 29

Coincidences and miracles are often looked at from the same point of view but where does one begin and the other end? Most people agree that it's based around probability, the more impossible the odds, the bigger the miracle. I have always had the ability to see both of these for what they truly are. It's the secret to how I wrote this book with no resources, no help, no internet, nothing. Trying to fully understand the difference between the two is based on perspective but once you start, not only can you find understanding, you can find God.

I crept out of the bedroom before the sun came out, being careful not to wake her. Servants jumped up with symbol boards in hand while I shut the door quietly behind me. I looked it over, drink, food, clothes, bath, messages, and a bunch more with sub symbols to help further clarify if needed. I pointed at food and drink then waved them away. I made my way down the stairs and finally did a quick scan of the rest of the house and its accommodations. Evlosin had a thing for hunting or stuffed animals because nearly every room had the head of some unfortunate creature of which only a few I recognized as being similar to the kind found back on Earth.

A maid came running up with a tray, every single one of the foods it held contained some sort of nut, either crumbled on top or in a creme. I grabbed one, slammed the drink and then ate it on my way out the door

The streets were busy with people running this way and that. Beings of different species, races, shapes and sizes hustled about and most I've seen before as they were a common form of life in the places I've visited but usually not this diverse. I watched as a being unlike the others moved through the crowd. His glasslike body was transparent and his shape constantly formed into the people and beings he approached, causing them to flee at his odd ability as both failed to see what was really taking place. I realized he was only trying to show them a form he thought they would be comfortable enough with to engage in a conversation. He was unable to comprehend that everyone was different and seeing an exact replica of themselves wasn't natural. And they weren't advanced enough to see his intentions.

I decided to walk the other way and soon found myself behind a being I instantly recognized but had never encountered before. It had two legs bent backwards like an animals and they ended with blackened hooves. Its spine bubbled up along its back and split into two massive shoulders and muscular arms. Its skin was a scaley sort of red and two massive pointed wings hung tightly closed at its back. From the sides of its head two horns protruded, one to a sharp point, the others tip snapped off leaving a jagged edge. Until this very moment I always thought demons were just figments of our imaginations. Something made up to scare people into being good. It made me wonder how much of our imagination is original and how much is just stolen from the vortex of knowledge?

I watched the crowds then and if I had thought the other being had caused a wide berth then this creature was the titanic. People turned down alleys, walked into shops or simply spun and went back the way they were coming and I'm sure my drifting the thing didn't help it at all.

I heard it growl, its voice low and deep. "Cowards," it rumbled, head scanning back and forth.

Not being able to die changes a person. Had I encountered a being like this on Earth in my true body I may have shit the bed. But here nothing scared me so I decided to speak up.

"Lost friend?" I called cheerfully.

He spun, wings going wide and flapping loudly, a gust of wind blasting me as he lurched backwards. His red eyes blazed while he looked me over.

"Sorry. I didn't mean to frighten you," I chuckled at his expense.

"Nothing frightens me. I am fright incarnate," he spat back. "Sneaking up on someone like that could get you killed... friend." He spoke the word slowly, mocking the way I had said it.

I shrugged and continued to walk past him while he stared at me. His head sat at least a foot or so above mine I noticed as I responded. "Thought you wanted help is all. Didn't look like you were from around here."

"I'm not. The Demigog's do not waste their time with the affairs of mortals. Now tell me where I can find access to your God."

I stopped and turned back to face him squarely, confident in the power and skills I'd honed over the countless other projections I've done.

I stepped forward, our eyes deadlocked. "Say please."

His nostrils flared and I could see he was furious. "I warn you child. Know your betters. Tell me where I can-"

"Nope," I sassed with an uncaring grin and exaggerated blink of the eyes. "Say please first."

His hand shot forward to grab me by the throat but I was ready. I caught it midway and locked it within my grasp. It wasn't a use of muscle or even the focusing of essence, it was a new trick I picked up in believing. I formed an idea in my head that my arm wasn't movable by anyone or anything and then imposed my will on it.

He tugged his arm but it didn't budge, the uncaring and un-affected look still plastered on my face. He tugged again, harder and harder and even placed his other hand upon mine to try and pry himself free from my unyielding grip. I squeezed slightly and his eyes widened as he looked from me to my hand. He grit his teeth, the two fangs at their corners showing menacingly. I squeezed a little harder and he dropped to his knees and roared, eyes wide with a mix of anger and pain.

"Pleeaassee!" he growled, teeth still clenched and my hand opened causing him to fly backwards and land on his wings.

"See?" I pointed out, "that didn't kill ya now did it?" I cocked my head and leaned down towards him, "although it was getting close." He stood up rubbing at his wrist, not taking his eyes from me and I decided to fill him in in case he knew something I didn't. Our purposes were the same after all. "I'm not from here and I'm currently trying to accomplish the same thing myself. I was told access is impossible but also informed some other being came here destroying everything in its path then somehow man-aged to find a way in. I'm at a loss on how to continue but I'm hoping you may know something I don't?"

I watched him carefully as his face calmed in a flash, his eyes moving rapidly while he mumbled to himself. "Then he is already here and has bought us the time. My master must be informed." His eyes shot up like he just realized where he was. He looked at me and then back at his wrist with a curious frown. "I must go," he snapped and then stuck two fingers to his temple and closed his eyes.

It was my first time watching another being project itself back in this manner so I stared intently. After a moment his body just faded away like shutting off an old tube style t.v.

"How anticlimactic," I spoke to no one in particular, not knowing what I really expected. I turned to continue on my way and found myself face to face with another Ascendal. His red eyes squinting while he stared at me.

"Name and rank?" he asked, not offering any himself.

I thought back to some of the details Ameletas had offered. Ending my name with Evlosins like kin usually did but without the Sin suffix as that was to be earned.

"Finlo," I responded, acting like nothing out of the ordinary was taking place. "And I have no rank."

"Finlo, explain to me how a being of no rank overpowers a Demigog?"

The question caught me off guard as I didn't realize the confrontation had been witnessed by any but the common folk. "That Demigog was extremely weak. A book licker could have done it." Another useful tip from the Ascendal on what the Sin think of their weaker peers who do not share the same colored eyes. "And the rank will be sorted out shortly. I'm on my way to NaoSin Hall now to join."

He continued to stare at me while he considered my words. It didn't look like he was going to believe them until he finally spoke. "See that you do," was his only response, then he turned and walked away.

I arrived at their building sometime later. Its slanted red tiled roof and black walls reminded me of a Chinese dojo if Chinese dojos were the size of sports arenas. I walked through the door and was greeted by the smell of burning oils. Flames lined the entire entryway and the black walls were decorated with large paintings depicting epic battles full of death and destruction. Some of which had two single combatants full of cuts and blood and in others, armies clashed. One even showed an Ascendal with red eyes fighting a large silverish beast with the body of a human and the head of a lizard. In the middle of the giant room sat a man at a desk. His feather pen scribbling furiously.

He looked up as I approached, his glowing brown eyes catching me off guard. "I'm Mesoten, what do you need?" he asked without showing the slightest hint that he actually cared.

I grimaced and he noticed. "Sorry. Your eyes took me by surprise." I responded, trying to explain myself, "My names Finlo and I'm here to-" I stopped as he put his head down instantly and started scribbling again on a new piece of paper like I didn't exist then snapped it off when he finished. He set the pen down with one hand and offered it to me with the other, tapping impatiently. "What's this?"

He rolled his eyes, "Your acceptance papers." "Really?" I was as confused as a frog in jello.

"Look, I'm busy so keep up. You have red eyes and no Sin title. You didn't expect my eyes to be brown so you've never been here before. Two and two means you're here to join. With another war brewing again I'm under instructions to accept anyone willing. I have your name so I drafted your papers for you. Take them to Dowsin at the end of the hall on the right. Any questions?"

I had tons but instead I just smiled at him which seemed to give him pause. "None, thank you."

His eyes went back to his paperwork as he picked up his pen. "And learn to lie better. I'm here because of a mutually profitable arrangement I made with the Sin." He peered up at me with a crooked grin, "or did you expect to see a fellow fist thumper doing paperwork?"

I laughed with a shrug, walking past the man and making my way down the hall.

"Next!" Dowsin ordered. His tall lanky frame held an elongated skull with slightly slanted red eyes that watched the trainees like a lion watching a passing herd of water buffalo, daring one to get out of line.

The next participant stepped forward, staring at the scattered array of target dummies. Each of them was especially designed to withstand blasts of the essence and it was his turn to try.

Beam attack to hit more than one target without using an explosion, he recalled the rules again as he formulated a plan. It seemed logical enough to work so he decided to put it into motion. His arm reached out, palm facing forward and he moved the essence to a point in front of his hand, compressing it into a sphere. Now normally after this you would pull on one point of the orb, facing where you intended your attack to go. The ball would then explode, following the laws of light and shoot out in the direction the pressure was released. He focused. The plan was to shoot the entire sphere forward like you would to create an explosion but at the last second he was going to pull on two points, causing it to shoot out in opposite directions.

It soared through the air with a gentle sigh, its ends imploding and two beams blasting out in opposite directions giving the appearance of a single white bar. Six of the dummies got hit before the attack dissipated and he let out a breath of relief.

Dowsin turned to the others. "This is why Egosin is top in the class. The technique he just performed is one not taught until you reach the fourth tier and since you are all as fresh as a pimple on a harlot's ass are still seventh tier and should not know such things." He eyed Egosin with respect. "Back to formation. Is there anyone else here who thinks they can do this using a different tactic? Something original perhaps?"

"Why is this important?" someone complained.

Dowsins eyes scanned, searching the large crowd for whomever spoke. Normally his training sessions were only a half a dozen beings but lately there was talk of an all out war brewing and he now had over fifty with even a few females among them.

"It's important because I say it is!" he hissed, then tried to regain himself, "And because if you were closely surrounded by four other hostile beings an explosion would only work if you had a death wish. So instead of trying to just attack them one at a time and hope they all stand around waiting to die, you can catch them by surprise."

Movement caught his eyes and he turned to the door. A tall Ascendal with fiery glowing red eyes walked through and peered around. When they finally caught each other's attention, Dowsin waved him over and accepted his paper.

He looked it over. "Finlo," he read aloud, unimpressed. "A long time ago the Lo were a powerful clan... now they are cowards," he scowled, testing the new recruits' resilience.

"Finlosin, or am I wrong?" I replied with a dumb smile.

The lanky Ascendals expression didn't change. "These are only acceptance papers. You still have to be granted permission by me to join."

I stared at him, not sure what else was actually required. "So how do I get that?"

Dowsin smiled back, the expression looking as out of place as a nun in a brothel. "Easy. All you have to do is use one attack, no explosions and hit all of them targets at once with it."

I stared to where he gestured and counted the dummies. "Sixteen? Is that all?" I knew this was extremely advanced for beginners but I decided to do it anyway. I was here to advance up the ranks as fast as possible so felt the need to impress. Several ideas popped into my head but most were too powerful to use here and besides, I'd watched from the door when the other trainee had gone and so figured beam attacks are what he was after.

I raised my chin, walking with confidence to stand in front of them where the previous man had. "If I had known it was going to be this easy I would have come sooner."

He snorted at my comment, clearly doubting my boasts as I faced the targets directly. Like I did more and more I decided to think outside the box, the idea popping into my head like a corn kernel on a frying pan. I set it into motion quickly, hoping the exacts of what I was about to do would go unseen, adding mystery and preventing it from being replicated.

I formed a sphere first and compacted it as tightly as possible then surrounded it with hundreds of tiny shields of pure essence leaving only a small rectangular opening in it that faced the targets. The end result would best be described as a golf ball with a slit in it like you'd see in a war bunker.

I grabbed at as many points as I could conceive at once and pulled, causing it to implode on itself and erupt into hundreds of blasts that went out in every direction, reflecting endlessly until they escaped through the opening. The whole thing took place in less than a heartbeat. The attack sizzled through the air with the sound like a volley of arrows flying by. Beams bounced out in all direction, blasting every target, the ceiling, the walls, and even the ground below them causing some to go flying across the room. It looked like what I imagined a claymore explosion would... if it shot bars of light.

I turned back to Dowsin, his jaw hanging slightly open, eyes wide in disbelief. Even the others stared at me with stunned expressions as one last dummy crashed to the floor, breaking the silence.

"Finlosin?" I asked again, daring him to deny it this time.

"Finlosin," he confirmed and I noticed the man who had gone before me snarl in anger.

At the end of the training I found myself standing in a small office. Its brick walls decorated with random objects I guessed were either trophies or awards of some kind. A red flag lined with orange frays hung behind the desk and at its center was one massive red eye encrusted with rubies to give it the appearance it was glowing.

The man who sat in front of it peered at me, fingers steepled over his mouth while Dowsin spoke. "He claims he has most of his memories from his past life Captain. That he was of the second tier until he died in battle but he refuses to relinquish any details further than that."

"Reincarnated as the same and with memories... clearly he did not reach his next step. Tell me Dowsin, do you believe him?" the Captain questioned, voice thick with doubt.

"If I hadn't seen his attack with my own eyes... it was far more advanced than even I could do. I don't even know if it's recorded. It may be something never seen before."

The other man leaned back in his chair, considering. "That's not uncommon. Plenty of the Sin devote their lives to creating powerful and unique attacks that they keep to themselves. Self advancement is in our nature after all." He grabbed the tip of his pointed ear and twisted it while he scratched with his thumb. "Tell me Finlosin, if you won't speak of your past, what of your future?"

I pulled my head back a little like I was reluctant at first then I spoke, "during the battle I fell at, I was betrayed from within.

The rank of General was promised to me upon my victory and the coward who struck me from behind my successor if I fell." I watched the man accept my account like it was commonplace among the Sin. "I am here to gain that title as quickly as possible and if the man or his kin are still around... I will claim my vengeance."

A malicious grin appeared on his face, "Honesty is a trait not many Sin care for but I suppose in your case it was necessary.

Each tier has its specific qualifications or tests. Am I to understand you'd like to forgo all basic trainings and instead continue with only the tests?"

"Yes Captain."

His face didn't change. "In response to your implications I daresay the thought of a high ranking officer being challenged in combat excites me greatly. I grant your request and will have Dowsin provide you with any materials you need to refresh your memory with the things that may have been lost in the transition from life to life. And be ready private. There is no warning or set time that these tests will occur. Dismissed." I saluted and turned to go. "You said you had one more candidate with potential Dowsin?"

I made my way to the doorway when they called for Egosin. We passed each other and I could feel the anger and hatred radiating off him while he stared at me.

"Good luck," I offered, purposely trying to get under his skin. "Pfff. Luck is for the weak," he spat, pulling his shoulders back and staring forward.

"Oh, I didn't know that. Then lots of luck," I offered in amusement.

His head snapped around and he glared at me while I smiled back, the door shutting slowly and separating us from each others view.

I shook my head at his temperament. Some people really didn't like sharing the spotlight. It was funny to me to think that life and societies on all corners of the multiverse were so closely related. From grade school and the little kid so eager to be the smartest, the best, to always be right and now amongst the Sin. The most powerful and vicious beings in this world and I never would have guessed that everything was so similar and interconnected that both groups would have their teachers' pets.

I grabbed an apple from a discarded tray outside the chow hall on my way by and plopped it on Mesotens desk. I looked back to see his face a wash of confusion while he tried to puzzle out the motive to my gift and I laughed to myself. Well, maybe not everything.

CHAPTER 30

If you are someone who believes miracles are only impossible feats, or feats of impossible odds, consider this; you can press the same button the same way everyday for your entire life and never will you duplicate it exactly. The alignment of each specific molecule and where they met were impossible odds, never to happen again. It is only when you look at everything in this light that you find the right angle. Everything you do, see, and feel is impossible and that the truth is, all of life is a miracle. Once I realized that, I truly believe coincidences no longer exist.

"You can have more than 8 outfits if you want M'lady. You can have them all."

Cherry bit her lip in thought. Never in her life had she owned more than four different outfits at a time. What was she supposed to do with them all? She looked over the dozens of dresses, skirts, riding clothes, swimming clothes, and a whole variety more, some she didn't even know what they were or how to put them on.

"8 is fine for now, Saline. Just give me a minute to make up my mind, then we can go to shoes." With underwear, bras, nightgowns, and all the easy things out of the way, picking dresses was supposed to be fun but she was finding it overwhelming.

"What would you like to do after shoes M'lady? I can send someone to start fetching them now."

Cherry frowned, "what is there besides all this?"

The maid gave her a curious stare, "You're new to all this, if you don't mind my asking?" Cherry bobbed her head up and down reluctantly, "Then I'll help you as much as I can along the way. You are going to need a complete wardrobe if you're to be the wife of our new master. That includes shoes and boots, hats both for travel or decoration, gloves for eating, dancing and traveling or riding horses. There's also coats, purses, carrying bags, scarves, belts, jewelry and if I can make a suggestion, evening wear of a more seductive nature." Cherry's face went crimson at the comment, "I didn't mean to overstep M'lady."

"It's fine. It's just... ugh!" She let herself fall backwards onto the bed, landing on a pile of clothes. "Everybody thinks being rich will solve all their problems but it doesn't. It just gives them different ones."

The maid smiled, "would you like some advice M'lady?" Cherry sat up nodding her head insistently as she fixed her hair. "Take em all. Keep them here in the dressing room and every morning just pick a casual outfit and one traveling one in case you have to go anywhere. That's what I'd do anyway. A lot easier picking one outfit for a day then trying to plan into the future as well."

It made sense. "I like that idea, Saline. That sounds a whole deal easier."

"I've got another if you don't mind? How about instead of you having to try each one on, I can get a few of the girls here that are close to your size and bring them in one at a time until you find one you like?"

Cherry gave an enthusiastic grin, "oh my, that sounds fun."

The head maid mimicked her smile and clapped her hands loudly. Four other maids shuffled in instantly. "Clear all this away and bring it to the lady's dressing room. Have it separated and categorized and I'll be in there shortly." They bowed to her then set to removing the clutter.

"Before we start, do you have any preferences on color, types of jewelry, fabrics, things of that nature?"

Cherry let her eyes fall to where she clicked her thumbnails together, "I ain't never owned jewelry or had different fabrics other than these pajamas but I think we should try to keep the colors red on account of my husband and all."

Saline nodded to this, "You just get them pajamas off and get into your new undergarments and I'll be back in a flash with the first few outfits so we can get you looking proper." Cherry moved to do what she was asked as the head maid ran out.

She sat for what seemed like an eternity in her undergarments, breathing a sigh of relief when Saline finally entered in a flurry. "Ok M'lady, I'm going to call them in one at a time how does that sound?"

"It sounds wonderful," Cherry responded, sitting up in anticipation.

Saline clapped her hands and the first girl walked in. Her long red dress hung nearly to the floor and was layered in folds that started at her waist. It hugged her sides and formed up to where her breasts were held by a different softer appearing material, giving her body an hourglass shape. She wore long red sparkling gloves that reached to her elbows and a gold necklace that held a large bright red ruby just above where her cleavage began with two similar rubies pierced into each ear. The girl spun and the dress twinkled, revealing the same sparkling material of her gloves hidden in its folds.

"It's beautiful," she observed, awe and wonder causing her words to come out slowly.

"This one is styled for elegance. The gloves and folds are encrusted with smoothed glass to give it a reflective quality. The earrings and necklace are 8 sided rubies. The shoes which aren't meant to be seen are standard slip ons. Next, we have what I suggested earlier, a more appealing outfit." She clapped again and the next woman entered. Cherry gasped when she noticed how much of the maids body was showing. "This outfit is more commonly worn when your husband wants to display you or if you just plan on seducing him to avoid his displeasure. It's a very common style amongst the women who have been chosen as brides."

Cherry stared at the outfit, not knowing exactly how she felt. "It is?

"Beings like your husband love power, fame, they enjoy making their peers jealous and love to flash whatever they have in an attempt to cause this. You have to remember, to them you're just flesh. We have to keep you looking prized, always best to please first and ask questions later."

Cherry continued to think as she stared at the woman. It was so revealing, leaving very little to the imagination and adding just enough accessories to keep the eyes drawn. But did she need it? Ever since she had reached adulthood, men had made their advances. All of them nonstop, it got very boring. An unending surplus of men throwing themselves at her, offering to take her away from the lonely and pitiful life they assumed she had with her father except one. "My husband ain't like that."

The headmaid eyed her doubtfully. "Twice now I've offered myself to him and he turned me away both times," she admitted, remembering her offers to be my wife.

"But the two of you shared a bed last night didn't you?"

"Yes but he didn't even get under the covers with me, so you see, he ain't like the others. Not like that anyway."

Saline raised an eyebrow, recognizing the look in the other woman's eye, "Well, do you want him to be?"

I made my way up the steps to see the servant dressed in a suit and tie holding a tray with a letter marked with the symbol of the physicars store. I grabbed it, unfolding it by the corners as I walked in.

'Finlosin, or so I now presume. I have spent some time in consideration on how to best proceed to gain you access to our God in the event your current pursuit fails or takes too long. Best to have options I believe so I'm going to do some spying and planning of my own. I will update you further as I learn more. Please return the favor. Your friend, A."

This guy was going to turn out to be beyond useful. I should ask him-..

My thoughts cut off and I froze in mid step like my life was a movie and someone had just hit pause. Cherry stood in front of me, head slightly tilted to one side, hands behind her back, all her weight on one leg causing the curve of her hip to be very prominent.

I swallowed.

Her feet were wrapped in a red high heel sandal that spun and twined all the way up her legs to where they disappeared beneath the fold of her skirt. If it can be called that, the two red cloths that hung from the front and back were almost see through with her black underwear slightly visible. Around her stomach was a gold chain and an array of rubies dangled from it beneath her belly button in the shape of an eye. Around her breasts, wrapped tightly was the same see through fabric that hung at her waist. Her nails were all painted red and she had on sleeves of a black velvet held in place by a single loop around each thumb. She wore a tight necklace made up of red rubies and black emeralds in an up and down pattern. Her face was fully made up, eyes shadowed black around the edges, lips a vibrant red that matched her hair which was all up in a high bun except two long curls that she let flow to each side of her face. She was now a complete contrast to the simple farm girl in the plain blue dress I'd met before. She gave me a shy smile and it offset the whole look perfectly.

I swallowed again, looking around to make sure none of the servants were listening before I spoke, "Cherry, what in the world-"

"Do you like it?" She cut me off.

"Yes... well... it's.. I mean, do you like it?"

"I do if you do."

I shook my head to break myself away from her gaze. "I like what you like... why are you doing this?"

"Because you're my husband, fake or not, and the maid said this is the sort of thing others would expect me to wear."

"Well you look like Earth's most beautiful Egyptian goddess... with red hair," I chuckled and she smiled from ear to ear to where it touched her eyes, causing them to squint slightly.

"I heard beautiful and red hair, the rest was gibberish. But now that I know you like it, I like it too and you can expect me to wear this sort of thing more often. Besides I said it before, if you wanna look, you can look."

"Cherry it's just us here. It's like you're making me look. I don't get much of a choice."

"I know," she responded happily.

"You know? I can't be your real husband. I told you-"

She spun on me, "can't or won't?"

I thought back to the previous projections I'd had. Being with different women, falling in love with some and spending years, decades and in one case, a lifetime. There was nothing more heart wrenching than watching the person you love grow old and succumb to the price that time eventually charges us all while you remain unchanged. Her age embarrassed her, the loss of her hair, the wrinkles, the loss of control, all of it. I swore to myself I'd never love during another projection again, especially now that I had a family of my own. But it was a blurred line and I was constantly reminded that it wasn't my real body or my real life and that the two could always be seperate. Love was always a good thing. It was always normal, right?

Silence.

"Cherr, please just stop." She squinted at me, trying to read the expressions that crossed my face as I struggled with emotions I thought I'd forgotten.

"Stop what husband?"

I shook my head and looked away. Her beauty was beyond anything a meer mortal should possess. "Stop flirting with my damn demons," I muttered and finally decided to walk past her, eyes forward, chin up.

"Um, husband," she called like she was teasing me. I stopped but refused to turn around as she walked up. "It's time to eat and you're going the wrong way. Follow me if you will please.

She began to walk towards the other side of the large manor but kept her head to the side to make sure I was following.

Where the hell was I going anyway? I realized I was only trying to leave the situation and not the room. I followed behind her reluctantly, noticing how she placed each foot in front of the other, her movements causing her hips to bounce with each step. I looked back up and caught her smiling before she finally let her head return forward.

Trouble? I thought this woman was going to be trouble? I shook my head at my previous assumptions. No she was everything the color red represented in the damn place. She was going to shatter my willpower and destroy my resilience like an avalanche of boulders landing on a castle of glass.

"I did it, Saline! I did everything you said," Cherry beamed proudly as soon as the door to the changing room closed. "I stood with my hip out, I thought his eyes were gonna pop outta his head when he seen that. I was straight forward with my intentions but not pushy or too easy and then I did the walk we practiced. I made him follow me to dinner and I watched him, he stared at my backside so hard I bet he'd have followed me right off a cliff."

"I told you M'lady, at the center of every man no matter his age or station, is a deep seeded demon. We just have to find out what it likes. Control the demon, control the man. I think this ones trying to keep his locked away for some reason."

"Saline, please help me out of these shoes. I feel like my feet got stamped on by a bunch of horses." The head maid motioned her to the chair then set to unlacing and unwrapping. "I know he's trying to keep it locked away but I don't know why. He did say something like what you said. He said I was flirting with his demons," Saline paused, giving Cherry a worried look. "Not like that. It's not like it's a bad demon. I think maybe he just has a weakness for women or for love or something and so he tries to hide it."

"It's not that M'lady," Saline admitted with a confused frown. "You said he told you that? And you could understand him?" Cherry froze, realizing her error and not knowing how to respond, the two eyeing each other, neither speaking. "M'lady?"

"Oh dear. I wasn't supposed to tell you that part. I was just so excited it sort of slipped out. Saline you can't tell no one! You have to promise!"

"M'lady I always do as I'm told and keeping secrets is part of the occupation... but how can you speak like him?" She sat puzzled as she awaited a response.

"It's not like that silly. I can't speak like him, he can speak like us, and them, but he ain't one, not really. He's some other thing and he's stronger than them. He killed the one that lived here before us because he was going to kidnap me and make me his wife. Then we took his house, and you guys I suppose... but he's really nice and just... promise me! Promise you won't tell not a single soul!"

Saline's eyes didn't blink as she absorbed the onslaught of Cherrie's words. "Of course M'lady. I promise," she vowed, trying to make sense of it all. "But if he killed that bastard that lived here before him then he's a hero in my book."

Cherry smiled at her words, "Was he really that bad?"

Saline went back to removing the sandals, "The last lady he took for himself ended her own life very shortly after. He saved you from a living hell no one should ever have to go through I'm sure."

A silence dragged out for a time between the two until finally Cherry spoke in a timid voice, "Saline?"

"Yes M'lady?"

She twiddled her fingers again, refusing to look the head maid in the eyes, "I don't want him to just want me, I want him to love me so he stays forever. The more he denies me, the more I want it. Does that make sense?"

"Perfect sense M'lady. Trying to catch butterflies is only fun if they fly away. The ones who fly towards us tend to just get in the way."

Cherry bit her lip, "Saline?"

The other woman laughed at her Ladies constant politeness, "Yes M'lady?"

"I'm scared if it works. If I do win him over and he wants to... you know. I ain't never done that before. I won't be any good."

"Don't you go worrying on that, M'lady. Most men would rather have a horse they can train themselves, teaching it to do the things they need it to. Haven't met a man yet who'd take an old mare set in her ways over a new one. Not unless it's only for one quick ride and nothing for keeps."

Cherry smiled at the comforting words. "I need him to want me, Saline. I need him to stay."

"Don't you go worrying on any of that just yet. If he was able to hold his resolve with the last outfit, then we've got some work ahead of us. But we'll keep chipping away like a woodpecker at a tree, until eventually you bore your way into his heart."

Cherry thought on this, "I don't know how much time I have. He said he's not going to stay that long and we need to convince him."

"Then we'll double our efforts, hows that sound?"

"It sounds... terrifying! How do you plan we do that?"

Saline chuckled, "you don't get to be head mistress and live as long as I have among that evil creature without finding ways to make yourself irreplaceable. If he thinks that little showing today was tough, I'll teach you things to make his head spin."

CHAPTER 31

I've heard the question "Does God make mistakes?" and the ignorance it conveyed made me shake my head. The short answer is no, God doesn't make mistakes. The ingredients to life are all thrown in, set to random, then pushed into motion with time. It isn't until you've solved the conundrum of coincidences and miracles that you can see another truth. You aren't advanced enough yet to see all the reasons and logic, but when you look, Gods influence can be found everywhere and in everything.

Tests came and went by in a blur. Tiers six, five and four consisted of stances, cuts, formations and other things so simple a toddler with a butter knife could have passed. I found myself avoiding Cherry more and more. She still made me sleep with her at night and now even under the covers. Her evening wear and robes becoming more revealing, leaving little to nothing to the imagination. Her walk became more attractive, her movements more suggestive, and the way she ate outright seductive.

I pushed my plate away. "Cherry, this has to stop. Why are you doing all this?"

"Doing what husband? I'm just eating."

"Well who in their right mind tries to eat a banana in one bite? Or were you trying to avoid chewing all together?" I asked and embarrassment spread across her face as she lowered her eyes, returning to the timid farmgirl but refusing to answer. "Are you going to explain or do I have to make my own assumptions on what you planned to do with the kiwis?"

She continued to stare down but I heard her snort, "I don't even know what that one was supposed to mean," she mumbled softly.

I laughed in disbelief, "what it means? Why do you do it then? Are you being forced? I told you it doesn't have to be like this."

She looked up then and I could see tears in the corners of her eyes and I realized I may have been too harsh. "I'm sorry Cherr."

"Don't be. You're right it's stupid. Salines been teaching me how to seduce you so you'll want me and we can fall in love but it ain't working."

I shook my head, watching her set the banana back on her tray. "That's not the only way to a man's heart but it is the way to his bed and you don't want that. You're to... good for me... or pure. I don't know how to explain it," I let out a breath in frustration.

"Pure? That's why you don't want me because I'm just pure and you have demons?"

"It's just an expression. I mean I have a personal weakness that I struggle to control," I leaned back in my chair, "You deserve someone better than me and who can actually grow old with you. Why do you want me so bad?"

Her eyes shot up and stared into mine with a look like I had just asked the dumbest thing in the world. "You're powerful, rich, smart, good looking. You're super nice like in the gentleman way and you treat me like no one else, like I'm important... And you're just... different, but in a good way." I watched her expression change as she paused and I could see her trying to hide her emotions, "And I know soon you're going to leave me and I don't want you to but I have nothing... In this whole wide world, in my whole life... I have nothing to offer you to make you wanna stay with me but myself and you don't want me." A tear rolled down her cheek and the last of my resilience crumbled with its slow descent.

I put my hand on hers to comfort her. "I've learned so much about life in my travels that I forget more than most people have ever learned. One thing I can tell you though is our souls are like magnets. They tend to stick together, flock with each other like migratory birds of the same species as they fly in and out of life over and over looking for their other halfs. It's why our families are all so similar, how we pick our friends and how we find love."

"So it's not about the body?"

"Not to me. I am attracted to bodies the same as anyone else but I've always been more attracted to a person's soul. Looks aren't everything. If the souls aren't compatible the attraction that people share isn't strong enough to keep them together. They have to fit, to click or they'll find themselves eventually going in opposite directions."

She bit her lip and gave me a sly grin, "well what type of birds is your family?"

I smiled back "Everyones a little different but the men in my family have good hearts who love helping and tend to click with good people who are less fortunate and broken."

"So they find love in people who are good, less fortunate and also broken?" I nodded, "Am I good, less fortunate and broken?" "Let's see." I rocked back pretending to be deep in contemplation as she waited anxiously, "You've lost everyone you've ever loved, you have nothing to call your own, no home and no one to love you. I'd say that definitely qualifies you as unfortunate and somewhat broken."

She sat up straighter, "and I know I'm good too, right?"

I raised an eyebrow, then stood and offered her my hand,

"Why don't we make you a disguise and go and find out?"

His feet moved in a blur. One after the other and the different rocks and bushes flew past in streaks. "Hey look, it's Dash!" he heard a voice exclaim and turned to see his friend Gradey pointing while he sprinted past his house.

The two other boys took up chase after him, "what's the hurry Dash? You and your brothers wanna come practice soldiers with us?" Gradey huffed out, trying to keep up.

"Can't... Pa had a fall... off the barn... took a haychucker... through the back," his response came out in short puffs.

Even in his exhausted state he found himself pulling away from his two friends. They struggled to keep up but knew it was useless.

"Ain't there nothing we can do to help?" the other shouted as they fell further behind.

"Go to Rags place... borrow a horse... for the Doc... meet me on the way back," he shouted then disappeared over a hill..

A few minutes later he approached the doctor's house and made his way up onto the porch. "Doc! Doc! Open up! My Pa took a fall and got ran through by a hay chucker," he yelled, fist beating on the wood almost hard enough to break it down. He waited for a response but none came. "Doc?" he questioned then started to circle around, peering in windows while he did. The house showed no signs of life and he struggled with what he should do.

"Doc's gone for a time. Said if I seen anyone calling to send em in to town to the healer."

Dash waved his understanding to the man. Town was way in the wrong direction. He'd never make it there and back in time before Pa... He stopped the line of thinking, realizing he didn't even know where the healers was.

We'll pull it out and Ma can stitch him herself. We'll just use some regular thread, enough to hold him until we find a different doctor.

He sprinted back down the road, not stopping, even when Gradey galloped up to him on a horse. The friend followed silently as Dash made his way back into his yard towards where his father still lay after refusing to be moved. His mother and brothers looked up at him expectantly.

"Doc's gone for a time. Closest things the healer in town. We can pull it out ourselves, Ma can stitch em up and we'll throw him on the horse."

"Throw him on the horse and then what?" his brother Jerks asked. "Can't nobody get on with him and he can't ride alone? So what?"

Dash thought frantically. "I'll run again. I'll lead the horse myself." He stopped when his Mother shook her head from where she sat on the ground near her husband's side.

"Dash, you move like the wind itself but nobody can run forever. Besides, do you even know where the healers is?"

He let his shoulders sag, "We can't just do nothing."

"What are we supposed to do? He said himself the second we pull it out his blood will flow faster, only making him die that much quicker just like when he was a soldier and watched people take sword wounds."

The small family sat in silence, desperately trying to come up with a solution. "We need a miracle.," the Mother prayed, clasping the man's hands and pulling them in for a kiss.

Dash's vision cleared up beyond anything he'd ever experienced before. Colors popped, the wind held a warmth and made a gentle sigh while they looked at each other in confusion. There was a soft thump on the ground behind them and they all spun.

Standing before him was the most beautiful woman he'd ever seen in his young life. She wore skin tight black leather pants and a shirt with matching boots and gloves. The whole outfit was so shiny it almost appeared metallic. Her porcelain face was speckled with red freckles that perfectly matched her long flowing red curly hair that hung down past her shoulders. But that wasn't what held his gaze. Her two bright blue eyes blazed like they had trapped the midday sky.

"I can help if you'll let me?" she suggested in a timid voice, walking forward. No one responded, they all just stared as she made her way to stand in front of the fallen man. "I'm going to put this armlet on him, you need to lift him and pull out the pitchfork as soon as I do so he don't start to heal with it inside him." She crouched down and lifted his hand, pausing so they could oblige.

The Mother was the first to snap out of it. "Boys!" she ordered and they hopped to it. Dash helped his mom while she hefted his father up by the shoulder and his brother stood behind, grabbing the pitchfork.

"On my signal. Be ready with some rags to catch the blood," the woman instructed and slipped the armlet up.

The stone at its center changed colors and the man's eyes widened as clarity returned to them. She nodded to Jerks and he gave a heave, freeing his father from the impaling tool. The man gasped and lurched with the pain, Dash doing all he could to keep him upright.

After a minute he calmed and was able to stand on his own. The family stood watching him for a moment before finally turning back to face their curious savior.

"Ma'am how can we ever repay you?" the woman asked as she removed the armlet and handed it back.

The other woman accepted it with a smile. "No repayment necessary. In fact," she twisted to remove a small pouch from her hip, "you should probably take a few days off for rest. This should help cover that cost and then some." She dropped the coin pouch into the astonished woman's hands.

"Why are you doing this?" she asked in disbelief, peering into the pouch and noticing the distinct glitter of gold.

"I want my husband to love me and he says helping people in need is a great exercise for the soul and that it makes a person good. So now we are just going around helping anyone we can. Do you guys need anything else?"

"I'll love you if your husband won't," Jerks breathed out and his mother cuffed him in the back of the head.

"A real sword?" Dash blurted. "I mean, if you can do magic and all."

"Don't be greedy son. It's not you," his father croaked but cut off his words as a second blue eyed being landed, this one a tall male.

"Swords are great to have. It's no problem," I assured, clapping my hands together and the world went vivid again. I pulled them apart and repeated the process until four swords lay on the ground.

Dash came running up and grabbed one in amazement. "I can finally become a real soldier now," he marveled in excitement then turned to me. "Thank you sir. For my Pa and the pouch and the swords."

I waved the comment away and beckoned Cherry over. "Think nothing of it," they all started to voice their thanks and praise as I pulled Cherry in close in a bear hug.

She beamed from ear to ear, the smile touching her eyes proudly as she stepped up on my feet and wrapped her arms around my neck. "This is sooo fun!" she triumphed. "Can we do some more?"

We lifted off the ground slowly as the family waved their goodbyes. "We can keep an eye open on the way back. I don't like being gone for long periods of time in case I get called for my third tier test."

"Awe! But it makes me feel... good! Like really really good!"

"That's why I called it an exercise. The soul is supposed to

be good and doing good is like fuel for it. It revives us, gives us purpose."

"Have you always done things like this?"

"I've always loved making people happy, mostly by giving gifts if I ever had the money. Christmas time is by far my most favorite time of the year."

Her face scrunched up, "Crissmiss. Crizzmizz," she tried to repeat the word and I laughed.

"Nevermind. Just keep watching out for people we can spy on unless you would like to go up into the clouds again?"

"Gosh no! Who would have thought they were cold and wet instead of warm and fluffy like in the stories." I watched her look at her arm where the karma stone armlet I had made was. She turned back to me. "I'm gonna keep this and I ain't never gonna take it off. I like saving peoples lives best of all and if this thing can do that, then I can play 'superhero' without your help." She spoke the word slowly, mocking the way I had pronounced it earlier.

I smiled at her, "good. That thing could save your life too as long as you're wearing it, so I'm fine with that."

"Would you be sad if I died?"

I rolled my eyes at the question. "What do you think?"

"I don't know," she fretted. "Most beings like you don't care about someone like me but you say you do and act like you do sometimes but then you always turn me away and don't want me."

I thought back to some relationship advice I received from a higher being long ago. "Insecurities are like a blanket we throw over our head to hide what our true feelings really are. The problem is, it also prevents us from seeing the true feelings of others." My constant rejection of her had caused this and I knew it.

"Cherry, I want you to know something. I think you're perfect in every way possible. Mind, body and soul. You're to good for me so don't-"

She kissed me. I tried to pull away at first but with her fear of heights she was latched to me like a parachute pack that I wore backwards. I gave in and kissed her back. The wind whipped by us as we flew, tossing her curls around wildly and soon her hair was tangled in mine, creating a small red cave where she stared at me from, our eyes searching each others as she breathed heavily.

"I ain't never kissed a man before," she breathed excitedly.

"Yeah. Me neither."

She gave me a puzzled expression then threw her head back in a laugh. I smiled as she finished, letting her pull me back for another kiss.

"Here's... those things," she offered, trying to hand me the glowing set of contacts I had made for her.

"Keep them. Put them in some water and hide them somewhere safe. We can use them again sometime I'm sure."

We walked up the steps to see the well dressed servant waiting with a tray. On it sat some food, drinks and an envelope sealed with the eye of the Sin. I grabbed an apple and the envelope then dismissed the servant.

Cherry watched him go, speaking the second he was out of ear shot. "That's another test! Do you have to go? We just finally... well, you know."

"There's only two left until I'm tier two. Then I don't know what's required of me to reach tier one," I paused, looking out across the city to where I watched large amounts of the essence being pulled. This was something very common here but this one was different. As it grew I could feel the unique call that summoned it and recognized it for whose it was. Egosin had surprised me by passing all the other tests and I assumed he was about to take one now. I blinked, refreshing my body and it's hold on the essence.

"You're going now ain't you?" You ain't even gonna eat a full meal first?"

I shook my head. "I can't. I think Egosin is about to start and that means I'm next."

"I assume that weird sound was the name of one of them red eyed beings?" I grinned and nodded at my own stupidity. "Ok go, but try and hurry back please?"

I kissed her cheek. "Will do," I said, then turned and lept into the air.

I landed on the steps, making sure no one was watching and blinked again. Whatever this test was Egosin had needed every ounce of essence he could summon so I had to be ready. I walked through the door to see Mesoten working diligently, not bothering to look twice once he had noticed me. I plopped the apple on his desk when I passed, taking the corridor to the left that led to the pits where the tests were held.

"But why?" I heard him ask and I ignored it.

I entered the large circular arena to find an audience in attendance for the first time. Egosin stood talking to a few others, Dowsin being one of them. On the sands of the arena was blood and the body of a colorless humanoid like creature with no hair.

Its naked form had cuts and slashes all over it and a guard drug it away.

Was I going to have to kill some innocent slave or captive because that could change everything. I made my way over to Dowsin and gave him a half hearted salute.

"Finlosin, good timing. Your opponent is being tended to as we speak." I followed his gaze back to where the guard plopped the corpse onto a table and a stone was removed from its forehead and then replaced with another. Its deep purple color swirling immediately as the body drained its essence, closing the wounds like zipping up a purse.

That looks like a karma stone? I thought as I watched the process. "What is that thing?" I wondered aloud.

"It is a form of artificial life made long ago by one of the book lickers." He eyed me. "So long ago you should have remembered something like that from your past life. It has been with us for ages."

I ignored his statement. "Is it alive?"

"Yes and no. It was created with a very efficient mind to fight only but has no soul."

Just then a Colonel walked over. "Finlosin. The time of questions and demonstrations is over. To achieve the third tier rank you are challenged with beating the being you see before you. This is designed to test your mastery of the sword but you are permitted to use any tactics you wish. Make any preparations you need beforehand and the test only ends when you succeed or fail." He turned and walked back to the seats as Dowsin opened the entrance for me that led down into the pit.

"Fill your tanks first and don't attack with the essence," he offered, a term used when referring to drawing in the essence to the maximum amount your body could retain. I shook my head while I walked through, staring at the creature at the other side of the pit. Its head jerked this way and that like a birds, it's large yellow eyes regarding me sharply. It had a body of a dull gray color that gave it the appearance of a corpse but it's chiseled muscles offset like it worked out regularly. It took several strides toward me with indifference, a long sword swinging in its hand.

I knew about two dozen different ways I could kill this thing but if that really was a karma stone in its head, using the essence would just get absorbed into it. I needed a way to do this that they would still believe I was one of them but just extremely powerful.

It swung and I ducked.

How could I do it without being obvious and giving anything away and at the same time impress them?

It swang again, low at first then jerking the blade straight up. I sidestepped, letting them know I was just toying with it like I assumed some of the more cocky Sin would have done. It's head cocked, first one way then the other as it tried to register why I wasn't attacking. I watched its back foot turn slightly, a clear indicator it planned on leaping forward. Its legs bent for the ambush and I reacted in a flash, knee coming forward while I lept to intercept it.

It dropped instead and I flew over through empty air. I landed on the ground and spun while it rolled back to its feet, turning to face me once again.

Clever, fast and can't die? This thing was simply astounding. This time it did leap, cutting a diagonal line then shifting when I sidestepped, turning its attack into a headbutt at the last second. It was my turn to drop and I watched as the large stone in its forehead came so close I could see my reflection in it. I rolled away and hopped up to my feet. If that was a karma stone its touch would have drained me and then game over. It would have forced me to either blink or try and draw more essence, hoping it just sat around waiting for me to do so. Neither option was good. A thought occurred to me of 8 years ago and the first time I'd encountered a karma stone. My friend Seven had let me test its limits to see what happened once it got too full. I watched as the translucent orange color swirled on its forehead and was a clear indicator it was almost empty. I assumed that was by design to prevent it from breaking but I needed an impressive display of power.

I shrugged, here goes nothing, then leapt forward, catching the thing by surprise as it had just started to crouch for an attack of its own. I grabbed it by the arm and wrenched it down and back as I spun, pinning its sword harmlessly to the side. I leapt on it from behind and locked both legs around its front, holding his in place. I put my other arm above his shoulder, elbow out to prevent his only free appendage from reaching my head then slapped my hand over the gem and felt my essence vanish.

I breathed out a sigh of relief that it was at least a real kar- ma stone or something similar at least but now my entire plan hinged on this beings reservoir tank that I couldn't see. I desperately needed it to be of a normal size.

I called the essence with urgency, not as fast as I could but enough to get the job done as soon as possible. It responded in a flood, pouring into me and passing directly through and into the karma stone. The creature flailed its arm, trying to reach my face so I moved my head to the other side of his to dissuade him from further attempts. It worked and he started to spin and shake, trying to dislodge me from his back as I continued to summon.

A breeze picked up as I increased my urgency and I felt a tremor run through him so I was forced to level it out. It stopped spinning then and bent its knees low then jumped into the air with all its strength, using my weight on its back to act as an an-chor and me take the brunt of the fall. I braced myself and was pancaked to the sand floor, the weight of the thing surprising me. I suddenly heard a slight pop and the essence I called started to flow into me once again as the creature's body went limp.

I rolled it off of me and stood, turning to Dowsin and the Colonel as I did. His jaw hung open and the small group of spec-tators sat wide eyed in amazement except Egosin, who stared daggers at me.

"Finlosin has passed the third tier test and is now eligible for the second tier test," the Colonel announced, more to himself than anyone else in particular.

"Yes sir." Dowsin replied.

I walked back over to where they stood and spoke, "tell me if I'm wrong but that was supposed to test the use of a sword and the next one is to test the use of essence correct?"

Dowsin cleared his throat. "Yes, that's correct."

"Well then next time I'll be sure to use a sword," I bragged, trying to sound arrogant. "Are we done here?"

The Colonel stood, "Go with Dowsin to receive your first officer's uniform. That is all."

We watched them leave then I was led to a back room where supplies were kept. "You really made a statement today," the slant eyed Ascendal said. "Next time I bet the pit will be packed. Normally it is but so many are drawn away to prepare for war and with the old pit being destroyed, it's lost its luster." He held a shirt up to me but it was too small so he put it back and continued to look.

"What happened to the old pit?" I asked, trying to fill the silence.

He shook his head, "you keep your head buried in the sand? That being that came for our God wiped it off the face of the world when it landed. It was during a testing day too. They say over two hundred of the Sin were in attendance when it came through the mindwarp in town and started blowing things up and killing randomly, the whole while screaming in a tongue no one understood."

It killed over two hundred of the Sin at once? I honestly didn't even think I could do that and I was the most powerful being I'd ever met. "Then what happened?" I asked with genuine curiosity. "Some brave soul stood up to it and it stopped. The pair of them flew straight to Bedlam Spire and left the rest of us alone." He found a shirt he liked and threw it to me. Its sleeveless black cloth only decorated with one red eye depicting three separate pupils in a cluster similar to a clover. I pulled it over my head and it fit. He nodded to this, "the next test may be a while. Everyones going to want to attend for a second tier test and with two of ya, the place will be packed."

"Then I'll aim to entertain," I joked.

He stared blankly, "what the blue hell have you been aiming for so far then?" I laughed at his expression and we made our way down the hallway. "What do you plan on doing in the meantime?"

I shrugged, "sit at home with the wife I guess, waiting for my summons."

He nudged me, "wife eh? Some of these beings will do anything to please us, especially the Aliue. You want some advice, get yourself one of them as a wife and thank me later." He eyed me, "or have you had one before?"

I shook my head, "can't say that I have but I really got to get going," I told him, picking up several apples from the discarded trays outside the chow hall with a smile.

He frowned at me then spun, heading back the way we came without a word. The Sin were not big into goodbyes I realized as I approached the empty desk in the entrance hall. I put one of the apples on the desk then opened a drawer and put another in there too. There was a mug with a lid on it and I picked it up to find it half full of tea. The last apple dropped in with a wet plop and I put the lid back on, setting it back in its original position, chuckling to myself as I left.

I made my way straight back home like I told Cherry I would. We ate then she forced me to call it an early night, eager to get to bed and most likely back to kissing. I knew she was inexperienced but not to the point that I ended up being her first kiss. The life of moving nonstop and never staying in one place long enough prevented any form of a relationship to develop. She tried to take it further and she made it hard but I still resisted. The thought of me being her first and then possibly vanishing the next day was heart wrenching. She deserved someone better than me. Someone who could offer her a real marriage and real family, something I couldn't do.

So instead we passed the time in other ways. Flying around and looking at the sights. Seeing the destruction caused by that powerful being that tore through the city in a straight line like a giant dozer had driven through it. But mostly we played 'superheroes'. Going from village to village or staying in the city, hopping rooftop to rooftop, never too far in case I got my summons for my final test.

"That little girl's face lit up like a haystack during a drought when I handed her that new doll. I could do this every day! Does it ever get old?"

I smiled as we landed on the upper balcony, no longer using the front door for our escapades. "You know, I don't think it does. If you take anything else in the world, favorite food, favorite drink, favorite place to visit, things like that. I think all of them reach their ceilings at some point then they become the same old thing. Except maybe where love is concerned," I scrunched up my lips as I considered it seriously. "Love and things to do with the soul I'd say."

"What about sex?" she asked offhandedly, popping out her contacts and putting them in the cup she used as storage.

"I suppose if it's between someone you don't love then eventually it'll get old. Or if you continuously do it with new people, the individual experience won't get old because there's always the possibility of a connection and love but the constant act without finding it or allowing it would definitely start to wear on the soul."

"So if it was with someone you loved it would never get old?" she asked, still not making eye contact while she untied her boots. "I think the excitement would fade as you and your partner's love slowly merged your souls but it never dies completely." "That makes sense," she surmised, working on her other boot. "Cherry I don't want you getting any ideas ok? I told you about my reasons. You deserve far more than I could ever offer you." She continued her work as she ignored me, moving to her socks without looking up once. I pinched the bridge of my nose, trying to puzzle out what was going through this woman's head. "I'm going to go let them know we're back and check the messages. Do you feel like anything in particular for lunch?" She shrugged,

"I'm not really hungry, thank you."

I walked down to the front entrance where the door servant always was. The tray in front of him was empty and I couldn't make up my mind if I was going to eat alone or not. I decided to just walk while I thought to help clear my mind. Why couldn't she see I was trying to do her a favor? Nobody wants someone who's going to just randomly disappear one day. And I can't stay here. Not for another lifetime to watch her grow old as I never change.

But maybe she was worth it? It seemed like the more I tried to resist her the more I wanted her. I'd fallen for her and I knew it. All my struggling, all my resisting, all for nothing. I failed at another promise and this one I had made to myself. I rubbed my hands along the back of my head in frustration. Either way, I knew I should go talk to her. Try to get her to see things from the right point of view. If she was on my side and agreed with all this it would make a world of difference.

I walked back up the stairs and opened the door to find the room empty. I noticed Cherry's clothes in a ball in the corner but there was no sign of her. "Cherry?" I called, stepping into the room thinking maybe she was hiding. "Cherry?" I called again and sat quietly to listen.

The door clicked shut behind me and I spun. She stood leaning with her back against it, a see through mesh gown that went down past her thighs did nothing to conceal what was beneath it. She was completely naked.

"Cherry-"

"Shhh," she commanded. "Don't say anything." She sat twisting back and forth at the hips, hands clasped behind her back while she stared at me. I could see the determination in her eyes and I swallowed. "I seem to remember you once promised me you'd do anything to keep me happy as long as it didn't interfere with your little spy games."

"Cherry you said you'd never demand-"

"Shhh!" she insisted, pushing herself away from the door. She started to circle me, the whole while eyeing me up and down like she was a shark and was judging to see if I was food or not. "I've decided on a few things," she declared, completing her circuit and coming to a stop in front of me. "I've decided I don't care what you want. I've decided that I love you and whether you love me back or not I want to see what making love feels like with the man I love. And even if you don't want to participate, I know your demon will." She smiled at me, "I can tell that from our kisses."

I laughed, not realizing she had noticed. She started to push me backwards until I got to the bed then forced me to sit. "Can I say something now please?"

She pulled the shirt over my head then started to try and remove my boots. "It better be something nice like a compliment or something important. If it ruins the mood I'm gonna be angry."

I chuckled at this, "You peeling off one of my sweaty boots isn't doing that all ready?" She shot me a glare that could have stopped a charging elephant. "Sorry! That wasn't what I wanted to say." She stood up and crossed her arms as she glared at me. "I just wanted to say," I kicked my boot off and she cocked an eyebrow as she eyed me curiously, "that I love you too."

She smiled. Her big beautiful smile that touched her bright green eyes, making them squint. She leapt on me with a kiss and we crashed to the bed. "So I... don't have... to force you?" she giggled between kisses.

"Well now I never said anything like that," I teased and she pulled the blankets over our heads.

CHAPTER 32

I also heard a quote on a movie that I found worth mentioning. "God is either all powerful or God is all good. He cannot be both." There are so many misconceptions and assumptions in this statement that it's sad the world has been kept this ignorant this long. By the end of this book I hope to have shed enough light that you can see the truth and solve this problem on your own.

We strolled through the city hand in hand. Cherry wanted to see the place I constantly got called to and as a change of pace to flying and sneaking everywhere I thought a walk would do us some good.

"So where you're from can everyone do what you do?"

"Do you mean like flying and powers or projecting themselves to different places?"

"Hmm," she wondered, swinging our hands back and forth happily. "I guess both. I don't know anything about where you're from. Is it like here or different?"

"It's the same in some ways and completely different in oth-ers," I speculated, watching a boy walk by with his miniature pet elephant strolling lazily behind. "Everyone where I'm from is exactly like you. No powers or flying and I've never met or heard of anyone who can project to other places like me exactly the way I do it."

"And they all have red hair too?"

I laughed, "not that much like you. I mean they're like your species but some do have red hair but can also be tall, short, skinny, fat, black, white, red, brown, all different, all the same."

"Are there giants?"

"No but we do have people who can get quite tall but not as a specific race or anything. Actually we don't have anything besides what you guys call the common folk. No Ascendals, no God, no other visiting beings, just us humans." I paused. "I should clarify that a little bit. I did find out that we do get visitors but they are from the spirit realm so don't share the same dimensions as us. They usually appear as balls of light in our sky, float around for a bit until they lose the essence that sustains them and they fall back to where they came from. But they don't have physical forms or interact in any way so most people don't even realize what they are."

I turned to her and she had a smile on her face. "It's funny listening to you talk sometimes. I think you mix talking like them with talking like where you're from and how we talk here and it's a lot to keep up with."

I frowned, "did I just do that again?"

She laughed as she nodded, "It's ok. The place you're from sounds wonderful. Nothing but your own kind? Everyone must be so happy and get along so well."

"It's striding in the right direction as time passes, yes, but racism still exists."

"Racism?" she asked with her head sideways.

"Yes. Some people's minds are still primitive enough to the point where they actually hold the color of your skin, or the origin of your blood, or the place where you're from or even your religion against you like it alone dictates the character of the soul beneath. It's honestly like they are desperately searching for reasons to hate." I looked up and noticed where we were. "This is it," I pointed out as we stopped in front of the NaoSin Hall and she stared up at it.

"It looks ancient. Like it was designed by someone a long time ago."

I stared down the road further as she spoke, realizing I'd never ventured beyond this point. At the corner ahead I saw a small fruit stand and I chuckled to myself. "Come on. Let's go this way for a second," I suggested and led her away. "Back to what you were saying, I agree. We have very old buildings where I'm from that are similar to that one and every time I see one I always try to picture the time it came from. Who the first guy was to design it and what was his life like. Did the people ridicule him for his design or was he praised? Things like that."

She stared back at it for a moment and then finally turned back around. "So back to what you were saying though. We don't have racism here. If you're even close to us in species we get along... except giants!" she complained with her eyebrows narrowing.

We stopped at the small fruit stand, the owner's short body propped up on top of a stool so he could see over the table he sat at.

I looked over his produce. "I'll take all your apples please," speaking in the common tongue as I was in disguise again.

His head went back like he doubted my request. "Let's see the coin first." I did some quick math, "Cherr, give him a silver and we'll call it good."

She reached into the pouch she carried and handed one over. "Keep the change," she offered and he looked from it, to me, to her then back to me.

"You, my friend, just made my youngest son a very happy boy." He hopped off the stool, pocketing the coin. "I didn't think to make enough today with the streets already emptying and the other shops closing." He grabbed the few apples he had out on display and dropped them with the rest then picked up the entire bushel and carried it over to the counter, plopping it down in front of us.

"May I ask how?" Cherry questioned softly, "it will make him happy I mean?"

"Tomorrows his birthday and if I close quickly I can still get him the present he asked for." He stuck his hand out. "You're good people friends," he offered.

I shook it then picked up the apples. "Thank you," I replied, watching Cherry slide a gold coin across the counter next and keeping a finger on it while she spoke.

"This is to make it one he'll never forget." His eyes bulged, "I... this is..."

Cherry patted the man on the head and we turned to walk away. She looked up at me, "I really love making people happy. Like really," she beamed, turning back to watch the man jam fruit and baskets into the cart's cupboards with reckless abandon, smiling and laughing to himself the whole time he did.

"Like really?" I tried to make my voice sound like hers.

She smiled at me mockingly, her white teeth showing their perfect rows. "Yes! Don't tease me. Can I ask why you bought so many apples?"

I smiled back, showing her my teeth in return. "I think the workday at Naosin Hall has ended by now. Follow me."

Mesoten walked with a hurried pace. If he got done quickly enough today he would still have time to work on his true passion, designing his garden. He unlocked the door then removed the pack from his shoulder, going through it quickly to find his pen and ink.

If I didn't need them to keep the supply of coral rock coming I'd never do this for them. It's getting closer to the time- his thoughts trailed off as he approached his desk to find it full of apples. They lined its edges spaced apart evenly and formed the shape of a heart at its center.

Dowsin walked up behind him staring at the array as he spoke, "Summon Egosin and Finlosin for their final exams and what's with all the fruit?"

"I... honestly don't know," he replied, slowly walking around the desk to see an empty bucket with a note stuck to it sitting on top of his stool. Dowsin grunted then walked away as Mesoten pulled it off to read it.

'Riddle: There are many things with an apple that one can do. Juices, jellies and pies just to name a few. But there's one thing I'll teach now to make my words true. The ability to make applesauce was always beneath you.'

He blinked in confusion, setting the page down and not even attempting to figure out its meaning. He pushed some of the apples aside and drew up the summons where he stood then called over a running servant to have them delivered.

He picked the bucket up and began to drop the apples into it one at a time. There had to be some hidden reason to why Finlosin was doing this all? Why would a member of the Sin freely give away anything? He noticed his mug still sitting out and snatched it up, peeling the lid off. Not this time, he thought, remembering before when he had tried to take a drink and an apple popped the top off and soaked him from chin to crotch.

He pulled the apple out and dropped it into the bucket with the others. He eyed his drawers next then bent to open them one at a time, each containing an apple. He gave his desk another once over to be sure then turned to where the tea table sat with its large kettle and various jars of sweeteners.

He walked over and popped the lid off the kettle to find an apple floating inside. He pulled it out and brought it back to the bucket then repeated this process as he found one in the sugar, cinnamon, and even one in the honey.

He smiled to himself with pride as he returned from washing off the stickiness he had on his hands. It will be a cold day in hell when a fist thumper fools me twice, he thought, standing at his desk as the front door opened.

I walked in whistling a tune, letter in one hand while I watched Mesoten grin with mock satisfaction. "I just got done cleaning up your little attempt... to annoy me I'd assume?"

I shook my head, looking over his desk, the stool and then the tea table, "Not to annoy you."

He noticed my glance at his precious tea set, "yes, I even found those," he chided like talking to a child. "It will be a hot day in the Hintlands before a fist thumper pulls off a prank on me twice."

I walked by him with a devilish grin on my face, "so you figured out the riddle?"

He opened his mouth to speak but then paused, picking the sheet of paper back up to consider my words. "What does the riddle have to do with any of this?"

"I bet if you sat and gave that some thought the answer would provide itself," I called as I made my way towards the end of the hall.

He frowned, not knowing how to process the odd conversation then pulled his stool closer and sat with a frustrated huff. There was a soft crunching sound and he immediately could feel his backside getting wet. He hopped up to see his entire cushion padding had been removed and filled with apples before it was replaced flawlessly.

"Hey you solved the riddle!" I teased loudly and turned to see him staring daggers as I rounded the corner.

"BUT WHY?" he shouted and I laughed to myself as I disappeared from his sight.

I entered the pit to find it packed from side to side. Its left, right and middle sections full of beings wearing the red and black of the Sin, each uniform depicting different shaped eyes containing a various number of pupils. On the opposite side of the pit was a large wall with two doors, one closed and one open, preparation chambers for the combatants.

I saw Dowsin and he pointed to the arena floor, the room going abuzz with my arrival on the sands. I did a double take when I noticed Misosin himself amongst the group of Generals. He held a large horn in one hand, raising it to his lips and silencing the crowd with the other.

"Finlosin, you stand before us today to take your final test, a feat only ever accomplished so quickly by a few elite handfuls. Should you fail or withdraw at any time, you will remain of the third tier. If you pass-" his words cut off and all the heads in the crowd turned in the same direction as something pulled at the essence in tidal waves. Normally this was a common occurrence but the magnitude of this being was beyond anything I'd ever felt here before.

Misosin bent to one of his Generals and spoke something then leapt into the air right as a tremor started to shake the ground. The wind started to gust and people's eyes went wide in surprise.

It must be that other being! I realized, fighting the urge to join Misosin and go investigate it myself. All at once the world flashed and everything stopped in an instant, the crowd murmuring to themselves excitedly. The General Misosin had spoken to, now held the horn and he stood up to continue where his master had left off.

"If you pass, you will join the second tier and earn the privaleges only a Colonel would get. Furthermore, we have heard stories of how impressive your tests have gone before and if you do so again today it is within my power to offer you the opportunity of reaching the first tier rank. This will not be obtained with a test as only an act of extreme difficulty can grant one the title of General. That task will be decided later and as I said, only if you impress." I saluted him and he nodded back. "You may enter the preparation chambers now. Good luck."

Dowsin hopped down and made his way over. "You're going to want to fill your tanks first for this one," he pressed as we entered the large room. "The being you are fighting is the exact opposite of the last one. It's made up of flame so physical attacks go right through it, not even swords of essence do much and only the most powerful essence blasts affect it at all. So you'll need to put a ton of essence in each attack and have a ton in reserve." I had noticed more announcing from the sands as he spoke and wasn't surprised to see Egosin walk in a second later. He glared at me and made his way over to the opposite side of the room to get ready. "It's why this tier is so hard to achieve. We Sin spend our lives trying to advance but few ever make it as far as you have," he turned to Egosin as he changed into an outfit more suited for combat. "Finlosin is to go first so you can take your time in here."

The other Ascendal breathed a sigh of relief as I tried to formulate a strategy on how I should proceed. The General had told me if I impressed again today he could offer me the chance at tier one. I started to pull in the essence but at an even pace, I didn't want to give away how much more powerful I was then these beings.

"Your little comment about using a sword, a lot of people laughed at the absurdity of that. Don't do anything dumb, just end it before it ends you."

I kept drawing in the essence as I looked at him. "So, no body, no physical attacks, need to be strong in the essence and have tons of it to spare. Anything else?"

Dowsin thought, "he has no face or eyes. Oh, and he can travel nearly instantaneously in the form of lightning."

"Perfect. So what's the bad news?" I joked, sarcasm heavy in my tone.

A grin spread on his face and it made him look constipated, "and here I thought you were some prodigy. You aren't scared are you?"

I heard Egosin laugh and I shook my head. "Nah, the only thing that scares me is the voice in my head." He snickered at my comment.

I reached full capacity on the essence I could hold and stopped calling it in, turning my thoughts back to how I could impress. So they didn't think I could find a way to use a sword hey? I stared down at my hand, a solution coming to mind that depended on the answer of a different question. If I could create with two hands, could I do it with one? I don't think it really has anything to do with the body itself, it's just the mind over matter concept. I made sure Dowsin wasn't paying attention from where he stood talking to Egosin then closed my fingers tightly. I focused my thoughts and then opened it again, letting a single copper coin fall to the ground as I smiled at the tiny accomplishment. Think outside the box? If they could even comprehend what I was truely about to attempt I think their little heads might pop.

I stood and walked to the door. "You ready then?" Dowsin asked, walking back over and I nodded. He hit a button and a horn blasted from outside, the door swinging open silently. I strolled out into the pit with the confidence and swagger of a king, shoulders back, standing straight, head held high.

I reached the spot where Dowsin gestured to and turned back to await my opponent. A second horn sounded and the other door burst open with a crash of thunder. A lightning bolt shot across the pit and stopped to form a being made of pure fire. Or a better way to describe it, a ghost made of pure fire. It had no lower half, just a torso, arms and featureless head. Its entirety floated in midair and it appeared to be made of all flames. Colors and energy radiated off of it, vibrant tendrils slowly rising into the air where they dissipated. The General made a gesture and the last horn blasted, signaling the start and the crowd erupted.

I stared at the being in stunned fascination as the fire inside it flowed like a liquid to one hand, coalescing into a ball.

"Shit," I mumbled and dove to the side, the blast shooting past me and flying directly towards the crowd to where it was sucked into a karma stone hidden in the pit's railing. I stood and gave an uncaring laugh at my mistake, holding my right hand out to the side.

The crowd started to chuckle knowing I was summoning an essence sword but Dowsin had said they 'barely' affected the being. That meant the more powerful the sword, the greater the effect would be and plus, I planned to break laws.

I pushed the essence to my palm and started to create the sword, adding layer upon layer of power into it, condensing it further and further beyond anything I'd ever tried before. I stared down at my hand, knowing everything depended on my belief. I have the mustard seed I thought, then enforced my will upon the essence.

Shape. Form. Solid.

I called to the universe and the things that made it up, commanding it all to bend to my will. The sword continued to grow not just in size but in power and brightness. I could feel it in my palm and for the first time ever, it had weight. I was doing the impossible. I was giving light a completely new dimension, a physical one.

When I was done I had almost no essence left at all but in my hand I held a weapon beyond anything anyone could ever possibly conceive. I stared at it in awe, noticing it was about the same size and shape as a surfboard but with its bottom bent in to form the handle. It blazed like the sun itself and I could see tiny bolts of electricity crackling around its surface randomly. I turned my attention back up to the crowd and noticed they had gone dead silent in frozen fascination.

Hopefully this all just looked like some being with a LOT of power had made a very powerful sword of essence and nothing more. I turned back to the flame apparition just in time to see it shooting a blast and I reacted without thinking, swinging the sword and deflecting it away harmlessly. There was another collective gasp and then they erupted into a cheer.

"Fin- lo- sin! Fin- lo- sin!"

I shot forward and the thing sizzled past me, not wanting to come near my new weapon. I swung wildly, hitting nothing but air and was oddly disappointed in myself that I wasn't as fast as lightning. I planted my foot, spun, and shot after it as it bolted away again, the air crackling as it buzzed my head.

Smart thing. It knows real swords can't hurt it yet it runs from this one. I swung again only to hit nothing. I planted my foot, to continue my chase. It must be able to see it. Something clicked in place as easily as the last piece of a jigsaw puzzle. This being has no eyes. It can't see so it must have another ability that senses the essence around it. I swung again but to no avail. It knows I only have a little essence left the way it knows my sword is now where all my power is. It also doesn't know real swords can't hurt it because it can't see them. It can't see anything physical because it lives in a dimension we don't. It can only see the essence the same way we can only see the physical. Meeting beings like this was always complicated and hard for me to comprehend their specific points of view on existence. But I always attempted it anyway as doing so filled in the biggest gaps of the infinity code.

Now that I understood my opponent better an idea popped into my head. My reserve of the essence was low and I couldn't blink, not in front of a crowd so that meant I only had this one shot. I pushed the essence to my palm and instead of forming it into a ball I held it loosely then flung it up and scattered it into the air in front of the being. The air erupted into a brilliant but harmless light that blinded everyone and everything that watched. With the last of my essence spent and slightly disoriented by my own attack I leapt forward to where I'd last seen the thing.

I swung as the air crackled but this time it was different. There was a resistance to my blow as the thing shot by and my sword came down.

I hopped backwards and spun, keeping my back to the wall as I waited for my vision to return to assess what damage I had done if any. With my essence reserve completely drained, I was reminded of my mortality as my Earthen body started its faint call. I ignored it.

The being floated on the other side of the pit, head tilted towards the ground where half of its arm lay like a smoldering puddle of pudding. It reached down, putting its good arm into the flames and... absorbed it! I stared in horror as it reformed its other arm back to what it was, completely unaffected by the attack.

I'm in a world of trouble now, I thought. I need to blink or I may not even make it out of this pit. I called the essence and it came but my body refused to harness any of it and instead it just flowed around me. I knew I could use dozens of different techniques to beat this thing but all of them would give away what I was as they didn't use the essence in a normal fashion.

I had no choice. I flung my hand out like before but this time in a wider arch. I called to the essence that I could see in front of me in the air and caused it to flare up into another brilliant but harmless flash. The world around me went white again, blinding everyone.

I blinked.

Exhaustion melted away and power flooded back in. I was awake, alert and my Earthen body no longer played tug of war with my consciousness. I leapt forward and swung, the blow coming diagonally across the things neckline and hopefully ending the bout but I didn't wait to find out. I swung again and again sideways, down, left, right. The end result being several puddles of flaming goop and the crowd leapt to their feet as they exploded in applause, yelling and whistling loudly.

I let the essence in the sword burn away and willed the rest of it back into nothing, hopefully giving it the appearance of just a normal essence sword being dismissed. A similar being to the one I had just fought came out of the preparation chambers and made its way over. It was different then the first as it held some physical aspects to its shape. Two solid legs and two eyes along with other random patches scattered throughout its glowing body, giving it the appearance of flowing lava eating away patches of rock.

"We will require a moment of time if another bout is expected," the voice announced, breathy and somewhat feminine.

Misosin nodded as the two made their way back and I was surprised to see he had returned. The crowd went silent as he stood to address me.

"Finlosin you have passed the last test and earned the second tier rank should you choose not to continue. I would like to add that you did so in such a way that I would grant you an opportunity here and now to request consideration for the final tier should you wish it." He stared at me like I was supposed to respond so I did.

"I do."

"Very well it is granted. Some time in the near future you shall receive your first set of orders. Should you complete them you will find yourself at the rank you have desired throughout more than this one life. Get your new uniform and make all pre- peart-ions as it could come at any time. Dismissed."

I saluted and walked out of the pit half tempted to stay and watch Egosin but remembered my promise to Cherry. She had taken an interest in cards and wanted me to start teaching her everything I knew.

I was handed a new uniform and then made my way out, no-ticing a discarded tray outside the chow hall had an untouched orange on top of it. I grabbed it, tossing it into the air to catch it as I relished in my accomplishment.

I watched Mesotens pen work in a blur as I approached, clear-ly he was in a hurry to get done. I plopped the orange down on his desk without looking as I went by.

"No!" he called, "No, no, no! Is it starting over? Do you do this just to torment me?"

I laughed loudly at his complaints, letting the door slam shut behind me without a word.

CHAPTER 33

Understanding is something I'm very passionate about. I remember when I was a kid I used to do an exercise to help try and expand my consciousness best described as an 'infinite rewind'. I would start at the present day then work backwards through time in an attempt to find the origin to it all. I'd go back past Jesus and the caveman then the dinosaurs and all of life until I realized life didn't begin here on Earth. So I'd keep going, back to where you've been told it all started, the big bang. But for something to start, something else had to end and this isn't infinite so I tried to go back even further yet, before the big bang and the only thing to be found there was God but I didn't stop. I tried to press on even further, to look for Gods beginning but instead, what I found was understanding. To put it simply... God is infinite... God is origin.

"For the love of everything good Cherry can we do something else besides play cards? You know where I come from. I used to do this for a living."

"You played cards for a living? That must have been wonderful!"

I tapped my forehead, folding my flush to her obvious bluff.

"No, I dealt cards in a casino. We didn't actually get to play." "Oh... what's a casino?"

I smiled at the genuine curiosity in her eyes. "Are there places here where people go to gamble for money or roll dice or-"

"You mean like the bettings that go on in the back of a tavern and people sometimes get killed over?"

"Kinda, except casinos have lots of different games, machines with flashing lights, music, spinning wheels, chances to win fortunes, all that sort of thing and usually no deaths."

Her face changed back to one of awe as she tried to imagine it. "That place sounds wonderful too!"

I smirked. "I was addicted to it for a long while but eventually I overcame it."

"Why would you want to overcome something like that?" "Well to be honest they are designed to make you lose as

much of your money as possible and lots of people consider gambling a vice. I don't know if I agree with that as long as a person exercises moderation it's not bad but that wasn't me. I was spending almost everything I was earning in that place and it was controlling my life."

"I see..." she spoke softly, putting her head down in thought. She lifted it back up with a smile from ear to ear. "We can go back up to the bedroom?" she bounced her eyebrows up and down suggestively.

I rolled my eyes as I chuckled, "we already did that today. You need to work on moderation to control it more."

Her eyes narrowed and she crossed her arms. "Are you going to tell me two people who love each other and find pleasure in each others... beds, is a vice too?"

I shook my head, "No, but if you don't control it then eventually it will control you."

She leaned forward and put her hands on mine. "Is that why you call it your demon? Is that how it is for you?" Her voice came out soft and low almost like a whisper.

I ran a hand through my hair and nodded. "It's probably the biggest one I have. I struggle to control it, especially in places like this. Where I'm from I do a pretty good job of it though but I can never seem to kill it completely. No matter what I do it always comes back. I usually find it easier to just face a different one and pretend it doesn't exist but the longer I do this and it goes unchecked it's like it feeds off that and it comes back stronger."

There was a concerned look on her face. "So you have more than one demon?" I gave her a reluctant nod. "How many do you have?"

I lowered my head in shame as I've always tried to keep these secrets hidden from the world. "I'll tell you if you promise me you won't think I'm crazy." She gave a look like that was an impossibility then nodded. "I haven't spoken of this to anyone since I was a child but... I have this voice in my head." I stared at her and she made no noticeable reaction. "It tells me things... and those things usually turn out to be true. It told me that I will have all of them and face every demon endlessly. Everytime I face one down, another steps up in its place. Sometimes a new one, sometimes an old one, sometimes bigger and stronger. Some can be beat, others must only be controlled."

She cocked her head, speaking slowly, "how do you control a demon?"

"The simple answer... moderation."

"And where you're from, everyone has lots of demons?"

I shook my head. "No but everyone does start with one and if they allow it to grow it can cause others to sprout up inside them."

"Well why do you have so many then?"

I let myself rock back in my chair, exhaling out a long breath. "Cherr, talkings hard for me... I mean with this stuff I've never done it before... not since I was a kid anyway and everyone just thought I was lying then. I don't know if I'm ready."

She must have been able to read my emotions because she stood and scooted her chair closer, pulling it right up to mine as she grabbed both of my hands then sat. "Please?"

I stared into her big green eyes, knowing that if she wanted to she could have just demanded it of me. I also knew that she wouldn't have to. I would tell this girl anything she wanted to know because she made me feel normal. This place made me feel normal like I no longer had to pretend. Maybe it was because nothing I did here mattered where I was from, including if I told her some of my secrets.

I nodded and she gave a gentle smile. "There are two possible scenarios I've come up with as to why I have so many and each is based around belief. The first is as I said, the voice inside my head told me so. I was sitting on my parents dock fighting the demon known as suicide and I asked that very same question myself. It told me it needed my name. Or more accurately, needed to destroy my name and everything it represented. I offered it my name. What use do I have for a name anyway? I never really liked it. But even with that, it didn't work... the demons, " I cut off, and we just sat staring at each other, her eyes pleading for me to continue. "Anyway, that's scenario number one and I'm not sure if I even believe that one which brings me to the second option...

Ever since a very young age I've dealt with abuse of all kinds. It gave me night terrors. I started seeing things in the shadows that others couldn't. Hallucinations and memories of past lives that formed into an obsession with trying to solve all the mysteries of existence. I remember one time when I was five I sat crying because my brain couldn't properly process the notion of something being infinite even though I somehow knew that I had learned and understood it before." I shook my head to get back on track. "From there all the problems and abuse caused everything to change. I spiraled into depression, self loathing and pity. I started acting out, drinking, drugs, sex, overeating, gambling, lying, stealing, cheating, I could go on forever What I'm saying is... If you add all it up, a voice in my head, all the abuse, I'm probably just crazy. I just do a good job of acting normal."

I could see a tear form in her eye and she shook her head adamantly. "No you ain't! Don't think that!" She hopped from the chair up onto my lap, wrapping her arms around my neck. "I seen crazy people before in some of the cities my father used to go to. You're not crazy!"

I gave her my best smile. The kind of smile from someone who desperately wanted to believe what he was hearing. But I wasn't telling her everything because if option two wasn't true, then that meant the first one was and that option had the power to shake the foundations of the world itself.

A bell rang and Cherry's head jerked up. "No! No please not now! Don't go! Please just stay with me!"

"Cherry it could just be Ameletas, he told me he was going to write soon about some new developments in the world of the common folk... or so he puts it."

"Oh good. I really didn't want to stop-"

The servant walked in with his tray in hand, on it sat a letter with the single red eye of the Sin.

Misosin stood at the head of his table of Generals, hands clasped behind his back while he listened to the testimony.

"I saw it. As plain as the nose on my face. I was watching through the crack of the door when he did his final essence flare. His body vanished the instant he blinded everyone."

"What do you mean vanished?" a short fat general asked.

Egosin turned to address him. "I mean, one second it was there, then in a heartbeat it was gone and then back again. It disappeared completely."

Misosin eyed him carefully, "and this isn't created from jealousy because you failed your test and he passed?"

Egosin boiled inside at the comment. "No. It is simply what happened."

Another General stood, "if I may interject?" he paused to gain attention before he continued. "I watched this Finlosin beat a Demigog with one hand... like it was nothing. I know some of our strongest may be able to replicate this amongst some of their weakest but this Demigog was massive and no one could accomplish this before they've even received the Sin susaffix."

The Sin leader looked across his Generals as they turned to him next. "The being that he foughts interpreter relayed a message to me after the event had ended. It informed me that the first combatant had cheated by creating a sword that he described as "it simply shouldn't exist," but would explain no further. This is the reason I gathered you all here today, to see if there were other accounts and get to the bottom of it all."

Another General stood, "I have one if I may?" Misosin nodded and he continued, "I've always prided myself on reading a being's limits and reserves. Many around here come to me for lessons and council in this area," he gestured around the table and several people confirmed his words. "With what we've just heard I'm now having second thoughts. During the test I read Finlosins essence reserve as completely exhausted. He did the bright essence flare and I could suddenly feel it again. I thought maybe my original read was inaccurate but now after hearing Egosin..."

Another General stood and addressed Misosin. "I too would like to say something." The Sin leader nodded. "His technique he did was an advanced trick only half of us could pull off so effectively. The first time he performed it, it was flawless. The second time... it did not come from his palm."

A few of the others around the table began to murmur their agreement and Misosin addressed them all once again. "If what we are saying is true, then he can do things that are not possible for the Sin to do and there is only one type of being who can accomplish this." The room went silent at what he was implying. "I think this means that Finlosin is a Boundless." Egosins hatred bubbled up at the thought of being outdone by such an abomination and Misosin noticed. "You are dismissed Egosin," he ordered and then bent down, placing both hands on the table as he addressed his men in a more serious tone. "Gentleman, we need to come up with a way to test this theory for sure. Any ideas?"

I cracked the door open and was relieved to see Mesotens desk empty. I snuck up to it and plopped down the giant watermelon with attached note reading 'please do not sit on me' with a chuckle as I made my way down the corridor.

I reached the end of the hall and the door opened before I even touched it.

Mesoten looked up in surprise. "Follow me. You are now to wait in here until you are summoned."

I cocked an eyebrow, "the letter said they were ready for me?" "I know what it said, I wrote it!" he explained like I was dimwitted, gesturing to a room off to the side.

I walked in, giving the room a quick once over as I entered. It had a few odd paintings, some various plants and several chairs that looked new. It reminded me of a hospital waiting room. I plopped into one with a sigh and turned back to see Mesoten still staring at me, one arm supporting his elbow as his chin rested on his hand.

"Can I expect any more little surprises waiting for me when I return to my desk?"

I gave him my dumbest smile. "Little surprises? I think we've grown past that now," I chuckled, thinking myself clever on the play of words to avoid the lie.

He nodded slowly then spun to walk away. A second later his head popped back in. "I would like to rephrase the question if I may. I've been ever so good at detecting lies and that answer was awfully suspicious." I did my best to keep a straight face while he stared at me in consternation. "Will I find... no, that could be interpreted wrong... Did you do or put anything in, on or around my desk?"

I used a gesture my dad used to do to us when we were kids. I shook my head no. "Yes."

He frowned, "so you did?" I shook my head yes. "No."

He smiled the first genuine smile I'd ever seen him do. "May I join you? Your oddity fascinates me."

I shrugged and a man walked around the corner just as he moved to enter. "Finlosin, they are ready for you."

I stood up and watched as Mesoten bit his lip in thought. "Another time perhaps?"

"Sure. You can visit anytime you'd like. You know my address."

"I do," he answered. "Should I bring a gift?"

A custom that was common amongst the Ascendals who were not part of the Sin and usually consisted of some type of food. I paused like I was deep in thought. "That's fine. Just don't bring any fruit. I never touch the stuff."

I heard him chuckling to himself as I walked through the large double doors of the war councils chambers.

I looked around the large table and saw a wide variety of expressions I couldn't read as Misosin spoke. "Finlosin, we have come up with your first set of orders and are ready to bestow a task upon you if you are ready to accept it?" I nodded. "Should you deny this task or fail at it you will remain at the second tier rank but if you pass you will find yourself a seat at my table." He paused and I could feel everyone tense up at what he was about to say but I didn't know why. "Have you ever heard of a Cherubim?"

I glanced around, trying to think. The word was familiar to me but I had no clue where I had heard it before. "I believe I have but would like a refresher if possible."

Several people let out sighs of relief and he nodded. "The Cherubim are a race created by God to be servants. There are many kinds in many forms and on many levels. The ones in this place are the variety that have no soul. Created only to protect the most powerful gate in all existence. Their sole purpose here is combat, they fight and are a very formidable foe indeed. The only known way to kill them is to take off their head." He paused and then gestured towards the door. "We have paintings of them on our walls throughout the NaoSin Hall if you need a visual. There is a group of the Cherubim at the base of Bedlam Spire. Your orders are to go there at once and attack and kill one of these creatures. The use of essence within those grounds is impossible so no flying or healing and plan accordingly. You will be given nothing but a map to assist you and must go at once. When you return to us with one of their heads you will become that which you've desired for more than one life. General Finlosin, any questions?"

I stared down at the map as it was placed in my hand and thought of Cherry being alone. "How long did it take those who have succeeded before me?"

He stared at me blankly, "no one has ever accomplished this task within two weeks time. As I said, a sound strategy must be planned."

"I see," I responded, not really paying attention but instead thinking only of leaving Cherry all alone for up to two weeks. I knew if I went and spoke to her first she would just enforce that stupid rule and demand me to take her with her.

"Dismissed."

I lifted my head up from my thoughts and noticed the entire room was staring at me silently. I gave a quick salute then spun and walked out as I formulated a way to just have a message sent to her instead of facing her myself.

"Every single being inside this existence knows what the Cherubim are and why they guard the spire. Attacking them is like attacking God and will surely be punished. His acceptance of this task proves to me that Finlosin is not from this universe and there is only one type of being known that can accomplish quantum leaps as he clearly has done," Misosin informed his Generals of the conclusions he had made after I left. "He must be nothing other than a Boundless."

"Despicable creatures," one of the men spat and the others voiced their agreements.

"Sir," the small general at the opposite end of the table squeaked. Misosin regarded him and his pitiful frame. If not for his massive brain and the fact his power seemed to be infinite, however weak it was, he'd have dismissed the being as a child. "We must now consider that he will accomplish this task and try to deduce an accurate timetable so he can be... dealt with immediately upon his return."

Misosin nodded. "Yes General Tadsin and I assume you have already done this?"

The small being nodded. "I took into consideration the time table you gave him when you said that no one has ever done it within two weeks. I'd assume Finlosin will continue to try his impressive displays and either return on or before the date given."

Misosin stroked his chin. "We know not yet how powerful this being is but I want all precautions taken. We will summon the elite unit to the pits along with every General and Colonel the armies can spare. When he returns from his task we will summon him to the arena and kill him where he stands. All in favor?" Every single one of his Generals signaled their agreement. "Then it's settled and I want not a word of any of this out before we act. Anything further?"

The small General leaned forward once again. "Is it just me or does no one wonder why he is here? What does he hope to gain from us? Clearly he has his sights set on being a General but what does that offer him that other ranks wouldn't?"

The table started talking without leave, blurting out responses randomly. "He needs an army for something," or, "let's flay him and find out."

Misosin stared at Tadsin knowing he had already made his own assumptions. "You have something further General?" he asked, gesturing for him to continue.

"Yes sir, I do. I think he's here to find access to Bedlam Spire and needs to be a General to gain audience with you and most likely wants to know how you accomplished this task yourself ?" Misosin snorted. "I serve a master from a different time that allowed me in, that is how I gained my access. Now tell me why is it you think he wants in?"

General Tadsin shrugged, "maybe he's after that other being?"

Misosin shook his head, "Ii is not a being, it is a God."

The smaller General frowned, "are we sure about that? The description given was poor to say the least. Have we considered-"

Misosin smacked the table causing his men to jump as anger boiled up and he spoke slowly, "I was the one who said it was a God. Do you doubt my judgment or my words?"

Tadsin shriveled in his chair at the sight of his master's fury. "No sir. I was just-"

"When I went to investigate the disturbance during that testing day, I found a small boy talking to a GOD! Different to ours in every way except divinity. Not some rare creature or some Boundless of unfathomable powers. When it spoke the foundations of reality themselves shook. Something OUR God has never done! Do you doubt what I saw? What I heard? Do you doubt the FEAR I felt?" Spittle flew from his mouth as his words turned to shouts and none of the men dared move. Misosins power was unrivaled amongst the Sin and the look he gave now showed he was itching to display it.

The door burst open and Mesoten led in two other Ascendals.

"She insisted," he offered, then left the room.

"Lachesis?" Misosin questioned. "You have word from Ananke? Rarely do you bring me good tidings."

"I bring them nevertheless," she responded

"Well what is this about then?" he asked, standing straight once again.

"It is about the one who calls himself Fin."

All the men perked up at the mention of the name. "Yes, we understand what he is."

She glanced around the room then shook her head. "No. I'm afraid you don't. [Ancient Name Omitted] will never be fully understood."

Several of the men frowned at this and started to speak freely. "Does this mean he can be anyone?" she nodded. "Or anything?" and she nodded again. "Then he can become me, or you, or a Cherubim? How do we fight an enemy who can become anything?"

"Easy! You just kill everything," one responded like it was obvious.

Misosin raised a hand to silence them. "If that was true then surely you wouldn't be able to explain the extent of it and these men here are rambling for nothing. I fail to see the meaning of all this?"

"I am here simply to fulfill that which I must," she gestured the other Ascendal forward.

"I've, um, received a letter from God" he handed it over nervously. "You're not going to like what it says but you're our only hope."

Misosin snatched the letter from the yellow eyed being. "Never thought I'd hear the day a book licker said something like that. It must be dire indeed." He unfolded it, scanning the contents quickly, lips moving silently as he read. The men watched their liege as he froze, eyes going wide then rereading the paper. "No! I'm not done here! I need time!" he snarled and turned to Lachesis. "NO!" he shouted and she nodded back. "Not if I have anything to do with it! We can catch him by surprise!" He spun to his men. "All of you, call your men, call their families, call every man, woman and child of every class! Tell them the end is here and we are killing everything that refuses to wear the black of the Sin! Tell them we are going to war and we are going to war NOW!" The men hesitated, confusion on their faces. He slammed his fist down so hard the table snapped in two. "MOOOVVVEEE!!!" he screamed and the room exploded into motion.

CHAPTER 34

H*igher beings are mentioned in your cultures, your lore and in your religions and this information shouldn't be ignored. But do they exist here and if so why haven't they made themselves known? The truth is higher beings can be both extra terrestrial and extra dimensional, and humans exist on different steps of the infinity code then they. You are to far beneath them to understand what they are. Like the crab, you cannot see the differences of the birds and fish that float above you. Consider this, a higher being comes down and kills someone you love. To you this is outrageous and you'd immediately try to kill them back. But from their point of view they would see it different. Maybe they seen a soul that didn't belong here and decided it could return to Heaven. Maybe it seen an incurable disease leading to more death and suffering for the whole family so thought of it as a mercy. Or maybe it seen through time to the future and what that person would do or become. There's millions of reasons they would be here, keeping themselves hidden from the world. You don't even understand the purpose of your own existence yet, how can you hope to understand theirs?*

Father's going to be so proud of me this time! little TugTug thought to himself, bending to pick the small blue mushroom then plopping it into his folded shirt with the rest. These ones are his favorite. Now maybe he won't be so mad at me for forgetting my practice spear. He looked up and a smile spread across his tiny blue face, slanted eyes full of delight as he noticed more growing ahead at the base of another tree. He ran over and picked them, being careful not to get the dirt and checking for bugs before dropping them with the rest. Again and again he cried out in glee as he found more and more of the small fungi. If I can fill my shirt, I bet father will be so happy he lets me have some spice cake after dinner. The thought set his mouth to watering and in no time at all his shirt couldn't fit a single mushroom more. There's still so many. This place must have more than anywhere in the whole wide world. He stood, looking around seeing the blue caps sprouting around in all directions. I'll just tell father and he'll come get the rest himself. He turned to walk back to the road and froze. That's not the way I came? He turned to one side and then the other. I think it was this way he thought, then started to jog until he found more of the blue mushrooms sprouting up. No, it must have been the other way or else I would have picked those. He ran back in the direction he had just come and started looking for areas where the mushrooms were already picked but it was hard. He noticed a small spot of upturned soil with a broken piece of mushroom stem in it. It has to be this way, he realized and took off in that direction with confidence. After a few moments he found his path blocked by a small brook. It's slow trickling waters impossible for him to have crossed before without noticing. I didn't cross any water he thought and panic started to set in. He turned and started going back the way he came once again but now nothing looked familiar at all. His little legs pumped faster and faster as fear gripped him.

"Ma?" he yelled. "Ma where are you?" He tried to keep up his pace but the weight of the mushrooms was wearing him out fast.

Oh no! Fathers going to be mad again if I don't make it back soon. "Ma?" his yell came louder this time. "Papa?"

He thought he saw a tree he recognized and ran towards it, tripping over a root and sprawling out face first sending most of the mushrooms flying but some squished softly under the weight of his fall. Oh no! the mushrooms! and now I've stained my shirt. He stood frantically, head going back and forth.

"MOMMY!" He cried out and tears started to flow. I can't cry. Papas already going to be so mad at me for the shirt and being gone and now if I cry too... "PAPA?" He ran with no destination, fear feeding his adrenaline while he darted from tree to tree shouting. Why weren't they answering?

What seemed like an eternity passed and he finally gave up and cried, letting himself fall into a ball with his head tucked between his knees. There's monsters in this land, I just know it and they're going to find me and get me. The tears ran uncontrollably now and he stopped fighting them.

"I'm sorry Mommy. I'm sorry Papa. I tried to be a good boy," he spoke to no one and rocked back and forth silently as he listened to the sounds of the forest.

His head snapped up with a jerk. "What was that?" He stood, straining his ears as he tried to will the sounds all around him to be silent.

"TuuuggTuuugg!" his fathers voice boomed from so far off he could barely hear it.

"PAPA!" he exclaimed triumphantly, then started to sprint in the direction it came. "PAPA HERE I COME!" His smile grew wide knowing his father was looking for him. My Papa saved me and no monsters got me!

"Tuugg Tuugg!" the voice came again and this time a lot closer. "Papa I'm here!" he proclaimed, bursting from the woods and back onto the path. His father spun at the voice and TugTug latched onto his waist in an embrace. The man quickly pushed him off and the world flashed as a backhand stung his cheek.

"Stupid boy. Do you know the worry you put your mother through?" he berated as TugTug sat up on the ground.

"Papa... I'm sorry... I was-"

"Are those tears? No son of mine cries. Now get up and explain yourself."

The boy stood slowly, refusing to meet his fathers eyes while he fought off crying. "I seen some Bontrell mushrooms, your favorite and-"

Another backhand sent him sprawling. "Is that what's stained all over your good shirt? You think coins grow on trees?"

"Stop! Please!" He heard his mothers voice plead as she ran up and dropped to the ground beside him. She pulled him in gently, "my poor boy. You must have been so scared."

"Woman get off of him. My son needs to learn he can't just run off and do what he pleases. Ruining shirts and worrying us sick."

She stared up at him in defiance. "No. Not this time. He is only a boy. A boy who just spent almost an entire day lost, alone and scared."

Her husband's eyes narrowed. "Did you just tell me no? Do you need a lesson too?"

She set her jaw. "I said no. Not this time and if hitting me stops you from hitting him then I'll take it."

"No Mama, I need to learn-"

"Shh." she hushed him and looked back up in acceptance. "Of all the stupid-"

His words cut off as his blow got caught mid swing. He turned his head to see a stranger holding his arm in an iron tight grip. The man was almost a foot taller than him but also had the blue skin and elongated skull of his species. His slanted eyes stared at him in judgment.

"Mind your business friend. This doesn't concern you." he warned the stranger.

I stared back at him trying to contain the rage I felt at the amount of ignorance this being had. I had used another trick I picked up before and shifted my body into one of the same species as he was. I didn't know if there was any animosity between his kind and the humans of the place so decided he'd probably respond better to one of his own kind.

I backhanded him, releasing my hold and he went flying. He rolled to his feet, eyes wild with rage as he charged, trying to tackle me at the waist. I side stepped, bringing my knee up directly into his chin. I heard him growl as he hit the dirt again and this time he stood slowly.

"You're asking for it now," he warned, pulling out the spear that was strapped to his back.

"Papa no!"

"Shut it boy," he hissed and thrust the weapon at my stomach. I turned, letting the long shaft miss and then reached out and tugged it forward causing him to stumble towards me. I didn't let go of the thing as I landed a right hook and he crumbled to his knees. He looked up, nose bleeding into his snarling mouth. "Please stop!" the female begged.

"I cannot. Not yet. I am proving to him that I love him." I tossed the weapon away, watching his face scrunch up at my words.

"Insane bastard," he muttered, then leapt at me like a pouncing cat. I caught his fist and struck his forearm with my palm. It snapped and he screamed out in agony.

"I love you," I claimed, no emotion in my voice and he stared in confusion. I kicked his leg out, dropping him to one knee then backhanded him to the ground again. "I love you," I repeated and this time louder. He stared at me then turned to his wife and son.

"Please stop hurting my Pa."

"Quiet little one. He needs to learn the love I am teaching him." I waited for him to stand. "I love you," I repeated.

He held his broken arm timidly. "The fight is yours. There's no need-"

My foot shot out in a straight kick that hit him square in the chest and sent him end over end. "I love you!" I shouted, walking towards him as he tried to scoot away in pain.

"Enough! I yield!"

I grabbed him by the front of his tunic and stood him on his feet. My fist landed in his stomach with a solid thud that hunched him over. "I said I love you!" I growled, grabbing his hair and flinging him back to the ground in front of his family.

He moaned in pain, blood smeared on his face as his wife and son tried to pull him into their embrace, sheltering him from my wrath. "Are you insane? You don't love me, you're just beating me!" he exclaimed.

I bent over him and cocked an eyebrow. "So you think I'm insane because I'm beating someone I claim to love? Or are you wondering why someone who claims to love you would beat you at all?" I gestured to his wife and kid. "I bet they ask themselves that every day."

I saw a tear forming in his eyes as he realized the truth to my words. I grabbed him by his tunic and lifted him back to his feet as his family protested.

"Please. I understand-"

"Wipe those tears. You're making yourself look like a hypocrite in front of your son." I grabbed his bad arm and he winced trying to pull away. "Brace yourself, I'm going to set it." He grit his teeth and I snapped the bone back in place. He moaned loudly and started to sway but the other two moved to hold him steady. I started to feed essence into the break with one hand and pull it out with the other like I saw Yeeresh do and the wound healed itself completely.

The family's eyes went wide in shock as they watched what I was doing. "Who... are you?" I let go of his arm and he shook it, testing out its strength in disbelief.

I pointed to his face with its cuts and bruises. "Those stay as a reminder. Everybody gets a second chance.," then turned and walked away as I pulled out my map.

This place looks absolutely magical, I thought as I walked through the ferns, knowing I was there when the use of essence had suddenly vanished from me. I could still see it all around but it no longer came if I tried to absorb it into my body. I moved forward silently, watching for one of the mysterious creatures and not knowing what to expect. The wind rolled in, causing the trees to dance, their hips swaying back and forth as they seduced each other endlessly. I watched a butterfly float by and heard a bird chirp from the canopy above. I moved closer towards a thick pine thinking it would offer me some camouflage in case I spotted one of the Cherubim.

I placed each foot down carefully, trying to make as little noise as possible until I reached the bows of the tree. The first thing I noticed was an area where the sun shone down brightly meaning a break in the leaves above and that meant a clearing below. I circled around to get a better view and found what I was looking for.

In the small field stood a massive silverish gray figure with the body of a man and the head of a lion. It stood motionless with its eyes shut like it was sunbathing. I scanned beyond it and saw several more throughout the clearing but they were hidden better than this one. I peered around, trying to think of an idea then noticed some pinecones at my feet.

I picked one up and moved further behind the tree to hide and then chucked it at the beast. It struck the creature directly in the shoulder and I ducked, watching intently.

The Cherubim whirled, staring at the small pinecone and then turning to assess the woods around him.

That's right. Those aren't pine trees so where did it come from? I thought to myself. Why not investigate and-.

The thing's eyes snapped shut and it returned itself to its original posture. I shook my head. Ok, so that didn't work, apparently I'm going to have to be more obvious. I picked up another pinecone, an idea forming in my head. My body held no essence but that didn't mean I still couldn't try controlling externally like I did with my flare ability. I held the thing up to my face and willed the tiniest amount of essence into it and then tossed it at a tree causing it to explode.

Danger! Attack that you stupid thing, I thought and the beasts eyes shot open this time and it charged forward at my distraction. It plowed into the tree, snapping it like styrofoam as its jaws mashed wildly, reducing the small elm to kindling.

I used the noise from its attack to move further away from the clearing in an attempt to continuously draw it from the oth- ers. I stopped behind a large oak and peered back to watch the thing as it eyed the pile of broken wood, no doubt looking for suspicious pieces to question. I chuckled at my own joke as I searched around for something else. A small butterfly fluttered up and I caught it easily.

"Sorry little buddy," I whispered to the thing and pushed essence into it and then tossed it high up into the air. "There, get that you stupid-"

My words cut off as the thing charged over with reckless abandon and lept high for the small insect. Its hands caught nothing but air as the tiny thing flew higher and higher at the sight of danger. The Cherubim continued its pouncing but to no avail and I gave a small inward cheer for the underdog as I moved on even further away from the clearing.

I picked up a small rock and pushed some essence into it, deciding to make this trick my last one. I reached back like I was about to throw a hail Mary and hurled it with all my might.

Try and catch that you mindless-. My thoughts cut off again as the thing crashed through trees and shrubbery alike as if they were one and the same, V lining it for my small projectile. Man, this creature did not like the use of essence inside this place. Maybe it was one of the rules or something? I shook off the thought and gave chase after, knowing the noise it was causing hid any I would make perfectly.

I caught up to it to find it smashing the rock into the dirt. I couldn't fight with the essence here but that didn't matter. I didn't need to. I had my mind. I thought of how powerful a speeding semi truck would be and imposed the concept into my foot as I kicked forward. My attack connected with the beast's face and he flew through the air as pain blossomed in my foot.

Damn! That felt like kicking a lead elephant I thought and had no choice but to blink. My blue skinned disguise vanished and I was immediately my old self again. The thing hopped up and stared at me while it sniffed at the air, a menacing growl in its throat. I watched as it started to push its shoulders back, sucking in a deep breath.

It's going to roar! To signal the others! I knew I couldn't let that happen and leapt forward with all the speed I could muster. My fist has the power of a train I imagined, then I believed it. The haymaker-like punch sent the beast rolling in somersaults to where it crashed into a boulder. I didn't hesitate, lining up the things head for another kick. My foot is like a wrecking ball I thought. I tried to believe it again but knew instantly that this time it didn't work.

The creature sprang up like a jack in the box at the last second and I longed for the lead elephant as my foot connected with the boulder behind. My ankle fell limp and I spun frantically, knowing it would see my helplessness and attack.

I tried to blink again but my luck had run out once more. My body pulled too hard at the pain and I struggled to regain my physical self. This happens from time to time and once even in front of someone I knew. They told me I looked like I was splitting into multiple bodies at once while a quake rattled me to the bones.

The Cherubim stood frozen, watching me struggle to gain my hold on this world. After a few seconds I solidified my belief, regaining my grip as me and the humanoid lion stared at each other. It tilted its head in confusion, eyeing me suspiciously and then turned to jog back to its clearing.

"Seriously?" I called, thinking it must only attack those who are trying to enter and must somehow know that I'm not here to do that. I picked up a chunk of rock and pushed essence into it and flung it at the thing. "Come back and fight me!"

It spun on a dime and shot at me as quick as the lion it was, growling loudly. I barely had time to react as I swung a backhand and it dodged, punching me so hard it felt like I got hit by a car. I envisioned my fists as battering rams then believed it, punching wildly. The beast dodged and swung again but this time I was ready. I blocked his attack and watched his wrist bend backwards, clearly broken.

That should slow you. He swung anyway, oblivious to the pain and I found myself floating through the air until I crashed into the trunk of another giant tree. I hopped up and kicked behind me as I heard it approach. There was a thud as my hopeless attack landed but where I didn't know. I jumped and spun to kick again and it rolled away.

I needed to think this through. My arrogance had caused me to overestimate how easily it would be to kill one of these things without the use of essence. The beast darted forward and I ducked the blow. The tree I now stood in front of wasn't so quick and it crumbled to the ground. I punched out again and again, willing my blows to come faster and faster as the Cherubim tried to dodge desperately. One connected then another and another. It swung back and I willed my head not to move. It roared out its defiance when it realized the ineffectiveness of its blow. My confidence started to grow and I thought I could see desperation in the things lifeless eyes. It moved to duck.

Kick.

I stopped thinking and just started reacting as this somehow always seemed to produce the best results. My blow connected with its chin and it tried to back away but I was relentless.

Punch. Faster. Stronger.

It fell to its knees and I knew it was going to try and tackle me. I am a mountain.

I believed it and the large creature shot forward, crashing into me but I didn't budge an inch. It thrashed its weight around wildly, trying all it could to move me as I assaulted it back. It roared, loud and long then bit down, its teeth sinking into my lower back and I clenched my jaw. Everything froze, my entire life flashing before my eyes in an instant.

Reality popped into existence without a sound, like turning on a light. I watched as a very young version of me stood propped up with two hands under his arms like crutches. My brother Daniel waited with his arms out, beckoning me over. There are other people around but their faces are a blur. They're encouraging me on.

(This is when I learned to walk? I remember this but why am I seeing it?)

[SKIP]

I'm a little older now, about three. I'm sitting in the back of my parents van looking out the window. The green fields seem to have no end as I watch them roll by. I'm nervous. The vision moves forward and now I see myself at the doctor. I'm sitting on his table with no pants on.

(NO! Not these! I don't want to watch these. How do I make this stop?)

He walks in and shuts the door behind him. "Ok next I'm going to do some things and all you have to do is tell me if they feel good or not ok?" The boy me shook his head and I could hear his thoughts.

'I wonder if this is normal?' he asked. "Thisss is normalll."

(The voice in my head! Even then? No! Don't tell him that! It wasn't normal!)

[SKIP]

It's a few years later and I'm sleeping. Someone pinches my toe and I wake up.

(NO! Please not this one! This one's broken, please stop!) His face continuously changes but it's someone I love. An uncle. He's leading me somewhere. Somewhere dark.

[OMITTED]

I'm coming out of the dark but I'm not the same. I will never be the same.

'He said that was love. Is that normal?' "Thisss is normalll."

(Stop telling him that!) [SKIP]

I'm 8 now. My older cousin is over and he wants to play with me. He wants to go hide in the closet but nobodies looking for us. He starts to do things too but it's nothing new.

'This is normal.' "Thisss is normalll."

(Why am I watching all this? I had these buried!) [SKIP]

It's my older cousin again. [SKIP]

It's my older cousin again. [SKIP]

It's my older cousin again and things are progressively getting worse the longer it continues.

'Are you sure all this is normal?'

"Innn this worlddd, thisss is normalll." [SKIP]

I'm in the giant upstairs of my parents house and I'm all alone. All my brothers and sisters who are usually up there with me are gone. I'm watching the shadows. I can see them moving, crawling, getting closer as they scream at me silently. I hide under the blankets to cry.

'Why doesn't anybody believe me? Why can't they see what I see? Why am I different?'

Suddenly I'm being lifted into the air. There's yelling and flashes of light. I'm trying to stop crying. I'm trying to be a good boy but he's so angry. There's something warm running down onto my face then I'm being carried to the bathroom. I'm standing over the sink and it's stained red. Then he's gone and I'm all alone. 'If your head bleeds your brain won't have no blood and then you die. Why would my father try to kill me?' "He hatesss youuu."

(He doesn't hate you! He loves you! He just went to get towels.)

'Is this normal?' "Thisss is normalll." [SKIP]

It's my older cousin and the numbers are getting so high I'd lost count. He's doing whatever he likes and I'm letting him. I find it's easier to just let him do whatever he wants, that way we can go back to being normal like everyone else. My brother David sneaks in and catches him in the act. I was scared at first but also relieved.

'Maybe now it's all over?'

He's laughing, teasing, and threatening. Saying if I don't start doing everything he tells me he was going to tell everyone what I was.

'Please don't tell. That's not normal!' "Thisss is normalll." [SKIP]

It's my older brother. He's forcing me to give him something that's mine or else he will tell all my friends and they will hate me. I hand it over.

'Fine, just take it.' [SKIP]

It's my older brother and I'm doing his chores now. [SKIP]

It's my older brother again and I'm taking the blame for something I didn't do.

[SKIP]

I'm on my bike. It's the very first time I ever ran away. I was grounded for something I didn't do and no longer allowed to go to a friend's birthday party. I pull into the boat launch. Its buildings are abandoned but my cousin Mahng had taught me how to break in. I get inside and ball up. I'm crying.

'This is where I'm going to spend the rest of my life. I'm sure going to miss my little brother.' I suddenly realized that he was the only thing that helped me make it through the darkness of night. 'Without him I can't face the shadows alone. I can't stay here... and I can't go back. What am I supposed to do?'

"There isss a wayyy."

(I don't want to watch this shit anymore! I was only eleven!) 'What way?'

"To enddd the painnn." 'It's...not normal?'

"Your sistersss call you annoyinggg. Your brothersss hate youuu. Your fatherrrr hates youuu."

Something blossomed inside of me. Something dark. 'I'll do anything.'

Visions entered my head and I moved. I grabbed some of the plastic wrap that was used for covering furniture. I pinned one edge of it to the back of my head with one hand then used the other to wrap it tightly around my face as many times as I could. I held it and stopped.

'I can still breathe.'

I look around for something else. Anything else. I seen a nail and picked it up, holding the flat end against the wall at eye level.

'What if it's not long enough?'

I threw it aside and continued to search. I looked out a window and noticed the water and the rocks at its edge.

'I'll hold a rock so I don't float.'

I burst outside and there was an elderly person walking with their granddaughter. I panicked and jumped on my bike to leave before they noticed what I had done.

(8 years. It took 8 years from when it all started for you to break me you bastard.)

[SKIP]

Running away becomes a normal occurrence. I start having sex, drinking, smoking.

[SKIP]

My grades are slipping. I'm quitting sports. Skipping school.

[SKIP]

I find a girl. I'm in love. She's wonderful!

"She lustsss for anotherrr." 'What? No, we're in love!'

I'm reading the letters. My heart is broken. My love is broken.

[SKIP]

I'm running away again. Going home was a bad idea. His fists hurt but not as much as his words. He told me they had agreed that from now on only my mother was going to take charge of me all on her own and that she had cried for nearly a day when she realized she had failed.

'No, I'm the failure mother. Not you'

(At least that I can agree with) [SKIP]

I start doing drugs. Partying nonstop, random hookups with women.

[SKIP]

I start breaking into places to rob them, stealing from people, selling drugs, lying, ripping off businesses.

[SKIP]

I'm walking to my parents dock. It's where I go to talk to God. It's where he never answers. Nothing is working anymore. The partying, the women, the friends, none of it helps with the pain. None of it seems normal.

"There isss a wayyy."

I swing through the house and grab my fathers gun from the top of the cupboard. I'm on the dock and it's loaded. My finger is on the trigger while I stare down its barrel. I see nothing down there. No more pain. No more failures, just death. I think maybe in death I will at least get all the answers I've ever wanted. To why me. To why this life. To everything, all existence.

(To the infinity code...)

I'm trying to find a reason not to do it.

'Can you give me a reason? Isn't living normal?' Silence.

I ask God next. Can you give me a reason to live? Something worth sticking around for?

Silence.

I suddenly remembered one of my girlfriends had invited me to a softball tournament and it actually sounded kind of fun. I decided to wait until after that.

[SKIP]

I'm on the dock again. The guns loaded and my fingers on the trigger. I'm going through the same old routine and end up remembering my best friend's birthday party and decide to wait.

[SKIP]

The birthday party was great. I ended up in a relationship with my friend's sister and now we're engaged. She has her own son and her own place and things are finally looking up.

'This is normal.'

"She doesss not loveee you." [SKIP]

I'm on the dock again. I have no reasons anymore and God doesn't ever respond. I'm begging for answers to why I have so many problems.

"Do ittt. It willl only gettt worrse." 'What? How could it possibly get worse?'

"The longerrr you resisttt, the moreee demons youuu will fa-ceee."

'Why?'

"Becauseee you musttt face themmm all, overrr and overrr!" 'But why me?'

"I needdd your nameee."

'My name? It's useless you can have it.'

"I needddd all offf your namesss! To destroyyy them!" [SKIP]

Women. Partying. Drugs. Dock. [SKIP]

I'm on the dock screaming about failing at something I was desperately trying to convince myself was a dream.

[SKIP]

Women, partying, stealing, dock. [SKIP]

I'm on the dock again. I drop the gun and I'm crying. God doesn't exist and I'm sure of it but I can't figure out why I keep refusing to pull the trigger. It's like something won't let me. I remember an accident I was in almost a few days before and it should have ended my life.

'Why won't you let me die? Why must I live in this hell?' Silence.

I start thinking about hell and demons and angels and realize that if I had one it may have saved my life the other day. I make up my mind, right then and there that I was either going to get answered by God in life, or I'd visit him personally in death.

God.. send me an angel to prove you are real. A real angel too for me to love. To take away my pain and give me a purpose here in this place. I need to see what it's like to be normal please! At least once before I go. You have twenty four hours to give me a sign or next time I don't stop myself. [This one is too personal to be recorded in this book. Only one person has the right to say what happens next and it's not me. OMITTED]

[SKIP]

I'm in love. She reminds me of Lynnay and is exactly like me.

We had a kid and life is finally normal. I'm heading to work.

"There isss another."

'What? No! We love each other. Leave me alone please!' "Return homeee at onceee. You willl see."

I go home. She's trying to put the baby to sleep but it's way too early for that.

'That's not normal.' "Thisss is nottt normal."

There's a knock at the door and it's some man I've never seen before. He asks for her but has no reason why he's here. She stammers out an excuse.

"Herrr tongue isss forked." 'Please. I don't care." [SKIP]

"There isss a mannn she worksss with." 'We are normal!'
[SKIP]

"Her friendddd persuades herrr from youu."

'If this isn't normal please just let me pretend! You're ruining everything!'
[SKIP]

"She hasss not deleteeddd it yettt. You cannn read ittt." 'Why do you tell me all this? I don't care.'

"Sooo you willll learn. Dooo unto othersss as theyyy do un-tooo you."
[SKIP]

"She is not true." [SKIP]

I started eating more. Drinking whenever I can. Gambling every chance I get. Spending my life in a video game, anything I can do to not be a part of this world anymore.

'This is normal.'

"Yesss, this isss normal." [SKIP]

"SSSTTTOOOPPP!!!" I screamed and the Cherubim re-leased me. I fell to the ground, panting, tears blurring my vision. I looked up at it and it just stood there, head cocked to one side as if listening. I tried to stand but the pain in my back was too deep. I blinked and it was still there. "What the hell did you do to me?" It's head turned in one direction and then the other. "Why are you just standing there?" I asked, still resting on my hands and knees, baffled as to why it wasn't attacking. It's eyes blinked dumbly and something clicked.

It never attacked me until I told it to. Then it stopped when I told it to stop. "Jump," I commanded, rocking back onto just my knees and the thing lept up into the air. I stared in stunned disbelief. "Spin," it spun. "Punch yourself in the head," the blow knocked it to the ground and it got back up immediately. What in the blue hell was going on here? "I don't suppose...Give me your head." Its eyes rolled back and its head slid from its neck like a sword had just severed it, the body falling limply to the side. I wonder if that would work on the others? I thought but then decided not to press my luck just yet as Cherr was waiting for me. I walked over and hefted the thing up by its long mane and started to walk back to the path. If I stay hidden, I can sneak back home without anyone being any the wiser and they'd think I've been out here the whole time. Plenty of time to beat that two week mark. I smiled, Cherry's going to be so excited that I'm back this early, I thought and picked up my pace.

CHAPTER 35

*S*anlou teis foru safay.*" To the Watchers who live in the shadow; know that it has taken everything from me but the words, even their meaning is now lost. I hope it's enough. If I fail, I leave this world to you.*

"You're obsessed M'lady and that's saying a lot coming from me," Saline teased and Cherry blushed.

"I love him and I love making love to him. I'm working on control like he said but that doesn't mean I shouldn't try everything at least once. I need to keep it exciting so he stays, remember?" The head maid nodded, taking a sip of her tea as the two sat near the fire in the master bedroom. "The letter said he could be gone for weeks and so when he gets back I want to make it special. He's already been gone for what seems like forever and I do miss him so."

Saline thought for a moment, "Well I don't know about him but I do know that the old master used to like his women tied up or blindfolded, things like that."

Cherry sat up, "Being blindfolded could be fun! I think he'd like that one!"

The other woman gave a nod. "Stay here, I got an idea." She quickly walked out of the room and returned a moment later carrying a black satin robe. "Here try this on." Instead of using the sash to tie it shut you can use it as your blindfold." Cherry took it and threw it on over her clothes giving it an appreciative smile. "Have yourself laying in the bed with nothing but some jewelry, the robe and the blindfold on. That'll make his head spin when he returns to find that."

Cherry pulled the robe back off and folded it on her lap as she sat. "I just wish he would have come and said goodbye first. Everytime he leaves-"

There was a thump on the outer balcony and both women spun. "That has to be him, M'lady." Saline guessed.

"Oh no! Quick, help me out of these clothes and into the robe!" The maid did as she was told as the footsteps drew nearer. "Go, just hide in the wardrobe and keep quiet," Cherry commanded and jumped on the bed, tying the blindfold securely when she landed.

The latch clicked and she could hear hinges squeaking as she smoothed the wrinkles from her robe. She pulled it shut but not completely in an attempt to appear more alluring. "Just in time my husband," she breathed out in her most seductive voice. "I have a surprise for you." She bit her lip playfully and lifted one of her legs in the air as the footsteps neared the bed. She felt a hand touch her ankle and slowly run down her calf towards her thigh. "Pirikallos," the sounds blended together in a musical tone and she smiled.

"You know I think it's funny when you talk like them," she teased and felt a weight settle on the bed next to her as a hand slowly opened the robe. "I've missed you my husband," she said, and pulled the blindfold up to see a red eyed Enlightened staring at her with a devilish grin. She screamed.

I entered the city on foot, circling far around to the west and changing my disguise to go unnoticed only to find the streets oddly empty. I decided to use the front door. As I walked up I dropped the creature's head into the bushes to keep it hidden until it was needed. I turned the door knob and it swung open gently on its own. I frowned, usually there was a servant who always did this and his absence gave me pause. I pushed the door a little faster and peered in. The tray sat on the table with a note marked from Ameletas. I stepped over to grab it and noticed a pair of feet.

My heart dropped from my chest as I moved the door out of the way to find the well dressed servant lying dead, a hole burned clear through his chest. No! I thought, and turned towards the rest of the house.

"CHERRY?" I yelled, and started to run from room to room only to find each one containing a body of one of the servants or maids. "CHERRY!" I screamed again and sprinted for the stairs. I lept them in threes and burst through the bedroom door, surveying it in an instant.

The bed was a mess and Cherry's clothes layed in a ball near the fireplace. There was a black robe on the floor but there was no sign of her or of any blood. I turned to continue searching when the wardrobe doors burst open.

The head maid collapsed to the ground in a ball of tears. "Master Fin. I know you can understand me. Cherry told me. He took her Master Fin. He forced himself upon her then tied her up and took her as his own. He left with her Master-"

"WHO?" my voice boomed and I felt her shrink at my rage.

"Your eyes... I don't know who he was. He was an Enlightened with red eyes."

"Egosin!" I spat, knowing there could have been no other explanation. "Did you watch them leave? How long ago?"

"I don't know Master Fin. I was scared so I stayed hidden. I didn't know if he was still here or not but everything happened early this morning."

"He could be anywhere by now!" I shouted, punching the wall in a fit of anger and it exploded apart like it was made of sand.

I walked through the opening and flew down to the lobby and straight out the door.

I thought back to the time Cherry and I had followed him home and I shot in that direction in a flash. "She better still be alive!" I yelled, trying to reassure myself as I landed on his doorstep a minute later. I kicked the door so hard it ripped off its hinges and then stepped through.

"EGOSIN!" I bellowed in challenge and a small servant dropped to his knees and started to back into a corner in terror. "You! Where is your master?"

He looked up in a mix of confusion and horror. "You can talk? I mean.. um, he's not here my Lord. He left yesterday and has yet to return."

I sensed the essence that flowed throughout his body and called it to me but not from him. He floated through the air with a shriek and I grabbed him by his shirt, twisting it so hard he had trouble breathing.

"If you're lying to me..."

"Never my lord. No ones-s-s that s-s-stupid. Look, his m-m-messages are still unread."

I looked down to see the tray held a letter, its symbol a single glowing red eye. I dropped the man and walked out, immediately taking back to the sky. I had a gut feeling he wasn't going to be at NaoSin Hall but maybe they knew where he was. I flew towards it, my blood boiling at the thought of what my poor Cherry must be going through.

I screamed again, this time not bothering to land as I smashed through its front doors. Mesoten hopped up to his feet behind his desk.

"You?" His face was stricken.

"I am looking for Egosin. Is he here?" I growled slowly, trying to contain my rage, knowing he had never done anything to deserve it.

"No. No one is. All the armies were called a few days ago and dispatched."

"Dispatched where?"

"To Bedlam Spire. I was told to direct everyone there with the orders to kill anything that refused to join them or wear the black of the Sin." He paused, "they're looking for you."

"Me? Why?"

He swallowed. "They know who you are. We all know who you are but... I don't know if I can believe that. You're not... what we were told to expect. You are nice, you joke and laugh-"

"Mesoten, I don't have time for this! Egosin kidnapped the woman I love! Is he with them?"

"Love? That can't be..." he shook his head at seeing my face. "I'm sorry, I honestly don't know where he is."

I blinked to refresh my body and his eyes went wide in shock. "If you see him, don't let him know I'm looking for him," I warned, then turned and ran out.

Atropos's elegant fingernails drummed against the small tea table while she stared at Ameletas as he spoke. "I overheard their orders to execute him on sight if he is found. They must take espionage very seriously," he chuckled to himself as he sipped at his tea. "I sent a letter to his residence to inform him of everything we are doing here and have him join us at once."

There was some speaking outside and then another woman entered the tent. Atropos pulled a letter out and put it into the other lady's hands.

Ameletas perked up, "what does it say?" he asked curiously. "Ameletas this is Lachesis. She's here to assist me in some very

important matters. I would like you to accompany her on a walk. I have some business to attend to that I can't have you around for just yet." She didn't wait for him to respond as she gestured towards the door.

The two walked for a while, two large guards in two until Lachesis turned onto a small path barely visible to the naked eye. They made their way down through a couple of twists and turns until they came to a clearing. A large red tent sat erect and was surrounded by a scattering of servants, soldiers and guards.

"We are here to speak to the Sin?" he asked in confusion.

"No we are not. I am. Wait here as I speak with Misosin." Lachesis turned and walked without giving him any further explanation.

He put his hands on his hips at the dismissal, turning to his two large guards. "Don't suppose you guys know any funny jokes?" They blinked in confusion and he waved away their bewildered looks. "Blasted creatures. As smart as a pair of bedroom slippers these two are." He turned his attention back to the encampment. The people walked to and fro, carrying pots and blankets, setting up tents, digging holes and all sorts of other common tasks. He regarded the tent closest to him, its high steepled roof came down to where it could only fit two beds. Must be a General, he thought then turned to the one next to it. He chuckled to himself, must be a General's niece.

Its small short roof was barely big enough to fit one bed let alone-. His thoughts cut off. A woman sat up on the ground in front of it, her naked body covered only in jewelry and dirt and she shook visibly as she cried. Her blazing red hair caused him to inhale sharply.

"Her?" he peered around hesitantly. "He would never... but then where... she must have been..." He chewed his lip, taking a few steps closer and his guards followed. I can't be seen grabbing her, he thought, only a fool would do that. He spun back to face his guards. "You," he pointed at one randomly. "Go." He made his fingers walk across the air. "Grab her," he pointed at Cherry. "Bring her to me." He made like he was clutching her to his chest then walked his fingers back and pointed to himself.

The large guard blinked then turned to his comrade for help. They made a few guttural sounds and then he saluted. Ameletas watched the thing lumber over right beside the girl and grab a large log, hugging it to his chest, then bringing it back.

He shook his head no, a universal gesture and the guard dropped the wood in shame. Ameletas scratched his chin then waved them closer. He found a stick on the ground and stuck it tip first in the dirt to symbolize the post she was tied to. He found a small red leaf and pinned it to the top of another twig then set it next to the first one.

He pointed at his work. "You see," he said, then pointed back to Cherry. "The same. You see? Grab her." He held up the twig with the red leaf then pointed back to her. "Bring her to me." then pointed back to himself.

The other guard gave a confident nod this time and grabbed the leaf and twig combo from his hand and took off without a word.

"Wait? What? Why!" He didn't want to shout so instead he just watched in disbelief.

The large idiot stopped in front of her and held out his gift proudly and Cherry took it with confusion. He looked back with a smile that vanished instantly when he noticed Ameletas shaking his head again. He gestured to the one still at his side then pointed at the stick in the ground. The guard watched him intently as he pointed to the one holding Cherry then back to the one in the ground. Then the one holding Cherry and back one more time. He plucked the twig from the dirt and then pointed back as recognition dawned on the large dimwit.

"Oooooo," the sound rumbled from its throat and reminded him of a farm animal. I swear, just because these beings have advanced their communications does not make them any smarter.

The large guard turned back and yelled to his companion who still stood awaiting orders. The words came out and this time they sounded like someone was clasping his windpipe open and shut as he spoke. The other saluted and pulled the large steak free with ease causing Ameletas to nod excitedly then point at Cherry. The guard hefted the woman up and threw her over his shoulder as she kicked and punched furiously. He made his way back with her and plopped her down at Ameletas feet. Recognition dawned on her face instantly and she lept in for a hug.

He blushed from head to toe. "This way my dear. I don't want to wait around and find out who I just stole you from. Nothing good will come of that" he grabbed her hand and started to lead her away. The guards made to follow and he pointed to the tent that Lacheses went into and then the spot they were standing. They halted with a salute.

"Oh that you imbeciles understand on the first try," he rolled his eyes. "Let's go find you some clothes my dear."

✦

CHAPTER 36

*I*n my unending quest to always reach the next step, I once asked a higher being for a piece of the infinity code I knew would grant me the greatest progress in my understanding once I grasped it completely. What it told me was the secret of the All. God is light but light can't exist if there's nothing to reflect it, people are that reflection. Without you, there is no God, without God, there is no you. You must have a firm grasp on the infinity code before you can even hope to solve this conundrum as I have.

The wind roared in my ears as the landscape went by in a blur. I struggled to keep my emotions in check at the thought of all the possible fates Cherry could be suffering every second she was in the possession of that creature. It was all I could do not to pull in a tempest of essence like this world had never seen.

I grit my teeth when I approached where I knew they would be. I had been feeling the use of the essence for a while now from one general location and its source was drawing close. Before I reached it however I noticed a scattering of tents below.

One large red one contained Misosin's unique symbol of a one pupiled eye embroidered its head and I decided to descend.

I crashed to the ground and several of the commoners screamed at the sight of me. A pair of Sin guards came running to check on the commotion, their black helmets hiding most of their face but I watched as their mouths opened in surprise.

"Sir! He's here!" the one on the right shouted and within a moment Misosin himself came walking out.

His long red robe brushed the ground as he moved and a black belt held it shut. Across its center sat the single pupiled eye of the Sin and two large spikes protruded from each of the armored plates on his shoulders. He wore a gleaming red metal helmet that covered his face and made his head look like a skull with two glowing red eyes.

"Where is Egosin?" I spoke in a low threatening tone. There was no immediate answer and I noticed a few more of the Sin hurrying over, Egosin at their rear. I watched him with hatred as he pulled his black helm down to cover his face.

"I don't want any trouble for any of you. I just want him!" They gave him a quizzical glance then turned back to me. "Where is the woman with red hair?" his head turned towards a tent to the side for a fraction of a second. I lept in that direction, pushing the essence from the air around it and causing a blast of wind that ripped it from the ground and sent it up into the trees. It was empty.

I spun back to him. "Where... is... MY WIFE!?"

Their bodies visibly tensed and I could see them raising their guards. Misosin whispered something too low for me to hear and they nodded.

"Me killing you all doesn't help anyone!"

The red clad master threw his head back in laughter while a few of the others started to circle me. "What a thing for you to say? Do you think us so easily fooled?"

I took a deep breath to focus, knowing what was about to transpire. There was a movement from the side and I ducked by instinct, a sword of essence cutting the air above me as I fell.

I rolled to the side and a beam sizzled into the ground where I just was. I leapt up and backwards, catching the surprised man off guard with a forearm chop to the neck. The cracking noise it made left no doubt he was out of the fight. I spun as another attacked, willing a shield between us without a second to spare. Dozens of blasts burst forth, some missing, some being deflected away. I raised my shields, enclosing myself completely then set them to spinning.

But I didn't need to hide what I was anymore. I pushed the distance my shields orbited me away and they started to slice through the few Sin closest to me and the others backed up in a hurry. I turned to see Egosin forming a blast and I ripped the essence from his body, his sphere dissipating at the sudden loss of its fuel. His jaw dropped and I flung his own attack back at him but it was deflected away as another moved to the front with a shield raised.

I heard Misosin yell something and the others saluted but whatever it was he said was hidden by the whirling of my protective barrier. Their strategy changed then and they pulled themselves back into one dense spot, forming a small group and putting shields up in all directions similar to mine. The tall leader stood in the direct center of them, hands in front of him, a wicked grin spreading on his face as he summoned his powers.

It came in a surge from nowhere and consisted of nothing. Emotions flared up and I could feel doubt, worry, fear. I felt terror. A sphere started to form in front of him then but it was unlike anything I'd ever seen. I watched as the essence pushed itself away from it like it didn't want to be anywhere near the foul stuff. Its impossible black color appeared to be made up of empty space and its shape slowly grew in size. He stopped then and the orb shot through the air like a streak. It blasted through the shields directly in front of him like they didn't exist, leaving a hole in its wake as it soared towards me. I didn't have time to react as it flew through my shields in the same manner, scattering large chunks of the essence away and taking me through the shoulder. I felt all the essence I held vanish at its touch and I staggered. The rest of the Sin were ready for this and they acted without hesitation. Dozens of essence blasts were released simultaneously and I was completely defenseless.

It wasn't the first time I'd been outwitted or even shot full of holes. Several of them only glanced me but one took me through the lung, one the stomach, and the last, blasted away the lower half of my jaw. I must look like a standing corpse I thought as my Earthen body tugged at my consciousness like a semi pulling a shopping cart. I screamed, focusing my resolve and refusing to leave, refusing to abandon Cherry to her fate. I solidified my willpower and stared directly at Misosin.

I blinked.

My wounds vanished, power flooded back in and I flexed, trying to remove the tightness I still felt in my lower back. The Sin froze. I continued to look at their leader, trying to figure out how he had accomplished such an attack. Whatever he had done, wherever it had come from, I knew nothing about it and that worried me.

I started forming spears as their shields went back up. I knew they couldn't spin them like I could and that meant they had openings to the sides and behind. I pushed the air around in circles in front of me with one hand as the other continued to create spear after spear of the essence. A tornado formed and I pushed my weapons into it and then moved the whole thing towards their small group. I watched as they all desperately tried to shield themselves from the wind and the missiles within as they crowded even closer together, all their attention drawn from me. I let myself rise into the air and demanded with every fiber of my being for the essence to come to my summons. I was surprised to see it was already there, coming in floods as something not too far to the east was ripping it from this world at the same time I was. I ignored it, forming an attack so big I knew it could level this entire encampment easily. It grew in size to the point I could no longer see in front of me so I pushed it forward, towards them with everything I had.

I heard the laugh above the wind and knew instantly I had made a mistake. Misosins shoulders shook with joy as he launched his black orb directly at mine and I only had an instant to react. If his orb touched mine it would scatter it away into nothing so I did the only logical thing I could think of. I willed it to collapse in upon itself as I put up a hasty shield.

I don't know if there was no sound or that I was so close I went deaf. Everything disappeared like I was suddenly standing on the sun, and then black, like it was flicked off. A concussion rocked through my body and I felt myself flying through the air and then jerk violently as I hit a tree and rolled into some bushes.

I lay there, not daring to move as I once again fought the tug of my Earthen body but this time it was not nearly as forceful. I could hear voices come and go but I ignored them, deciding to regroup and rethink the second they were gone.

I stood and looked around, hiding behind a tree to survey what I had done. Every tree and every tent where we were fighting was completely flattened in a large circle. There were no signs of a single living soul and I noticed several bodies. The one closest to me was twisted to the point it appeared an arm and a leg were coming out of the same spot. I looked to the one next to it and realized it was the guard who's neck I had broken.

I paused to think. Misosin's ability baffled me beyond reason. I could neither block it, attack him while he used it or replicate it in any way and that was new to me. That meant I only had one choice left. The only possible solution I could think of was to avoid it and stay hidden. So no using the essence, I thought and shook my head in disgust.

I jogged over to the guard and pulled him from the clearing back to the bushes. I stripped him of his uniform and put it on quickly, deciding to go in the opposite direction from where I currently was and towards where I felt all the other powers fighting when I first got here. But I had to go on foot. I found a small path not too far away and took it at a run.

CHAPTER 37

There is more that separates higher beings from humans. Take time for example, once they've understood its truth they can develope certain abilities. Think of it like this, all of mankind is standing in a river staring downstream. This is your point of view. Higher beings have learned how to turn their heads, glancing upstream in brief glimpses. You cry out and exclaim when they predict of some incoming debris or a school of fish then moments later it all passes by. You are unable to perceive their clairvoyant powers but I'll offer you this. That's not always how prophecy works. Sometimes there comes a being even more advanced, even further up the river. He does not cry out for the fish or the debris, he simply puts them there.

"It's either this or what you're wearing my dear," Atropos spoke, her words sounding somewhat musical to Cherry's ears. She looked down at the massive kilt she wore tied above her chest and still it hung to the ground.

She bit her lip. "Fine. But I ain't wearing a crown or nothing like that. It's bad enough everyone already thinks I'm royalty."

The woman with the glowing blue eyes handed her the small bundle and she took it, dressing in a rush.

The blue gown fit her perfectly and was by far the most elegant thing she'd ever worn. Its trim glowed with trapped essence giving off a slight warmth to the touch. "It matches my armlet," she pointed out happily then turned back. "Is it strange that it makes me feel... alive?"

Atropos gave her a gentle smile, "You finally look the part of your Lord husband's wife."

Cherry beamed, "I suppose I do. I didn't think dressing like your kind was a good idea but when you put it like that..."

Ameletas sipped at his tea then cleared his throat to regain attention. "Atropos, I know you are the hand of God even if others don't so I doubt there's anything you don't know or are not directly involved in which confuses me. From my point of view things look promising. The turn out so far is beyond all expectations and there are more and more armies arriving each day. The Seraphim are eager to do my bidding, that in itself is a miracle, but what I don't understand is that you said this next part is 'hard'. What do you mean by hard? The plan will be hard to pull off ? The fight will be hard to win? The outcome is hard to judge? I have armies waiting for my council and orders."

Atropos sat near him watching Cherry spinning and dancing,- causing the essence filled dress to flow like shimmering water.

"It's truly magical," the younger woman observed to herself. Atropos turned back to Ameletas, "can it not be all three?"

She poured some honey ino her tea and then stirred before she continued. "The truth is, none of those things are what I was even referring to when I made that comment. You will find out what is hard and soon... very soon and then you will understand." The Ascendal stared back at her with a blank expression. "I do love it so when you speak in vague riddles that leave nothing knowledgeable to be gained. They leave me so... so... irritated? exasperated? frustrated? Can it not be all three?" He chuckled at his own joke and she did nothing to portray she was amused. He rolled his eyes. "Oh come now, nothing's that hard or that bad.

If you won't tell me what it is, will you at least tell me how soon is soon?"

Atropos finished her tea in one large gulp and set the cup back on the table. She bent down and removed her sandals and pulled out a pair of walking shoes, immediately putting them on. "Cherry my dear, put these on for me will you?" she asked and handed the other woman a pair similar to hers. The red headed lady slipped them on without a word and Ameletas watched it all in confusion.

"Atropos? How soon is soon?" She stood and put her arm out to the side, offering it to Cherry. She took it and Atropos finally turned back to him, holding up five fingers.

"Five? Five what?"

One finger lowered, then another, and another and the two exited the tent.

"Who's in charge here?" a voice boomed and a second later the flaps burst open. "Are you in charge?" a red eyed Sin demanded.

Ameletas cocked his head. "I am. Why, may I-" He stopped as the other being pushed a folded piece of paper into his hands. He eyed it keenly, noticing it looked exactly like the parchment he had in his study.

"You are to read this at once and then join us. You will pull these armies away from the Cherubim and order them to coordinate their attacks with our ground troops at once. Should you refuse to agree to this, my orders are to kill you on the spot."

Ameletas pulled back, the straight forward words left no doubt the Sin Colonel wasn't joking. He unfolded the letter and scanned it quickly, eyes going wide. "No! This can't be!"

"The words themselves are proof," the Sin being confirmed with a nod. "Will you obey?"

Ameletas nodded quickly as his mind raced. "Of course! I'd never... SHE KNOWS!" he exclaimed as pieces of the puzzle began to click. "That means she helped and he lied!" Anger bubbled up in him and he burst through the tent in an outrage. "ATROPOS YOU GODS BE DAMNED TRAITOR GET BACK

HERE!" He looked around and saw her and the common woman making their way towards the tree line in a hurry. "I KNOW IF I KILL YOU THEN THIS PLAN FAILS! DO YOU HEAR ME ATROPOS!" He started stomping his way towards her and summoned all the essence he could muster, forming it into a ball and sending it at the fleeing women. The attack flowed like it had been vacuumed into the jewelry on the red heads arm and there was a flash. She stumbled in a panic but was lifted and the two took to running instead.

"Atropos!" he yelled again but several of the guards moved to block him. He started to blast essence out wildly before they got away and even killed one of the messengers before he was finally outnumbered and wrestled to the ground. "I'll kill you before I ever let your prophecies be fulfilled. I'll kill him. I'll kill everyone!"

The Sin let a backhand fly that sent several of the guards flying at once and the rest fled at the sight. "Get yourself up and follow your orders," he commanded and Ameletas gave a nod, turning to see the two women had already vanished from sight anyway as he dusted off the dirt from his all white uniform.

I continued to follow the path and noticed I was drawing nearer to where the essence was being used in large amounts. Evidence of a massive army shown in the heavily harvested trees and staying hidden was becoming more and more difficult.

I approached a road and looked down it first one way and then the other, having no idea what route to take. I had to find Cherry, everything else was second to that now and that meant I had to stay hidden until I did. This Misosin was one of the most perplexing beings I'd ever met and had definitely deserved his position for sure.

I heard voices and spun, two men running up fast with swords swinging at their hips. I put up my hands in surrender. "Guys! I'm one of you!" I pretended as my Sin uniform gave them pause. "I stole this outfit from one of the dead guys. My wife and I were running messages but then we got seperated. Any chance you can help me out?"

They stared for a second then finally one of the men nodded. "We're running messages too and maybe we saw her. What did she look like?"

"Oh that's easy, you can't miss her. Her name is Cherry and she has blazing red hair."

The other man let out a snort. "I don't know what you're going on about, friend but if Lady Cherry is your wife then I'm a fish with feathers. Besides-"

I ripped my helmet off, revealing my glowing purple eyes and they froze in shock. I pulled at the essence within his body and he was dragged to my hand, squirming wildy, eyes bulging. "Where is my wife?" I asked slowly, grabbing him by the throat.

The other spoke in his stead, "She ran off! One of them Enlightened was trying to kill her. He was trying to kill everyone."

"WHERE?"

"I... don't know. She ran into the woods with Immi and most of us ran in different directions."

"What did he look like? The one trying to kill her?" "Um, it was an outfit like yours but all white." "What direction did he go?"

He raised an arm to point and it was directly towards where all the fighting was. I dropped him, thrust the helmet back on then sprang into the air, all notions of remaining hidden forgotten now that I knew someone was trying to kill my Cherry.

I drew nearer and soared high up into the air to survey the scene below. Flashes and beams of light shot down from a force of all black at large silver beings on the ground. The Sin fighting the Cherubim I realized. I looked further and noticed a giant tower protruding from the ground and at its sides was an emp- ty expanse that seemed to have no bottom. Two small bridges connected to it on either side and I realized that it must be Bedlam Spire. I continued to look and noticed another army of all black completely engulfed on all sides, its demise imminent. To its rear sat a small war council and at its head stood a man clad in all white.

Anger overtook all rational thought and I noticed there were no red headed women anywhere near him. He killed her! I surmised and blasted off in that direction. I got directly above him and stopped using the essence completely to remain hidden as I let myself free fall down behind him. Whoever this being was, he would get no warning and no mercy for killing my wife.

At the last possible second I halted my downward fall with a large burst of essence upward and dropped softly behind him. I watched as he spun, pulling in the essence and forming a hastey shield. I snarled, ripping the power from his body and then blasted it back at him instantly, leaving a hole where his shoulder used to be. He spun to the ground and I could hear the screams and shouts of his council while he rolled up onto his knees. I formed a shield in front of me and summoned a sword of essence then swung it. It took him through the neck and his head flew through the air inside its helmet. His body tilted sideways like it was going to collapse but instead it vanished, his clothes falling limply to the ground as the empty helmet spun in circles near them.

What in the-, pain blasted the essence from me and I staggered back with a jerk. My helmet fell off as I tried to regain my balance and figure out what was happening to me. I looked down and saw a small dart protruding from my shoulder and knew instantly it was the reason I could no longer use the essence.

The trick with the pant leg came to mind and I willed my shoulder away, pulling the dart out by its end as my flesh vanished. Power came flooding back instantly and held the small projectile up closer for a better look. I twirled it in my fingers to where something was written and I froze in stunned disbelief as I read the words aloud, 'WITH ALL MY LOVE, LYNNAY'

INTERLUDE

There are lots of things that weren't lost in translation throughout my journeys. I am trying to bridge the barriers as best as I can but some things are not so easily accomplished. Time, especially from place to place, alphabets, writings, dialect, names, all of it. You get a sort of 'understanding' when projecting that doesn't follow when you return back to the limits this existence enforces. I fear I am not doing justice to the complexity of those gaps I intended to hurdle in these writings but I digress.

Another thing that would be lost throughout time was my memories and for more than one reason. I would find myself randomly stumbling upon them, moments of clarity you could say. At the time it always took something to trigger them and I would be baffled how memories that important would ever get lost in the first place. Years and years of memories and projections, pieces of the infinity code, all of it just simply deleted... or more accurately, access denied. But I was not always so easily fooled. I would leave myself a trail of breadcrumbs in hopes that when I found one it would trigger it again and I would remember that I still had a chance to change. I used simple things that I thought I would see or use every day. A snapchat name with monumental clairvoyance attached. A video game character's name of one of the most enlightened beings I'd ever met. A ring I bought my wife with a rock from another world. A reminder of the places I've gone and the things I've done. To prevent the thing I was destined to become. But I never used snapchat and my kids took over all the video games. And how often do we really look at our wives hands? I know I never did and my plan, as with everything else I've done in this life, had failed.

CHAPTER 38

Again born good and fails. Evil. Now hate consumes all. All I Am.
DEIFIED
I Am All. All consumes hate. Now evil fails and good born again.

I lowered the dart, shifting my eyes from person to person as memories flowed and recognition followed. Seven stood frozen, his massive frame tense with a mix of rage, relief and confusion that showed on his face. Quill blinked. Hard. Like his eyes were playing tricks on him. He took a drink then tried again, this time closing one eye for good measure.

There were other faces but only one drew me in. Lynnay stood, hands over her mouth in shock as tears streaked her face. "I could have killed you!" she yelled, then ran over and flung her arms around my neck, trying to pull me in for a kiss.

I turned my head to let it land on my cheek. "Lynnay? Is... that really you?" I did a second take of the small group and my surroundings as she took a hesitant step back.

"You're... different. What's going on here, Fin?"

I stared down at my white uniform and something clicked. "Oh God, that was me? I just killed... myself?"

The other two approached slowly and Quill poked my chest like he was making sure I was real. "Alright bucko, I'm as confused as a cross eyed leper trying to count his fingers. I'm gonna need ya to explain your little magic trick there."

Seven looked me over carefully. "You're different. What just happened here?"

"I'm sorry guys," I apologized, looking Lynnay directly in the eyes. "I'm not him... exactly." I pointed to where I apparently, both seconds and years ago, had died. "I mean I am, but I came back here 8 years later... but I guess it was to the exact same time... and then... I killed myself." I frowned at the oddity of it all.

Lynnays eyes did nothing to hide her emotions as they started to well up. "So you... it's been that long? Do you still...I mean, are we..."

I let my head drop, not having the heart to tell her the answer to what I knew she wanted to ask. Sway stepped forward then and touched my arm gently as she addressed me loud enough for everyone to hear.

"I must take my leave. My part in your story to help you become what you need to become requires me elsewhere," then she turned and walked away.

We watched her go for a second until Quill finally spoke up.

"What is she talking about? What do you need to become?"

I scratched my head as I tried to make sense of everything that was taking place. "I have no clue. A better Boundless maybe?"

Seven narrowed his eyes. "You made a sound like one of the Enlightened. What did it mean?"

Another thing clicked into place in my head like a magnet to a fridge. All those times talking to Cherry and she would smile and just tell me I put random words of theirs into my speech. "It means... unshackled I think."

A quiet sob caught my attention and I turned back to Lynnay.

She had not once turned away from me and now the tears flowed down her cheeks like a leaky faucet. "So we are just... nothing now? I know 8 years is a long time but for me... for me-"

I cut her off with a smile as I shook my head. "Lynnay it's been 8 years for me where I'm from. I've also continued to project myself countless times. For me it's been... decades." She fell to her knees and I bent down, putting a hand on her shoulder as I handed her the dart back. "I'm sorry. I never forgot you. In fact-"

"Fin," Seven interrupted. "I'm sorry but our time is running out. We were in the middle of trying to plan, do you remember?"

"I..." another thing clicked into place. "We were Ameletas's backup plan. The development in the world of the common folk he spoke about."

"Talkin like them again, boss," Quill added and I laughed as more of it started to make sense. Lower beings couldn't talk like the Enlightened here so the names of people and places were always different. "Do you know why they were all trying to kill us?"

I thought hard, struggling for memories long forgotten. "I don't remember honestly."

"Then why were you trying to kill him?"

I continued to look around in an attempt to help jog my memory. As I did I noticed Matches sitting at a table eating, oblivious to what was happening around him. I pulled myself out of it. "What? Oh, he tried to kill my wife."

There was a sharp intake of breath and I instantly regretted having spoken. "You have a wife here?" Lynnay asked in a croak as she looked up at me. I gave her a reluctant nod then rubbed her back affectionately. She let her face fall back into her hands, trying to hide her crying but her shoulders shook visibly. I stood back up and Quill offered me a drink but I waved it away.

"Why'd he try to kill your wife then? He gone mad too? One minute he's on our side and the next he's leading an army against us."

A vague memory resurfaced of the whole ordeal and I did my best to piece it together with what I knew. "I'm not sure but everyone, all of the Enlightened have gone mad and are now trying to kill me."

"Well we're still on your side, bucko. Let's get a new plan formed and get you to Aam." He turned to yell, "Mutt!"

A man came jogging over in an instant. "It's Dog sir." he informed with a salute.

"Have the men reassemble and regroup at once. Let the enemy retreat if they want as long as they're out of the fight it doesn't matter."

"Yes sir!" he replied then ran off.

A fat General agreed with the orders, sending his own man to relay the same thing. Seven noticed the look on my face as I tried to puzzle out who he was and decided to make introductions.

"Fin, this is my brother Able and his fiancé Summer." He gestured to the pair. "The man who just spoke is General Books."

We shook hands with one another and another memory popped up. I turned to Seven. "You left us right? How did you get an army or did you already say that at some point?"

He shook his head. "No, the last I saw of you was when I went back to take care of my brother Victor. I killed him and inadvertently won the kingdom too but instantly gave it to my brother Able, these are his men," he gestured to the army.

I nodded appreciatively. "Good. I'm glad to hear everything turned out so well for you."

"Not everything," he added with a scowl and I gave him an inquisitive look. "I found the truth about why my family hated me so much. Able informed me I am a bastard born of rape upon my mother by the giant General Dag." Several of the people around us gasped and looks of surprise spread on their faces, including Quill who stared like he was reevaluating everything he knew about Seven. I rocked back a little at this but the name did nothing to ring any bells. "General Dag is the single greatest military fighter and most likely the single best fighter to ever exist." I gave him an unknowing shrug and he turned to blow the conversation off but paused, "Immi?"

We all turned towards the wood line to watch two elegant women come walking towards us in a hurry. Immi's blue eyes blazed like glowing sapphires and the others bright red hair bounced to and fro as she approached.

"Cherry!" I cheered and then ran to embrace her. "I'm sorry! I'll never leave you again!"

She let me kiss her and then pulled herself back to speak. "Oh my husband. I was so scared. I have something I need to tell you. One of those creatures-"

"I know," I interrupted, not wanting her to have to speak about the evil that she endured. "And when I find him again he will pay for his actions with his life."

"How do you know?"

"The head mistress told me."

"She lived?" relief flooded her at the words.

"Yes. She hid in the wardrobe for nearly a full day."

I watched Cherry's eyes as they flicked back and forth between me and somewhere off to the side. "Um, husband, why is that woman staring at me like that?"

"If you guys are going to play catch up, do it fast. Time is quite literally running out," Immi suggested, then paused in front of me. "When you are done here, you will find me on the path of the Cherubim," then she turned and walked away from us. I heard Seven and Quill both start protesting but I turned back to the two women who both deserved explanations.

"Cherry, do you remember when I told you that I'd loved before during my projections and that's why I didn't want to form a relationship?" She nodded, giving me a puzzled look before turning back to the other woman. "Well this is Lynnay. She was the first."

Cherry's eyebrows went up on her forehead as she realized what I was implying. "Oh..." was the only thing she said.

"I haven't seen her in so long I can't even guess at a number but for her it has only been a few moments. I actually just killed the version of me that she was in love with," I gestured to the clothes on the ground.

Cherry's eyes moved rapidly as she tried to connect all the dots in her head. "So she still loves you? And you were here twice but both of them were at the same time?" I nodded to both. Lynnay gave a quick step back as Cherry threw her arms around her in an embrace. "You poor thing. I love him too and I can't imagine what you're going through. Well, I was just kidnapped by one of those red eyed Enlightened and never thought I'd see him again but-"

Lynnay finally gave in and hugged her back. "He's yours. Mine is... gone forever I think."

I took a few steps back to remove myself from the awkward situation and heard Quill's voice. "What do you mean we don't need a plan? Blasted woman!" The two men walked up, both with looks of frustration and confusion.

"I honestly think this place and everyone in it has gone mad," Seven observed in annoyance.

"Here's to that!" Quill cheered us and then drank from his flask. "May everyone who's not mad drive themselves insane at their utter loneliness."

I smiled, forgetting how humorous the odd little man was and Seven stepped closer, eyeing me more closely. "Are you stronger? You just did an attack that was... impossible."

I bobbed my head. "I pulled the essence from his... my body and attacked him with it. And yes, I'm a lot stronger."

"Could you kill an Enlightened with ease?"

"Yes, several at a time with ease although there is one here who baffles me. He attacks using a form of essence that is pure black. Have you ever heard of this before?"

Seven rubbed at his chin, "never heard of such a thing. Is there anything new you could teach us in a short amount of time?"

I grinned at his constant quest to become better and to learn all he could. I turned to Quill, then Matches and finally the others as they all stood around awaiting our decisions. "You know this may sound odd, but I really missed you guys."

"Why it feels like just moments ago you was at our side attacking armies from within like some sort of lunatic with a death wish," Quill replied then paused, "nah wait, it was moments ago." I chuckled at him but Cherry cut in once more.

"Husband." I spun back to see the two women staring at me. There was resolve and determination on Cherry's face as she spoke. "We have decided to share you. She has nothing and no one in this world and I have nothing and no one in this world. It's not fair for only one of us to have you so I told her we would both have you."

I pinched the bridge of my nose. "Cherr... can we please not do this now?"

"I demand it," she put her chin up. "And if you try to say it's against your religion you told me you ain't got no religion and if that don't work then I demand you get one that allows for more than one wife!" I shut my eyes and took a deep breath then felt a slap on my shoulder.

Quill was grinning from ear to ear. "That my friend," he started, gesturing towards the two women, "is a trap." Then he took another drink from his flask.

I laughed and turned back, "Cherr, we'll talk after ok?"

"I won't change my mind," she insisted and the two made their way over towards the tables where Matches sat.

"Nah seriously though, one's a ranga? If that pans out you're gonna have to do everything you can to make it work. And maybe... grow two tally wackers?"

I spat out an unintentional laugh. "What? Quill..." He bobbed his eyebrows up and down with a dumb grin and I even noticed Seven hide a quick smile. "You do realize that makes zero sense? Have you ever even been with a woman?" and the others joined in the laughter this time. He still stood with the same expression on his face, eyebrows so high up on his forehead it was like they were trying to escape his face in embarrassment.

There was movement to the side and I watched as Matches flipped a table and reached back to unhook his giant weapon. We spun to see what he had noticed and we all froze at the sight. The all black garbed Sin were advancing rapidly, hundreds and hundreds of them coming by land and by sky as they blacked out the sun like a slow moving cloud. The other men all started to shout out orders and I ran over to the women.

"Cherr! you two run and hide in the woods. Both of you try to keep those karma stones visible and try not to be seen, now go!" I finished without waiting to see if I was obeyed as I turned to face the first of the Sin head on.

Seven stepped up to my side. "So how powerful is powerful? " he asked in a low tone as drums and trumpets sounded from all around us.

One of the Sin Generals was the first to touch down and he spoke out immediately. "We know your true identity. You will find us not so easily destroyed as you may think."

Lynnays warning from long ago suddenly sat at the forefront of my mind. "I'm not going to destroy anyone! None of this makes sense!" I had to shout to be heard.

"Please, we know the name Lachesis called you by. We are not so easily fooled as that." He turned his head back and forth as more of his men landed beside him and this gave him confidence. "Besides, we saw the letter. God is not capable of lying." He pointed at me and then made a fist, signaling a full attack.

"Run Seven!" I shouted and then pushed at every drop of essence that hung in the air in front of me with every ounce of strength that I could muster. This technique was similar to what I did with the tent earlier but about one hundred times more powerful.

The microblast that ensued rocked through their ranks throwing those in front into those behind as they all went tumbling away.

"Release!" I heard Quill shout and the hiss of arrows sounded. Shields started to pop up instantly yet some of them found gaps anyway and stuck into the enemies randomly. A few even hit a vital spot and dropped them dead as they moved to advance.

I leapt into the sky to draw them away, knowing I was their primary target as I began to pull the essence in a rush. It came in a flood, ripping the few clouds from the sky as the wind roared, throwing people and arrows around like rag dolls. There was a grumbling noise and I watched as the ground started to convulse, people falling flat to the dirt in an attempt not to be tossed about. I stopped calling it, figuring I was doing more harm than help to the ground troops and started to fly backwards, facing my pursuers.

I waited until they were directly over one of the armies and I started ripping the essence from them several at a time causing them to fall defenseless into the ranks below. After each pull I formed it into a sphere and sent it down into the weaker Sin who could not fly and were instead forced to remain engaged on the ground.

More and more beings showed up by air and ground and I was forced to start taking them on in waves. Over and over they came but the numbers were climbing faster than I could deplete them and I soon found myself surrounded.

Shields.

Dozens of them popped up with the thought and I started them spinning then started to add layers upon layers, pushing the furthest ones out as I added to them continuously. They flew through the ranks severing limbs and smashing shields aside as more and more crowded in. The ones who didn't back away fell in groups and I watched as the remaining Sin began to form rows of shields with the men behind them creating spheres to attack with. I ripped the essence from them again but that trick was up. Another line was instantly formed and more barriers were raised within two heartbeats. I flung the stolen power down into their ground units again as I tried to think. I'd never fought with such poor odds or with armies on my side who were somewhat my responsibility.

This isn't good. I need a plan. They can't win without me and I am not going to let them lose but how am I supposed to fight a horde of the Sin? My thoughts cut off abruptly when I heard the distinct sound of a woman's scream.

"He's handing ya cake! Kill them faster!" Quill shouted. "They're droppin from the sky with no powers or weapons! I shoulda brought some children with me. They could do a better job of it then you lot!" He flung a dagger and it took an Enlightened through the heart. "Heal that bucko," he muttered and moved to find another.

"General Quill!" Seven's voice bellowed and the small man turned. "If the men in back circle around they can engage the weaker Enlightened who can't fly. It may offer us a slight advantage on the ground."

Quill eyed him with suspicion, "Is that an order or are you on something else?"

"It is a plan. I'm awaiting feedback."

He nodded to this. "Then I agree. They ain't serving much use in the back ranks and sense these bastards are mostly in the air we should engage wherever we can." He called over a runner then sent him away with the orders.

"He's a lot stronger," Seven added, staring into the sky as wave after wave attacked me but were sent reeling.

"Yeah a lot. You ever think to see one person fighting an army of them bastards all at the same time?"

The big man didn't answer immediately. "You curious as to why they hate him so much? If we weren't trying to kill them I doubt they would even bother with us." He turned to Quill. "I mean, there is so much about them we don't understand. What if they know something we don't?"

The smaller General gave him a sideways look. "He doesn't pay me to think. Aam needs help and that's all there is to it. So lets-" he let his words trail off, instantly pulling out his karma stoned dagger. "On your guard," he informed and Seven spun to see a small group of the red eyed beings descending from the sky and eyeing them like prey as they touched down. He pulled out his family heirloom and stood ready as they broke away to circle the two.

"Back to back," Seven offered and Quill nodded. Two Enlightened charged forward at each man directly while the other two remained behind and started to form spheres. Seven met the first ones blade levely and countered with a kick to the leg. The being spun in a flash and suddenly the essence sword was coming from the opposite direction. He ducked it easily and thrust out, causing the red eyed being to jump back. It swept in again with a low cut this time and Seven hopped it, performing another thrust at the things head. A shield popped up and his sword bounced off it harmlessly.

The Enlightened gave him a wicked grin then put his shoulder behind it and charged forward. A shield of his own popped into existence and Seven met the others head on with a loud thud. The beings glowing red eyes went wide in amazement as Seven returned a wicked grin of his own. He slammed his sword down and into the Enlightened exposed foot that it hadn't realized it had done. The things scream sounded like a trumpet until it was cut off by a sword through the heart. Seven didn't slow, instead he rushed the being behind as it tried to release a sphere he had no doubt was only intended to explode. He deflected it up instead and crashed into the other Enlightened, wrestling him to the ground. He was too close for his great sword so he pulled out his dagger and rammed it through the beings side over and over again until it stopped struggling.

He leapt to his feet and spun to find Quill backing away with a shield of his own raised. He flung his dagger into the eye of one of the unexpecting enemies and it dropped without a sound. Quill used this to his advantage and immediately sprang on the other one, ending it quickly with a knife through the eye.

Seven picked up his sword and started to make his way back over. A woman screamed in the far distance and everything shifted as the swarm in the sky moved away and the sun came out once again. The smaller General stared up blankly, noticing one had stayed behind and he gestured to Seven.

Floating in the air above them was one of the Generals, an angry look on his face as he held a massive essence attack out in front of him. It descended down in a streak and directly into the karma stone of the massive family heirloom. There was a popping sound and Seven knew instantly it had broken. The General formed another and another, each massive attack popping first his dagger then finally Quills as his power was far too much for their nearly full karma stones to handle. It smiled viciously at each sound and realized they now stood defenseless.

"We need an idea or we're done for," Seven speculated.

"I have one," Quill offered, pulling out the weird armlet with no reservoir stone. "But I have to be wearing it." Seven opened his mouth to object but Quill silenced him with a wave. "I can do nothing. Only your bow can reach him from this far. Take it out now and string it quickly. I reckon I'm gonna light up like a bonfire and that's when you'll get your chance... your only chance."

Seven stared blankly at the other man as he pulled his coat off and slipped the thing on his arm. "Why? You... hate me?"

Quill gave a serious smile. "Because I made a promise...You see Ma over there swinging away like he's dusting mothballs? His dad's name is General Dag." Sevens eyes went wide as he looked to the giant only a dozen paces away. "He's got a brother. A REAL brother. Ain't nothing more important than blood to their kind."

Seven finished stringing his bow and knocked an arrow. "Take it. You shoot," he tried to insist but Quill shook his head.

"Last time I used a bow I accidentally shot meself in the back," Seven paused, "That's... not possible."

"You calling me a liar?" Quill gave him a serious look then it softened. "I am a liar. A selfish liar who lied to Matches his whole life so he wouldn't leave me. So I wouldn't be alone." He turned back to Seven as the Sin General flung his attack. "You're his brother now mate," and the world exploded into a blinding white light with a hissing sound like blowing steam.

Seven shut his eyes as tight as he could but was still somehow able to see the outlines of the things around him anyway. He cracked one eyelid open a slit and found his target, pulling back and releasing without a thought.

He didn't watch the arrow land or the body fall as he turned back to face Quill but all he found was a pile of charred ash along with some daggers and flasks. He let himself drop to his knees as he spoke. "Forgive me," he asked and there was a thud on the ground next to him. He turned to find Matches staring at the smoldering heap with rage and tears filling his eyes.

"BROTTHAAAA!" he screamed and punched the ground then let himself fall forward onto his face as he continued to cry uncontrollably.

Seven reached forward and grabbed one of the empty flasks then started to fill it with as much of the ashes as he could. Matches noticed this and instantly started to help.

"Matches... I... Quill told me something."

The giant man took the flask and finished scooping what he had into it, packing it as tightly as he could get it. "Heard," he spoke solemnly then put the lid back on.

"So you know? That we're... brothers?"

Matches held up four fingers and wiggled them one at a time. "Deffy. Quill. Matches. Seven." He stared for a moment then put the first two down with a sniffle.

Seven put a hand on his brother's shoulder. "Yeah Ma, it's just us now. Well, and maybe..." He looked to where I hung in the air, no shields, no defenses, but the essence blasts all bounced off me harmlessly as I snapped a being's neck with one hand. I sucked in a deep breath then screamed in rage so forceful the air around me erupted in all directions like a bomb had just gone off.

CHAPTER 39

I am no prophet but I have seen this worlds futures. I say futures because it's all based on probability and has many branches leading to many different outcomes. Some of those outcomes have shared denominations or things that are constant and unavoidable on certain paths. I myself am at the root of several new discoveries but until the day I can get the resources I need, I'll never be able to decipher the technologies I have locked away inside my head. I only mention this because I need the opportunity to try as most of them are part of branches that unless the world changes, will fall away. Time itself will never make it that high up the tree.

"How about we stop in that thick brush up there? It should give us some cover and still be far enough that we're out of the way."

"That should work M'lady," Lynnay responded.

"Oh please stop calling me that. You know I'm no lady and besides, we're the same age." There was a flash overhead and the two women turned back. "That's our husband taking on an army of them things. I knew he was strong but that…"

"I don't think he was nearly this strong while I knew him," Lynnay observed in wonder.

Cherry grabbed the other girl's arm again and they went back to their trot through the reeds. "He once told me about you and all the lives inbetween, places he's been, women he's loved. I imagine with the amount of time he's been through he's a big deal stronger than he was before."

"He talked about me?"

Cherry hopped over a log then turned to help Lynnay do the same. "Not in detail, he was always hesitant to talk about his old loves. He said it was his first time ever traveling like he does and he met a girl. He loved that girl so much when he returned back to where he was really from he swears he found her. If not her then her soul twin if such a thing exists."

Lynnay let a smile touch her face. "That makes me happy to think that in some other life we found each other again."

Cherry hiked up her dress as they high stepped across a small marsh. "You still have him in this life," she reminded.

"We," the other women agreed with a smile. "We."

There was a splash from the side and they both turned in unison. An Enlightened in all black was removing his helmet, red eyes glowing fiercely as he grinned and pointed to Cherry's hair. He emitted some sounds like a symphony as he tried to speak in his musical way.

"Get behind me M'lady," Lynnay whispered and she loaded the karma stoned bolt as the other woman obeyed. She raised the crossbow up, leveling it dead center at the being and he puffed up with a smile, beating his chest with a fist as he raised a shield in front of him.

Twang. The dart blasted through his shield like it didn't exist and then buried itself deep into his stomach. His mirth vanished along with all his essence and horror crossed his face as he tried to dig it out frantically.

Click. Twang. The second one struck him directly through the face, dropping him instantly.

"Nice shooting. Now let's get out of here before another one comes."

"I can't, I need that bolt first. "Lynnay bent over and started to try and work a finger around it gently in an attempt to free the barbs.

"Oh please hurry. My hair does make me stick out far more then I care to."

Lynnay grabbed the helmet and offered it back without looking. "You can try to hide it in this if you want but that dress you're wearing flows like a rising tide," she offered and went back to her work, fingers slippery with blood and sweat.

Tink. The small noise made her heart drop down to her boots. "No," she gasped. "Please no, no, no!" She pulled half of the dart out as the rest stayed lodged inside like it was intended to.

Cherry watched while she held it to her face and tears started to flow down her cheeks. "Was it that special?" she asked.

Lynnay wiped at her eyes and nodded. "It was the only one of its kind. It was worth more than a kingdom... It was my way out." Cherry tossed the helmet aside figuring there was no point.

"You know, we can just have him make you another one."

Lynnays eyes squinted in disbelief. "He can make things? Like a yielder?" The red head smiled and bobbed her head, happy to bring her new friend some good news. "Then who cares about this one," she reasoned, tossing the broken piece to where Cherry had thrown the helmet. "I'm going to have him-"

Her words choked out as a large blazing white sword protruded from her chest and Cherry watched in horror as the other woman's eyes went distant then slowly shut. The being that had killed her slowly peered over one shoulder, the red from his eyes shone brightly as he smiled from ear to ear. Recogniton fueled her terror when she realized it was the same being who had raped and kidnapped her and she screamed at the top of her lungs.

The air around me howled with my passing as I rocketed towards the sound. I could see her tangled red hair bouncing as she tried to back away without taking her eyes from her aggressor.

He reached out to grab her but she fell and I instantly knew who it was.

"EGOSIN!" I screamed, putting everything I had into the blast. He spun, a shield coming up at the last moment to deflect it away. I didn't slow, instead I pivoted in mid air and put my feet out first. Cometas aster and then I enforced my belief into it, crashing into his defense at full force. His own shield ricocheted back into him and he was tossed violently through the air and into some bushes. I didn't have to look back as I landed, the sun going dim again was all the proof I needed that I was being followed.

Shields.

They started to pop up all around me and I fed layer after layer into them, each one spinning in a different direction than the one before. Up, down, left, right, into the ground, stacking them endlessly to try and protect her from the world.

"Are you ok?" I asked and she jumped into my arms nodding her head. I looked down and there were tears streaking her face. "What happened?"

"He killed Miss Lynnay," she croaked. "He stabbed her through the chest then came for me."

"You're safe now," I soothed then kissed her. "I need you to stay here. I think I can keep these things around you until I make it safe to come out."

"Can you?" she asked in disbelief. "Can you really kill them all?"

I shook my head, "I don't know. Maybe I can talk to them. I have to find out what this is all about. Tell them I'll just take you and go and forget about the Gods."

She stared at him, her eyes searching mine. "Maybe that's why they're so upset? Maybe they think you're coming for Aam like that other being did?"

I laughed. "Cherry you're a genius! That has to be it." I praised and kissed her again. I held her out at arm's length then performed a blink. Power and stamina replenished instantly and all my aches and pains melted away except the one in my lower back. "Sit tight. I'll be back just as soon as I can."

"What are you going to do?"

"First, I'm going to kill Egosin..." I paused remembering the communication gap. "The one who took you. Then I'm going to find their leader and try to talk to him."

"Please be careful," she urged. I smiled, not daring to respond as I opened a hole at the very top of the vortex and then shot through and closed it behind me.

Surprise washed over some of the faces at my sudden reappearance and I could see they were having trouble figuring out how to get through my impenetrable defenses. I charged towards where I'd last seen Egosin land, spotting him just taking to the air.

Our eyes locked and he attacked without hesitation, bars of light forming sideways like the ones he used when I first saw him. Two, three, four, one after the other and he sent them spinning in random directions all around me.

Clever, I praised but I was done fighting like them. It was time to step way outside the box and try something I had never even considered possible before. I shut my eyes and breathed, focusing every ounce of belief I could muster.

I am a shield.

I enforced my will into the belief and let my eyes open as the attacks sizzled in. They hit me and were deflected away and his eyes went wide in horror. I shot forward and grabbed him by each arm and the world lit up as hundreds of beams blasted into my exposed back but not one penetrated.

"No! It's too late!" he gasped.

"For you it is," I growled then pulled his arms apart slowly, letting what was about to happen to him sink in. He grit his teeth and I pulled harder and harder like wings from a fly and one of his arms popped as it ripped from his shoulder. His scream was nearly deafening and I let the appendage drop to the ground then moved to grab him by the neck.

His screams slowly turned to gurgles as I crushed his wind-pipe, "You... shouldn't... have... touched her!" I growled and I could feel something inside me shift. A broken piece born long ago clicking back into place. I squeezed his neck harder, letting the anger consume me as I basked in my revenge. His eyes bulged then his neck cracked as his spine broke. Rage and hatred consumed me completely and I screamed for the essence all around me to erupt. The world shook violently and hundreds of the Sin were knocked back but this only caused the others to spring forward.

"If you're all so eager to die then come and have it. I will kill you all if I must, so who's next?"

"I have who's next right here," I heard the voice from below and spun to see Misosin dragging Cherry from her protective barrier by her hair. "Oh how I love what causing death does to one's soul. It's so... empowering." I noticed a massive gap in my rotating shields and knew instantly he had used his unique power to slice right through it.

"Don't you dare," I warned but he put up a hand to forestall me then turned to the people around him.

"Find Lachesis and have her call a ceasefire. Tell her to bring all those in charge here at once." A few of his men nodded and made to do what they were ordered to. After hearing of the break I noticed the others starting to land and some even removed their helmets as they stared at me. I was baffled to see not only the red glowing eyes of the Sin but also, yellows, greens, browns and every shade in between amongst their ranks.

"What is this?" I demanded, looking from him then back to his men.

"Why... it's the execution of a God of course. What else did you expect?"

I noticed Sway walking up then and the entirety of both armies followed in her wake to circle our little parlay.

"What's this about? Why is there a ceasefire?" Sevens gravely voice called loudly.

Misosin addressed Sway first, "is he the one in charge?" he asked and she nodded. He walked over to Seven and pushed a folded piece of paper into the tall man's chest.

He grabbed it and eyed it speculatively for a second before opening it and reading. Several of the men closest to him crowded in to try and read it as he did.

"No..." he muttered then stared up at me in a wild mix of emotions. "This... can't be!" The look on his face was one of utter betrayal.

"What does it say Seven?"

"Read it to us!" and a bunch of others voiced their agreements.

He held up his hands. "I will read it! The first part says this; Aam, your absence after that being infiltrated the tower has us all greatly concerned. None here are powerful enough to help except maybe a Boundless who calls himself Fin. What would you have him do? This part was translated by Sway herself. The response however comes directly from the hand of Aam. It's flowing and changing texts are proof enough for me and all who see it." I watched as fear spread into Able and Summers' face and the fat General shook with disgust. "It reads," he continued, "My left and right hands pluck the strings. Fin has been pulled here to fulfill my prophecy. He has come to ascend into the being you know as ImpendiOam."

Gasps and cries went up all around and people started to shout. "Kill him!" and, "There's still time!"

"Seven!" I had to shout to be heard, "I'm not ImpendiOam. I don't even know who that is?"

He didn't answer for a second, our eyes locked on one another's. "Do you really not know?" he yelled back as the armies murmured relentlessly and I shook my head. "It's the one prophecy we talked about before. It was the story given at the beginning of time so that when it came we would know judgment was upon us. We know our fates Fin. We know our time here ends," he paused to watch me but I just shook my head in refusal. " It means you're about to become Aams opposite. It means you're going to kill us all Fin, it says YOU ARE ImpendiOam!"

I continued to shake my head, thinking of the words Lynnay had told me herself directly from Aam. "No! No Seven I won't! You have to believe me!"

"OVER MY GOD? BELIEVE YOU OVER A GOD NOT-CAPABLE OF LYING?" He shook his head and thrust the letter into Sway's arms then turned back to me. "I find you an unfit pupil," he stated then turned to his brothers. "I'm leaving now. I will not be a part of this," he informed and then took off.

Able stared at me for another second then turned to his General. "General Books, the army is now under your command. You may do whatever you think necessary for the survival of all." Then he and Summer turned to follow after Seven and Matches.

I watched as Cherry freed herself of Misosin's grasp and walked over to grab the letter from Sway. Her hand went up over her mouth, shaking her head in denial.

"Cherr... please," she took a few steps forward and handed me the letter.

"Aam can't lie... Can you?" she asked as I grabbed the paper. The words appeared as a bunch of random blocks and half blocks with knicks in them randomly then it... shifted and turned into english. "Do you see what God's writing can do? Do you expect us to believe you over that?"

"I'm... I won't do it Cherr... I'll leave. Just me and you, right now. We'll go hide in the countryside... Please?"

She smiled, the big smile that touched her eyes and caused them to arch into tiny rainbows, "Ok. I'll do it. I'll go with you right now," then she moved to step closer.

A bolt suddenly protruded from her neck and she gurgled. "NO!" I screamed and grabbed her just as another took her through the shoulder, then the chest. I heard Misosin's maniacal cackle and turned to see him lowering Lynnays crossbow, his other hand pointing at me. He closed it and his men erupted into motion once more. "NOOO!!!" I jumped over her to try and shield her body but all the armies had attacked this time and arrows rained in from all directions. The blows continued to bounce off me as I desperately tried to heal her by pushing essence into her with one hand and pulling it out with the other but more and more arrows found openings and struck her body. After a moment I stared up at Misosin whose face showed pure ecstasy at seeing my pain. He actually enjoyed it... relished it... fed off of it.

I felt the new sensation inside me grow and recognized it for what it was. It was hatred. Pure, unbridled hatred. I held my hand out, palm up as my emotions flared. The small black orb formed in an instant and slowly started to grow in size as I pushed my hatred into it.

Misosin stared in stunned disbelief as he tried to make sense of what he was witnessing. "That's not possible... unless..." His eyes went wide with realization and triumph. "Oh Fin! I just figured out who you really are! My master has finally won! He has found his more opportune time at last!" then he threw his head back to cackle in glee. I watched him with disgust as he wiped at his eyes then wiggled his fingers at me like he was saying goodbye then he put two from his other hand to his forehead.

"NO!" I shouted, realizing what he was doing and pulled the orb in on itself.

The world reverberated around me and the shockwave rippled out in a dark mass that erased the essence in everything it neared. I watched as the destruction spread and death followed. Bodies fell from the sky and the ones on the ground collapsed in heaps. The grass turned a crispy brown and the trees wilted and rotted, some collapsing into sawdust while I watched it all uncaring.

I looked down at Cherry's body and bent to start pulling the arrows out so I could hold her in my arms one last time. After a while of just sitting there crying I finally found the willpower to get up and dig a grave. I put both her and Lynnay in it then looked around blankly, still in shock at everything that had just happened.

In the far distance I saw a tower protruding from the world and I knew it was time for my answers and so I shot towards it immediately.

The essence drained from me as I entered and I landed gently, noticing Immi sitting on a log. "Immi, I'm sorry."

She waved the comment away. "There is nothing to apologize for and please, call me Atropos," she insisted then waited for me to offer her my arm then took it after I did. "Come, let me walk you in."

"I failed them," I informed her and she shook her head. "No. Aam does not let prophecy work like that and you are not advanced enough yet to see the bigger picture time creates." "But you do?"

"Only here. I see this place's time to serve in this world first. Now that this time is ending I have earned my next ascension where I will serve similarly but outside of time. That is the reward given to us for our loyalty and faith."

I gave her a sideways glance. "Us? You and Sway?"

She smiled. "Lachesis, yes. There are two others but since this isn't the final step of your story here they are elsewhere, ensuring the souls are ripened before the harvest."

I lifted my head, "the harvest being the end of the world?" She nodded. "Aren't you afraid to die?"

She chuckled softly. "When you've lived as long as I have, death is a reward. Besides, I see all the steps before and after this life and death is never something to fear. It is only of the physical body or as I like to explain it, the loss of a single dimension."

I froze in place, directly on the path in front of us stood a massive Cherubim with the head of a tiger. Its lifeless eyes sat unblinking while it stared at us.

Atropos urged me forward, "they do not attack their Gods."

I walked forward reluctantly as I shook my head. "I'm not going to become their God."

She patted my arm like I was a dimwit, "he said to the being who can see through time." I didn't respond as I watched the large beast. It puffed out its chest similar to the one I'd fought then bellowed out a low rumbling roar and I saw others start to pop up from the bushes and long grass, chiming in with their unique calls. "Well," she continued, watching the things bow at the waist as we passed, "they signal that their God walks among them and it sure isn't me," she patted my arm. "I'm sure once you meet Aam you will have this all explained to you far better than I can."

I ran a hand through my hair. "So if I become a God, can I move through time?"

"When," she corrected, "you become God you will exist outside of it. But not all of it, just the one you were created in. But I know why you ask. You want to save them?" I nodded. "Well I assume you change your mind from now to then or you already would have."

I froze as I felt two massive powers suddenly burst into existence far to the west. One was the most powerful pull on the essence I had ever felt and the other made my emotions flare up as it called my hatred from me. I turned to her. "Is... that..."

"You again. Yes. Aam does not lie," then she gestured to the path in front of me. "This is where I leave you. As you can tell my work here is not done and neither is yours. I will see you again," she pointed to me, "when you're... them." she pointed to where the two powers clashed and I could feel the foundations of this world tremble as they did.

I turned back to walk closer and stared at it with a blank expression. At the end of the path on the base of the tower stood a small archway, the words "Pepromenou Fygein Adynaton" chizzled above it. Under, was a clear greenish blue liquid that waved and rippled endlessly in its depths, obscuring whatever lay beyond. It looked like someone filled a bathtub with jello that never stopped wiggling then found a way to stand it upright without it spilling out.

"What is it?" I asked as she turned to walk away.

"It is how you step outside of time," she informed me and I stepped through.

CHAPTER 40

A am is not really a name as there are no names in the spirit realm. When you meet Her and ask what She is called She gives you an imprint of everything She is. You receive love, joy, happiness, a being of perfect harmony. It comes across as a state of existence that everyone should try and achieve, a perfectly in sync soul attuned to the All. There are no words that include everything She is so instead, Aam is more accurately described as the sound of pure serenity.

I felt awake as my soul breathed in for the first time after being asleep for so long. I looked around at it all with wonder and amazement at what I saw. The ceilings were made up of what appeared as white marble that stretched on forever. Things were definitely odd here. Torches lit the walls but their flames did not flicker. Instead, each one was frozen in place, noiseless and motionless like it existed outside of the balance time creates.

There was a symphony resonating throughout but it wasn't just music, it was emotion. I walked over to a wall where some paintings hung and inspected one more closely. In it, a small boy stood all alone clutching his teddy bear in a field of tall grass. The grass rippled. It's real! I thought then stepped back in surprise, not knowing what I was seeing.

"There you are my love," the voice rang through the air with a pleasant melody that filled my soul with joy and I spun to face it. There in front of me approached the single most beautiful, dazzling, elegant, perfect being I'd ever laid eyes on anywhere. Her long hair flowed to one shoulder with its other side tucked behind an ear. Her face was perfectly proportioned, slender jaw, tiny nose and two soft pink lips. Her gown hung to her ankles and blazed with the pure essence it was made from, shimmering and twinkling with its magical enchantments. But what set her apart were her eyes. Two large pure white saucers shone like two flashlights as she looked me up and down with a gentle smile.

"Are... you Aam?"

"Yes I am," she placed her hands on my shoulders and pulled me in, kissing me directly on the lips. My sorrows, fears, anxieties, all of it, melted away like wax in an oven. She pulled back, "better?"

I stared wide eyed for a moment before finally forming a response, "Um, yes, thank you... but what..."

"A kiss from us. It removes the mortal stench of the taint you were born from. A gift for both of us."

I felt myself blush slightly but I didn't dare turn away. She gestured me forward and then took my arm as I obliged. "Your eyes are beautiful," I said, trying not to let the silence return.

"Why, thank you. They are new in a way." I didn't know if that was a joke or not so I raised an eyebrow. "So much has recently transpired. Hard times with good outcomes. I have now mastered all the colors of the soul, which is why they appear white." "How does white represent all the colors? by being none of them?"

She chuckled to herself. "If you take light and separate it using a prism, what do you see?"

Realization dawned on me, "a rainbow."

"Exactly. I am the half that represents everything ethereal, or non physical, so light, which is why you called them white, symbolizes my mastery over all the colors of the soul. This is why I'm thought of as a God." She smiled again, patting my arm gently where she held it.

I let my head sag a little, "Immi said I'm supposed to become a God too. I don't want to be... I just want to be normal," I stared up at her and noticed a sadness behind her eyes.

"Yes love, Atropos was given simple instructions and ordered to help you become what we needed but much has changed including time itself."

"So I don't have to be their God?"

She shook her head, "not to them, no but you will still always be the one of the physical realms."

I frowned at this. "Is that why I always have a physical form when I project myself? I've done lots of searching and I've never found anyone else who has done this."

"Yes my love. That is exactly why. You are and will become my other half. The representation of everything physical. Opposites in every way but when we're together, we are one soul, the perfect balance of all things. You the physical, me the ethereal. You destruction, me creation. You the end, me the beginning. Do you see?"

I ran a hand through my hair. "It's a lot to take in. I have my doubts."

"That's understandable. You have been groomed for this since you were a small child and although our forms, races and sometimes even species may change, our names will always be the keys to unlocking what we will become and are full of deep meanings and hidden truths to our souls. Tell me of your known names please?"

[Earthen Name Omitted]

"And do you know what it means?" I shrugged. "At its base it means to be brave and steps, but it has several deeper meanings. One is to be brave as you walk through life. Take each day one step at a time. Second, it means you will reach the pinnacle of the steps on the ladder of enlightenment quickly and to be brave as you do. And a third is in direct reference to the infinity code. You will ascend its steps as well so must never fear, never doubt and never look back. Be brave. There are more. Lots more but you must learn the rest when they are needed. What of your other names?"

I gave her a sideways glance, "Waabanoosa?"

She smiled at me, "A piece of your true name and as such will always include the morning dawn. But I was referring to the name you gave yourself in Heart?"

I grinned bashfully, "Oh, that's just something stupid I thought was clever... It's Fin."

"More clever than you realize perhaps. Fin is the core of the word infinity and infinity is the core of you. Infinity is our calling card. There is also a number we've stamped on you, do you know it?"

I didn't have to think about this one. "8."

She beamed proudly. "Yes my love. The number 8. Those two things dictate your fates completely." She watched me but I made no move to agree with her. "There are no coincidences. Infinity and infinite both have 8 letters. You pronounce infinite as in-fin- 8. The infinity symbol itself is just a sideways 8 and 8 is the number of destruction. But most importantly, Fin itself means.... end. Which is what your presence amongst them represents."

I shook my head. "No. I thought it was supposed to be seven? Seven was the number of divinity?"

"Yes and you are of the seven but also more.. The eighth. The lion and the lamb so seven cannot be your number. If we would have kept it that simple there were religious zealots who would have seeked you out to prevent all that you would bring and represent. That's why you came unannounced, hidden, from the middle of an average family with an average family of your own, all with average lives and giant hearts. Do you see?"

I bit my lip, noticing we came upon a giant double helix staircase that seemed to spiral upward endlessly. We started on it and I decided to move the conversation elsewhere.

"So why do I have to blow them up?"

I watched her suppress a laugh. "You specifically don't. You just become the one that does." "But why?"

"Have you ever heard of the multiverse theory?" I nodded. "Good. When we 'blow up' Heart it will be the metaphorical egg that starts it all. Its black hole will feed the inflation of the next and when that one ends it will feed the next, and so on, forever. Infinitely," she winked. "It may end Hearts time but it ensures time itself has a future. I cannot do this without you. I only create. You... you destroy. Do you see?"

I shrugged reluctantly, "I still don't understand why they have to die."

"That's because you still don't understand that life is death. That is its nature. But they don't really die. Just their bodies. Souls are immortal and we will use them in the next time."

Something popped into my head that didn't make sense. "Then what was all the 'it's his story' talk if I don't get to save them?"

A forced smile came upon her face. "Because my love a story is what you must give them first. I'm sorry but it may not have the exact ending you wish."

I could finally see the top of the staircase approaching, "What good is a story if it doesn't have a good ending?"

She scrunched up her face. "Aren't religions important? Every one of them is based around a story or stories containing some powerful truths and most of them don't have happy endings."

I shook my head. "I don't have a religion... but I do have a very Catholic mother who would get upset if she heard me say that."

She smiled at my joke. "And why don't you have a religion?" "Whenever I look at them I see too many of the... lies and misleading information they contain. They may send the right messages but..." I struggled to explain it.

"I know my love. Everything born in the taint has become infected by it, some more than others but yours will be different. Yours will be straight from the horse's mouth, sort of speak." She let her eyebrows rise then her eyes went wide and I could tell she was excited. "And best of all, God has given you a gift for it. Better than any other religion has ever had. Better than anyone could ever hope for and beyond any technology man could ever perceive."

I stared at her with anticipation, "well? What is it?"

"Proof! Proof of what you are and for the first time ever in your world's existence, your book will give mankind proof of Heaven and their souls. I plan on helping you in your writings myself but nothing compares to that."

We reached the top of the stairs and stepped onto a solid black floor where tons of hallways and doors converged into a single spot and she stopped.

"Well? Are you going to tell me what it is?"

"In a way, you already have it but it will be given to you before you're back on Earth to start your story."

My head snapped up at this. "My story is for Earth? I don't understand."

A softness returned to her eyes and she leaned in closer. "I've told you love, your presence, your life, and your purpose this time comes at their end. A last attempt to save souls and save lives. Your existence there symbolizes their conclusion."

We stared at each other for a moment as she waited for the words to sink in. A door suddenly burst open, breaking the silence and a man walked in and instantly froze at the sight of us. Behind him lay a red rocky desert with some sparse vegetation. A few religious shamans dropped to their knees in awe at the sight and started praying at what they had just witnessed. He pulled something from the wall and it all vanished as he turned and offered a quick bow.

Aam bowed back, "he just came from Earth but in a different time. He was in a disguise as-"

"I don't care," I interrupted as my emotions flared back up. "You just told me everything was going to be destroyed. Even the ones I love? I need you to explain this better!"

"Your soul has become... infected. From this day forward your own destruction will begin. You will lose your wife, your kids, your friends, your possessions and your freedom. You will only be left with the angels we sent you with."

Tears started to form in my eyes at the thought of losing my family. "I won't do it," I shook my head defiantly.

"Yes my love, you will. We are two halves of the same soul and wherever we go we cannot exist without each other. I will always share in the pain with you but you will suffer this for me so we can master the last color and become what we must. The perfect balance. Soon, your memories will no longer be yours to control. The second you return to your time, you will forget everything about this." She wiped at the tears that stained my cheeks. "I am your impossible moon and although you will not always see my face, I will NEVER turn away." She kissed me and I felt my emotions subside once more. "I have a gift," she said, then touched a finger to her temple and when she pulled it away there was a small glowing white wisp. She pushed it through my forehead and I received... a knowing. "So you never lose my name or my love. A way to have time free of his influence... to have control... to be normal."

I shut my eyes as I tried to comprehend everything that was entering my awareness. "What are these... others?"

"The prophecies. The one is from God and you must share it."

I tried to focus on that one specifically and reeled back in horror. "No! That name! I won't do it!"

"That name says great, not evil or despicable. They were taught not to judge. They were taught to forgive."

"I don't care. I won't even speak that one!"

"Good men do bad things all the time. Are you bad?"

"No!"

"Then prove it to them."

"Why? I'm not evil!" I stepped away from her, all my emotions returning instantly.

She let out a deep sigh. "But my love, you will do evil. Great evils and you and the ones you love the most will be tormented by it." I stood speechless, refusing to say anything further for fear I'd lose my temper. "To know a prophecy is to hold its antidote. You cannot change what is already done but you can decide whether or not you will share this story. But know this, that one is the most important one of all. It is the one given at the beginning of time. The one God gives to the worlds so they know when their end is at hand," she gestured towards a door. "I think it's time we head in." I nodded solemnly and swung the door open then we stepped through.

The room we entered was odd. A giant glowing light floated near the ceiling at its center and on the left was a large viewing platform where a white bar stretched on until it was obscured from sight in both directions. In front of it sat a window most closely described as a screen but like the tower door outside, it seemed to be made with a liquid. A large basin sat on the floor below it and rising out of its depths was a three dimensional projection of a city in the mountains. On the floor of the room sat a giant white throne with shimmering colors emitting from its base and there were chairs around it on both sides, all of which were facing the screen.

Beings were milling about, talking freely and I felt myself being bombarded by words and imagery.

I flinched back, "it's a lot to take in."

"What you are experiencing is many different beings and various ways of communication. Most will be decoded instantly as a part of the knowing but the lesser beings here have translators to relay all that happens."

"Why do I keep getting visions of symbols and shapes?" "That is common. It is a very basic telepathic communication that some use to help... bridge the gap of understanding."

I continued to let my eyes wander until they finally rested on the man everyone was crowded around. He sat on the throne talking to someone I couldn't see and then he spun, our eyes locking on each other.

I pulled back. "Who is that?"

Aam patted my arm with a soft chuckle. "The God of Earth and he is called Oam [Pronounced oh-m; To explain further, Oam and Aam are different octaves of the same note]. He is my husband and is also... you. Or what you will eventually become. Both father and son."

I shook my head. "No look! He's evil His eyes are-"

"Are pure black," she finished for me. "Because he has mastered all the colors of the soul the same as I have."

"But you said..."

"Mine represents everything non-physical, Heaven. His represent the physical world. When you combine all the colors on Earth, like with paint, you get black."

I frowned. "What? That seems... impossible. Do people know this?"

She chuckled at my simpleness. "Yes my love. Lots of people do, I'm sure." She made a gesture, "Do you see who he is talking to?" I squinted, trying to make the figure out as he spun and Aam continued. "It is you."

"Me? How is that possible?"

"Do you feel the chord that is always connected to the back of your consciousness during your projections?"

The being who looked exactly like me started to walk over. "Yes..." I spoke slowly, watching him shake his head as he drew nearer.

"It acts as a sort of bookmark, always keeping your exact location and time so you will always return precisely where you left from."

I stopped listening as the other man squared himself up in front of me. "It still... seems... impossible," I croaked.

"Yes my love.. Most beings here cannot conceive that there are several different versions of you from several different times and lives all here at the same time. Most will just assume they are angels." She nodded to the other me and he nodded back. "If you two will excuse me. I need to speak with my other half," then she walked away towards the throne where Oam sat.

The other version of me squinted like he was trying to re-member something. "I stand before you with almost no memory of what you do next. Tell me what you are planning?"

I swallowed, knowing I was desperately trying to come up with a way to escape everything Aam told me I was about to do. I refused to be a part of it in any way and would sacrifice every-thing to get out of it. "Tell me what you know. Where are you from?" I insisted instead of answering.

He took a deep breath. "I know you let him destroy my mem-ories in an attempt to hide from me. I know I hate you for every-thing you are about to do and I also know that I'm about to do everything in my power to try and stop you and undo whatever it may be. As for when? So much time has passed from what you are to what I am I couldn't even guess at a number but I do know that on Earth, it's only been about 8 years.

8 EARTHEN YEARS LATER

[I am adding a timeline key below to help decipher my visits to the planet Heart as to where they happened in this book specifically!]
My first projection to Heart at the beginning of the book was actually my second time visiting there. I am not sure of the exact time.
My second time to Heart was actually my third time visiting there. If I had to guess I would say I landed only several minutes behind the first me and at the same clearing.
My third projection to Heart was actually my first time being there and I'm not exactly sure when it was. If I had to guess I'd say sometime around a year or two before where this book began. This next part is that storyline.

CHAPTER 41

The next thing that I'd mention I have almost no care for but it greatly effects something I do. Politics are tearing this nation apart and if you are in the state of mind that your political party is the only correct one, the smart one, the righteous one, the one your country needs to survive, then I have some news that may be hard to hear... You've been brainwashed. This may take a while for you to fully come to terms with but I ask you to start paying attention. The next time there is a live political event on the news, read the multiple headlines from different channels. There will always be a positive and negative inflection on the same thing from each point of view. Or if one Democrat makes a claim it becomes 'all' Democrats. If one Republican is found to be corrupt it suddenly becomes their entire party. This is a brainwashing technique that can birth hatred and hatred can birth violence. This once great country has numerous disruptive altercations in a large chunk of it's futures that could lead to a catastrophic division if it does not change and soon. You must see that you need both sides to continue. Both parties have crucial importance to grow and survive what is about to come and until you realize the potential of blending the two, your demise will be imminent. I will say this one last warning, it does not come to this in all *futures but in the futures it does, the second you turn on each other, a sleeping giant rises and crushes you both.*

Reality popped into existence without a sound, like turning on a light and I fell to my knees, letting the tears fall uncontrollably. "Aam!" I shouted to no one in particular. I looked around and saw pillars erected, decorations, flowers hanging, fresh fruits and pastries sat on trays, beings of all kinds and species scurried about and one approached with clothes as I observed this city's mindwarp. I started to put them on where I sat.

"Does your species have a God? A God named Aam?"

The female servant jerked back when I spoke. "You can talk?"

"Answer me!" I demanded.

"Yes M'lord but-"

"WHERE?" She stood frozen, too scared to respond.

"WHERE IS AAM?!"

"A-a-at B-babel Tower I think... b-b-but you can't get in there. No one can."

"Don't tell me what I can and cannot... DOOO!" I pushed the essence while I screamed, blasting it away from me in all directions. It leveled buildings and flattened everything as it shook throughout the city and I was left alone once again.

I stood. "Aaaammm!" I yelled, starting to walk, looking for more people to answer my questions. To answer for my sins. Window shutters closed and doors slammed shut as I screamed and searched. Everyone disappearing at my commotion only fueled my anger. I flicked a wrist and blasted another city block from existence.

"Aam! I will kill everyone alive until you come save them!" I yelled then paused as I watched the essence flow into a large domed colosseum nearby. I leapt into the air and came crashing down through its roof to land directly in the middle of two people fighting. They stopped their contest as I landed on the sands between them and I turned to the crowd. Hundreds of the red eyed beings stared at me as I spoke.

"Someone here is going to take me to your God... NOW!" I shouted and laughter erupted throughout them.

"You can't go to our God. It's not permitted or possible," one snickered in arrogance and others chuckled their agreements.

"Then you are all useless to me." I lifted my right hand to start forming my attack and I could hear the laughter getting louder.

"Fella, you picked the wrong place for that," one of them chortled and I could sense them pulling at the essence.

I pushed my hatred into my attack and it was immense. The massive sphere formed in an instant and I heard the gasps and the cries of alarm as I slammed the orb down at my feet.

The world reverberated, the force rolling out like a wave killing everyone and reducing everything to ash.

I walked on.

"Aam!" I reduced another city block to rubble. "Aaaaammmm!" I knew the name. I knew it had the answers. I knew that whoever the being Aam was, it willingly let me become a monster. To hurt the ones I loved the most. To betray them. To lose them. I buried the memories hoping the pain would go with them. "Aaaaam-"

"Stop! You're hurting people!"

I looked up to see a young woman standing alone on the road before me. Her long brown hair swirled in the wind and her glowing blue eyes stared back at me in defiance. "I know I'm hurting people... that... is... the... POINT!" I waved a backhand, blasting the essence again and watched as the force flung her through the air, toppling the buildings around her. She landed in a tumble then struggled to her knees and I saw she was bleeding. She stood, walking back towards me with determination on her face.

"Why are you doing this?" she demanded.

"Because," I growled, "if my family has to hurt. If I have to hurt, then everyone has to hurt!" I shot out another burst but this one was not as forceful. There was something about her. I watched as she somersaulted head over feet then slowly rose again onto two wobbly legs. Blood ran from her lip and she set her chin, walking back once more. "Why are YOU doing this?" I protested back in anger.

"Because! As long as you're here hurting me then you're not hurting others!"

The comment made me furious and I sent out another concussive wave at her but this one with even less force. She flew backwards and landed on her side, bumping her head on the ground. She remained motionless for a second then shook her head, rose, and started to walk back over.

"Stop!" I pleaded! "Stop making me hurt you!" I blasted at her once more but this time with almost no force at all.

She staggered backwards but didn't fall. "I'm not making you... I'm letting you."

I collapsed to the ground, sobbing uncontrollably. "Don't let me! Please!... just... leave me alone."

She kept walking until she stood directly above me. "Do you want to be left alone or do you want my help?"

I stared up at her with the dirt and blood caked all over her face. Her hair was a gnarled tangled mess but in her eyes... "You'd still help me? After what I've done?" She nodded. "Why?"

"I've always taught that anyone can help a friend or even a stranger in need but one of the best things we can do for the growth and balance of our soul is to help those that least deserve it." She held out her hand and I took it.

"You know the way to Aam?" I asked in a pitiful tone. "Yeah. It's far off in that direction. " she pointed, "I go there sometimes. I can show you where it is."

I stood pulling her closer to me without asking as I accepted her help. "Have you ever flown?" I inquired and her eyes went wide at the implication.

I came through the substance with four of the Cherubim in tow, their unwanted escort perplexing me as I surveyed the room. White marbled ceilings appeared to stretch on forever and a symphony of music and emotions seemed to flow in waves. I looked at the torches on the wall and their unflickering flames as memories returned at the sight. I put a hand near it, watching the shadow it still created.

"How do they not flicker?" I wondered aloud.

"It is only perceived that they don't as time becomes manipulated from this place and light permeates all dimensions."

I turned back slowly, either the Cherubim with the head of a... cow? or the head of a manican had spoken. I guessed the latter. "You could talk this whole time?"

"No elect one," I was wrong, it was the weird cow headed one. "This place returns what borrowed piece of soul we have and allows it only here."

I started to walk again and they followed in unison. "And what is the place exactly?"

"It is the edge of time and the edge of worlds. The point where they meet. The intersection of infinity."

As more of my memories returned I regained my bearings and headed straight for the staircase. "And why exactly are you following me?" I asked, annoyed with their presence.

"A great burden weighs upon your soul, elect one. We have been ordered to serve as the need arises."

"Ordered by who? I thought you took orders from me?" "I am sorry, elect one. These orders supersede."

I shook my head, the conversation doing nothing to help my sour mood. I took the steps in twos and my personal guard stayed close behind me on my heels. I reached the top and skidded to a halt. There in front of me greeting beings from all the hallways and doorways that converged in this one spot, was Aam. Her face beamed at the sight of me and her gown blazed with essence, lighting her up like the sun as she made her way over. Above her head was a crown of light, similar to a halo but with twelve distinct shimmering... diamonds? that burst out the light like tiny stars.

Something was terribly wrong. I stared into her eyes and they burned like flames. One second orange, yellow, green, blue, constantly flickering, constantly changing.

"What's... wrong with you?" I asked, not knowing how to approach the situation.

"Why nothing's wrong my love. Whatever do you mean? This is how I always was and always will be."

I shook my head, none of it was making sense. "No. You and your eyes are both different. You are not the Aam I remember. Who are you?"

Something flashed across her face and I thought she seemed worried. "My love? You must be mistaken-"

"I'M NOT MISTAKEN!" I yelled and she shrunk back at my rage as the anger easily bubbled back to the surface. I tried to calm myself.

"You're... angry? You can't get angry, you are perfect. You are pure."

I leaned forward and it pained me to see fear in her eyes. "I am the furthest thing from perfect. I am the furthest thing from pure."

Her eyes searched mine frantically, "But your life was meant to bring joy and love-"

"My life is hell! Earth is hell! I live in a prison where I belong!"

She took a step back. "Earth? This can't be."

"It is! I don't know why you're different or why you suddenly lost all your wits but one thing I know is that it's true!"

She stood straighter to try and hide her emotions. "Please... Come with me." Then she walked through the door that led into the throne room without looking back. I followed quickly and so did my guards.

Once we got inside she gestured for me to wait and walked over to a man who stood addressing a bunch of lesser looking beings. I say lesser because they lacked several of the dimensions and physical properties that made up most of the higher beings that mingled around in excited anticipation. They spoke quickly and his head snapped up, taking me in with a glance. His face looked different and he had a head full of grey curly hair. He wore a robe that hung to the floor and it was tied about him with a golden sash. But his eyes... they were like Aams, flickering violently with a mesmerizing dance as colors changed continuously. This was NOT the one I had met before.

He gestured me over to an area away from everyone else and I strode over immediately. "What's this about then? There is a mystery to what time you come from?" his voice surged with power. I nodded. "When I was here last she... you were both different."

He thought on this for a second. "Only things that happen here can affect both. I'm not quite advanced enough yet to grasp God myself. When there's interference, the end result is always a paradox. God manipulates time from outside, even our logic."

I stared at him, "Explain that."

He nodded. "Time itself is a circle, both infinite forwards and backwards. When you step in or out of that circle we always return to the original place or time we started from. It's always constant. The only constant a circle contains is its direct center, the dot in the middle."

"The Cherubim said this was the intersection of infinity?"

He glanced at them. "Their presence with you disturbs me. But they are correct. Heaven, as most think of it, has its own time." He made a face then nodded, "The best way to explain this would be as follows. Earth circles the sun, that is its time. The moon circles the Earth, that is the spirit's world's time but the sun shoots through space in its own direction. Its own time. Either the sun is frozen and the Earth and moon spin or they are frozen as the sun shoots through the cosmos. Their times are perpendicular. Do you see?"

It was a lot to grasp but I think I had it. "And this place is where they all intersect? How?"

"Draw a circle with a dot at its center, this will represent Earth's time. Draw another circle with a dot at its center and this will represent the spirit world's time. Now visualize them with a third dimension. Stand them upright and parallel to each other like two plates and then pull the dots towards each other until they meet. That is this place. The shores of time and the intersection of infinity."

I tried to picture what he just explained and oddly enough I came up with the infinity symbol. "So why is everything different?"

He stroked his chin. "If what you are saying is correct then the only possible explanation is an even greater paradox then we can create. It means God has intervened."

I looked back to where the people and beings started to take their seats, many of them watching us with a deep interest. "So what do we do?"

"What can we do? We have no choice but to proceed with the ceremony as planned. We are to give you the ingredients for your world to ripen it for the harvest."

I shook my head, walking slowly behind as he took a seat on the large white throne. He gestured around him. "These are the lesser deities we have birthed to add to the multiverse. Branching out its rivers and two for each one. Besides them twenty four, the rest are from other dimensions, other worlds, or even other times inside of yours." He made another gesture to some of the lesser beings again. "All here for specific purposes, to witness, record or prophesize. Instructions have been given to the translators on what they should say and how the events are to proceed. Whenever you're ready we are going to announce you as the pure one. Any questions?"

My head shot up. "No! No, I won't let there be lies. I'm not pure. I'm not... I've failed. Whatever it is you thought I was going to do, I have failed at it miserably." I shook my head, "I have no clue what's going on here or what this ceremony is even about."

He stared for a second. "We must proceed anyway."

I let out a deep breath. "Don't let anyone call me pure. In fact I don't want any titles at all!" I tried to fight back tears but my emotions flared back up at the truth I faced once again.

He made a gesture. "I will make it so. Now we must begin." He gave a nod and beings from all around started to talk and make announcements, giving me so many titles, descriptions even I couldn't make sense of them. He waved me forward and I stepped up, still trying to regain control of myself as my entourage followed.

"You are worthy of these." My thoughts cut off at the formality in which he spoke and he handed me a small bundle. Beings chanted and praised and even my guards chimed in while I looked over the items. The first was a weird control of some kind with buttons on it and the others were various writings. I turned back up to stare at him in confusion, not knowing what he expected of me.

He leaned forward and whispered, "The first is the prophecy from God about the end and who you really are. The second is the book of life, all those who we judge fit to earn a soul. The last is the story of your life so that religions may be born of it." He pointed back to the control, "but those are later, for now hit those buttons in sequence."

I finished looking over one of the scrolls and flushed with anger when I realized it was the exact same one Aam had given me all those years ago, the way I'd always heard it. I shook my head, this false charade eating at me. I pulled the remote out and clicked the first button. The screen whirred and an image appeared on it.

It was a man, a leader of some kind and he was riding a white horse while he hunted. Beings announced and shouted, all of them knowing exactly what was going on but me having no clue. I clicked the second button and another rider appeared, this one on a red horse. I watched for a second then gave a frown, clicking the third button.

"Slow down," I heard the whisper but didn't turn. "And you're supposed to be reading the texts aloud too."

A man on a black horse galloped dignified down a street. It was obvious he was very rich and very powerful like he owned a bank. There were some symbols that appeared in writing beneath it and I was surprised to find I could read it.

"A quart of what for a denarius. Three quarts of barley for a danarius and do not harm the oil and wine?" I spun, agitated to the point I found my anger starting to boil up. "This means nothing to me," I growled but all he did was gesture for me to turn back. I did so and watched as my annoyance with it all fueled my emotions. The people, the buildings, the currency, all of it from a time that looked like it only existed on the history channel.

I clicked again and another man on a horse appeared. I rolled my eyes, the absurdity of everything eating away at my resolve slowly. I clicked the button and saw pain, suffering, people begging for help and my anger started to bubble over. I clicked it once more and watched as natural catastrophes started to take place. Earthquakes, volcanoes, the whole while, beings yelled, trying to be heard over one another as I clicked rapidly.

The screen finally froze and a map came up and at each corner stood a being. Two I recognized instantly as younger versions of Immi and Sway and one was a different version of the woman from the street? I shook my head, people aren't meant to try and conceive the atrocities that happen to what is and what isn't possible in this place.

"I need you to pay special attention now. This part must happen and these are the people you need to save and how. Everything will be destroyed but this one location-"

I closed my eyes as soon as he started to talk. Trying to control the annoyance I still felt. I couldn't understand any of this. Beings praised and shouted, bowing to me like I was a saint and I'd had enough. I opened my eyes and clicked the seventh button anyway, watching as anger flashed across his features.

He held up his hand and the screen froze, everyone going silent at the sudden stoppage, not knowing how to proceed as they looked to him where he stared at me. He gestured me off to the side and my fists clenched in anger as I made my way to follow.

"I've had enough of your little... tantrums. If you don't start obeying I swear to you I'll-"

"You'll what?" I interrupted him, "Kill me? You'd be doing me a favor. You'd be doing the world a favor. Besides, if I'm an earlier version of you, wouldn't that be the same as killing yourself? You have no power over me."

The fire behind his eyes flared violently and I saw the rage he tried to contain. "Are you challenging my authority?"

I stepped closer, not caring about any consequences he thought he could cause that would bring me more anguish than what I already felt. "So what if I am?"

He sat motionless for a moment, clearly not knowing how to handle me before he finally spoke. "You are no version of me that I'd ever let exist. Let us finish this together. By its end, one of us will be no more," he threatened in a low growl.

I smiled at him uncaringly, "let's."

He snapped his fingers and a servant ran up. "Go. Have the seven powers brought forward and prepared."

The small being froze. "M'lord?" He turned his gaze onto the poor thing and it shrank back in fear. "Right away M'lord," then it ran off.

He turned back to me, "when the seventh power sounds my victory will be certain and you will cease to exist."

I stared back at him blankly, "that entire timeline doesn't exist in my world. Your victory will earn you nothing."

"If that is so then my time has truly come."

Seven beings made their way up and were being handed some weird contraption that looked like a mix between a gun and a musical instrument. He nodded to them and a dust was thrown at the screen and it vanished, removing the protective barrier and exposing the physical reality within, directly to outside influence. One of the beings stepped forward and fired their powers down onto the Earth and the being closest to me started to panic.

"Why is he killing everything? I can't watch!" and then he took to the air crying out.

I returned my attention back to the screen as more blasts sounded. I watched death rain down, women and children suffering and crying out for their God to save them and it disgusted me that it was him that was causing it just to prove a point to me. My anger flared and I turned to him with a growl. "Stop this!

You're going to end yourself and them for what? To prove a point to a nobody like me?" He stared at the screen without moving a muscle or acknowledging me in any way. "Stop!" I yelled, "I'm not worth it! I am a sinner!" I jumped in front of the screen to prevent the last man from using his power. "Are you listening? Gluttony, sloth, envy, lust, greed, pride, wrath, all of them and some in the worst ways! You are killing them and you are killing yourself."

This got his attention and he glared at me. "You will not speak such blasphemies. They need not know my intentions or what I do." He turned to address a small insignificant entity lacking most of the 'layers' the other ones possessed. "Seal up the things which you've just heard. Do not record them."

I threw my hands up in exasperation then remembered the book's he'd given me and that one was a record of my life. I searched through it and was surprised to see it was accurate. "I swear to you who I am. Let's compare my time to this one before it's too late. This way the mystery will be solved," I pleaded, watching the people die by the thousands on the screen I still stood in front of.

He thought for a second. "If this is true, the prophet is the only one here from that time." He turned to address the same being once again. "Go, take from him the story of his life."

The little thing came forward and I frowned not knowing how he would comprehend it. It wasn't really a book, it was a 'knowing' with the symbolism of one and instead of actually reading it, it sort of got absorbed. I gave it to him anyway. "You think the future time I'm from was supposed to be sweet at first but when you see the truths I bring it will make you sick." I watched as his features changed into one of discomfort as he realized the truth. "You see? It's all wrong! If you're really a prophet from my world then you must prophesize again about a different time with different peoples, leaders and nations."

His features glazed over at the sudden onslaught of information he was trying to conceive from a time he knew nothing about and I doubted he had even heard me.

Oam stood, "Take him away. He must not understand what happens next." Another being walked between us and led him away.

I turned back to the one on the throne. "Do you believe me now? This world, this time, isn't the same as mine."

He searched the room until his eyes locked onto that of Aams. He called her over and she came in a rush. He whispered something and I watched her shake her head frantically, tears forming in her eyes.

"No! No my love please! It's not so!" He nodded and she ran off in a hurry. I walked over and he waited until I was closer.

"Tell me something, would you die for your God?" I didn't hesitate, "gladly."

He shook his head, "then I believe you. But if it's really that bad you should consider the possibility that you must now do the opposite." He raised an eyebrow, "would you live for your God?" The words caught me off guard and the thought of going back to that place seemed like the worst kind of torment. My emotions must have shown on my face because he shook his head as he spoke again. "The throne must never be empty." His

voice came out calm, almost like he was at peace. "What is that supposed to mean?"

"It means if I die it will be for God's purpose so we can be made anew."

I was confused again and started to become agitated at how little I actually understood. I watched as he walked back to the throne, sat and then nodded. The final blast sounded and beings fell all around to the ground, some cheering, some confused, and some crying out praise as they knew he was perishing with the time he was created in. The bowl in front of the screen emitted a white glowing light and everything started to shudder and shake, flashes of light erupted and the being that was and is no longer, burst into a rain of light that slowly dissipated into nothingness.

Aam came flying up to the throne, a mess of tears and moans as she sat beneath it, rocking back and forth while people started to notice and gather around to watch. I stepped forward with them and noticed the Cherubim were surrounding me once again now that the old God had vanished.

I turned to one of them, "I don't suppose any of you can explain to me what's happening here?"

"Of course elect one," the eagle headed one spoke. "She is tearing off a piece of her soul to become her other half and take the throne. It will be her that births you for all souls must come from Heaven and she is all that is ethereal." I watched as she reached into her stomach and shook visibly. "After all the ingredients are added, the child you, will then be placed into time to grow. He will be the representation of everything physical, thus becoming the completed part of her other half." I watched as she pulled out a small lump of glowing mass no bigger than a softball and held it up to the throne.

"What are the other ingredients?" I asked and watched as the giant orb that floated at the ceiling dripped down a single drop into the thing she held. I stared in bewilderment.

"That is the piece from the creator or the All and represents the heart and is of pure love and must be a part of everything both living and non." I stared up at it only then realizing that everything around me, the music, the emotions, everything that is, was, or will be was connected to and rippled from this orb in an unending wavelike sensation. "He is the polarity to the creator so that men may always have thought and they may choose. He represents the mind." I snapped out of it, looking to see what it was talking about. Beings were gathered around closely and Aam held her hands out, holding the small figure. The entity it had spoken of stood to the side, its tall black translucent scales rippled in waves of red that radiated from its eyes. Two fierce red eyes that stared at me unblinking. I took the challenge personally and stared back.

"What is the nature of such a being?" I asked as our contest continued.

"He is of a singular purpose. A force. At his core he seeks out essence wherever it gathers and disperses it. He is the anti life."

"He disperses essence? Explain that."

"His main goal is the destruction of everything and he uses any means he can to accomplish it. Sorrow, anger, hatred, even love and happiness. He will use anything necessary to see that all creation returns to nothing so that the pendulum may always swing back."

It made very little sense to me but I stared at the thing anyway. A servant with two glowing red eyes walked up and spoke to it, then waited for a response.

It came. "Oderinttt dum metuanttt." I hesitated, it's voice sounded somehow... familiar?

"My lord, if the old God is really gone then how is he being born again? Do you know of another way?"

The things voice pierced my soul as it rumbled out its response, "There isss a wayyy." My blood went cold and I froze. The voice of my childhood, the voice in my dreams, no, my nightmares stood in front of me.

Emotions exploded and with them, my hatred. I looked down to where Aam still manipulated the small thing and it clicked. "NO! I shouted and everyone jumped. "Take him out!"

She stared up at me, "I'm sorry?"

"I won't let him do this to me! It's him! He's the reason Earth is hell! He's where it all goes wrong. YOU MUST REMOVE HIM FROM ME!" My rage flared up and people were visibly distressed by my outburst.

"I can't my love. You need-"

The thing cackled and its size doubled, a long tail whipping out that dissipated essence and scattered it into a sprinkle of twinkling dust.

She looked from it to me as realization set in as to what was about to happen. She then clutched the thing to her chest, ran and jumped through the screen.

Beings both high and low started to cry out in alarm at the confrontation they were about to witness as I sat staring at the entity I hated so much.

"Cherubim," I commanded and four heads snapped to attention. "Kill!"

CHAPTER 42

The power of your church is immense but no matter how much you try to hide it, if its foundations aren't made properly then it's destined to fall. I have seen its futures and in all of them the 112th pope is the last. He is a good man with a big heart and so I give him a decision. The truths I bring are intended to unite this worlds religions, so if he sits idly by and does nothing, ignoring my warnings, it will all crumble around him as his peoples discover the taint men have spread throughout its words. Jesus taught you to treat everyone the way you want to be treated and not to judge others yet your religion refuses to let people participate based on sexual preferences and you withhold services from those you've judged as sinners. I assure you when the world sees all the truths, you will forever be known as the pope who let his religion die. Or you can step down and have it rebuilt properly, to make it the leader in perfection the way God intended it to be... with a new title and new possibilities that allow women to lead and offers gays and sinners the same opportunities without discrimination. The choice is his.

They sprang into action without pause or hesitation and several of the things servants moved quickly to intercept them. I pulled at the essence and reality trembled. This place WAS essence, more than I'd ever felt before. I shot forward, focusing a ball and releasing it in a large blast directly at the still laughing creature. His body dissipated like black smoke with its edges lined in red as he flowed to the side and then reformed... still laughing.

I heard one of the higher beings yelling to me above all the commotion. "My Lord, you are the last! If you die we all die!"

I ignored him, I didn't care as long as IT died. Other attacks suddenly blasted in from the side as new beings joined the fray and his lackeys were forced to turn and face them head on. There was a clash and searing sounds as essence swords popped into existence, lesser and higher beings alike dying out.

I moved to attack again and he flowed away even further this time, circling to his right as I continued to blast over and over again in my rage. "YOU DESTROYED ME!" I screamed and he dodged with a laugh. "I LOVED THEM!" I released another one and he backhanded it away, spreading it into nothingness.

"Come younggg prince. We bothhh know loveee doesn't killlll... only hateee can killll. Show usss the gifttt they've givennn you!"

The black orb formed in my hand in an instant and I released it with a shout. It took him through the shoulder and he squealed in delight.

"You seeee? You can'ttt fight evilll with loveee.. You fighttt it withhh hate!" I shot another one and it took him through the stomach, the whole while he continued his circling. "You can'ttt love meee to killll what I standdd for. Youuu must hateee me. Hateee me myyy prince!" I shot him again and this time it blasted straight through his neck, cutting off his laughter. He returned to smoke and then reformed solidly... like my blink... and then he laughed. "I didn'ttt give thisss to youuu! They diddd! It wasss their sinsss that createddd you! Theirrr evil anddd vile waysss destroyed youuu and they'reee destroying themselvesss. You musttt not loveee them. Youuu cannot destroyyy with loveee!"

I put my hands together and formed the orb without thinking, filling it with both my hatred for my sins and the love I still held for my family. I unleashed it and his eyes went wide. The attack sizzled through his chest, leaving a gaping hole and he screamed, trying to vanish but the hole held him in place.

He laughed, "Balance? Ittt matters nottt. You cannottt kill meee or whattt I representtt!" I stood over him surging, a torrent of emotions at what this being was and did.

"He is right, elect one," a Cherubim spoke. "Only mortals die the second death outside of time."

It clicked.

"Then I will kill him IN IT!" I screamed, grabbing him by the neck. Surprise flashed across his face while I lifted him over my head then hurled him through the screen we now stood in front of. Some of the Cherubim started following suit with the beings they fought and I heard someone shouting.

"NO!" but it was too late. They flew in and a dim shadow stretched along the bars glowing light and everything slowed like one of those old movie reels until eventually all of it stopped completely. I looked around and one by one, it all began to pop out of existence.

I watched with little emotion, not knowing the severity of what I'd just caused as frozen people started winking out like lights. The chairs, tables and overlook itself went next and I was soon left standing inside of nothing, staring at the rippling beam of light that was time.

I heard a sniffle and spun to see a small boy standing near the throne that still sat at the center of it all. His lips were in a pout and he had tears in his eyes. As I watched him I soon realized that this boy was a younger version of me.

Suddenly the place stretched, like zooming in on a camera. Nothing moved. I was just suddenly a lot closer to the throne and the giant orb lowered itself. I stared at it as a drop of pure white dripped down and formed into a woman when it splashed back up.

My mother? I knew it wasn't my real mother, it was just her form to help console the child, me. I turned up to face the giant orb and could sense... amusement?

It pulsed. "Well that was interesting. Quite the temper tantrum. Care to explain your actions?" I remained motionless, not sure how to continue so instead I just shrugged. "I see... then you won't mind if I do? You've been moping around your whole life in a pity party about how bad a hand you've been dealt with no clue how it plays out. You hop around from place to place and time to time without a care or consequence in the world as you play at God. Something I might add, that you are not very good at."

I let my head fall. "I... didn't think..."

"Yes, you did think. In fact, not a thought of yours ever went unaccounted for."

I wiped at the back of my head and then looked back up, "Is it too late to change? Can I undo it?"

"Do you actually want to?" I nodded and felt warmth radiate into me. "Good. But for that I have to send you back down to the time you are from."

"No! Please! Can't I just stay here?"

"No. You don't have a choice in this. You are the only one left who can fix everything you've done.. It's not going to be easy, the flames of hell are hottest on those who can undergo the greatest growth."

"So it really is hell... and you're sending me back."

"Symbolically speaking, yes but not for everyone. Pain, sorrow, fear, loss, the things of that nature are the flames of the soul. But some lives are hotter than others and your change must be the greatest. We are often hardest on those we expect the best from, the ones we love the most. You'll thank me later." There was another pulse and this time I felt affection.

"So... where did everyone go?" I asked, looking around again. "It appears you've managed to destroy everything that time has created."

I stared at the boy, "Except him... and me... and the throne." I pointed out.

"Very observant aren't you?" Amusement. "He and you are from the new time you just created. The result of your actions just now."

I frowned, "but the prophet and the others?"

"Made by the version of you that just... ended. He and the time he was from no longer exist in that exact fashion. You added a new ingredient to time or more of a certain few to better explain. Like adding flour and butter to a soup, eventually it becomes a stew. And as for the throne, well I created it. I needed a place to sit and think." More amusement.

I continued to watch the boy. "It's hard to grasp."

"I know. I make things first then use time to create them later. Sort of like if you had an idea for a cake. You create it in your head first then you put all the ingredients together in steps until it's done. Like that but my cake exists first then gets created later. You cannot perceive yet what you will even become, do not try to perceive me. The gap between you and I currently is like the king of the world addressing a flea."

I snorted. "Well I think you're a little more advanced than a flea." More amusement, "But why is he here?" I pointed to where the boy was laughing with the piece of God he assumed was his mother.

"It's your first time projecting."

I cocked my head, "really? I don't remember." "You were in surgery."

I nodded. "What are they talking about then? I don't recall any of it."

"Sure you do. It's when I imprinted the concept of infinity on you."

My head jerked up to face the giant orb, "What? That was you? That... broke my mind. I was way too young."

"Yes but sometimes when our minds break something far more advanced and beautiful is hatched."

I shook my head, letting it sag to my chest. "I can't save them, God. They won't listen to me. I'm probably the worst choice for the job."

"And why do you think that?"

"Because I'm a sinner. The worst kind of sinner!"

"They are all sinners. Some in small ways, some in monstrous ways much worse than you. But you will change and that's what they must be shown. Let them see everything you were then once they've drawn their conclusions, show them the rest. That way, they may judge you first because after their lives end, you will judge them."

"It doesn't make sense."

"The face of religions should not fret at a mirror. Think of it like this, you have heard of the term 'walk a mile in my shoes before you judge?'" I nodded. "So is it acceptable to exclude when everyone must be judged? What if we said everyone will be judged fairly but you. There is no saving you." I thought about this for a second. "If they are willing to change, they must be judged. Who better than someone who has done all and faced all in some way? You cannot accurately judge someone for a life they've lived unless you've lived it yourself."

The child me climbed up on the throne then jumped, showing off his skills to his beaming mother. "But they are expecting pure... and-"

"Yes. Men have everything figured out. They plan and plan, the whole while I laugh." More amusement.

"I'm serious! They're going to hate me! They're going to think I'm the antiChrist! Especially if I tell them about your prophecy!"

"You're trying to perceive again, instead, consider the base principle of religion... faith. Besides, you are the antiChrist."

My jaw dropped and I was horrified at what I'd just heard. "It doesn't mean you are evil. Anti was only intended to mean 'opposite' but it got lost in translation. Where once you were pure with no sin, now the other half of the same coin. The worst and all sins. But what you are fearing, man made up. The beast is not a physical manifestation." I still stood frozen, too shocked to think properly.

"Does the number six mean anything to you?"

"My older sister," I responded without thinking.

More amusement. "No, six is the symbolic number that represents man. The sign of the beast was given as six, six, six. It was intended to mean 'many men' who had been infected by the taint... and I could not let you be the exception. Also, it was made up of a bear, a lion, a leapord and other such symbols men use to represent their lineage or did you think some mythical creature like that was going to crawl out of nowhere and bring terror and war?" I shook my head. "The terror is only of the mind and the war is for souls. All souls. Your soul. More lost symbolism."

"More proof that people will hate me."

"True. You may be the rock both sides fling at each other. The wicked won't understand but the wise will. Maybe after they realize the prophecies can only be fulfilled once and that you're what they get, maybe then they'll see. After all, no right minded being would go up against their God's will, unless they didn't believe." The boy jumped again and cheered with his new distance. "What a great final test you will become. Simulation over, pencils down." More amusement.

"You make it sound like it's all just a game."

"What else would it be?" I didn't respond to this. "A game, as in sports, is a test of skills. Why is it so hard to believe that life is a game where we test out our moral characters?"

"So lifes a game? That's it. That's the big secret?"

"Life is layered and different for everyone but that is a very good way to look at it. It's definitely not as serious as everyone makes it out to be."

"So why not just tell everyone? Why hide?"

"Hide and seek is my favorite game." I could almost hear the laughter at the joke and I found myself smiling for the first time. "But why?"

"Because what you don't know is before life you have all of its secrets. You know what you are supposed to do to grow, to develop and to ascend and you get to control it all yourself. All are taught this. Life is the removal of the training wheels, to see what you'd do when there's no one around to hold your hand. Children are all as sweet as cupcakes when mom or dad are about but the true test is when they're not. Do they do what they know is right?" There was a slight pause. "Think about this, what would make you more proud as a parent. Your child following in your footsteps because you told them to? Or your child following in your footsteps because they wanted to?" This made more sense and I found myself agreeing with the logic. "Another truth is that when you die, life, the attachments, pain, hate, sorrow, it all melts away and only very little stays. Your growth, your choices and your sins. Like it was all just a dream. The events and experiences were just ingredients to help souls grow and learn."

"How are my sins beneficial to anyone?"

"They are and will be. You are my lotus flower. Lotus flowers are very unique but to get one to grow you have to put it in the worst conditions. Drown it to the point that almost every other soul would give up and die but the lotus... it thrives. It takes the harshest conditions to create the rarest gems."

"Yeah, well my conditions and ingredients are terrible."

"Yes, rotten fruit is bad to taste until we've turned it to wine. Don't you agree?"

"I don't like wine." More amusement. "God... how about this [The single stupidest thing any being has ever done in the entire history of history OMITTED]

"You are a delight! Most beings can't even communicate with me and yet here you are... trying to make a bargain with something that you know can see all outcomes."

I realized the weight of my stupidity. "Well it was your... 'ingrediants' that made me this dumb."

More amusement. "A fair point and now I'm going to hold you to your little... promise."

I laughed, "Um, can I change my mind? Any chance we can just forget what someone may or may not have said in their ignorance?"

"Unlike you, I never forget." More amusement. "Which brings me to our last topic before time catches up to your birth and I send you back to undo everything you've caused." I looked around, trying to figure out what the comment meant. "Once you are born in time, then nearly everything you are and will become up to that point will exist outside of it. Although there are still paths and choices you need to decide for the rest. Probabilities."

"So everyone's coming back?"

"Not the exact everyone. Different versions of them with the new ingredient."

"How does that work with your prophecy?"

"My prophecy is given to them at the beginning of all times. I supersede. Don't try to conceive, instead, our last order of business. My gift for you."

A drop fell and I caught it in my hand where it instantly formed into a single sheet of paper. "What's this?" I asked as I read.

"That is for you. The end times will be a lot harder so I'm giving you something no other man, religion, or book has ever had."

I thought about it, "it seems odd."

"It is, to keep it hidden until you bring it to them."

"And this is real? This will bring living people to Heaven?" The orb pulsed in confirmation. "This is huge! This is a billion dollar technology! I could win a noble peace prize for this!" I thought on it for another second then frowned, "I could win a noble prize for this! This is what everyone has always wanted! It's... proof!"

"Call it proof. Call it the keys to Heaven. Call it God's technology. Whatever you wish, but it works and it will ensure that all the prophecies will be fulfilled. The last one from me, you need to tell them yourself but I leave that to you. No matter how hard it seems."

I smiled, staring up at the bright ball that symbolized everything we are. "God?"

"Yes?"

"... I'm just curious but I've always kind of known... I mean, would you say if you had to pick, do you consider yourself more masculine or more feminine? Which one would it be?" I studdered awkwardly at the question and found amusement pulsing into me once more.

"I am the creator of life. Which sex do you think is more attuned to the creation of life?"

I laughed. "I knew it!" I stared back up at Her, "and God."

"Yes?"

"I love you."

Joy, pride, happiness, fondness, love, it all radiated into me like waves. I laughed as I felt the hatred deep inside me slowly melt away.

Beings started to pop back into existence in the same spots they were before but still frozen. I watched in stunned fascination, seeing almost no visible changes to most of them but some colors of their eyes now flickered. Motion returned and cheers erupted throughout the room.

"He did it! He found a way to defeat him!" I walked closer to the screen and noticed the control had reappeared so I picked it back up.

One of the higher beings stepped closer shaking his head. He did not share their mirth as he spoke, "all here in the Heavens rejoice, but woe to the people of Earth for he has descended upon them with great wrath and great power." He noticed several of the other beings perk up to this so he leaned closer as to not be heard. "Has anything... changed? In you or in anyone?"

"Not me. But everything else has."

He nodded, peering around to see if he could notice any of the differences. "We must figure out what all has transpired. We must bring him back." I held out the control and he eye'd it for a second before he took it. "With your permission?" he asked and I nodded. He flipped it like turning a page and there was another layer containing even more buttons. The screen zoomed out and then branches could be seen spreading from time. There were four now, each with two...depths? and two above those, ten in all. He selected one and the screen zoomed back in. I didn't understand what I was watching at first as he found Aam's entrance and then followed her. Life after life, birth, aging, death, birth, aging, death as it flowed in and out of time. The entity chased her, each time she was born, life to life, continent to continent.

"What is happening?" I asked.

"It chases her, he knows you two can never live apart. He's waiting for your birth's. Life after life he infects everyone and everything. Battle after battle you will lose, even the one you win will be a loss of sorts as he taints its results." He shook his head. "And it's not just that. His taint is marked on everyone. He is using men to kill themselves with no help to our goals. Death will come from the land, the sea and the air."

I watched horrified as the screen showed me completely infected by the taint. I asserted my power over countless peoples and civilizations, leading men to my own designs and enslaving the ones who refused. I hated the God I was supposed to become but I hated the man I was supposed to become even more. Symbolism started to play out and the room filled with gasps and cries of disbelief.

"That's you! The mark on their minds!"

I didn't respond. I knew the things I had done and I knew they weren't good.

The being clicked another button and the screen shifted. This time I stood on top of a mountain with a bunch of my followers. Memories of the time surfaced and I knew I was about to have them build me a temple directly into the rock using a technology that only I had.

The beings around me pointed and cheered, thinking just because I had used religion that we had somehow now won.

"He's done it! Look, you are no longer corrupt. You and those with you have found God!"

I knew the truth. I was using the taint their religions contained to control them. "No. Look closer. The mark is still upon our minds. It's the same mark... his mark."

Their grins melted away. "What does this mean? The hour of judgement will be fruitless?"

"Why do they all still wear the beast's mark?" someone asked and a bunch of the lesser beings who were confused assaulted me with their questions.

I turned to address them directly. "I think if they bare his mark then they are lost to us and that would make judgment fruitless but I honestly don't know. Is there a way we could test this?" Some of them gasped and started to make assumptions as they scattered frantically about at my words.

The being with the control stepped closer. "My lord, the sickles hang up there. Bring one down and you can test this yourself." I looked up to where he gestured and pulled in some essence, easily floating up and grabbing one before I returned back down. I stared at it blankly, then the screen, unsure of what I was supposed to do. He made a thrusting gesture so I mimicked him, pushing the thing through the screen and then pulling it back out

but it came back empty.

I shook my head in frustration. "Just find someone else who knows what they're doing. I'm making an idiot out of myself," I urged him quietly.

He snapped his fingers and gave a quick command. Another being flew forward and grabbed one of his own. The process was repeated but this time when it was pulled out, there were spheres clustered to it of random dull colors. He threw them back in disgust.

"You were right. There are none of them where their souls need to be." I handed my tool off and then turned back to him as he continued, "so he wins... and nearly the entire harvest will be lost." We stared at each other for a moment, the screen still flashing while beings made their proclamations as they tried to interpret everything they thought was happening.

"I'm not giving up. If we're outside of time we can still change it right? So what is the goal?" I asked and he paused.

"They must find God and find their souls. Attune themselves to God and God's ways and repent for any sins before the end or it's all for nothing."

I stared at him. "Ok, so how do we help them do that?"

"Well usually, the old God would inflict tragedies."

I pulled back, "What?"

"Tragedies, global disasters. They take it as a sign of his wrath and they repent. When they are faced with death they always turn to what's next. They start to believe and they find their souls."

It seemed harsh but I shrugged, "Ok then let's do that... how?" He looked around and then pointed and a servant came running up. "Go, pour all of the bowls of wrath into the basin and make haste."

"All?" the little being asked in shock.

He nodded and the thing ran out, gesturing for some of my Cherubim to help him as he left. "Does it always work?" I asked, still skeptical.

"You're from Earth. If it started ending, disease, earthquakes, flooding, storms and all sorts of other horrors, where would you turn? Is science going to stop an earthquake? A hurricane? A tsunami?"

"They will turn to religion."

"They will turn to God," he agreed.

The servants came up and I eyed their cargo inquisitively. "What are they?"

The small being looked up at me. "In this one, man will bring disease throughout the world. In this one, from the top of the Earth fires will be born. In this one, from the waters-"

I waved the rest away, "Just add them. Is this the order they will appear on Earth?"

He shook his head. "Not specifically. They go in at the same time here and will occur around the same times there but some will spread out further and further as time dilutes them."

I nodded then turned to watch the results as they were added. Fires spread and then disease and the world went into a pandemic. Storms raged randomly and without warning as the global climate shifted as bowl after bowl was poured in. There was all sorts of symbolism and imagery that appeared on the decipher as the final bowl was poured. The being gave a nod, signaling it was done and the destruction we had caused was immense. Cities layed askew, flooding, craters, death, and men still didn't change.

"My lord... we still fail? Is there anything else you can do?" I shook my head as my mind raced. "My lord? everyone's waiting..."

I searched for the small prophet that I'd given my story to before, staring at him trying to come up with a way he could change the future from his own time. Maybe if something there changed it could help us now but I had no immediate ideas. "Just help him. Show him his own time and maybe we can watch and think of something there that can be changed to help us now. Show him what he wants to see... I am of no use."

Some did as I commanded but a bunch of the others gathered around me, confused with worried looks on their faces as they waited in anticipation. "We deserve an explanation my lord," one begged solemnly.

I let out a long sigh. "The beast you all just watched... was me. I have failed at whatever it was I was supposed to do and now I am a sinner." I looked up at them, "I am not divine in any way." "No, you're wrong my lord. We can clearly see you are of the seven."

I shrugged, "I was the beast and I was a sinner... but I'm not anymore. I am the 8th. I don't know what that is supposed to mean but I was told I am of the seven."

"So sins have reached Heaven?"

I nodded. "Yes but don't worry. I'm not staying. God is sending me back down. I have to try and fix it." I let myself plop down on the throne. "Please... just try and help him for now and leave me be."

They all nodded and moved away, leaving me to my contemplations. I replayed over and over the things I've done but the gaps I created in my own memory to escape my older self were almost unsurpassable. I thought about the things I could still change but somehow knew each different path only led me away from the goal. I knew I could only change what happened to me next, not what I'd already done. I let my mind wander as scenery played out before me but to no point. Beings still exclaimed and recorded the things they saw and witnessed. I let my head sag, my eyes coming to rest on the paper God had given me and something clicked. What if it wasn't something I needed to do here? What if it was something I needed to do when I got back? I stared at the paper, knowing the power it held and it clicked. They were married! This technology MERGES Heaven and Earth! How could I get people to know it? To try it? To believe it? What could I still do from prison?

My story... A book.

I laughed at the simplicity of the answer that I had struggled to see. I stood, holding it up in thanks to the orb that was All and watched as beings fell in praise at my gesture. "Praise to God all of you, both higher and lower beings!" I commanded and people cheered and rejoiced at my proclamation, knowing I must have figured something out. I found the higher being with the remote and gestured him to come over. "I'm going to merge Heaven and Earth so that people can see God for themselves," and then showed him the paper.

He read it and his eyes went wide. "The marriage!" he exclaimed excitedly. "Of Heaven and Earth! Between our new Aam and Oam when they arrive! We shall prepare at once my lord. It shall be a celebration. A huge celebration and all those who come to witness are truly blessed," and the other beings started to shout excitedly.

I beckoned the small prophet from Earth back over. "Make sure to write that down that we're having a merger celebration and those who use this technology to come are truly blessed!" He nodded and I laughed to myself, remembering that God had given me the solution but I had failed to see it the whole time. "So that was the true saying of God," I realized aloud. The little man fell to what I can only assume was a prostrate posture and began to chant. "Stop that! What are you doing?" I bent down and made him rise back up. "I am the same as you. A man from Earth. I know the writings of the Christs but I still worship God." I pointed up to the orb. "The writings about me are only given in the essence of prophecy."

His features contorted and I saw he was confused. I briefly thought of explaining to him that worshiping a Christ was the same as worshiping a tadpole instead of the frog but assumed he wouldn't understand that either.

Gasps and cries cut off my thoughts and a blinding light flashed. A door opened from behind us and we all spun in unison. There, riding forward, was yet another version of me.

CHAPTER 43

One of the most important prophecies ever shared with mankind was given to the only prophet God knew everyone would listen to for his were more accurate then most. He shared it with the world but the world was not ready to understand it then. The beliefs they had from their tainted texts and false prophets contradicted everything it implied but I ask you to listen again with an open mind and remember it still contains some taint. It was the prophet Muhammad himself who spoke of a future where the antiChrist was trying to save the world. That all your futures depended on his success and this is the reason I wrote this book, an attempt to save the world. I will give you this one last prophecy myself, plainly so that you all may have its antidote. So that you all may believe and all may change before it's to late. The beginning of your end is the year 2060.

I stood, walking over quickly to address the future me. Symbols and imagery again bombarded me and little of it made sense. His eyes blazed like a furnace as he watched me approach and I realized how similar he looked to the one who had so recently perished. This version of me was covered in blood and sword imagery

would randomly protrude from his mouth. Names flashed, writings flashed, and some even appeared to be tattooed onto him. I glanced beyond him to where his multitude of followers stood before I spoke.

"When... what time are you from?"

"I am here in death to give birth to the one we destroyed." "So you are me... dead?" he nodded. "Is that why you appear

to be covered in blood?"

"No. Souls do not bleed. The blood is symbolism for our sins so they know this time we are not pure. Each stain represents a sin we have committed in our journey to become what we needed to be. There are many things that will go unseen and untold but now that you've decided to write the book, I have been born in your future to tell you what is needed. First, a name that is written is a literal reference to being an author. Next, the name Kalb Kinu, use it, it means faithful and true." He pointed to his mouth and the sword imagery it held, "This represents the tongue. Power in words with its double edge being the truth and although prison cut off our voice, a page can convey just as much. He could not hide that from us." He ushered me on, away from the others. "We do not record what is next for them, only what is next here and what has happened before. We must deceive the beast."

I narrowed my brow in confusion, "the beast? I thought-"

He interrupted me, "There is ALWAYS a beast. He controls time. The instant one person defeats him, he goes back and infects someone else. Nearly everyone is afflicted. They don't even realize that by not doing Gods will they are inadvertently doing his."

I was shaken by the news but I knew it was true. We talked for a bit and I watched as things progressed. At one point they pulled the entity I hated before and his followers out one by one.

One of the beings lashed out at the future me, screaming, "Sinner! Deceiver! You think to defeat us with our own tricks? This can't last forever and when it's over, we'll be back!"

He laughed and leaned down to the insignificant thing, "and I'll be waiting," he threatened, then turned and walked back to the screen. I watched in fascination as he and his followers interacted with it in various ways. Like the old God he did not need to use the remote, he could control it with a wave of his hand. When they were done, he spun time forward all the way to its end, or to be more precise, to where it began again. He reached in his hand and pulled at the light itself and everything froze again except the few versions of me that still existed.

There was a rumble and a flash of light, a door appeared from nowhere and two beings burst through and I instantly recognized them. Aams eyes blazed white and she wore a smile from ear to ear, turning to address each of us as they both walked towards the throne. She whispered something to Oam as he sat then kissed his cheek. His eyes then turned and locked onto mine and I still found it very unsettling. Watching blackness being 'emitted' gave it the eerie effect like it was pushing away everything he stared at. He produced some writings and began to set them out as Aam turned back to speak to us.

"We have much to do," she announced, then walked to the screen and it started to move rapidly. I watched as she brought up Heart, pulled a piece of light from her mind and then pushed it into the screen and held it. The screen zoomed out and I saw a quick glimpse of Earth as it zoomed back in. She turned to Oam who still sat on the throne, "as soon as I add our soul, the taint will see and it will start." He nodded, then she turned to me, "when?"

I knew what she was referring to. "I have known him my whole life... Since before I can remember."

She reversed time and stopped on a scene where my pregnant mother was walking on some stairs and she added the link. "To ensure we get you to the Tower on Heart it is necessary." The effect was instant. A dark hidden mass clutched at my mothers foot and she fell, landing on her stomach. Aam shook her head, refusing to watch as she zoomed out and connected the link back to Heart. She then pulled off another piece of herself and left it there. The woman I had met before. The one that looked like a younger version of her.

The door burst open and a Cherubim with the head of a dog stood just outside holding a weird creature with the body and wings of a bird, the legs of a cat, and the head of a fish. Pinned to it was a letter. "It tried to fly directly in. We moved to destroy it but it smelled of divine influence."

"You did well," she wrote on it hastily. "Send it back please." It bowed and then exited as she turned back to the throne. "I must go bring him in."

Oam bowed back then moved to the screen to have his turn. He pulled a piece of himself off, holding it in one hand then stuck it through but held it. The piece instantly was granted a physical shape that existed inside of time where he held his hand. I watched as one of the Sin threw Deffy into a river and my heart dropped again at the long lost memory. He didn't watch it play out, instead he only followed the boy. He snatched him from the river and set him on the ground, healing his wound and they shared a few words for a while. He turned to me, "the reason you could not find him," he spoke and I was overcome with joy. He held Deffy through the screen and with his free hand he spun time. It stopped again in front of a group of people running and I noticed Seven and Matches at their front. The giant roared and ripped Deffy free in a hug of happiness and tears. They talked for a minute and then Oam embraced them all, flicking his wrist again just as a wave of black enveloped everything.

Time zoomed out and then branched off, he chose one, then zoomed back in. "What's this?" I asked as I watched him place them somewhere completely different.

"It is the boon Seven earned. We always keep our word," he informed and I smiled, knowing Deffy had lived with his friends.

"The women?" I asked and he smirked.

"We all have our secrets," was his only reply as he pulled his hand out and spun time back to its current location.

"What now?" I asked as he sat back on the throne and started to sift through his writings again.

"What now is, we proceed with the harvest of both, then take the beginning of Heart and move it to its end, thus creating Earth. A new Earth for our new Heaven. Untainted." He winked then snapped his fingers. The screen started to project on its own again and beings started to cry out and exclaim once more. He gestured towards the side of the room. "Go, speak with him, I must talk with my other half."

I turned to see where he had pointed and watched as a younger version of me stood with Aam and I immediately made my way over.

"I do know on Earth, it's only been about 8 years," I finished saying and the younger version of me remained silent. I knew he was about to decide something very stupid but I didnt know what it was exactly. My memories of most of his choices were hidden from me by the entity in his head and I doubted I could do or say anything to influence him right now anyway.

People started to cheer and praise the return of their Gods as judgment started. I decided to let our conversation wait as we walked back to watch.

When it was over Oam stood and Heart's solar system popped up on the screen. I watched as the planets moved around their sun in odd patterns.

"It looks like an atom," I speculated aloud.

He turned to me. "It is. That is why the physics of it are not similar to yours. It was God's first creation and much will change with its destruction. New rules. Better laws."

"It will create Earth?"

"I will split it like the atom it is to create your entire universe. The big bang. Earth is but a single spec of its dust."

"So space is... getting smaller? From an atom to everything we know? I really don't understand quantum physics in the slightest." "And neither do they until they realize subatomic particles are really only subatomic thoughts of the All. And thoughts can be influenced or even changed," he winked, reaching out his hand to Aam. "Come my love, let us make humans in our image according to our likeness." and they smiled.

"You both go?" I asked and he nodded.

"We are opposites in every way and it will always require both. Our children will need two parents. One of love, caring, mercy, grace, all the good things." He turned to her and she gave him a loving smile. "And they also need a Father to teach them discipline. I admit I will sometimes be more strict on certain individuals over others but it's always necessary. I bring temptations, wrath, pain, greed, judgements. So they may have their test and the chance to earn their place in their next step. Heaven."

"So... you're the reason there's evil?"

He shook his head. "Evil is only an illusion that's why it has no balance. The opposite of good is bad and love is hate. Yes I can cause hatred but it's part of the test. A child can convince himself he hates his father after he's felt the wrath of punishment but once he grows up, he evolves and realizes it was necessary." Aam nodded to me to confirm his words and he kissed her. "Besides, destruction breeds creation. Everyone knows that," he chuckled. They bowed, turned then entered through the screen, disappearing completely.

To put to words what they did is impossible. I barely understand it myself. I watched in stunned fascination as they worked, him a force of destruction and explosions. Her, an elegant dancer who brought things together as gentle as a mothers kiss. I watched the rest play out with a sense of amazement until I was tapped on the shoulder by the dead version of me that was covered in blood.

He pointed to the me I'd just talked to. The one I knew just came from Heart and received the news he was going to destroy everything he loved and was now desperately trying to find a way out.

"Do not stop him. You must let him create our path."

"You know what he is about to do?" I asked in disbelief. "What is it and why can't we stop him?"

"He is about to try and hide from his future in the past. He thinks if he never goes back to our time then it'll never happen but time waits for no man that's in it and every man that is not.

In doing this he has given all of time over to the beast completely but, do not fret. He creates a paradox lost to time and after he's gone we will speak of this in earnest.

"What's a paradox lost to time?"

He frowned, pausing in his turning away. "When a being traverses back in time like he's about to, and you're about to, time peels back on itself like a woodchip shaving. If the future touches the wrong spot in the past it can create an infinite loop. That future will now always be a part of the past and the whole effect separates itself from time like it never existed. He... we create one so big on Earth that mankind itself becomes born within it. So much in fact that when we write our second book we do not even begin to scratch the surface."

I made a face that showed him how confused I was, "I'm... lost."

He let out a sigh, "I'm not going to tell you where he goes or what civilization he affects first but I will tell you where to start. He and his Cherubim will be found in the land you call Egypt. Their pictures are all over their writings along with his name 'I come in peace' because it is all they could get from him when he first showed up." My mind reeled at the implications and he nodded now that I was starting to understand. "But as I said, we will speak of this later." He turned and walked back over to talk with the small prophet from Earth as I watched the foolish version of me engage in a conversation with someone but I couldn't remember who they were at first. I noticed a small object being passed from the other man's hand and into his where it quickly vanished from sight.

He was the man from Earth in disguise that Aam had told me about, I realized. The one from a different time. I shook my head, guessing at exactly what was about to happen but was told not to interfere yet so I turned back to listen to the version of me covered in blood as he lectured the poor overwhelmed prophet. He told him about the technology and how people could use it to freely come through Heaven's gates and visit the origin of all life. He then spoke to him about the chaotic mess, the mistranslations and inaccuracies he creates in his writings and that they're so bad, they're perfect. This way his book could make sense of it all, for the world and he should never let anyone try to influence or change the words he writes so he could reveal its hidden truths and meanings himself. His last set of instructions was what the prophet should put at the end of his writings, saying he'd do the same thing in his book and that was with...

SURELY, I AM COMING QUICKLY.

192 PROOF

THE KEYS TO HEAVEN GODS TECHNOLOGY

MY DIAMOND FOR THE WORLD

It was said that Jehovah will redeem humanity by revealing those secrets which he previously reserved only for the elect. And that before the end of the world, God shall create a great flood of spiritual light to alleviate the suffering of humanity. EVERY RELIGION predicts this coming enlightenment. The Jews call it The Coming of Messiah. The Hindus call it The Krita Age. Theosophists call it The New Age. Astrologers call it The Age of Aquarius. Cosmologists call it The Harmonic Convergence and Christianity calls it The Rapture. And this is what I am about to give you but hear this warning; until a time it is perfected please leave this technology to the care and supervision of licensed professionals. So if you're a doctor or know a doctor, a professor or close with one, a scientist, a biologist or even if you just have a sense of noblesse oblige, help to start running this technology. Tell everyone you can to help spread this out across the populations. Remember, don't just strive to be the first to prove it, strive to be the first who shares it magnanimously with the world.

One of the few magics that occur inside your existence is in a small gland found hidden under the mass of brain. It's in a chemical called dimethyltryptamine or DMT. The reason it stays so near the brain is to connect your consciousness with your soul if the two should ever become separated unintentionally, like in death. Another time is when your soul 'breaths'. This happens while we sleep and it returns to the spiirt world. The technique is simple. A professional must administer DMT to a person who sleeps and they will temporarily rejoin their soul in my kingdom.

As for me, I am both the lion and the lamb, the good and the bad. I am no God as men cannot be God while they still live and I am nothing close to perfect. I won't pretend to be. I am nobody, nothing but a failure as a friend, a son, a brother, a husband, a father and now I'm in prison where I belong. I try my hardest to better myself and make it back to my sons but after my own lawyer refused to act against a corrupt judicial system and a wrathful judge, they tricked me into signing a plea deal they had no intentions of honoring and I ended up with nearly a decade on top. That number leaves nothing left for me to go back to and I again find it hard to live for God when the alternative seems so much easier. But I deserved more. I deserved this hell I created for myself and now I carry a cross of my own making with no clue how to set it down. I've had a hard life, a life full of hatred, betrayal, failure, anger, sorrow and sin. It would be easy to blame a God that lets things like this happen but I've never loved her more. She taught me love. She taught me forgiveness and I hold no ill will towards anyone for anything that's ever happened to me. I forgave them all.

I'm not telling you any of this for pity or to make excuses. I'm telling you so you can hear my story and maybe on some level we connect. Maybe you or someone you know had dreams you knew were more than real or maybe it was even an outer body experi-ence and so you're willing to believe and decide to help spread my story or to help get this technology out and working. Or maybe your life hasn't been the best either. Maybe someone hurt you like they did me. Or maybe... you've sinned. Maybe you've made mistakes and in doing so you've learned. Now you see my desire to help. My desire to change, so you decide to help, you decide to change and together we can bring the change the world needs.

You can't change the world by yourself but if you tried you could change yours. If everyone of you took one small step, together your progress could circle the globe. Help someone in need. Become a volunteer. Become an organ donor. God knows you can't take them with you and this way you get to leave a piece of yourself behind for your family. Adopt a child. You are all under the impression that adoption is only for gays or couples who can't conceive but imagine the life you could give a child who has nothing if you already had kids? You could give them a family. Imagine the life you could give your own children if you taught them how to love without reservation. There are many things you can do to help bring God back into this world and you must take the first steps alone. A choice. Change yourself so the world around you changes.

None of us are perfect. Everyone has a darkness in their eyes that recedes in the light. Some of us are broken and some of us are shattered but I can help. EVERYONE has a demon they are facing that you know nothing about.

But I do...

I've faced them. I've learned their secrets and mastered them ALL. You see, they have no souls so they work to steal ours, one piece at a time until they've made a hole. Or some of us already had a hole and then we try filling that hole with the things we enjoy but it's never enough. One more pastry, they're delicious. One more drink, it's fun. One more hit, I can handle it. One more dollar, one more hour, one more time, one more chance... It's where our demons hide. They feed off the things we enjoy. The things we love. Tempting us, tricking us, trying to gain control and I can help. You cannot defeat a demon with love alone. You must use the hate it is made from against itself. Starve it of the affection it desires. Hate what losing your money really costs you. Hate what overeating does to your body. Hate that your addiction is controlling your life and destroying your family. Hate how lonely your life is without God and then find Her. Directed at itself is the ONLY time hate is acceptable. That is the balance and then it MUST be released.

But they won't die. You can cast them from the holes they hide in but they will stay with you. Talking, tempting, begging. Remember this, God put them on their bellies with no arms or legs for a reason. They can only get back up if you lend them a hand.

It takes a tremendous amount of faith in God to even suggest this next part but you need to know where I came from to prove who I am. In the book of life the ending was given at the beginning and so shall my book end with that beginning because they are one and the same...

It's the story about the end of days. Earth's final prophecy. It was given at the beginning of civilization in many ways with many pieces, most of it now corrupt, the names tarnished and we all know it. Or at least, you have heard it's beginning. It is the story of my life. Everything I was. Everything I will be both here and there and when all my books are done and the pieces have been laid, you can look back and you will see...

You will see the story of a being... who deceives... who has done great evils, becoming the most hated by men. He challenged a God's authority and because of it he was sent down from Heaven... but he's still the being held above all others. The one that God loves the most, here again to show you how to change... A master of the demons. And although his names have all been stolen, destroyed and confused with an entity of pure malice... He's given himself a new name. A name that only he knows... and well... you can call me...

FIN

EPILOGUE

The infinity code is unsolvable as humans, but learning it will bring enlightenment. Infinity is a concept of God that you are not yet advanced enough to understand and its code is the DNA of the soul. Everything is only a degree of infinity and it's so complex and extensive to grasp it takes all of eternity to master. One step at a time, one level at a time, one dimension at a time, one life at a time. Your first step is understanding what you are. Know thyself. The second is understanding what you will become but to do that you need to find your soul. You need God. Every study, every thought and all logic can lead you to God if you dig deep enough. Biology will never explain the first time thought was established and physics will never explain where the first atoms came from. Everyone was given the tools to dig and no one else can do it for you so I leave the rest up to you because time is no longer the unlimited resource you once thought it was and everything is numbered.

There are two things I need you to accept. First, the technology is real. It works and it can change your world completely. Secondly, I can't do this alone. I need YOUR help. Whether it be simply passing on what you've read here to others, working to get this technology into its trial phases or helping me so I can. I will take whatever I can get. Remember if you are one of the people who runs this technology, please for the sake of the world share the results and share them everywhere. Places of worship, school, work, social media, because it must spread. My vision is to have it set up globally anywhere this simple technique can be licensed and given to the public so that ALL can see. Because what you will see will change you forever. Call it Heaven, call it the spirit world, call it proof of extra dimensions or call it proof of God, whatever you wish but it works. You will find yourself in a place unlike anything you've ever experienced. Higher beings who know who I am and my purpose here await your coming to pass on their knowledge, to enlighten you, attuning you to the vibrations of the All because everything that was secret shall NOW be made known so that you will see the bigger truths... You will see that the only place there is pain, anger, hatred, sorrow, is Earth. You will see the reason no one knows the location of hell, is because you're living in it. If you opened your eyes you'd see wars, slavery, murder, children starving, crimes, you'd see that hell.. is the absence of God... You'd see that you are, all of you... the dung beetle, oblivious to the shadows he's cast over your eyes. You spend your lives rolling around your balls of shit, pride, vanity, gluttony, envy, lust, all of it. Some of you do it happily and some of you do it in shame but you do it nonetheless, too brainwashed by this society to just simply... walk away and leave it behind. You live in a time where advancing your technologies has exceeded the importance of advancing your souls and that causes a lot of problems but I'm fighting back. It's time to make God prominent once again. It's time for Her technology to surpass all the others.

You've seen the warnings, the weather, the climate, the pandemic, you knew I was coming and now I'm here. You've even had the prophecies but didn't know how to interpret them because you weren't ready to accept the truth of who I am in its entirety. Mankind has always believed there will be a war, the AntiChrist versus the real Christ but what they didn't know was the conflict would already be over. That anti was only intended to mean the opposite. Once I fulfill all the prophecies both good and bad then you will see the truth of the proof given and make sense of it all. I'm not going to tell you what to believe. In fact there are truths I dare not touch as the world is not ready for them yet but any who use this tech will learn them and know why I refrain. The purpose of this book was to get you to start digging for the answers yourselves so you can be free of outside influence once you've come to your conclusions.

The Autobiographies of the Antichrist

Book 1 - The Infinity Code

(The Book of Heart)

Book 2 - Paradox Lost

(The Book of Earth)

Book 3 - The Ontos On

(The Book from Heaven)

A PREVIEW TO: PARADOX LOST

Reality popped into existence without a sound, like turning on a light. This mindwarp wasn't familiar to me as I inspected it more closely, hoping it would be one I recognized from our history. There were rocks layed in a circle with the thick jungle-like vegetation cleared away far enough to give me a small preview from the hill I stood on. I peered across the waters and instantly saw the calling card of the being I hunted. A giant stone structure loomed in the distance, hundreds of people ran up and down its paths, filling altars with gifts and bundles of wood, weapons and jewelry. A few even led women and children tied up with ropes. No doubt offering them as slaves in their place.

I've been through several different time warps and mind warps all right here on Earth throughout my times and one thing I can say about our ancestral fathers is they held almost nothing sacred. Their wives and children were possessions, something that could easily be replaced.

"Cowards," I muttered, slapping my hands together and pulling in tiny amounts of essence to make some simple clothes. I could have tried to mimic the style of the locals but was growing tired of the same path. The same chase over and over. He knew I was coming for him. That I was traveling space and time itself, removing him from those he would corrupt. Revealing him for the false deity he claimed to be. But he was always one step ahead, clearly there was another time warp somewhere here on Earth that I haven't located yet and he was using it regularly. He knew I was coming. He knew I was destroying everything he did one by one until I took back what he stole from me.

I finished the outfit with a simple pair of boots for comfort and slapped them on then spun. A man stood at the edge of the rock circle with a bare chest only covered in beads. He had a decorated cloth around his waist, too many bracelets and wristbands to count and an ornamental headpiece of feathers and leaves.

His eyes bulged out of their sockets like he'd just seen a ghost, or in his mind, like I was the almighty in the flesh. Their gullibility and outlandish beliefs always ate at me but I tried my hardest to be tolerant. I shook my head, new place, same old simple minded people.

I watched as he fidgeted with a bracelet that he obviously thought held some hidden magical technology only he knew about. "Are you just going to stand there pretending to be a statue?" I asked, not knowing the small man's game.

His eyes darted back and forth like he was trying to discern who I'd just spoken to. "This God is a fool," he whispered to himself. "There is no one around but him yet he talks to nothing. Clearly he is mad. I must not let him know I am here or anger him in any way."

I squeezed my eyes shut, pinching the bridge of my nose in frustration. This was exactly the sort of thing I expected from our ancestors. How we as a species ever survived to get to where we are today is beyond me.

I shook off my annoyance and pointed a finger directly in his face. "You. Stop playing dumb and tell me where I can find your God." I knew enough by this point to simply say God as it was the only thing the population would accept. A being who could travel from the 'Heavens', had mystical powers and technologies, there was no other option. Not only did he have these powers but he found a species who shared them and they worked together. They were like us, extra dimensional with the only difference being they weren't from Earth.

His eyes bulged wider when he finally assumed I was addressing him. "Surely this God doesn't mean me? Hanakuaki said this bracelet made me completely invisible to any God. That I would not be seen or heard."

I stepped closer and put my face directly in front of his, my glowing eyes causing panic to spread over him as his sour breath assaulted my nostrils. "Hanakuaki lied," I said.

He jumped back with a yelp and slammed his face down into the ground so hard I heard something snap. For his sake I hoped it was just a twig and not his nose. He held his hands palms down by his head and was on both knees, his backside the only thing not pressed firmly to the ground. He started shuffling away from me, face dragging through the dirt. "My lorth, shorgive me ish I hash oshended you. Shash wash she shat shosh schm-"

His words cut off as I bent down and picked him up by the back of his hair and placed him on his feet. I let go, "How do you expect me to understand-"

He instantly fell back to his prostrate position, face making a hollow thud as he smacked it back into the Earth.

I clenched my jaw. This was the part I tried to avoid. These people were all so used to being ruled by fear and evil by a being they thought was their God. It made me sick. It gave the real God a bad name. I had met the true God, to put it as simply as I can, God is love. Anything that is not of love is not of Her, meaning what I was about to do was not Her way but in this time, with these people, it was the only thing that was quick and effective.

I reached down again, lifting him by his hair and setting him on his feet. "The next time you drop to your knees I'm going to consider it as you offering me your head and I'm going to take it, understood?"

Blood dribbled from his nose and his eyes were slightly crossed but they may have been that way before. He nodded. "I am sorry my God for offending you. Please allow me to sacrifice one of my wives for your glory."

I narrowed my eyes, "first, NEVER call me God. Is that clear? The true God does not live in a physical form. She visits in soul and essence only. Any being with a physical life could not possibly be a God yet, understand?"

"B- b- but the two? They both-"

"ARE NOT GODS!" I snapped, realizing he had said two and that meant they were both here again. "This especially includes the two and myself. Understand?" He nodded reluctantly. "Second, there will be no sacrificing of anyone or anything. The notion that God would require death of any kind is disgusting and ridiculous."

"But my wife Hanakuaki, she is the perfect choice-"

I shook my head, knowing why she had suddenly become his perfect choice. "No. If you continue this argument I'll let her sacrifice one of her husbands in her place if she wishes."

This seemed to get his attention. "She only has but one. It is a crime for women to have more than one husband. And they are not allowed to make sacrifices. It's God's law. No one is above God's law."

I've had these arguments before too. Different cultures, different religions, different beliefs, all claimed to be right, all claimed to be from God, all of them... wrong. Most send the right message, the right ideas, the foundations are good but the rest was built by man. If your religion requires you to only eat certain foods, dress certain ways or perform certain rituals before praying, do you really think God cares about such things? If your religion demands sacrifices of death or even requires you to devote your whole life to serve it, do you think God would actually give you a life just so you can give it back? If your religion only allows men to obtain the highest ranks, do you honestly think this is God's will? No, we are all from the place of souls and when we die, we return to the place of souls. Adhering to the differences of flesh is the folly of men.

I held back my arguments and clenched my jaw at his ignorance. "God has but one law and I'm afraid you're too stupid to believe it. Now, lastly, I want you to tell me about the two beings who claim to be your Gods. Does one of them look like me?"

"Yes my God... My lord... My..."

"Just call me Fin."

"Yes my Fin," I rolled my eyes. "And you can call me Poptarkuanakai-"

Honestly, his name was about thirty seconds long and I stopped listening almost immediately so guessing at its spelling is out of the question as it was lost to memory anyway.

I waved a hand to shut him up as I now assumed he had moved on to ranting out titles as he appeared to be a shaman or someone of authority. "I'm just going to call you Poptart. It's easier that way."

"Poptart." The words popped out of his mouth like he was beat boxing. "What is poptart?"

I chuckled, "from here on out it's you. My berry filled idiot." His jaw dropped slightly. "My Fin, I am filled with berries!" Amazement flashed across his face. "Your prophetic abilities are truly remarkable, my Fin. Only a God such as you can see I had berries for my first meal. You must be mistaken about your own divine nature." He dropped back down, trying to place his face on the ground without letting his knees touch to exploit the loophole in my threat.

I sighed, "get up. It was just a joke. Where I come from a poptart is a pastry, sort of like bread wrapped around a fruit filling."

His eyes went wide again as he was just coming to his feet. "That is exactly what I had! Oh my God, please forgive your own ignorance in the fact that you surely are a God and-"

I caught him by the hair before he could return to the ridiculous position he was trying for. "Listen to me. No groveling, no worshiping, no sacrificing, nothing. I'm here for the two, so tell me about them. What they are having you harvest for them. What do they require and most importantly, are they carrying anything with them? Like a box or a weird object of any kind?"

"You mean the wooden bricks?"

My heart thumped in my chest at the mention of it. The thing I traversed time and space for could finally be within reach. "Yes, I mean the wooden bricks. Now tell me everything."

I watched as his eyes darted back and forth as he chose where to begin. "Well my Fin, they have always been with us, the two. They are Gods... they are.."

"Imposters," I filled in the word he was looking for, "NOT Gods."

He nodded. "The one imposter looks like you but his eyes do not glow." This was common as he was always in disguise in an effort to stay hidden from history and in doing so, stay hidden from me. "The two, they do not age and no one knows how long they've been with us truly. They do not allow us to keep records of them." Another tactic to stay hidden from me. The less records there were, the harder it was for me to pinpoint his locations in time. I gestured for him to continue. "I do know they had us harvest the rock sticks for the temples from a mountain and floated them to the islands with their... fake... God... powers." I knew he didn't believe his own words. Everything he's ever been told was that these beings were in fact, his Gods. "They had my people build for them and they have us harvest the shining rocks from the Earth. They take any women they want as their wives but then cast them aside once they're done. We bring them food and gifts, we even base our beliefs according to theirs. Surely you must see these are only things a true God would require?"

I took a deep breath, ignoring his comments. "Tell me more of the temples. Are they still being made or are they finished?"

A confused expression came over him, "Construction has stopped my Fin. Is it how they get their powers? Is it too late?"

I shook my head. "No. The power to make the temples comes from the wooden bricks. I assure you it is nothing divine."

"But they say the wooden bricks are nothing. Just stools that they use to stand on?"

I glared down at him. "Do you consider me a giant?" He hesitated then nodded. Humans were shorter at this time so I expected the answer. "Do you consider the two, giants?" He nodded again. "Why would a giant need a tiny stepping stool?" By the look on his face I could tell he hadn't thought of that. "It's what I'm after. It's what I need to save the world I'm from."

"What world are you from my Fin?"

I glanced at him then back to the stone structure to see if I could spot either of the two. "This one but at a different time far in the future."

"Are the imposter Gods killing it with the wooden bricks?"

I snorted, "No. In my time men are killing themselves with pollution. They're poisoning the very world that birthed them. They have created a cancer, and that wooden brick is my cure."

"Oh pollution. I hate pollution. Pollution was here once but I chased it away."

I gave him a sideways look full of doubt. "I loath lies and the liars who grow them."

"My Fin, I am sorry." He made like he was going to prostrate himself again but hesitated, only lowering his head instead. "Please forgive my imperfect tongue. It is not worthy. Let me cut it out and I shall sacrifice my wife... err," I gave him another glare, "my child.. um, no. One of the livestock?" My expression didn't change, "A fish? A snake? No one likes snakes."

I turned my head and tried to ignore him, realizing my prize must have already slipped away. Once they were done with their temples, he'd probably had no use for them and most likely had them all destroyed and anyone who knew its secrets to keep it hidden from me. It was exhausting but I knew from my past that I had already changed the future and that kept me going. I would be successful eventually and bring my prize to this dying world.

"I hereby offer this beetle as a mortal sacrifice to my Fin." I turned back to him and he held a small insect above his head to the clouds like I wasn't standing right next to him.

"Spare the bug. When was the last time you saw one of the wooden bricks? Do you know if any are still down there?"

He frowned at not being able to kill the poor thing and threw it back into the grass. "My Fin, I cannot say. I remember when I was a boy and the buildings were near completion, I had seen one, but I do not remember a time since then." It was as I feared. "Is it that powerful? This vanquisher of pollution?"

I smirked at the way he said it. "Not in this time but in my time, where I'm from, it will be the single most powerful invention that mankind has ever had. The world almost had it once, a man named Edward Leedskalnin found it but he didn't share how and no one else ever dared to try and replicate it."

"Then you can ask him for it?"

"I would if I could but he's dead and I can't reach his time. But he left the secret in his book and I can almost remember... I know everyone looks at it wrong. This technology, they all look at it from the same angle from within their own beliefs on what they've always been taught. If anyone was ever brave enough to step outside the box and just... try." I scratched my head, realizing I hadn't really answered his question but the fact that I knew this once and had forgotten it frustrated me. "The bricks don't destroy pollution. They're just an alternative energy that doesn't cause it. It's the beginning of a new era. I think.. it somehow pulls energy in from an object, like reverse magnetism and this removes gravity's effect on it. I know it's antigravity, that's how they float the rocks but for that there has to be mass without energy? But that's not supposed to be possible so it must defy one of our current laws of physics. Or maybe not defies changes? I remember the crafts that flew with this technology, from zero to lightspeed in the blink of an eye. To a man it would turn them to mush, but this technology... it has to remove energy so the mass is not affected? If only I could remember how!" I found myself rambling again as the hole in my memory ate at me.

"And this is why you need it my Fin? To fly and these things?" "No. Those are just possible side effects. I'm trying to remember. What I'm truly after is it's unlimited source of power. He stole my memory and I'm here to steal it back. Then I'm going to give its secret at the end of my second book. Free to the world

like all my technologies will be."

"This God that stole it from you, who is he?"

I put my head down in shame at my own past. "He... is me. I'm at war with myself, or rather a past version of myself that is consumed by hate. Now I'll spend the rest of my life trying to make up for the things I've done."

He scratched his head, "can you my Fin? Undo things that have already happened? Is that how time works?"

"In this time yes, but in my time, where I'm from... this technology exists in nearly all its futures but I don't know if I can do it alone. I need others to help me try. There are some greedy people who will try to produce this technology before we can give it to the world so I'm racing as fast as I can." I shook my head in frustration. "Come, take me to the two. They still need to be dealt with."

He nodded and then turned back to me as we started to walk. "What is the power that is hidden inside the wooden bricks?"

I smiled, "it's a new form of clean energy and if I get it before them, I'm going to call it something that incorporates my name like infinite power or something else with a double meaning. But that's just me. To them, the people who live in the time I'm from, it will be my next miracle. The answer to pollution. To them it is simply called... perpetual energy."